THE GODMOTHER'S APPRENTICE

THE GODMOTHER'S APPRENTICE

ELIZABETH ANN SCARBOROUGH

ACE BOOKS, NEW YORK

THE GODMOTHER'S APPRENTICE

An Ace Book
Published by The Berkley Publishing Group
200 Madison Avenue, New York, NY 10016

First Edition: December 1995

Library of Congress Cataloging-in-Publication Data

  Scarborough, Elizabeth Ann.
    The godmother's apprentice / Elizabeth Ann Scarborough.—1st ed.
      p. cm.
    ISBN 0-441-00252-8
    I. Title.
    PS3569.C324G63   1995
    813'.54—dc20   95-9745
                                                    CIP

Printed in the United States of America

10 9 8 7 6 5 4 3 2 1

*This book is dedicated with love to all of the Irish people who were
so kind to me, especially:
Mr. and Mrs. John O'Regan, Sr., and John O'Regan
Maureen Beirne
Cyra O'Connor
Jennifer Kiersey
and, of course, once more to Anne McCaffrey*

Acknowledgments

Many thanks to Maureen Beirne, Jason Beirne and John O'Regan for their services as tour guides, to Eileen Gormley for witty stories, to Sandra Darrow for advice on the Irish social services systems, to Katherine Kurtz for sharing the history of her house during the famine and to Fr. Richard Woods for *his* tour guide and chauffeur services. I am also indebted to the Famine Museum at Strokestown Manor, to Celtworld at Tramore, to the Dublin Traveller's Education and Development Group and to the folkloric works of W. B. Yeats and Lady Gregory, and many other fine books besides.

Author's Note

On "Cunla": The song quoted is an old night-visiting song. It's something a fellow would sing to let a girl know he was coming to see her. Such songs get a bit bawdy at times. Since there also exists a tradition of house spirits, both mischievous and helpful, it seemed to me that the song could apply to another kind of less amorous night visit as well, so I nicked it.

On Dialect: The use of misspellings in dialect is controversial, but part of the fun of this book was evoking the way things felt, looked and sounded. Also, the Traveller's speech is somewhat distinct from the general run of Irish accents. As a guide for the pronunciations, I used one of the publications published by the Travellers themselves, a book called *In Our Own Words* (Pavee Press). For the reader's information, many of the long *e* sounds are pronounced as long *a*'s and the *er*'s as if they were *ar*'s. Sometimes *u* sounds take on the sound of a short *o*. I've tried to indicate this and hope that by mentioning it here, it won't slow down the reading too much, but will give a flavor of the speech as you hear it. I've also tried to use the Irish terms for things even if they have a different meaning in America. The Irish slang is pretty much in context.

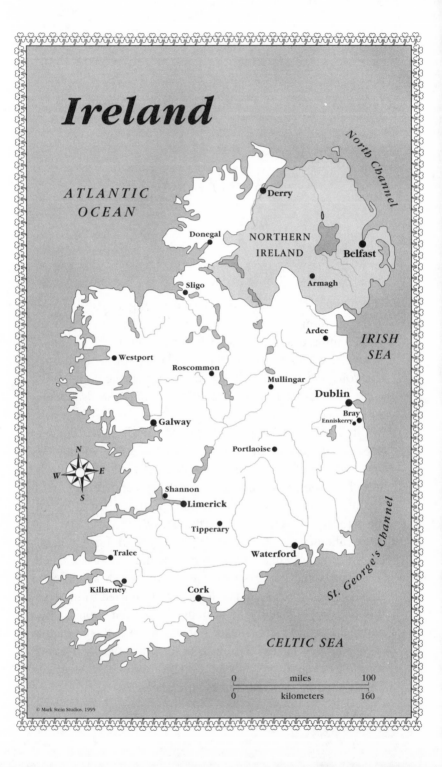

The Princess and the Toad

Once upon a time there was a princess who refused to live happily ever after. Having survived a difficult childhood, the death of her mother, an arrest for possession of illegal substances and the perpetual adolescence of her father culminating in his marriage to a woman who made three attempts to murder her, Snohomish Quantrill felt far older than her fourteen-going-on-fifteen years. She decided that instead of marrying a prince, which she was too young to do anyway, she wanted to be a fairy godmother when she grew up.

Marrying princes was not all it was cracked up to be. She knew that. Her father, Raydir Quantrill, had been the Prince of Punk before he became the King of Rock, and she definitely was not ready to take on somebody like him. Besides, she had been through enough counseling to know that you had to get your own shit together before you interfaced with somebody else's kingdom and all of its headaches.

The way she decided to become a fairy godmother before she was even a mother was through a counselor friend of hers, in fact.

Almost being murdered, once by a hired hit man, twice by your own stepmom, made you ponder on the meaning of your existence in a way that was difficult to communicate to most people.

Her classmates at Clarke Academy had welcomed her back with girlish squeals and touchy-feely hugs. They were so sorry she'd been hurt and were so *gen*uinely glad she was back, and had the hit man, like, *raped* her or anything? It was too creepy the way they drooled over the details they'd gleaned from the media. Some of them, she knew, were really, truly pissed at her because they'd been looking forward to attending her funeral and giving tear-choked statements for the six o'clock news. They acted like what had happened to her was some lurid splatter movie instead of her own life for the last month or so. But she had very real scars to remind her of the last attempt on her life, which had landed her in the Harborview ICU for two weeks.

Her dad wasn't exactly a pillar of strength either. He'd extracted his head from his ass long enough to join the search party looking for her, but in the process had found someone else as well. He fell in love with his fellow searcher, Cindy Ellis, hired her as his own stable manager to keep her around, and lately had spent most of his time trying to convince Cindy that he could change, he really could.

Cindy was nice, and she too had had a wicked stepmother, but Sno couldn't help being less than thrilled with her for taking up so much of Raydir's attention.

She didn't know what to do or where to turn. She was what they called marginalized. *Way* marginalized. On the surface, she seemed okay, even better. Her testimony, at her stepmother Gerardine's trial, was clear and unshakable enough to swathe that fashion slave in prison coveralls long enough for her wardrobe to go out of style and in again.

Meanwhile, Sno's grades improved because she didn't have any real friends anymore. Drugs had almost killed her, and she had no use for them. What she longed to do was to go back into the woods with the seven Vietnam veterans who had tried to protect her. They understood what it felt like to have your life threatened, to be wounded, hunted.

There was just one problem. They weren't in the woods

anymore. They'd returned home to their own lives and their own wives and daughters, who would take no more kindly to some outsider like Sno horning in on their relationships than she took to Cindy Ellis. So she spent a lot of time writing reports on World War II concentration camp victims, Vietnam, Cambodia, Bosnia, Somalia and the new gulag in Uzbekistan, until her teachers stopped being delighted by her industry and became concerned about her thematic choices.

The teachers spoke to Raydir, who in turn sent forth an invitation summoning Sno's former social worker, Rose Samson, to dinner one night. Rose brought along Felicity Fortune, a woman with long white and silver hair and a shimmery, floaty, asymmetrically hemmed, much-scarved outfit that looked like something the ghost of a 1930s movie star would wear to dinner on Rodeo Drive. Felicity was, Rose said, a bona fide fairy godmother.

Rosie went on to tell her a fairly complicated account of what she and Felicity had been doing while Sno was hiding out in the woods. They had helped a street kid, Dico Miller, by giving him a talking cat, Puss, which helped him get more handouts. Rosie and Felicity had also confronted the Asian gang harassing Dico and turned the gangbangers into helpful citizens. The gang leader, Ding, and Dico had even become friends and had discovered a mutual musical talent. Dico was supposedly pursuing his studies of the flute in Waterford, Ireland, while Ding wrote an account of his parents' experiences in the Vietnam War. Rosie and Felicity had helped Cindy Ellis when her wicked stepmother and stepsisters tried to take all her money and make her lose her job. They'd been instrumental in Cindy's meeting Raydir and rescuing Sno. And, while trying to help two neglected children who had been picked up by a child molester, Rose had renewed her acquaintance with a nice cop named Fred, and they had fallen for each other. Rosie and Felicity had been very busy and had done so much and helped so many people that Sno lost track of all the details, except that now Rosie was her own department head and there was a big shake-up in the state and city government and social services organizations because of what she and Felicity had done.

This was all a revelation to Sno. Before she was kidnapped, she had classed fairy godmothers with Santa Claus and the Easter Bunny. Given her recent experience, however, all it took was Rose's word and a peek at the creature Felicity carried in her pocket, and she was a believer.

Admittedly, it was all a little surreal.

"You recognize him, then?" Felicity Fortune asked, as if asking her to identify some microscope slide for an oral exam in microbiology.

Sno peered carefully into the pocket Felicity held open and looked into the popped eyes of the toad staring back at her with an extremely in-your-face expression. She hadn't actually seen the face before, of course, or the expression, but the attitude behind it was frighteningly familiar, even on a toad. "Nooo . . ." she said, taking a quick step backward.

"How about if she puts a little teeny motorcycle helmet on me, kid? Could you finger me then?" a voice said inside her head, a voice unlike her own, one she would never forget, menacing and mocking. Of course, all she heard the actual toad say was "Reedeep."

Still, she stumbled over an end table in her haste to back away.

"I'm sorry, my dear," Felicity said, quickly closing her pocket again. "No need to be alarmed. As you have so sensitively perceived, your original assailant, the "executioner" Robert Hunter, has been rendered harmless and now inhabits this toad's body."

"Yeah? What happened to his own body?"

"It currently houses the toad-body's original personality and is safely hopping around the psychiatric unit at Harborview Hospital, though I suppose a more long-range institution may be necessary at some point."

"Cool," Sno said.

"In an effort to partially redeem himself by undoing the harm he has caused, Bobby has twice saved your life and made your stepmother confess her crimes against you."

"Is she putting me on?" Sno asked Rose, but Rose, who was usually so calm and sensible and the last person you'd think would know a fairy godmother or an executioner-toad, only shook her head and added, "You can ask your father or Cindy Ellis what happened in your hospital room when your stepmother tried to kill you. You can ask your veteran friends how they knew you needed help."

"So, kid, let bygones be bygones?" The voice in her head was in no way muffled by the pocket fabric. It was the same voice as the hit man's, but with decidedly amphibian overtones.

Sno edged closer, pointing at the toad. "Let me see that thing again, will you?" she asked Felicity.

Felicity opened her pocket again. "Howsabout it?" the toad asked. "Compadres, eh?"

"No way!" Sno said adamantly and flipped the fabric back over the amphibian. To Felicity she said, "That's him, isn't it? How can he be a toad and still talk to me?"

"He's been practicing, obviously," Felicity said with a shrug. "Little else for him to do unless he wishes to remain as he is. Communication is, after all, the key to mending one's relationships, and Bobby here—Bobby the Butcher, as was his most recent, er, moniker—has a lot of mending to do."

"He almost killed me," Sno said. "With a knife."

"Yes, dear. Me, too. Also with a knife. Which is how he came to be as you see him now."

Sno looked over at Rose, who nodded but seemed a little worried. "I wasn't going to tell you about Felicity, Sno. But she was on your case all the time, trying to protect you. From what your teachers have been telling me, the trauma of your recent experience has been causing you a lot of pain. Is that so?"

Sno shrugged. "I don't sleep a lot anymore. But it's not just because I'm scared. Not really scared. I mean, Gerardine's locked up and now that I know this little guy's under control, what do I have to be scared of? Drive-by shootings? Traffic accidents? Earthquakes? Another kidnapping? Death by pollution?"

"That about covers it," Rose said with a weary and rather pained smile.

"Yeah, but that's not it. Not really. What I really wonder is what I'm doing. I mean, I'm glad to be alive and all that, but why?"

"Aha!" Felicity said, hoisting her arm aloft in one of the kind of grand dramatic gestures Sno had mostly seen used on late-night movies and by drag queens. As Felicity's silvery draperies flowed in harmony with her movements, small beads and sequins and bits of jewelry twinkled in the folds and billows. "An identity crisis, I believe you call it; isn't that correct, Rose?"

"Perhaps it's best if we hold off making any diagnosis until Sno finishes *telling* us how she feels, Felicity, hmm?" Rose said.

"Certainly," Felicity said with a nod. "Very wise. You show great promise for this line of work, my dear. Do carry on, Sno."

She settled herself with her hands folded in her lap, rings with settings like little crystal balls and old-fashioned mirrors clinking gently on her fingers. Her entire posture projected, "I'm listening." Her eyes, first pale blue, then silver, then gray, watched Sno intently. "Like those little holograms you get in jewelry sometimes," Sno thought, suddenly so fascinated she forgot what she was trying to say.

"Please. Go on. Do," Felicity prompted.

"Let me put it this way. Gerardine tried to have me offed because she was so hung up on her looks that she got freaked out by me being younger and cuter. But that's so dumb. What would killing me accomplish? She'd still be older." Sno shook her head. "It's so bogus. Her agent thought I could be a model, Dad thinks I'm going to be a model, but I don't want to just live on looks—hell, I don't even think I'm all that pretty. But I've been duckin' dudes who hang around my dad all my life. I want to do something else—something that means something. I almost got killed, and what had I done with my life so far? Bad or good? I'd like to make a difference."

Rose and Felicity exchanged glances. "Ahem," Felicity said. "I do have one or two little ideas. It might involve travel."

"The Peace Corps? I'm too young."

"Right now, yes. No, I had in mind something more immediate, though you'd need to train, of course. And have an open mind."

"I'd suggest," Rose said, "a very open mind."

"I was thinking, Sno dear, that with the empathy your recent experiences have provided you, you might make an excellent candidate for Godmother training."

"Really? I'm assuming we're talking Cinderella here, not the Catholic trip, right? I'm not old enough, am I? I always thought—well, excuse me, but I always thought fairy godmothers were old ladies who compensated for the lack of romantic involvement in their own lives by helping younger babes score—like a video dating service, only with magic."

Felicity arched an eloquent silvery eyebrow and said, "Fascinating. And who do you suppose these wand-bearing fossils were before antiquity set in?"

Sno shrugged. "I never thought about it."

In the time that followed, however, Felicity explained something of the work of fairy godmothers, and Sno could think of little else. Strange as it sounded, Sno recognized that what this husky-voiced woman with the holograph-colored eyes was telling her was real and important and that learning to be a fairy godmother was exactly the sort of vocational training she wanted.

And so it was decided. Raydir had already met Felicity, and he liked and trusted her too, though he didn't really understand who she was or what she did. Felicity, flourishing her silvery scarves like they were Superman's cape, told him that his daughter would be coming to Ireland under her "personal tutelage to study cosmology." He thought she had said "cosmetology," and agreed right away, saying, "It'll be good to have a background in that, in case you end up in modeling or show business."

CHAPTER 1

Solitary Fairies

> *"Who's that down there tappin' the window pane?*
> *Who's that down there tappin' the window pane?*
> *Who's that down there tappin' the window pane?*
> *Only myself, says Cunla."*
>
> Trad. Connemara song

There had been no house there for eight hundred years. No house at all. Only meadows with horses grazing upon them. Meadows with warring tribesmen marching over them. Meadows with Cromwell's brigands marching over them. Meadows with the patriots' footsteps whispering across them on the way to some assignation during the revolution. Meadows for poets to rant about and artists to paint. Sheep meadows. Horse meadows. Grass meadows. Meadows without so much as your stone fence or your round tower to distinguish them. Nothing to do for the likes of a hard-working house spirit.

But now there was a house. A house atop the foundations of the old house, the old many, many feet deep below the new. A great bloody barn of a house it was. Oh, a poor spirit would

9

be hard put to keep up with such a place.

That and dodgin' all them prowlin' cats who came from all over Wicklow to supervise the goings-on, just as if the place was to be a cat palace. Now then, that was a challenge. Cunla the night visitor, Cunla the toe-tickler, Cunla the window-tapper, was poor Cunla quick enough to become Cunla the tail-puller?

CHAPTER 2

Dear Rosie,

See? I'm doing my homework and writing my therapist like you said. Anyway, I hope the transmission is okay. I'm using the new laptop Raydir laid on me and I'm still figuring out the E-mail.

Raydir got very fatherly just before I left and, like I said, gave me this laptop and my very own gold card and told me to go buy some clothes for the trip. I didn't. I decided to wait till I got here so I could shop where the local people do and blend in a little better that way, y'know? I also had an idea that maybe fairy godmother candidates were supposed to dress like Felicity—sort of like nuns, only supernatural. They don't, though most of them don't dress much like anybody else I know either. Anyway, as you also suggested, I decided to keep a therapeutic journal about this trip, only I'm going to pretend I'm talking to you some of the time because writing to myself is a bore. So I'll write you a note from time to time but mostly I'll just let you read this when I get back. Okay?

Love, Sno

*   *   *

My Trip to Ireland
by
Snohomish Quantrill
Journal Entry—Beginnings

I'll have to get used to saying "Dear Journal." Right now it sounds pretty juvenile but I promised Rosie I'd let her read this later and maybe I'll let Raydir read it too if he's interested sometime, and maybe later, who knows? I might use it in my autobiography when I get famous.

So, maybe I should start by saying that I didn't always want to be a fairy godmother. When I was a kid, a couple of years ago, and my mom and Grandma Hilda were still alive, I wanted to be either a folksinger or maybe a journalist who went around exposing unjust establishment ploys to exploit people. I really would have liked to be a communist but that's been a lost cause since I was in fifth grade. My grandma used to be a hippie in the sixties and she had this great collection of tapes and vinyl albums (which I inherited) and she used to talk to me about how exciting it was at the peace marches and love-ins and stuff. She still had her love beads and her pink plastic peace sign earrings, bell bottoms and Indian bedspread skirts, which I used to play dress-up in. For a long time, when she went to California, Grandma lived in a converted school bus. She and her roomies handed out political pamphlets at concerts and published a little paper. Once the FBI even mistook her for Patty Hearst, till they found out she was six inches taller and pregnant with my mom to boot. I loved to listen to her stories, with some old album, Dylan or maybe the Lime-lighters, playing in the background. She was the one who told me why Joan Baez wrote "Song for David" for her husband in prison, and who Che Guevara was.

My mom always started slamming dishes around or vacu-uming when Grandma talked about the olden days. I think it's because she remembered the pretty recent past when she and

I were living in the tour bus gigging on the road with Raydir.
That's my dad. He's a rock star. I can sort of understand how
Mom felt. It's weird when the girls in your school talk about
your dad as being really hot—an old guy, but still with great
buns. What're you supposed to say to that?

Mom and I went to live with Grandma when the road got
to be too much for us. Anyhow, that's what Mom told people.
But really it was because she didn't like some of the pervs
who hung out with Raydir and gave me a hard time, even
when I was four or five. And then there were the bimbos. She
really hated that. So we went to Missouri and moved in with
Grandma in back of her beauty parlor. We weren't exactly
your typical sitcom family. Grandma had art students two eve-
nings a week and they studied everything from abstract ex-
pressionism to fashion design. I sat and drew with them, doing
costumes for my paper dolls to make them look like the characters from books, movies and TV.

It was a great time. Mom went out on dates and I went to
a regular school with kids and teachers I liked. Grandma and
I would make brownies together and she would gaze wistfully
into the batter bowl while telling her stories. I loved how she
smelled of sandalwood oil and the way she wore her hair long
and loose even though it was gray and she must have been
over fifty anyway!

Mom fussed over me and worried, even though we were
away from Raydir, that I wasn't growing up to be someone
the press would recognize as his heir. She thought I was a
little too straight, I think. She tried to get me to dye my hair,
which is straight and black like Joan Baez's used to be, purple
or fuchsia and get into leather or studs but even when I was
on the streets, I only got a little grungy, and that was as far
out as I'd go.

I know now that Mom must have really loved me to take
me away because she was still in love with Raydir. When we
fought, I used to tell her if she didn't give me what I wanted
I'd tell the judge I wanted to go back and live with my dad.
I've wondered sometimes if that's why it happened. If Mom
and Grandma getting killed in the accident was a punishment

maybe. Because after that, I didn't have any choice but to move in with Raydir in his new place in Seattle.

It went okay, I guess, for a while. Raydir hadn't known what to do with me, and he'd ignored me and gone off on the road leaving me in the care of whoever happened to be around the house. I had to move pretty fast to avoid some of the guys. They didn't care that I was just a kid. They seemed to think the younger the better. Actually, I was more grown up even then than a lot of them.

But I got along okay until Raydir decided we were going to be one big happy family (and my mom hadn't been dead a year even) and he married this famous model Gerardine. She was sweet as pie to me when they were going out but once she moved in, I could do like, nothing, but nothing, to please her. She never said anything while Raydir was around, but she had her claws in me every chance she got. It got so bad that I couldn't stand being home anymore. I ran away.

I didn't know where to go or what to do. I had been fooling myself that things would be okay with Raydir, that Gerardine would start liking me and that would make me stop missing Mom and Grandma. I had been in total denial, in other words, and all of a sudden, it just hit me hard. I knew a couple of kids who hung out at Pike Place Market, and I crashed with them. One of Raydir's pals had started me smoking a little dope, in secret, and I had some of that. It helped take the edge off. Raydir didn't even know I was gone till I got busted. He was on the road at the time and Gerardine could give a shit. Neither did I.

But then I met Rosie Samson, my caseworker. She listened to me and when I stopped talking because I was embarrassed or thought maybe there was something I shouldn't tell her, she just kept listening until I told it anyway. She wasn't taken in by Gerardine when she and Raydir came for group counseling. I was kind of mad at her for suggesting Raydir send me to a private school where I had to wear this dumb red uniform. But it worked okay. The school kept me out of Gerardine's way and everything was fine. Then Gerardine's agent came to visit and tried to "discover" me. He told me I could be what she had been. Unfortunately for me, she overheard.

That led to a whole bunch of bad stuff. But it also got me on my way to Ireland, on my way to study with an actual real fairy godmother.

The truth is, when Gerardine's agent originally suggested I might become a supermodel like dear old stepmom, I admit it appealed to me at first. I know a couple of other models, married to friends of Raydir's, who seem like okay people. I like clothes, I like fiddling around with makeup. But I have no desire to end up like Gerardine. She's the crazy extreme, I know, but I don't intend to take the chance.

I also never wanted to be like Raydir. His life seems so superficial and shallow. What I've decided is, I want to make a difference, do wonderful things for people, change their lives for the better. Like Felicity and Rosie. (More like Felicity, actually, since Rosie has to deal with politicians.) So I enlisted as a fairy godmother.

Raydir was unusually sweet about me going away (instead of him, for a change). Besides giving me this computer and an E-mail account, he also collected names and numbers from all of his Irish music friends of relatives and friends of theirs I could go see or call—as if! But Niambh Rourke, who is this terrific fiddler, lent me some books and videos of stories by Roddy Doyle, the guy who wrote *The Commitments*. The books were mostly in heavy dialect that I couldn't get into until I watched the vids. I checked out several other books on Ireland at the library too but I didn't have much time and you can watch a vid in an hour or so where it takes you a couple of days to read a book. I already saw *The Commitments* and *The Snapper* with school friends but I hadn't seen the third one, *The Van*, yet or the miniseries called *The Family*.

I also watched *Hear My Song, Widow's Peak, Da, Into the West, The Field* (MAJOR bummer!), *In the Name of the Father, The Crying Game* (Raydir didn't know about the last one but he wouldn't have cared). I relistened to all the old Irish albums and tapes I inherited from Grandma too, and read as many of the Irish folk and fairy tales from her books as I could before I had to leave.

With so much Iroid cultural exposure, you may ask yourself, why bother to go? But, you can't say I wasn't prepared! Anyway, I thought so.

Felicity and I flew Virgin Atlantic (Raydir knows Richard Branson from the days when Virgin was strictly a record company) to London. I brought all the suitcases I was allowed, because I want to bring back some Irish music when I come home and gifts for people and souvenirs.

I packed some of my favorite Clancy Brothers and Chieftains tapes as well as some of the old ballad standards I taped off Grandma Hilda's record collection. It's mine now and Raydir's fit of fatherliness extended to actually having the collection shipped from Grandma's house in Missouri about three weeks before I left.

We took the Virgin City Jet into London. Felicity said she used to take the tube, but after the long trip, and with luggage, she found it very hard to stand all the way and being an FGM, she kept giving her seat up to various needy types. I was disappointed at first not to see more of London but I saw all I wanted of the underground stations, as they call the subways there (they call their underground walkways subways, Felicity explained) transferring from the airport to the regular train at Waterloo Station. Every time we switched trains, I had to drag my luggage up flights of steps I swear to god were as steep as Mt. Rainier.

One of the perks of being an FGM apparently is that you don't need luggage. Felicity didn't even carry a purse—she kept producing anything she needed from her pockets, including the Odious Amphibian. She was very sensitive though, and kept him in the pocket furthest away from me.

We took the train east to Bath, which was where the FGMs were having their meeting. I'd never been to England before and was surprised to see that except for the parts that look just like the sets on PBS shows like *Mystery!* and *Masterpiece Theatre*, it looks a lot like Missouri, only neater, as if every blade of grass knows its place. And the animals looked friskier than I've seen them at home. There were a couple of horses kicking up their heels and chasing each other and even some

lambs gamboling—I guess that's what they were doing.
Lambs always gambol in books. I thought for a while it meant
they played poker or something but it actually means they're
running around being lambs in a cute kind of way. I hope no
one tells them about mint sauce any time soon.

There are neat little hedges surrounding each field, or stone
fences. And the rivers also look as if they are quite happy to
stay within their banks, thank you very much. I wish the Missouri would learn that. It'd save people a lot of trouble during
flood season. Maybe the English rivers are more peaceful because they know they can run right out to the ocean any time
they want to. The ocean's never very far away on an island
like England. You can't even imagine you're on the same
planet with an ocean when you live in Missouri. But Missouri
did used to have a lot of stone fences, though it doesn't have
many left anymore.

Grandma Hilda told me there used to be lots of them because farmers needed something to do with all the rocks they
had to dig up from their land before they could plow. It must
have been some rough job trying to plow back in England in
the old days, because they have a *lot* of stone fences. They
also have lots of stone houses (and some newer, concrete
ones), stone churches, stone barns, stone outbuildings, and
stone bridges, not to mention, of course, the castles, cathedrals
and all the usual stuff you think of when you think of England.

Bath is something else again. Felicity says it's very
"posh"—which means upperclass or fancy. She says it used
to be "posher," back when people actually took baths in
Bath—not the tub kind with soap and bubbles but like hot
springs, for therapy and relaxation. They were the original
spas, a cross between The Door where Gerardine used to go
and Olympic Hot Springs where you can go skinny-dipping
on the weekend. Grandma Hilda and I used to watch *Mystery!*
on PBS a lot and I especially loved Agatha Christie's stories,
so Grandma loaned me the books. Seemed Hercule Poirot or
Ariadne Oliver were always taking the waters someplace like
Bath. Back then, the resorts were so posh that at night, the
customers had to put on evening dresses and tuxes to go to

dinner. The place looks it too, even though now the baths are mostly empty and have been excavated as archaeological digs. They date from Roman times, according to the guidebook, and they've found coins and little scraps of pewter with writing on them that were sacrifices to the goddess Minerva, who was supposed to be in charge back then.

As for the town itself, I don't remember Dame Agatha mentioning that a lot of the fanciest houses are built in crescents or circles—which they call circuses here, though there are no clowns or bareback riders. There are, however these great old what they call Georgian buildings—after King George. I don't know what kind of a king he was, but judging from what I've seen lately, there was this major boom in the construction business while he was king. The contractors must have cried at that guy's funeral big time. The houses are all built from honey-colored stone and have fancy doors with stained and etched glass and pretty little postage stamp–sized gardens in the fronts. You can easily imagine horses and carriages driving up in front of them.

The Godmother HQ is in one of the houses on the fanciest crescent. It has a nice brass plaque with a date and the etching on the glass is all moons and stars, if you look closely, but otherwise it blends right in.

I was a little disappointed that there was no butler—a woman in a black dress and white apron let us in and the inside was pretty much what you'd expect; another PBS set, maybe from one of the Miss Marple mysteries.

There was a little wagon with a silver teapot and sugar and creamer and china cups and saucers in all different flower patterns. Mine was a lily of the valley. Felicity got a primrose. Everything had lace doilies on it and big cabbage roses and the rug was an oriental one so ornate I wondered if maybe it wasn't also aerodynamically sound.

Of course, I was especially interested to see what the other godmothers looked like and at first glance they seemed pretty much like any extremely varied group of dressed-up ladies having a tea party. Felicity was in pewter palazzo pants, a long tunic, a floppy vest and a scarf long enough for Dr. Who. I felt suddenly out of place in my comfy travel clothes, jeans and T-shirt from Raydir's last world tour.

To our right were two tiny little Asian women, and pardon the cliche but they did look like collector edition dolls wearing silky things embroidered in pinks and fuchsias. Next to them, a black woman with a hot-fudge voice talked seriously to the group. With her accent, she could have subbed for one of those people who introduce opera on FM stations. She was decked out in a flowing gold and orange dashiki and a lot of flashing silver jewelry. There were also two ladies in saris. And another wearing a long red satin broomstick skirt, a yellow velvet blouse with silver buttons all over the seams, collar and cuffs, and a lot of turquoise jewelry, was spinning wool against her knee with a long spindle. Her face and hands were brown and creased as saddle leather but her hair was still as black as mine. The rest of the ladies were white bread, all different ages, some gorgeous, some ordinary, but all of them wearing artistic-looking clothing like Felicity's, full of scarves and glitters and tiered skirts and droopy gauzy cardigans. One of the younger women, pretty in a country-Norwegian kind of way with curly blonde hair and a dimpled smile she kept the wattage turned up on, I couldn't help staring at because of her jewelry. She wore gobs of it, shiny gold and rainbow crystals formed into fairies, dragons, mermaids and unicorns that winked and twinkled in her hair, at her ears, throat, chest, wrists, fingers and even ankles.

"That's Dame Genevieve," Felicity said when she saw where I was looking. "An American like yourself. Actually, she represents her entire family, including a brother—though of course he can only be honorary, as he can hardly be said to be a mother of any sort. And the term 'godfather' has come to carry an unfortunate connotation in the United States." A certain creepy amphibian "reedeeped" from inside Felicity's pocket at the allusion to his former career.

The other American was a young Jewish woman with large brown eyes and curly dark auburn hair. "Merrilee is another trainee," Felicity told me. "Dame Prudence discovered her at an East Coast literary agency, attempting to make silk purses out of authors during the day, conducting a literacy program for inner-city children in her spare time.''

All of the ladies seemed like pretty upbeat types except for one in an iron-gray tweed suit and a gunmetal gray silk blouse with smog-colored tights on her legs and gray suede Nikes on her feet.

She clutched a clipboard like she was the director and everyone else in the room was an actor in her production. I kept expecting her to yell, ''Cut and print!''

She pissed me off as soon as she opened her mouth, because right away she started saying all kinds of nasty things about how Felicity had handled things in Seattle. If I hadn't heard different from Rosie and Raydir, I'd have thought she was a real dweeb.

''Who's the anal type?'' I whispered to Felicity.

''Dame Prudence,'' Felicity whispered back. ''She's our accountant. She keeps track of magical expenditures and receipts. Of course, there aren't many receipts these days.''

Just then this stunner of a senior citizen spoke up and it was clear right away who was in charge. She was a tiny little woman who wore her pale strawberry blonde hair up, cameo-style. You could tell she was really old only because she looked as if she might break. And her eyes! I have never seen anybody with eyes like that—this lady, you knew right off, had seen everything and furthermore, she understood it. Her eyes held whole rain forests of green, whole jungles. She was dressed in her own version of the godmother style in a long skirt and tunic jacket and lace-up boots, all in shades of green. The hems and edges of her clothes were trimmed with gold and silver embroidery in the shapes of Celtic knotwork animals. She wore big silver cuff bracelets and long silver and gold wire earrings in a spiral design with green stones dropping from them, and a crescent moon–shaped necklace that matched. She would have been perfect except for the slight hump protruding from either shoulder, under her jacket.

Everyone called the little woman Her Majesty.

''Who's that?'' I asked Felicity. ''That is one seriously gorgeous chronologically gifted individual.''

"Rather. Extremely well preserved for a slip of a lass barely five thousand years old, I'd have to agree." Felicity gave me a significant lift of her angelwing-silver eyebrow.

"You're kidding!"

"I'm not. She's Tatiana, Queen of Faerie, and she's not a day under five millennia. If you don't believe me, wait until she removes her jacket."

"The humps?" I asked, hardly believing my own suspicions.

"Wings, of course."

"Cool," was all I could think of to say.

In spite of how well dressed and interesting-looking everybody was, the meeting was still boring the way business meetings always are. I sat there and spaced out, thinking about the trip and all of the arguments and arrangements that went into getting me into that fancy little room.

One of the things I was thinking about was how good Rosie had been at persuading Raydir to let me come. I mean, if you want something done, ask a professional! It was a class-act guilt trip she laid on him about my post-traumatic stress syndrome. I especially liked the touches about how closely bonded to my vet buddies I'd become—Raydir thought that was a real insult to his fatherhood that other guys got to know his little girl better than he did so he compensated the way he usually does by letting me have what I wanted and giving me lots of money besides. I know I wasn't supposed to hear all that, but for an expensive mansion, Raydir's house has got really thin walls and really big keyholes.

Did I mention the girls at the academy had a farewell party for me? S'true. They kept asking if I wasn't afraid to go to Ireland with all the fighting and everything after what I'd just been through.

To tell you the truth, I would have been except that Ms. Eisner, our World Studies teacher, when she heard how I was going to Ireland, took me aside and explained the whole sitch to me. She said it's the north that's so heavy into ballistics and that the south is pretty much peaceful. I was surprised she took the trouble. I didn't know she cared (choke).

Actually, Raydir almost took me to Dublin with him once when U2 wanted him over there for a recording project. But in the end, Mom and I went to Grandma Hilda's and Raydir went to Ireland by himself.

Anyway, I told the girls at the party that according to La Eisner, the south of Ireland was peaceful and calm with nothing but lots of green stuff, guys with cute accents, diddly-diddly music, shamrocks, leprechauns and like that.

I was just kidding about the leprechauns, of course, at the time, but that was before I really got to talking to Felicity and went to the godmothers' meeting and took a gander at those humps under Her Maj's shoulder pads.

To tell you the truth, I was beginning to wonder, during that meeting, if someone didn't put a little extra something on the two lumps of sugar I had in my cute little flowery teacup.

But, as Ms. Anderson in English Comp would say, I digress.

When all the boring stuff at the meeting was over, and Felicity told her story with me for backup, she got a pat on the back and extra brownie points instead of being dissed, which is what that Prudence dame wanted to see happen. She arranged a little surprise for you, Rosie (no, I'm not telling), a gift from her and the girls. All I will say is it will come from Fortunate Finery, the Pike Place Market vintage rag shop that's actually a front for the godmother operations in Seattle.

Her Majesty thought it was great that I wanted to be a godmother too and said that Felicity taking me to Ireland was a "superb" idea. I mean, I'd have had a long trip home if she hadn't liked the idea, but I could have gone back to London and taken in a show or something, I guess. Or maybe just gone to Ireland and hung out, I dunno. But it was strictly no problemo. The godmothers are heavily into recruitment of whoever's interested, it seems to me. Her Maj was particularly nice to Felicity *after* she learned that I was in the picture.

Felicity noticed it too, touched me on the shoulder and

whispered, "My ace in the hole, as it were. So very glad you could come, my dear."

Her Maj noticed the gesture and raised an eyebrow. Felicity smiled and gave one of those airy dismissive waves of her hand. "I was just saying to Sno, Your Majesty, that I suppose we'd best get going if we're to settle in our hotel tonight before finding a flat to rent."

"Ah!" Her Majesty looked as if she was about to pull a rabbit out of her crown. Well, Zen crown. She wasn't really wearing one. You know what I mean. Rabbitness was implied anyway. She gave a meaningful look to another godmother, who took the cue.

"Actually, that won't be necessary, Flitters dear," this other mother reported like she was giving the minutes on the bake sale meeting. "While you've been away, we've been engaged in a new project from which you and your pupil will be the first to benefit. Her Majesty wished to put something back into the country of her and your mutual origin and so we've built a lovely new pied-à-terre a bit south of Dublin where one may recuperate while one is in one's—fallow state. We employed seventy-five different craftsmen in the building and decorating trades for a number of months!"

All the other godmothers applauded, especially the part about employing the workers. Because it was a good work to provide good work, I guess, the FGMs being into helping folks out and all.

Felicity certainly seemed thrilled. She clapped her hands together like a kid at a birthday party. "Oh, this will make the recuperation so much pleasanter! And provide an environment more conducive to teaching and research!"

"Of course, you'll also run the communications and operations center and be responsible for staffing and maintenance while you're there," Dame Prune-face added. She seems to hate to see Felicity enjoy herself too much—no, hate isn't the word. It's more that she seems *scared* when Felicity is having too much fun. Not serial-killer-is-coming-to-get-me scared, more like nervous scared. "And the training of the child, of course."

I didn't much care for the way she said "child," but she was already my least favorite candidate for someone I wanted to place a quarter under my pillow for my loose tooth.

Her Majesty nodded and continued. "There is also another matter of course, that of the apprentice's stipend. This is to see you through while you are under our tutelage, dear," she said, and held out this pretty little gold pillbox which she prestidigitated from nowhere, though she did have on long sleeves. The box was oval and had a design on the lid of a fairy landing on a flower—the fairy and the flower were all set with pearls and crystals. It looked like one of Dame Genevieve's baubles and she smiled at me when she saw me comparing it to her pins, necklaces, etc., etc., etc.

"Take it, child," Her Maj commanded, handing it to me.

"Gee thanks, it's gorgeous," I said, and started to open it. Wrong move! Everyone in the room rushed forward to stop me, as if the thing would detonate on opening. Her Majesty reached out and put her hand on my fingers.

"Gently, dear, gently," Her Majesty said. "You don't want your allowance to leak out until you and Felicity can determine how you can best spend it."

I looked at the pretty box again. It was too small to hold any money and I hardly thought the godmothers would pay me in drugs—fairy dust maybe. Or diamonds. Diamonds seemed like a possibility, from what I'd read. If so, I was glad Her Maj gave them to me in the little box instead of having them drop out of my mouth when I talked like they'd done with that chick in the old fairy tale. That kind of thing is just way too high-profile for good deed doing, as far as I'm concerned. I mean, you wouldn't want to go down Second Avenue in Seattle befriending the homeless with diamonds dropping out of your dental work. You'd get mugged. I didn't figure it was any different in Ireland. *And* it would be really awkward trying to explain to the customs cops.

I held the box out to the queen again. "This is real nice of you, Your Majesty, and I'd love to have the little pillbox but I don't need an allowance. My dad's filthy rich and he gave me plenty of cash and a gold card and all I have to do is call home for more. So you could—uh—put it in the poor box or something. I'm glad you think I'll be worth paying, though.'' That was as diplomatic as I knew how to be and I threw in my best smile for good measure, both out of good manners and caution. I mean, think about it! The Queen of Fairies! I sure don't want to cross that particular authority figure. I have no desire whatsoever to end up like Bobby the toad.

But I didn't have to worry. Her Majesty laughed a world-class laugh, like a whole New Age shop full of wind chimes and incense. "Bless you, dear, for your honesty and unself-ishness. I can see that Felicity has chosen wisely—in this instance. But what this box contains is not among the services offered by American Express, I'm afraid. Within this little container are the three wishes that will enable you to function, in a somewhat limited fashion, as a godmother. Guard them closely and use them wisely.''

Of course, I wanted to know what they were and almost peeked in the box again before I remembered not to.

"They're what you will need most—but only you can decide that. Felicity will help you. She herself will have no magic.''

"No magic?" I looked from Her Maj to Felicity, who shrugged and gave me what Agatha Christie would probably call a rueful smile. "Why not?"

"Because she overspent on her last assignment and she's run out," Dame Prudence butted in. "Do you think magic grows on trees? Its sources must be cultivated, coaxed, which is why I always urge the membership to use it well and hoard it whenever possible.''

Her Maj gave Prudence a look that shut her up, but said, "It's true, my dear. Magic is, fortunately, a renewable resource, but like any other it takes some time to replenish. When a godmother has undertaken as formidable a task as our good Dame Felicity, she depletes her store and must allow herself a fallow period in which to renew her own precious store. Felicity must rest as a field must rest before it is able to be fruitful again. And in the meantime, she must cultivate her sources and will have at her disposal only the powers and skills with which she was mortally born. Therefore, all that is available to either of you is within this wee box. Be careful.''

"Yes ma'am, Your Majesty," I promised, not knowing whether to clutch the box tighter or carry it as if it were made of glass. Nobody had ever given me anything so important. "I will. I really will. Thanks a lot."

CHAPTER 3

Jack of the Giant-Slaying Jacks

In many places around Ireland, but currently chiefly in Dublin, there lived a boy named Jack who was a prince of sorts, provided you looked far enough into the past to discover his noble lineage. For this lad was descended from royalty who had long ago lost the crown, the throne, the scepter and the kingdom. Nowadays what family he had remaining was not only common, but many would tell you they were the commonest in all of Ireland. In a word they were tinkers; in two, itinerants. To use a somewhat less pejorative word, they were travellers. In the far more pejorative but nonetheless immortal words of the great American actress, entertainer, and infomercial spokesperson Cher, they were "Gypsies, Tramps and Thieves."

That was dead wrong, as Jack would have told anyone. His folk weren't gypsies. Gypsies were them dark blokes from Egypt or something, travelled about Wales. Jack's people were Irish and they spoke Cant, not Romany, and they weren't tramps who travelled because they had no homes. They travelled because that's how they liked it. And they weren't thieves. Well, some were, maybe. But so were some settled people as well. And without as much cause. What did the commies call it? Redistributin' the wealth. Jack had nicked a thing or two in his younger days perhaps, but now he wouldn't risk it for fear of being jailed and leaving Mam all alone.

The busking was another thing. It was more respectable than begging. Not that there was anything wrong with begging, really—it was by way of being survival training, rather like those Outward Bound programs they had in America. Even the wealthiest Travellers would sometimes go where they were unknown and do a bit of begging, just to keep their hands in, so to speak. Of course, these days it was mostly the women did the begging, and the children. Less threatening. Jack himself was getting too old and too well grown to be an effective beggar. He looked more like a street tough and didn't inspire the proper pity and guilt on the part of the tourists. People had few qualms about calling the gardai if he tried to persist in his pleas for their charity.

Not good for business, growing up. That was why Jack learnt to play the squeeze box to accompany his singing on Grafton Street. Tourists thought they was gettin' somethin' for their money, like, if you played 'em a bit of a song. He was particularly touching on *Danny Boy* and *When Irish Eyes Are Smiling,* and if the day was slow, he might play a thing or two he liked for himself, just to keep warm.

He had to stay out there, rain or shine, he was that desperate for money. He was the man of the house now, his older brothers and sisters all on the road, and himself the youngest with Mam to look after, and her too old and sick to travel, too feeble to beg and too strong to die.

Just as he gathered his breath for another song, six young girls sat down on the fancy brick pedestrians-only pavement not five feet from him and crossed their pretty legs, nodded to each other and began reciting what sounded like some sort of sports cheer, in French. He grunted to himself. Tourists, run out of hamburger money maybe. Or just under the impression that this was some sort of free-for-all music session. Which it was, unless you were trying to make a living at it. Then it was serious business.

Stung by the injustice of it all and unable to cope with the joyful insensitivity of those who took the bread from his mouth because they had nothin' better to do than make a spectacle of themselves, he shrugged and headed off up to St. Stephen's Green. He imagined the park was like the countryside had been one time for his people, green with flowering trees and flowing streams. Cool ponds with swans mirrored in them. Of course, the old campsites wouldn't have had the fences around them too high for a man to jump, nor the little stone benches, nor the statuary of political and religious Irish heroes. But it would have been all lush and flowering like, sure it would, and free to all.

After an easy walk, he entered the Green and found a bench by the duck pond. Today, as often happened, it was also a swan pond. Four of the graceful milk-white birds glided on the surface, heads down as if admiring their own reflections. Jack watched them, thinking he should be able to make music that would sound as beautiful as they looked, but with a squeeze box, his music always sounded more like a duck or a goose than a swan. He leaned against the back of the bench. For a change, the weather was sunny with only a nip of a wind to bite into his clothes. A fine day altogether. Sitting in the sun, tired from his playing, the suspense of wondering if a coin would drop, the pretense of seeming not to care, he closed his eyes and let the swans swim behind his lids as he thought of tunes. He must have sat there longer than he realized, because the sound of a splash startled him awake.

Across the pond from him, three lads were throwing things into the water, trying to lure the birds. One of them held a stick ready, but out of sight of the pond.

They pretended to be friendly to the birds, throwing bits of fruit and bread that made Jack's own stomach growl. Three of the swans paid no attention but one glided closer, dipping its head to catch the treats, which drew it in closer to shore. It was crooning to itself in a pleased way that broke Jack's heart. He had never heard a swan sing before and remembered that when people talked of a "swan song" they were talking about the last song you'd ever sing and that seemed to be where this gull of a swan was heading. Normally swans could look after themselves—those graceful wings and reed-thin necks were fierce strong and quick. This bird seemed tame though.

As it drew close to the lads, the one with the stick stood ready while another looped his tie around the swan's delicate neck and pulled. The bird's wings flapped, but it was too far from the wicked little gobshite to do him the damage he deserved. The one with the stick hit it. Jack was on his feet, yelling, "Hey, layve t'bird alone, yez!"

They weren't so big, these lads, and for once he was glad he was large and rough-looking. Prissy little schoolboys like themselves tended to be afraid of Travellers anyway, though they'd call names and beat you with their sticks if they thought they could, but in this case they dropped the tie, dropped the stick, and ran away, just as a park custodian came up brandishing his rake.

The swan was trying to disentangle its neck from the tie, and Jack reached out to give it a hand when the custodian panted up to him and gave out to him, threatening him with the rake. "You there, out. I'll have the gard on you molestin' them birds."

"I never!" Jack cried, holding up the tie. "It was them lads as run away. Here now, what would t'likes of me be doin' with this thing?"

"No knackers allowed here, ye great lout, out!" the man commanded, and because Jack had to think of his mother and not be thrown in the jail, where Travellers had been known to meet with unfortunate accidents, he went.

He was halfway home and night was coming when he remembered his squeeze box. With any luck, the thick-headed custodian would be elsewhere. Wearily he trudged back through darkened streets, worrying that he would not have Mam's tea ready on time, but also worried that if he lost the squeeze box, he'd be hard put to find some other instrument with which to make his living.

He was stealthy as a cat making his way to the bench beside the pond, but the custodians and the gardeners had all gone home for the day. The gardai patrolled the paths after dark, but he was well used to avoiding them.

But what was he to do if someone nicked his squeeze box? He fairly choked on his own heart when he saw the bench was empty. Sinking to his knees beside it, he wailed, "Oh, no! Now what'm I to do?"

From behind him he heard a melodious voice say, "If it's the squeeze box you're after, it fell behind the bench."

"Did it?" he asked, hope replacing despair as he did a belly flop and stretched under and beyond the bench, fishing with his hand until he felt the instrument—safe and sound, for all its adventures. "No harum's come to it!" he announced to his informant, climbing to his knees and turning toward the voice with his reclaimed instrument clutched triumphantly in his hand.

But not a soul was there save the four swans, floating just off the bank of the pool. They watched him. Curiously, it seemed to him. Nosy, even.

He looked around for the person who had spoken to him, but nobody else was around. The swans glided a little closer. "I don't suppose any of yez saw the bloke told me where me box was?" he asked them, the way you'd speak to a cat, dog or horse. He did talk to cats, dogs and horses all the time. He had the gift for animals that his people were supposed to have—of course, he thought it was just that he liked them and took the trouble to think what they might be feeling or wanting. He never really thought it was some sort of psychic, eerie thing like people pretended for the sake of the gullible—a little something to give Travelling people an edge over the settled.

"I did that, and a small thing it was too, after the way you saved our Nuala," the same voice said, and he had the impression it had come from the second swan from the left, although of course the animal had no lips to speak with.

"Is it the swan that's after doin' the talkin'?" Jack asked, looking around lest whoever was playing a prank on him should spring from the bushes, laughing to bust a gut.

"It was but it never should have been *him*," said a husky feminine voice. "I should have been the one thankin' you, as it was my own self you saved from my foolishness. But my t'roat is still a little sore.''

This seemed to come from the right-hand swan, and even in the dark he could see the mark where the cruel tie had ripped feathers from her neck.

"*Jay*zus," he said, backing away. "Dat's t'queerest t'ing I ever heard of in me life. What sort of baysht are ye, talkin' like that?"

"You heard the story about the children of Lir?" the lady swan asked.

Jack nodded. "The four chiler of the oul King who's stepmam turnt them into swans." His mam had been a great storyteller in her day. Still was. She remembered the stories fine. It was her name and his own name and where they lived that she was after forgettin' all the time.

"The very ones!" the lady swan said, pleased. "Well, they were our great-great-grandparents."

"I never heard about them havin' any chiler. Didn't they all turn to dust when St. Patrick rescued 'em and turnt 'em back into people again?"

"They did but in the meantime, during all those years, what do you s'pose they did?" the second to the left swan asked. "They just swam around all those years, never took up with other swans? 'Course they did, and we're the proof!"

"That's why we can talk, d'you see?" the second from the right said. "Magical genes. We've got them, on account of being descended and all. That's why we can talk and sing—"

"Like birds," added Nuala with a dip of her head.

"Is there something can turn you back into people as well, then?" Jack asked.

" 'Nother stepmother, maybe," said one of the male swans, considering. "Fortunately for us, swans don't have 'em, being as how we mate for life, and witches don't take much interest in our sort. Not that there's all that many witches about these days."

"Even if there were, no witch could turn us *back* into what we never were," Nuala said.

"We'd stay well away from any witch who wanted to try, too," said one of her brothers. "Just because we're swans doesn't mean we've feathers for brains. Bein' birds isn't the best, you might say, but it's a far cry from the worst and that's true as well. We've our health and our voices and each other and that's what matters when you get down to it."

"True," Jack said. "True enough." He was still wondering if he'd accidentally sniffed too much petrol hanging out on the streets and was ending up as empty-brained as the kids who did it for fun, so now he backed away from the swan as politely as possible, bowing a bit and touching an imaginary forelock. "Well then, it was delightful to meet yer worships, I'm sure. And I thank you for helpin' me find me box. I got to be goin' now. Me mam's old and alone and will be missin' her tea."

And with that he turned and walked as quickly as he could from the park. But someone called after him, "We'll not be forgettin' you, Jack!" and another song like nothing he had ever heard before followed him down onto Grafton Street, though no one else seemed to be hearing it.

*   *   *

Journal Entry—Friday

When we got to Dublin it was pouring rain and blowing a gale, which Felicity says is pretty normal Irish weather for this time of year. We sat in the airport for an hour waiting for the ride that was supposed to pick us up, but they didn't, and all the rentacars were rented. So we ended up taking a cab all the way from Dublin to the house and it got pretty expensive, since Felicity had never been there before and gave wrong directions three or four times before we found the place.

I couldn't believe it was the right house! I thought it would be, you know, like a castle like the one Mia bought or a mansion like Sting's or one of the Martello towers like U2 used to have. But it was this big sprawling ranch house made of cinderblock painted white and topped with a tile roof. Quel bummer! I thought. There were a few skinny little trees tied to stakes but otherwise the house was set in this giant pasture of mud rapidly getting muddier and eroding in big gullies into the gravel driveway. The poor baby trees were drowned by the downpour and taking an awful lashing from the winds ripping up from the sea. The setting was unquaint, unstately, and as unbecoming a fairy godmother (or godmothers) as any piece of real estate you could imagine.

The downpour continued inside the house, we discovered when we finally fished the house key out of the mud puddle where Felicity dropped it as soon as she stepped from the cab.

At first I thought what I saw inside was what Raydir's gardener calls a water feature—a fountain or something. I complimented Felicity on her indoor waterfall.

Felicity did not look thrilled but she was cool. ''Ah,'' she said, looking up at the source of the leak. ''The workmen seem to have run out of tiles before they quite finished the roof.'' Then she calmly sidestepped the torrent sluicing down the white paint in the hallway and puddling on the new carpet.

''Where's the kitchen?'' I asked, setting down my suitcases.

She consulted the sheaf of papers Dame Prudence gave her before we left Bath. ''To your right, dear, if the plans were correct. All mod cons according to Prudence, who was quite put out about the extravagance.''

''Let me find the switch,'' I said, hoping it wasn't wet in there too, lest I get a bigger charge out of the situation than I bargained for.

The kitchen was bigger than the one at Raydir's house, though not as big as his bar. A central island split the room in two. On one side of the island was an oven, microwave, sink, dishwasher and cabinets. On the counter a stovetop had been installed. On the other side of the island, another cabinet and a kitchen table big enough to feed an army filled the room in front of a brick fireplace. Me, I was only interested in the contents of the cabinet. The upper cabinets were stocked with a few food items, plus what looked like fairly fancy crystal and china. The lower ones held tea towels, potholders, utensils, bowls and—hot damn, pots and pans. Seizing a couple of the biggest, I returned to the flood. I put the pans under the main part of the drip, the way Mom and Grandma Hilda had done when we all lived in Grandma's house in Missouri before Grandma could afford to have the roof fixed.

"How clever of you, dear," Felicity said, like I'd just recited the Declaration of Independence or high-scored at Nintendo. Godmothers, like you counselors, Rosie, are big on positive reinforcement. "Now, really, you must be off to bed. Surely you're exhausted."

Having made as certain as I could that I wasn't going to drown in my sleep, I hefted my suitcases and followed Felicity to a large peach-colored bedroom which contained a bed with a poufy coral coverlet and a chest of some light wood. There were no curtains on the windows, however. The rain drumming the bare windows was positively unnerving, even to somebody from Seattle, like me.

"We can hire a housekeeper tomorrow to help us settle," Felicity said. "We can ask her about blinds or window coverings."

I asked where the closet was and Felicity opened this cabinet thing—a wardrobe, we'd call it, or an armoire.

"Ta da!" she said, but the space where you could hang things was only about a foot wide. Seeing my skeptical look, she explained. "They don't use closets here, dear. They use clothes presses. Stone houses are too difficult to build little rooms into, you see."

I said okay. It wasn't like I'd brought a lot of dressy stuff anyway. Just three dresses I thought might be appropriate for doing good deeds in, plus my 501s, a few tees and sweats with choice slogans, some underwear and of course my Adidas and my Doc Martens.

Next to the "press" was the bathroom. "An en suite loo," Felicity said.

"My own little leprechaun's room," I said, just kidding.

She shook her head. "One can only hope *not*, dear. Leprechauns are not the joke Mr. Disney would have you believe. They are extremely territorial, as are most of the sidhe."

"She who?" I asked. I didn't like the way she made it

sound. "She who must be obeyed? Like in Rumpole?"

Felicity shook her head. "That's s-i-d-h-e, dear. Her Majesty's constituency. The little people or whatever. We'll discuss it tomorrow."

Inspecting the bath, I saw that it had a toilet, a sink and a shower but no mirror or medicine cabinet. "Maybe Her Maj got Dracula's decorator."

"Sno. Dear."

"Sorry."

Felicity left, and I brushed my teeth and used the loo, as she called it, before going to bed. I noticed then that the toilet didn't flush and I thought that was pretty strange in a new house, but no stranger than an indoor waterfall. Besides, it isn't cool to flush in the more eco-pc parts of Seattle anymore anyhow.

I dug into my bag and pulled out the "Honor Veterans— No More War" tee Doc gave me to wear in the hospital. It's sort of my lucky shirt now. The room was still pretty cold, even though the heat registers were kicking up quite a racket, so I kept my socks on and crawled underneath the coral-colored poufy comforter. A duvet, Felicity called it. But it was downright freakin' freezin' in there, let me tell you. I usually sleep cold, but after I rolled around trying to warm up various spots on the bed, I finally figured out I was just going to have to put more clothes on so it was back up, shivering all the way to my bag before I could haul out a sweat suit and leap back under the cover. I put my hand up against the register, but the little puff of warmth coming from it was about as much use as a whisper at a rock concert.

And the wind! We get some good blows at home, of course, but this was a hurricane-force howler! It boomed against the house and rattled like automatic weapons fire. I couldn't help thinking of Doc and the guys in monsoon season in Nam. That was *real* bullets and mortars, not just rain—and even the rain, they didn't have a nice safe house between it and them. I thought about the people in the cattle cars and camps, hungry, when here I was stuffed with too much airplane food. I pulled the covers up over my ears and told myself I was being dumb to mind the wind when I'd always loved it. I was thinking maybe you had something there, Rosie, when you said I'd been traumatized. I couldn't help wondering if it was like this for the guys when they first came home from Nam, part of them knowing they were safe but another part saying, Oh, yeah? But I told myself to get a grip.

After all, here I am with the same fairy godmother, whose *name* means good luck, for chrissakes, in a house built by the friggin' AFL-CIO of fairy godmothers. Where in the world could possibly be safer?

There was a lamp on the nightstand and I snapped it back on. Beside it was a book. One book. I hadn't noticed it before, though it must have been there. It was a book of Irish myth. So I thought, okay, I'll read myself to sleep. This was the kind of stuff Felicity wanted me to study so I started reading like it was a school assignment, and making mental notes accordingly, letting my concentration focus on the book instead of the storm.

The early stuff was about the settling of Ireland and the Tuatha de Danaan, who were supposedly Her Majesty's people, though at times it seemed as if even they were visited by beautiful people from the underworld, so maybe not. Maybe even the fairies used to have fairies.

I got disgusted and put it down when I got into the Ulster Cycle. Lots of the stories were about this boy named Setanta, who grew up to be known as Cuchulain, the Hound of Ireland. He sounded like a psycho to me. He had these psychotic episodes like the old berserker Vikings used to have. Whenever he got into one his hair stood out straight and he had to be dunked in cold water to keep him from killing everything in sight. A regular rageaholic. Nice role model. Then there was his boss the King Conor Mac Nessa and he was a pip too— and a misogynistic bastard who made a pregnant lady race his chariot horses to save her husband's life. She got back at him, but still, it was a really gross thing to do. Then later on the old lech, who seemed to treat the wives of his soldiers even worse than Axl treats his *own* girlfriends, took a newborn baby away from her mother because the kid was supposed to grow up and be beautiful. When the baby, who was named Deirdre, *did* grow up and fall in love with a cute guy her own age, the King tricked him and his brothers into surrendering and killed them, then kept poor Deirdre around in spite of the fact that she became anorexic and clinically depressed. Nice beddy-bye stories for the kiddos, okay! Then his Kingness arranged it so that he and the guy who did the actual killing of Deirdre's sweetie were going to take turns "hosting" her and I bet you spell host r-a-p-e. Frankly, I don't know how they got away with it since this was supposed to be during this really enlightened time in Ireland when both men and women were warriors, both ruled lands and had property, and women supposedly had status. Some status! Deirdre's folks were nobility who worked for the King, and it didn't keep her from being a victim.

Of course, if she'd been an ugly chick, it would have been different. Nobody'd have bothered her. As it was, it didn't matter if she was rich or anything, she was *victimized*, Rosie, by those rich guys, just because she was gorgeous. They said it was because the prophecy said she'd be trouble for Ireland, but really, she didn't do a damn thing but go off with a guy she liked. It was the King who caused all the trouble himself.

Like, I could identify. I wasn't doing anything to Gerardine either, minding my own business when, pardon me? she tried to off me three different times. If I'd been Dee-dee pooh, I'd have forgotten cute guys and become a warrior instead and then, if the King tried to give me any grief, I'da had *his* guts for garters. Oops. Sorry. Thoughts unbecoming a fairy godmother candidate. Anyhow, I sort of dropped off thinking it was weird how one of Ireland's great heroes weren't nothin' but a houn' dog. Or a reasonable facsimile thereof.

For a while I kept sleeping, thinking I was dreaming about Cuchulain, which was why I kept hearing howling in my dreams. But then it got so loud I woke up and looked to the window. Something looked back.

CHAPTER 4

Deirdre of the Sorrows

The day her mother was buried, Deirdre O'Sullivan thought, well, that's that, then. At last I'll get a good night's sleep, not havin' to sit up with herself through the night wonderin' if each breath will be the last. One of them finally was, as it had to be.

Deirdre thought she'd feel relief and, after so many years of taking care of first Da until he passed on, and then mother, no more than a little regret. They were so old they'd outlived their legs, their eyes, their ears, their bowels and finally their hearts and lungs. And through it all Deirdre had fetched and carried bathwater and bedpan, food and drink and medicine.

She had thought about how it was before they fell sick, or at least before Mam fell sick as well as Da. She'd remembered how they were when they were younger and still ran the only post office and news agent in two villages. How it was when she was a girl. But she'd been over those memories and over them and what she recalled the most vividly of her relationship with her parents was her father's anxiety, every time she'd shown an interest in far-off things or people, that she wouldn't be there when he passed on to look after Mam. And Mam's anxiety that she might take up with the wrong kind of lad until both the wrong kind and the right kind had found mates and married and had families running around them and, more often than not, moved away to Galway or Limerick or Cork, even to Dublin. Somewhere where there was a life with more promise to it than digging endless tiles of turf, which was the local industry hereabouts. Oh, very colorful that looked for the tourists but it was backbreaking work and now with the new electricity plant that ran on tidal power, there wouldn't be need for the turf anymore except for the odd fire here and there.

No, the memories and Deirdre had made peace with each other long after Mam had been any kind of company at all.

But to her surprise, Deirdre found she missed caring for the husk that had been her mother, nonetheless. She missed the washing of her and the feeding, the laying out her clothes and the changing of the bed linen, the trips up and down the stairs. Missed all the drudgery and sadness of doing the necessary for them as needed her that had shaped all of her days for so long.

Missed it so much, in fact, that now when she might go to bed properly, in her own room at night without worrying about Mam, she found she couldn't. So she sat in the chair where she had sat for so many nights keeping vigil and rocked.

She was waiting, she told herself, for the cat to cry to be let back in. Usually the cat came in at about nine o'clock, but tonight she hadn't. Did Popsy sense the change in the household, that Mam was dead?

As the evening wore on, with no cat crying and no Mam to care for, Deirdre felt as if her life had emptied out—as if it were a ribbon bow, knotted in the middle and convoluted, but basically tied together, which suddenly had had its end pulled and now lay flat and straight before and behind, without interest altogether.

The thought was utterly self-indulgent and too depressing to be tolerated. She couldn't bear sitting there alone in that small house with its cramped little rooms, the wallpaper on each wall a different floral pattern from the rug and the lino and the drapes, each of them different in each room and each clashing with every other like candidates at a political rally. And all of the space in between the rioting flowers empty empty empty. She had been born and raised there like her mother before her and had seen both her parents leave the world from this house.

She'd never raise her own children here, no. She was well past that now without some of those embarrassing-sounding artificial things the doctors were doing in London and parts of America. No, at one time she had wanted a man and children like other women but Mam had said wait and sure enough, Da got took with the sugar diabetes that very year. And it was one thing after another after that. Maybe she should do like some of those women she saw and get another woman to live with her? She was sure most of them weren't—what did you call it?—cheerful: No, gay. They weren't gay. Far from it, in either sense. Not even particularly lonely, if they were like her, far too set in their ways by now, too used to doing things as they liked. But some things were simply *easier* with someone else to share the burden. The only problem was, most of the single women she knew who were alone because a man didn't want to live with them, she didn't want to live with either. Not in this village anyway. Perhaps elsewhere.

She stopped rocking, stood up, plucked her cardigan from the back of the chair, and pulled it on while she hurried downstairs. At the coatrack, she took her slicker from the hook and started out the door. Then she paused. You never knew how long it would take to find a cat. She slipped her feet into her wellies and made sure her keys were in her pocket before opening the door and being swallowed up by the storm.

The funny thing was, she never actually thought she'd find Popsy. She imagined she'd go out, get rained on, become thoroughly soaked and go in and dry off and have a nice cup of tea and by that time be so tired she'd be ready for bed. No doubt just as she slipped between the covers she'd hear Popsy crying to be let in two floors down.

But in fact, despite the wind and rain, she heard Popsy's distinctive mew and that of several other cats almost at once when she stepped—or rather was blown—away from her doorway.

Oh, dear, Popsy hadn't found a tom had she, at her age? She hadn't been fixed, but she hadn't had a litter in years—that Deirdre knew about, anyway. They'd inherited her from a neighbor who died, actually, shortly after Da's death. The old girl had to be as old in cat years as Deirdre was in human years—which would have made kittens if not impossible then at least unlikely and inconvenient.

Deirdre braced against the buckets of rain the sky was throwing at her front and waded toward the sound, which seemed to be coming from the little close behind their house. "Popsy!" she called. "Here, you naughty puss! Don't you be playin' the tart at your great age. Come away with you now, pet."

The meowing stopped as Deirdre rounded the corner. All of the cat voices were silent. But at least a hundred pairs of glittering eyes glared at Deirdre as if she'd interrupted a high-level cabinet conference.

"Well, I'm that sorry I'm sure, yer worships, but a certain puss is going to miss her dinner and spend the night rough if she doesn't come along now."

With that Popsy gave a meow, ran forward from among all of her fellows, and rubbed a wet head against Deirdre's wet wellies. Then she disappeared back into the welter of cats, and the lot of them scampered off into the road.

The King of the Cats

Jack's mother, known to one and all as Mrs. Daly, the mother of fourteen, the widow of two men, God rest their souls, and a sickly, dotty old woman nonetheless believed by the gullible to be strongly empowered with both the evil eye and the ability to tell the future, thought of herself as Moira. Moira the young and graceful, Moira the child laughing behind the horses as they pulled the bright-colored caravan past green fields until she and her family—not the family she had borne, but the family she was born to—stopped to rest by the prettiest, clearest stream they could find. She thought of herself dancing with other Traveller girls, their shawls slipping round their shoulders in abandon as the men drank and danced closer to the fire and their mothers cooked up good suppers and fed babies and mended clothes and made lace for sale to the settled women.

It wasn't really that somewhere deep inside herself she didn't know that she was an old woman in a dingy room with a drafty stove, no toilet or running water and community cooking facilities that were beyond her know-how to make use of. She knew, all right, sad and sour and regretful because of it. People thought the poor were only depressing, never depressed, but the changes she had seen in her lifetime had weighed as heavily on her as a cartload of dead automobile batteries. Finally she had simply chosen to forget. Her illnesses gave her the excuse.

She saw what she saw and what she chose to see and wouldn't be argued with—except by herself. And this night, while she waited for Jack to come home, she argued with herself about whether what she saw was what she saw or what she chose to see, indeed. Though who would choose to see such a thing, given the choice?

The cat it was who gave her such a start. Not her cat, not really. Pets were not allowed in the halt, not cattle nor sheep nor horses nor dogs nor cats. But who could ever tell a cat when to come and go? They were like Travellers themselves, cats were, and came and went as they pleased. This one old battered black tom had taken to coming round her place.

She gave him a bit here and there, but he never allowed himself to be stroked or patted. So she was very surprised one evening when Jack was late coming home and Mary McDonagh came over to light her fire and share a bite of her family's meal. The other Traveller families knew that her son was all the family she had left with her and the women looked in on her from time to time, as was their way. Mary had quite a lot to do herself, with six chiler, three of them under the age of five. This evening she had come with a baby on her hip, accompanied by her twelve-year-old daughter, who also was carrying a wean, and a toddler clinging to their skirts. The old tomcat prowled around the door, reluctant to come in to beg while the chiler were there, but the toddler on the floor had shown no interest in him, as mother and daughter were involved in a bit of a discussion.

"You mustn't go spouting such nonsense, Ann. Isn't it enough trouble we have being taken for ignorant and superstitious without you blathering about funerals for cats?"

"I'm only repaytin' what I saw wit' me own two eyes," Ann said rebelliously.

Mary handed her the baby while she piled up a few turf tiles and got the fire going and put a kettle on before uncovering her little cracked blue dish containing some of the stew she'd made for her family that day. There was also a hunk of bread, which was dry so that old Moira couldn't properly chew it, though it was fine enough when she dunked it in her tea. The stew was harder to manage with her few bad teeth.

The fire was smoky. The little concrete block house was ill-made with a leaky roof and a chimney that didn't draft properly, but it kept her mostly dry. When Mary had hands free to reclaim her chiler, she sat down while Ann went to empty Moira's chamber pot in the single toilet provided for the thirty-eight families staying in the halt. That took her some time, as there was a bit of a line at the toilet usually, and another at the community tap where people were allowed to draw their water and rinse out what needed cleaning. Some ones never minded about the toilet, but did their business on the outskirts of the halt. When she was more able to get about, Moira had gone to the toilet once to find it overflowing. It was cleaner-like to go outside, even with the halt being built so near a dump.

"That girl," Mary McDonagh said, shaking her head. "My other ones is sensible enough. I don't know if puttin' her in school with settled chiler has been good for her atall. She's got all these fancy ideas about Traveller's Pride, does she now, and she's after puttin' the greatest store by the silliest things. Now she's claimin' to have 'the gift.' Says she saw a funeral procession of cats passin' by."

Old Moira nodded, chewing her stew, and stared into the fire. The toddler had gone out with his sister, and now there was just Mary and the two babies sitting on the floor. The tomcat came in and hunkered down by the fire to wait for his bit of stew.

"Says when she was out in the country the other day with her auntie an' they were covering different houses, selling flowers, like, an' there was a hill and a bit of space between one house and the next. Ann's swearin' she saw this thing, but it can't be. Even in a dump, I've never seen as many cats together as she claims—"

Ann returned then, her little brother cuddled against her with one arm, the clean chamber pot in the other hand. "But I did, Mammy, I did see them. Ever so many cats."

The old tom's battered ear showed signs of life, though he'd been pretending to sleep. "There was hundreds of them, I tell you, an' they was carryin' somethin' with 'em. Looked like a bitty wee coffin to me, like you'd put a dolly in. Covered with a purple cloth it was. Breda says there was a tiny crown as well, but I never saw that." She turned to old Moira. "Mammy don't believe me, Gran, but you've seen quare things in your day, haven't you?"

Moira had, though more to do with men than cats. She nodded. The child was beside herself from not being believed by her own family. Really, Mary McDonagh should know better. Sure, didn't the chiler get enough scoffin' from the settled folk? But Mary McDonagh put too much store by what the outsiders thought of her people and her chiler. Worked at that center in Dublin, she did, when she could get someone to look after the babies.

"We do have the gift, don't we, Granny Moira?" young Ann asked. "Jack says as you do. It's not always just made up."

"It's true enough when it comes to daylin' horses," Mary McDonagh told her daughter. "Some folk did have a way with them, but that belongs mostly to the old ways."

Moira opened her mouth, and her voice sounded rough even to her, too many cigarettes and too many days and nights shouting against the wind to her own weans. "Wasn't just horses, a gra'," she said, using the Cant endearment to the younger girl. "Was all God's crayturs."

"Like cats? See there, Mammy, Granny Moira has a cat her own self. Does he talk to you, Granny?"

"Aye, he makes his whishts known," she said.

"Well, then, I'll tell you true, I never have had animals spayke to me in my wakin' hours but after I saw these cats I had a drayum the next night. I spoke to these cats, and they spoke back to me. 'Cats,' says I, 'what're ya abou'?' Not expectin' an answer. But one of them, a wee little gray thing, said, "Oh, Missy, it's a turrible thing altogether but the King o' the Cats is dead. It's his funeral we're havin'. I told Eileen about the drayum and she said it was a true one because that same gray cat had said as much to her."

"That's just an old story!" her mother said. "I won't have you goin' round sayin' such things like an ignorant girl."

And she shoved her out the door and, without another word to Old Moira, took the rest of the family with her.

At the same time, the tomcat jumped up on Moira's knee and pawed a piece of meat from the stew from her bowl. He'd never done such a thing before, and when she tried to brush him down he bristled and dug in his claws, and she left him alone till he finished the stew.

"You're a greedy thing today," she told him.

"Need my feed, Gran," she thought she heard him say, a growly sort of voice inside her head. "If my father, the King of the Cats is dead, it's foul murder and I'm King of the Cats now and must avenge him. Ta." And he hopped down and was out the door.

"Cat, wait!" she cried, never thinking that he would. Old Moira had never seen or heard such a thing. She'd journeyed far and wide in her day, and the gift she had surely heard of, but she was always the one too busy with the chiler to bother much with animals. This was a wonder and a miracle and she had to know more. Had she been harboring a demon or a kelpie? No mind, the cat was travelling on and she would be right behind it, as best she could manage. Old she might be and slow, but she felt the sickness melt from her and the sadness go altogether as she struggled to her feet and wobbled out the door, into the fresh air, facing the road where the cat impatiently paced, staring down the road until it saw her, then springing away again.

*   *   *

The morning after Deirdre found her cat, Popsy, having a ceili in the alley with all those strange cats, no cats at all were to be found in the whole town. On every other doorstep, people stood calling, "Puss, puss, puss," and "Kitty, kitty, kitty," rattling can openers, rotating cans of tuna like incense in a cathedral. But there was no answering patter of soft paws on the paving stones, nor any kindling of bright eyes in the shadows, nor any yawning and stretching upon the windowsills, nor rubbing against ankles, nor licking of fingers, nor meows nor purrs nor chirrups of greeting. The town was as bare of cats as Hamelin Town was said to be bare of rats after the Pied Piper tootled through. The hearthstones and the rugs in front of the fires looked awfully bare. The front stoops, fenceposts and rooftops were naked as a monk's head.

No one had any idea where the cats had gone, nor seemed to care. It was presumed they were all out hunting. "*All* of them?" Deirdre asked the neighbor who advanced the theory. "Now, that is as likely as everyone in the pub agreeing on anything whatsoever."

She was not satisfied with the explanation, nor was she satisfied in any respect at all. She realized suddenly that she didn't just miss Popsy, she was actively jealous of her. She'd left. Gone. Escaped. Deirdre longed to do the same.

And then it occurred to her that she had to, really. There would be no old-age pension for her mother coming in now to add to the home-caretaker's stipend Deirdre earned to supplement her dole check. And there were no jobs in the village to speak of. Not that Deirdre wanted to speak of them. She wished to follow the cats, was what she wished to do. To lock up the house, take what little money she had saved and leave town. It would be nice to go abroad but truly, it would also be nice just to see a bit more of home. Why, here she lived within twenty miles of the Kerry Peninsula and she had never gone round the Ring of Kerry, nor seen Killarney, nor done any of the famous things there were to do in Ireland. By the time she was old enough to do it, her parents needed her help.

So it struck her as something to do to go to Galway and Derry and Belfast and Dublin, then on to Cork and back to Killarney, and see what work opportunities there were and how she liked those cities, but to do her searching the long way round, covering as much of Ireland as she could by public transport.

As for places to stay along the way, though she had no close relatives any longer, both her mother and father came from large families and there were aunts and uncles and cousins and in-laws of one sort or another, or friends of the family at the least, in most places Deirdre wished to go. The difficult part would be getting away from the relations long enough to go see the sights and look into the housing and job opportunities. The other part, of course, was gathering up the last of the jams she'd canned to have a little gift for each relative. And to write notes to those farthest ahead, informing them of her intentions and expected arrival time, and making a call to the ones in Tralee and Galway, where she was told that she was very welcome, they were sure, and they'd manage fine, really they would, in spite of the abruptness of the visit. For once she didn't back away politely, as she always did, but told them that she wouldn't be troubling them but a short time and— shamelessly—that it was the shock of her dear mother's passing, didn't they know, and she just had to get away. And of course they did see, having been through it themselves.

For her part she'd rather have stayed in guest houses, but it was out of the question with what she had left. Except for a couple of nights in the north, where she had no intention of relocating, being quite happy in the Republic, thank you very much, she was stopping with family. She couldn't help thinking how freeing it would have been to have done without the jam glasses, the excuses for coming, the excuses for leaving, the excuses for doing as she liked just this once, please God.

Her private time was on the trains and when she walked in the cities, unless, as in Galway, a talkative cousin cared to accompany her and show her the sights, which was quite pleasant. Her father's cousin in Tralee had said little but promised to speak to friends about a housekeeping position. Once, long ago, Deirdre had learned to type but now she couldn't remember where her fingers belonged.

No one paid her much notice, though people on the trains were always willing to chat and even share a bit of the food the experienced travellers brought with them. Deirdre broke open one of the jam jars and kept it for just such occasions, so she'd have something to contribute.

And she did see a fair bit of country. She stopped in Tralee long enough to take bus excursions back to the Ring of Kerry, which was stormy but quite beautiful with its cliffs and bogs and the forests of voracious but lovely rhododendron that had devoured the oak groves. Dingle was different-looking, gentler in places, more dramatic in others, with little villages full of young people, many of them foreign, and pubs advertising music that she couldn't stay long enough to hear. After the Dingle trip, she spent one more night with the Tralee relations, then took the train to Limerick. She had not been particularly looking forward to Limerick, as it was not a beautiful city, having often been destroyed by its enemies in the past.

But there she stayed with her cousin Kitty O'Regan and John, her husband. She was led by their son John, a man in his early thirties and a writer of music books and reviews, on a tour of King John's Castle and the Treaty Stone. Then nothing would do but they had to bus out to Shannon and see Bunratty Castle and the Folk Park, where the old house of one of their mutual relatives had been transplanted to show the tourists what Ireland used to be like.

And at last she did get to hear some music because when John heard she liked it, he dragged her away from his mother's fireside and out to a back room in a hotel pub where a folk club met. A young woman from Newry sang modern love songs while her husband played drums from all over the world. It was lovely, but at the same time it made Deirdre a little sad. Kitty was up ahead of them the next morning with a fry-up of sausages and bacon, black and white pudding and potatoes, tea and biscuits and before Deirdre left, insisted on sending a tall box of Cadbury's Roses chocolates with her.

Funny. She had thought Limerick would be the least hospitable of her stops, and it turned out to have been one of the best. Galway was a much more beautiful city, economically better off too, but her cousin's sister-in-law was not nearly as welcoming or warm as the O'Regans and obviously couldn't wait to see the back of her.

It was on the long, long stretch between Galway and Sligo that Deirdre saw the cats again. Not that she could have said for certain these were the same cats that abandoned her village. She saw several tortoiseshells and several calicos, but she wouldn't have gone so far as to say any of them was Popsy. However, since it looked like she was seeing every cat in the world, she felt safe in assuming that some of these would be the cats from her village, including her own round, furry friend. They walked in procession, three tails deep at least in most ranks, the line spread out for a mile or more.

And then the train was past them and she couldn't see them behind her—though the fields were shadowed with what *could* have been cats. The train made a long stop in Sligo and it was after that, near dark, about halfway to Derry, that she saw the eyes, like thousands of fireflies, massed along the tracks.

On an early morning walk to the Giant's Causeway, long before the tour buses arrived for the day—she'd taken the bus in the night before and stayed at the hotel—she saw that every stepping stone of the causeway had a cat curled upon it. She walked quietly among them, looking for Popsy. One stone after another, all those cats, and on the most prominent, next to the sea, eight cats lay surrounding a little purple draped coffin with a crown on it.

She spent more time than she would have imagined possible walking among the sleeping cats, because the sun was rising and the first tour bus of the day came rumbling down the hill. She watched it for a moment, and when she looked back, all of the cats were gone.

She took another side trip to Armagh to see Navan Fort and Ewain Macha, home of the Kings of Ulster. Then to visit the relatives in Belfast who were so happy to see her and were full of news—the death of a soldier, the disappearance of a young girl, in hushed tones—and with deep cynicism and fatalism and no little yearning, the proposed IRA cease-fire.

"Of course, that'll just make the UVF all the worse," her cousin Jimmy said, referring to the Ulster Volunteer Forces, the Protestant guerrilla equivalent of the IRA, as dedicated to ensuring that Britain maintained a presence *in* Ireland as the IRA were that it would not.

"Well, if the IRA doesn't respond," his wife said, "at least there won't be twice the killings—the horrid scorekeeping as if our lives were all pawns in some great nasty game."

That was all the mention made of *that*. There were happier subjects to talk about. Jimmy and Eileen's daughter Claire going to Uganda as a relief worker. The Irish performance in the World Cup. The scandals the British Royals were up to these days and the poor Queen, God bless her, how did she manage with such a family? And of course there were many remarks exchanged about what lovely people Deirdre's parents were said to have been, though neither Jimmy nor Eileen ever met them. They'd heard though, from Eileen's mother.

Deirdre slept well that night, in a snug little room that Eileen used for her sewing. And she dreamt of cats.

CHAPTER 5

Journal Entry—Friday

When I saw those big eyes glowing through the rain pouring down the window and heard that yowling over the moaning of the wind, for a minute I couldn't move. Then I fumbled for the light and knocked my little wish box and the book *and* the lamp off the bedside table.

I bent over to pick up my box and the lamp. When I looked back up at the window, the eyes blinked at me. About that time I heard this little sad "Meow." That must have been why the howling. Some dog had been chasing the cat and couldn't catch it 'cause cats can jump up on windowsills and dogs can't. Feeling like an idiot, I fumbled around until I figured out the Irish window latch. The cat, a small bundle of very wet gray fur, not caring at all that I got soaked to the skin from the blast that was blowing cold rain all over the room, acted like a hitchhiker trying to decide whether or not I was a pervert before it finally decided to come inside like it'd been screeching to do for the last five minutes.

I reached out to wipe some of the water off its fur. "Whew, kittycat, you had me scared there for a minute."

The cat ducked and blinked at me again and strode to the

52

door, where it stood expecting to be let into the house. "I don't know, cat," I told it.

To emphasize its point it scratched at the door and meowed again, only once, but with feeling. I obeyed. Cats are like that. But I expressed my reservations to our first houseguest. "If you're a tom and you spray Felicity's new house, we'll both see how good and kind fairy godmothers *really* are." The cat flirted its tail and sauntered down the hall. I followed, flipping on light switches. I wanted to make sure the cat didn't pee on something. I also wanted to see where it went. Felicity and I had been too pooped to explore the place before we turned in, but now, even though I hadn't had much sleep and it was the middle of the night, I was wide awake. Must have been jet lag.

The cat stopped in front of another door, which it pawed. I heard this noise behind me and jumped about three feet. When I came down my bare foot grazed something cool with the texture of bumpy leather, definitely alive. It was that gross little toad! It hopped off out of range, luckily for it, and like, *stared* at me with its big pop eyes. The cat hissed at the toad and batted at it but it stayed where it was.

"If I'd known it was you, you nasty thing, I'd have worn football spikes and stomped harder," I informed the toad.

"Snohomish, dear, is that the attitude with which you wish to start your new career as a doer of good deeds?" Felicity asked, flinging open the door, I thought, to her bedroom. She was dressed in this movie-star nightie—whaddaya call it?—a peignoir and a drifty, pale gray negligee. Her white-silver hair was piled on top of her head and clipped with silver combs in the shape of dolphins.

"He," I said, pointing to the toad, "started it."

The cat mewed and looked up at Felicity. Felicity looked down at her as if she was listening and then said, "Oh, very well, Puss, but I really think you could have let us get a good night's sleep first." With a sigh she turned to me. "Puss has asked me to make formal introductions, as you'll be working together somewhat. She inhabited a cat in Seattle, but I don't believe you've met. Puss, this is Snohomish Quantrill from America. Sno, Puss.''

This was too much for me. I mean, sneaky toads who used to be mob members and cats who clawed their way into *my* room but would only talk to Felicity without an introduction? Puh-leese!

"This is nuts," I said. "I wish I—"

Felicity looked up, and I should have paid attention to the warning in her face, I guess, but I was feeling left out just because I had two legs. Felicity and these critters had all known each other longer than I had known anyone and furthermore, they could all talk to each other in animal and I couldn't understand. I was at least going to finish my sentence.

"Could understand all this animal talk so I—"

"Sno!" Felicity said and gave this grimace in the direction of my hand. Then I looked down and saw that I was still holding my little pillbox.

". . . so I could talk to animals too," I continued, even though I realized now that I had just used up one of my wishes by bitching aloud while I was holding the box.

Felicity sighed.

"Well, I do," I finished lamely. Maybe it was okay. The box didn't look any different.

"Seems a sensible wish to me," the cat said—I swear it— clear as a bell inside my head. It wasn't like telepathy on TV, though, you know, not like it was me saying to myself or some announcer with a deep voice—it was this catty little scritchy voice. A catty little scritchy voice with an Irish accent at that.

"Geez, it worked," I said.

Felicity shook her head. "If you wanted to be able to talk to Puss, you could have done that without spending a wish."

"What do you mean?"

"Puss is the—shall we say reincarnation?—of the same magical talking cat of Puss in Boots fame. In Seattle, I imported her magic to a stray cat there to assist a young man named Dico, but ordinarily it stays right here, with her."

"At least till she becomes roadkill or dog food," the toad said—not in a toad voice, but in that same sarcastic voice that had threatened to cut me in the woods outside Mt. Baker. The toad had Bobby the Butcher's voice even though it was in a toad body.

"Too bad," the cat said, "St. Patrick had to be so hasty about driving the snakes from Ireland. You'd make a tasty snack for a python, wart-face."

"Puss!" Felicity said. Puss hissed at Bobby behind her back. Felicity picked her up and pointed her toward me, giving her ears a little brush with one hand. "Cut that out. You wanted to be introduced. This is Sno. Sno, Puss."

"Put me down this instant, you bold woman!" Puss said, squirming free and dragging her claws down Felicity's peignoir. Once she was back on the floor, though, the cat washed a paw and said, "Well, Sno, in the future, see that you leave that window cracked a bit for me, there's a good girl."

"Uh—charmed, I think," I said.

"We're that pleased to have you, dear," the catty voice said as if it belonged to Queen Elizabeth talking in brogue. "Normally I'd offer to be hospitable and sleep at the foot of your bed to make you feel more at home. However, I've a funeral to attend and just called in for a bit to catch up with Flitters. But don't be glum. If you're a pet and leave the window open as I asked, I'll bring you a nice dead rabbit when I return."

"Uh, no thanks, but thanks for asking. I guess I'll go back to bed now," I said, not sure yet that this wasn't all a dream anyway.

Felicity nodded. "You do that, dear, and I'll just finish up a bit of work here. And don't worry about the wish. When it comes to wishes, spontaneous is usually best. Even though you could talk to Puss or Bobby without a specific wish, now that I think of it there's really no place else to get such an honest and diverse viewpoint as conversing with the other animals."

"You really think so, Felicity?" I asked. I felt like an idiot just popping off and wasting a wish like that when Her Maj had told me it was all the magic either of us would get.

She nodded slowly and her eyes were twinkling like Santa's. "As a matter of fact, I think it was a stroke of brilliance. In many of the oldest tales in Ireland, as in most of the early fairy tales, people and animals conversed as easily with each other as they did with their own species. It's also told that Tuan, brother of the first man to set foot on Ireland, spent several lives as various animals before being reborn as a human. And then, of course, there are all of the people who were turned into animals.''

Well, having been on the streets in Seattle, I was familiar with *that* kind of animal anyway.

I said goodnight and told the cat it was nice to meet her. She had just been sitting there washing, but she looked up then with wide mint green eyes. ''Ah, I'm sure it was at that, dear,'' she said.

And I heard her say to Felicity just before I closed the bedroom door, ''Skittish little thing, isn't she?''

I slept really well the rest of the night, and my dreams were a whole lot tamer than real life had been on this trip so far— or was going to be the next day.

*   *   *

Cunla the window-rattler had had a fine time. He'd had his fears that the silvery woman, with her connections to the Gentility, would suss him out, but she'd never noticed hide nor hair of him, even when he punched the great hole in her roof and stopped up all her privies. He'd banjaxed her auto good as well. He was clever, was Cunla, and these days the autos had so many parts that weren't iron that a clever one such as himself had not a bit of trouble bollixing them up.

And the girl! She was that easy to frighten, the timid thing, with his rattling and tapping. He'd have had the duvet off her and her shriekin' round the room had it not been for the great nosy cat near knockin' him off the windowsill just as he was about to pry it open. He'd scuttled off under the eaves before the Puss was aware of him, though, and wasn't he the thankful one for the rain to wash away his scent?

Why, it was almost too easy. He'd thought these ones would give him a challenge, what with herself bein' one of the great ladies who had ordered the house built, but all the shimmer of enchantment was gone out of her and she was as helpless against him as any farmwife. The only place he couldn't enter was the room where the machinery was, for it carried the shimmer of them as spoke on the other end of it from far away.

He darted under the machine-room window and saw herself and the girl talking, looking down as if conversing with the cursed cat.

Cunla thought for a moment of letting loose the wee dog howling from the pen next door, but as he turned to look at it, the dog gave out to him with a series of great growling yaps and Cunla decided that himself on the one side of the fence and the dog on the other was the way it should stay. He'd made trouble enough for the night already. Mustn't use all the fun at once, but let it out slowly and with a bit of slack at times, to lull those within to a false sense of calm, the better to set them up for the next wee prank.

CHAPTER 6

The Christening Gifts

Grania O'Malley's christening had been the event of the village. "Ah, she'll be a beauty like her mother," her Auntie Cyra predicted.

"And she'll have Gran's kind heart as well," Auntie Margaret added.

"And that graceful way about her I've always had," Auntie Sinead, who was a bit vain, put in.

Her mother had a large family. Thirteen brothers and sisters altogether, and the church was crowded with them. Her uncle Gino predicted she'd be musical, like her grandfather. Her auntie Mary said she'd be a good girl. Her uncle Tim said, God willing, not too good to be any fun.

Then the church doors slammed open, and to everybody's dismay in stalked difficult Aunt Gobnait, whom Grania's mother had never liked, but had invited anyway, as it was the right thing to do, regardless. Unfortunately, the little backwater village in the far northwestern corner of Northern Ireland where Aunt Gobnait lived was having a postal strike and the invitation never arrived. Even more unfortunately, Aunt Gobnait seemed to be the only one in the family gifted

with the second sight that was a hereditary gift/affliction.
Yet more unfortunately, her second sight wasn't strong
enough to tell her about other people's good intentions—it
only let her see where she had been slighted, jilted, neglected, cheated or lied to and never gave her any insight
whatsoever into extenuating circumstances. And it certainly
never allowed her to see which behavior of her own had
prompted the slighting, jilting, neglect, cheating or the little
lies people told to try to avoid, to no avail, falling afoul of
Aunt Gobnait's formidable bad side.

"I heard you! I heard all of you fawnin' over this child
as if she was not filled with sin as any born of woman. And
I'll tell you this—she'll be all the things you say and it will
do her no good, no good at all, because by the time she's
sixteen all them qualities will combine to land her in so
much trouble she'll be slain for a strumpet! One of you at
least should have had the wit to ask the Lord that she be pi-
ous and chaste! But, no, you lot wouldn't think of that,
would you?"

Grania's mother burst into tears. She was the baby of the
family, born when their mother was sure she was done with
children, and her much older brothers and sisters doted on her,
all but Gobnait, who was next to the youngest and had re-
sented bitterly being displaced by the newcomer.

Everyone was most uncharacteristically speechless. Aunt Sinead clasped her heart, and Uncle Tim turned bright red and
looked as if he was about to explode, which was not good for
his blood pressure.

Then through the open doors came another figure, the aunt
Grania from Cork whose namesake baby Grania was. "Shame
on you, you daft old woman, venting your spite on a wee
baby!" she stormed at Gobnait. "I could hear everything you
said clear out in the churchyard where I was payin' off me
taxi. Imagine bein' given the sight and seein' nothin' but evil
in everyone. Not only that, but you've given the child no
proper wish at all so I'll do it for you and hope before God
that she has the sight and sees a damned sight better world
than you do! As for my own ideas about the child, I think that

with the wit of all of this family which so sadly bypassed you, the girl will be smart enough to see herself through any trouble her good intentions get her into.''

Grania had been told the story by her dear Auntie Sinead and the others as a sort of bedtime tale, not to scare her, but to reassure her of how loved she was. Years passed, and Auntie Sinead's heart finally gave out. The aunts and uncles seemed to fall like dominos after that. It was on the way to Uncle Tim's funeral in County Antrim that Grania's parents were killed in an auto accident. Grania was just thirteen when it happened, and thirteen had been a most unlucky number for her.

For who was it claimed to be the last of the family and her sole living relative but Aunt Gobnait, who took her out of school and away from her home and back up into the hills. She burnt Grania's jeans and pretty clothes and made her wear black wool, shapeless and scratchy and frumpy, to conceal her budding figure.

"It's for your own good," Gobnait told her with a sneer of satisfaction. "Am I not doing all I can to prevent the doom I see from comin' on you?"

And for the next three years, Grania could do nothing right. Her aunt had warned the nuns at her school that she was a problem, and so they were down on her right from the start. The kids in her class, who had all grown up in the same village, disliked her because she hadn't and mocked her accent. Her uniform fit poorly—her aunt saw to that—and she was always getting reprimanded for it.

She hadn't even got over the death of her parents when everything changed for her and it seemed like she just couldn't stop being sad. The sadder she was, the more chuffed her aunt was about it, and she found all kinds of hard work for Grania to do, which she didn't mind doing as long as it got her away from the aunt. But the chores gave her no time for her homework.

If it hadn't been for the story her other aunts had told her when she was little, she'd have believed she was a dead loss the way Gobnait told her and probably would have slit her wrists or something.

As it was, she figured that she belonged someplace, but it definitely wasn't with her Aunt Gobnait, and as soon as she was legal, she would run away. Except she didn't know where to go precisely but figured she'd work it out when the time came. The second sight her aunt Grania was supposed to have given her meanwhile kept her from eating the tainted meat that her aunt put on her plate periodically.

The first time she thought the meat was just a bit off, and gave it to a neighbor's dog, but the dog died. When anything tasted off to her after that, even if she was very hungry, which she often was, she found a way to get rid of it without eating it, though she never again fed it to an animal. She told herself she was probably just being silly—melodramatic, as the nuns said—but every time she had what seemed like an irrational fear, it also seemed to come true. Not all of her fears were connected with her aunt, though many were—the time she had to go to the loo just as lightning struck the metal molding on her bedroom window, the time her aunt sent her to the market and she for some unaccountable reason decided to go to a different one than usual and the one she usually went to, next to the bookmakers, was blown up.

On her sixteenth birthday, she was jumpy all day, because she remembered not only the birthday but what Gobnait said about it. Gobnait's prediction in this case seemed likely to be a self-fulfilling prophecy. If Grania was so rude as to make her aunt out a liar—or even mistaken—Gobnait was likely to kill her. But Gobnait said nothing about the birthday or the curse, and that was cause for celebration even if turning sixteen in the old hag's house was not. Grania sneaked out to go to the church to pray for her mother and father and all of the nice aunts and uncles who'd died just before she really needed them.

On her way back, she passed a checkpoint, and as she walked along the river, there was a good-looking young soldier squatting there with his gun. His heart didn't seem to be in it. He glanced up at her with such a sad, rueful expression, as if to say, "Well, there goes another pretty girl who probably hates me," that she felt even sorrier for him than she did for herself.

She'd given him just the tiniest smile of encouragement— not that kind of encouragement, just the sort to help him keep on a bit. Not politically like, just personally. Because the sixth sense didn't just warn her of danger—it let her know what other people were feeling like too, which was usually too bad, since these days she mostly read hatred or fear. But not in this chap. Not now. Right now he was feeling much as she did— homesick and afraid of the hostile people around him; alienated was the word. Like some kind of creature from outer space instead of just from another county or another country.

She'd been careful about the smile because she knew it could be dangerous—the girls at school still talked about the older sister of one of them. The older sister used to be a real beauty, they said, but she'd gotten caught shaggin' a British soldier and right-thinkin' people had done for her good—cut off her hair and stripped off her clothes and tarred and feathered her and beat the livin' daylights out of her, though not in that order. If she'd heard such a tale where she used to live, Grania would have said, "But that's bloody barbaric. That only happened in the old days." But she could just see her aunt getting a real jolt out of doing that kind of thing.

The soldier caught her hand, that was all, just long enough to say thanks. But as she looked down the river, Grania saw her aunt's next-door neighbor, who was almost as bad as Gobnait was, standing at the door staring straight at her. And she knew for dead sure she couldn't go back to her aunt's house, not then or ever, not even to pick up her things. Well, that was all right, then. She had been going to leave as soon as she was of age, and sixteen was when her aunt would stop drawing money for her anyway and kick her out.

She detoured into the news agent's and tried to think. What to do next? But her guardian angel must have been watching, because just then a bus drove up and she got on. She had a few pence she'd scraped together from the marketing, a perilous enterprise because her aunt was careful about checking receipts. Lately her health hadn't been as good, though, so sometimes she let it slip, and Grania held back a ten p here and there.

She had just enough to get her to the next town. She left the bus and headed down the highway, thumbing a ride. She caught one with a pair of tourists who stopped to ask her for directions. The luck was with her. They were headed back across the border into the Republic and were going all the way to Dublin. At the border checkpoint, the soldiers checked the ID of the driver and his wife but seemed to assume she was their daughter and waved them through. She rode with them into Dublin, arriving around half eight in the evening. Her hosts went to their hotel and she walked the streets all night, dodging drunks and snogging couples, walking like she knew where she was going, though she hadn't a clue.

She would have been afraid to be in the big city walking the streets alone at night except that it was so much less dangerous than where she'd just come from that all she could feel was relieved. Early in the morning, as the news agents opened and the morning papers were delivered, something told her to take a look. And there in the headline was the name of her village, and news of another killing. The face was one she recognized as the soldier's. He'd been killed, it said, in retaliation for what was believed to be the kidnapping of a young Catholic girl from the village. That would be herself, and there was her picture alongside that of the poor young soldier.

She turned away quickly and walked on her sore feet out to what looked like a main road. Since her second sight seemed to be saving her arse these days, she watched the cars and willed the right one to stop. Two dozen passed her before a jeep pulling a horse trailer stopped and a woman opened the door. That was all right, then. Grania hopped in without a second thought, and saw the baby in the child carrier.

"We're headin' home to Waterford," the mother told her. "How far are you goin'?"

"I'm just going to see my auntie in Enniscorthy," Grania told her, having a vague idea that Enniscorthy would be on the way.

It was, and the woman took her to a door Grania identified as being her aunt's house. She thought of staying there, but the town looked too big to her, small as it was. Probably silly to be so concerned that she'd be found this far from home, but Ireland was small and the border between the north and the Republic didn't prohibit people from travelling back and forth at will so long as they could answer a question or two at the checkpoint. If anyone was after her, they had only to cross over and come straight down the highway to find her.

So she hitched another ride out to another small town, further off the highway, where she chose another house to be her aunt's until the car that gave her a lift passed on.

She walked on and on until she came to another village, rather a tiny one this time, and here she stopped long enough to buy a soft drink and a packet of biscuits at a news agent's, then set off down the road to the countryside.

She walked a long time, looking for some uninhabited place where she might find a little shelter while she decided what to do next. Weariness weighted every footstep, while dread prodded her to hurry along.

She passed a wide spot in the road where a caravan was parked, the front of it guarded by old bathtubs and discarded windows and a sofa hopping with fleas. A pair of brown-and-white-spotted horses, their coats scruffy and dusty, their bones poking through, grazed in the field beside the caravan. The light from within the metal home looked warm and inviting, but she couldn't risk being turned in "for her own good" to be sent back to Aunt Gobnait.

A little country store was just closing when she arrived. The lady took a look at Grania's book bag and said, "A student, are you? Out for a bit of a holiday in the country?"

"I am that," Grania said. "Would you be knowin' where I could get a bit of shelter for the night? I've not much money."

"There's an abandoned abbey down this side road, but it's being fixed up as a farriery school by an American lady. Used to be you could have slept in the cottage, but it's all redone proper as a house with a lock and key for the lady's guests.

But could be some shelter there still. If you'll wait a bit, I could try to find something better for you, though. A young girl like yourself . . .''

"I wouldn't be puttin' you to that trouble, thank you, no," Grania said and left quickly, before the lady could ask the questions Grania could all but see on the tip of her tongue. Much as she ached for a bed and a meal, Grania couldn't wake up among folk who might see her face in the morning paper.

The road was long and rutted, overhung with trees and edged by thick brush. A small, dirty-looking pond sat in a depression just before she reached the arched stone ruins of the abbey. She could tell even in the twilight, even at a distance, that they would do her no good. The roofs had been removed for renovation. Besides, the property looked as if it was being worked on, and she did not want to be discovered by workmen. The ground smelled of wet char where brush had been burned back. Above the stone ruins, brambles ran rampant. She climbed the hill to their edge, to see if she could spot some other likely shelter. A chimney and part of a roof rose just above the thorny tangle. No smoke curled from it, and the roof had a hole. Slowly, carefully, painfully she worked her way around to the narrowest spot between herself and the house, and, using her book bag to mash down a path before her, made her way to the house.

A broken window gave her access, and she fell exhausted and bleeding from thousands of scratches onto a floor littered with tins, old papers and animal dung. It smelled of damp and mildew. She found a corner farthest from the holes in the roof and pulled a bit of rotting old carpet over her for warmth, then fell into a pit of sleep.

*   *   *

Balor of the Evil Eye

The man whose true name was Balor was as pleased with Grania's friendly gesture to the now-deceased soldier as everyone else was displeased. Of course, it wouldn't do to show it. He leaned back against the wall, the front legs of his chair tipped off the floor, his hands cupped behind his head. His legs were crossed and propped up on the card table in the little house. His whole posture was relaxed, but watchful, while the local lads worked themselves up over the incident. He was always cool, but he warmed himself with the heat of their vehemence.

"The bint set him up, I tell you!" Archie Graham, the local Loyalist leader, told his troops. "The boy never touched her—he didn't live long enough. She give him the whaddayacallit, kiss of death!"

" 'Scuse me, sir," said young MacFarland, a new recruit. "She didn't kiss him at all, sir. I was there, sir. She just smiled at him." He'd bear watching, that one. An inquiring mind was not a desirable quality in an armed fanatic.

"She did something, you can bet. I hear she was a hot little number. Besides, the Taigs are whining for peace now. If she and the boy hadn't had something on together, they'd not have blown the poor lad away and him with a widowed mother and all," Sinclair offered. He was practically drooling. He liked to think of all the screwing Taig women had to do to get those large families.

"They're claiming he done away wiv her, Arch," Lewis volunteered.

"I bloody well know what they're claiming!" Graham thumped his fist on the card table. Balor lifted his feet until he was sure the table wouldn't fold under him. When it seemed safe, he lowered his heels again. "But our sources tell us the little hoor got clean away. They saw her takin' a bus right after. And I say she pays. She wants to play dead, we'll give her a hand at a bit of realism."

You'd have to catch her first, Balor thought. She's taken a powder, and not even her dear old auntie knew where she'd gone. Inconvenient in a way, not to have her handy. On the other hand, there was much more speculation, and it kept the incident alive longer to have her missing, have a little something hanging in the balance.

Young MacFarland didn't look happy about all this, though

he wasn't stupid enough to ask further questions. Balor decided he'd have to take the lad under his wing—perhaps introduce him to some chemicals that would change his perspective, help him make a better adjustment to the group ethos.

Balor was good at adjusting to the ethos of different groups. In fact, he'd attended another meeting earlier in the day, with people of the opposite political persuasion, among whom he was known by another name. Both sides knew him as an outsider—a useful outsider. Each side was convinced he was passionately committed to its cause. He was known to buy drinks, supply chemicals such as those he proposed to lavish on MacFarland, and had been seen, personally, by members of each group, to calmly commit murder and plant bombs. He was above suspicion. It never occurred to anyone that perhaps he simply liked committing murder and planting bombs.

At least he wasn't hypocritical enough to confuse his interest in the suffering of his fellow human beings with political affiliation. He was perfectly democratic, nonsectarian and nonsexist about that. It didn't do to let on, however.

The old biddy who was the aunt of that girl, now, she was less honest. She was just like him, but she slathered religion all over her lust for pain. She'd have been aces in the inquisition.

He had been brought along as a friend of Breda Reilly's son Kevin at a gathering of a few of Gobnait Brophy's concerned neighbors. Gobnait was serving tea to those who came to offer condolences about her niece, and to decide what was to be done about her, the treacherous ungrateful little slut. Breda Reilly herself had seen what the girl done. And they were each sure the other knew who had killed the soldier, though none of them did.

"I only wish that before that soldier was killed, they'd have got out of him what he did to your poor Grania, Mrs. Brophy," said an elderly lady with soft white curls and pink cheeks as she smacked her ill-fitting dentures with relish over the girl's imagined fate. "True she was a forward piece, as Mrs. Reilly herself has seen with her own eyes, but still and

all she was one of ours and I hate to think of you worryin'
yourself sick over her maybe lyin' half naked in a ditch, where
the heathen bastard flung her when he'd given her that for
which she so plainly seemed to be askin'.''

Kevin Reilly, who certainly would have been capable of the
killing, though not perhaps in the timely fashion Balor preferred, was oddly enough the voice of reason among all the
speculation.

''I think you can rest easy on that score, Missis. Our sources
tell us the lass was never kidnapped at all. Turns out one of
the boys at the turf agent's saw her boardin' a bus. Remembered specifically because your lass is such a fine-lookin' girl.
Of course, we're keepin' that to ourselves for present. Headquarters is annoyed enough that we did for one of the soldiers,
whatever the provocation. Says it embarrasses them during the
peace process. How to break it to them that she wasn't raped
and murdered after all, I'm sure I don't know.''

''Fancy her causin' all that trouble then runnin' off like
that,'' another neighbor said. ''Must have been a tricky little
thing, your lass . . .''

''She's no child of mine, you know,'' Gobnait Brophy said.
''She belonged to my late sister and out of charity I took her
in when her parents were killed, though I knew I'd regret it.
I could tell from the time she was a wean that she was going
to be nothing but trouble.''

''You'd think she'd no idea where she came from, the way
she carried on,'' Mrs. Reilly said. ''Makin' cow eyes at that
little Nazi and him gropin' at her in plain sight of the village.''

''As you say, Mam,'' Kevin Reilly said. ''When you told
us about it, our first thought was to give the girl a bit of a
lesson—nothin' lethal, mind you, just a good beatin' to remind
her who she owed her loyalty to. But when you, Missis Brophy, reported that she'd been kidnapped, why, we figured the
bastard naturally took her for a ride later and disposed of her
after. So we made a proper example of him.''

''You only did half your job,'' Gobnait said. ''She's no
better than he was, and I say that even though she's my own
sister's daughter, and sure she'd turn over in her grave to hear

it. She's sly, that girl, and she knew she done wrong. In the old days, we knew what to do with girls like that.''

"Still do!" the white-bunned neighbor said with that blend of lip-smacking savagery Balor found so compelling in some women. "Oh, we still do, we certainly do."

"Then do it," Gobnait Brophy said.

*   *   *

"No love lost there," Kevin Reilly remarked to the man called Balor as they adjourned to the meeting place where the lads would decide what to do.

"None at all," Balor agreed. "Girl was evidently a piece of bad work through and through. Seems a shame to upset headquarters tellin' 'em she didn't get what she deserved.''

"It does. So what do you think, then?"

"I think," Balor said with a slow and deceptively lazy smile, "that perhaps the fellow at the turf agent's was mistaken. I think if enough of us look hard enough, we're bound to find her in that ditch somewhere around here, just as we predicted we would."

"Better that happens to her than that aunt of hers and the other old biddies get ahold of her," Reilly agreed.

Sure it's a great loss to the politicians that I've no interest in the peace process at all, Balor thought to himself, when I'm so skillful at getting others to agree on a mutual goal. Or perhaps *target*, a mutual *target*, was a better word.

CHAPTER 7

Journal Entry—Saturday

This morning, while waiting for the plumber, the appliance installers, the curtain and upholstery people and the garage hired to fix the godmothermobile, we had a wee gawk aroond the hoose, as Felicity suggested in a *Star Trek* Scottish brogue.

The rooms are all big ones—as big as Raydir's house in Seattle. There's a living room that would be ideal for house concerts, with Stonehenge in the middle of it in the form of the fireplace, which is built of three stone slabs, two supporting the solid mantelpiece, or altar stone, depending on your viewpoint I guess. A huge mirror tilts over the mantel so you can see your whole reflection in it—it's a little spooky, like something out of *Alice* or *Snow White*. The shiny hardwood floors are softened with thick wool rugs in shades of pink and green covered with dragons and flowers.

In the middle of the big round coffee table is a crystal orb supported by three rampant unicorns. The chairs are like velvet thrones, though the couches are just your normal flowery upholstered couches. My favorite thing was huge harp with a mermaid carved into the support post. It sat in one corner with a smaller harp and a drum next to it. The little harp has Celtic knotwork carved into the wood and seems to have some kind of letters. I ran my fingers over the carvings, trying to decipher them.

Felicity caught me at it and smiled. ''They're runes—usually you see them rendered more simply, but those were carved by one of the great magician/bards. Did you know that it's believed that all of the oldest airs in Ireland were learned by mortals who heard them while sleeping on fairy hills? Even the great harper O'Carolan was said to have acquired his tunes that way.''

I told her I thought the fairies needed a good copyright lawyer and offered to give them the number of Raydir's.

Felicity laughed. ''Fortunately for the bards, fairies had no use for such things or for royalties either, except for Her Majesty, of course.''

I took the opening to ask how she met Her Maj and got into the godmothering business.

She said we should finish the tour first, which didn't make me feel so much that she was evading answering as that the answer might take a while.

The dining room was smaller than the living room and was empty except for a big wooden table and chairs. In the center of the table was a bouquet of flowers that said ''Flitters'' on the card.

''Secret admirer, Felicity?'' I teased, thinking actually that they might be from you, Rosie.

But when she read the card, Felicity said, ''No such luck, pet. They're from the girls.''

I indicated the soaked rug and the pool the waterfall down the hallway wall had produced, where it overflowed the pans I set out last night. ''Water lilies might have been a better choice.'' We took time out to empty the pan and replace it with another while Felicity repeated her call for a plumber, then we explored the guest room next door to the kitchen. It wasn't as big as mine and didn't have a bathroom attached. Its furniture, the standard wardrobe, bed, chest and a desk, were overpowered by the bright red wall surrounding a sliding glass door set, strangely, right up against the hill outside, which was still scraped to bare mud and full of debris from the building. This struck me as decidedly weird, and even Felicity looked startled and pensive, as if she was starting to wonder about the contractor's sanity.

"You think the builder screwed up again? Looks to me like the view doesn't even justify a window. Nothing but mud. I wonder if he read the blueprints wrong or something."

She just shook her head. "Very strange indeed and as you say, hardly scenic. I'd much prefer it covered. Come, help me put a sheet up over it for now. We'll have the drapes for this room made first." So we scrounged around till we found a sheet with little yellow flowers on it and hung it over the window. Funniest thing. I felt, hanging the sheet, as if the doors were open and something was watching us from the other side, when I knew very well all that was there was a blank muddy slope.

I didn't see the staircase last night, it was so dark. I was a little surprised, this morning, to realize there was a second floor. Not that it was anything special, this staircase. Scarlett O'Hara would have considered it a dead loss. It wasn't spiral and it didn't sweep, it just went upstairs, but the newel post was carved with a tiny, chubby dragon. The landing was covered with stacks of boxes and there were seven beds set dormitory-style under the eaves. And three locked doors. One of these, at the head of the stairs, Felicity opened to reveal—ta da!—*more* boxes and *another* wardrobe. Inside it some clothing, God knows whose, was wrapped in plastic bags and hung up. The place smelled of cedar and the herby smell from the bundles of dried flowers tied to the rafters.

"We'll store our luggage up here," Felicity told me. Two doors opened off that room, besides the one we'd entered. One of the doors was to an upstairs bathroom.

The other one had a "Do Not Open. Keep Out. This Means You." sign on it and as if that wasn't enough, a picture of an open door enclosed in a big red circle with a red slash through it.

I jerked my thumb toward it and raised my eyebrows. "So is that the closet where they hide the skeleton or what?"

"No. Probably the sign's there because the builders haven't finished with it and it's hazardous, I suppose. Or possibly it's something electrical." She fished in the pocket of her big fluffy gray cardigan and pulled out a bunch of silver keys. She jingled them around a bit then announced, "This is the one that fits, but there's a tag on it too saying 'Do Not Open.' How very melodramatic. Still, dreadful things happen in stories to people who open forbidden doors. We can ask the builder when he comes by if he knows anything about it. Come along. I'll show you my rooms and I believe there's a pleasant surprise as well."

Felicity has two rooms. The first one, the one I thought was her bedroom last night, was actually an office. Even though the rest of the house was pretty sparse on homey touches, this room was already equipped with a computer, a fax machine, copier, police band radio, two phone lines, and two walls full of leaded glass-fronted bookcases, floor to ceiling, filled with what looked like volumes of fairy tales. All of the machines were on, the computer screen blinking data, the fax spitting a message which Felicity ignored, and the radio babbling in a low murmur. Another wall mostly held filing cabinets in a style to match the bookcases. The computer, printer, copier, fax and phones were all enclosed in the most enormous rolltop desk I've ever seen. It held the machines inside it like they were Pinocchio and company and it was the whale. It was fitted with little cubbies and crannies and nooks for paper and filing and drawers and shelves, most of them still empty. There were two phones, a portable shaped like a glass slipper and a touch-tone pumpkin. Another crystal ball, this one much more utilitarian than the one in the living room, and easily as big as a beach ball, sat atop a revolving bookcase full of dictionaries and encyclopedias of myth and folklore, language books, telephone books and a lot of other things I didn't have time to notice.

You know all those carpet stores they have down on Pioneer Square? Well, the rug on the floor by the desk made everything they have look sick. It was about five by eight and with the most beautiful intricate Arabian designs you've ever seen in your life and gold tassels at the corners. It was so plushy it seemed to ripple underfoot. You felt like you were walking on air.

Two big windows looked out onto another mess of mud and debris scattered over a neat stone walkway around the building. In some places where the ground was especially soupy so the sidewalk was flooded, planks or boards were laid on top of it. But beyond the stone fence enclosing the yard was the Ireland I had expected to see. Pretty rolling emerald meadows with sheep and horses grazing in them galumphed their way off to low mountains in one direction and in the other direction, the sea. Arching across it all, livening up the gray morning, a big double rainbow shimmered in all its pastel gorgeousness, hinting at the blue sky trying to push its way through the clouds. I know it sounds silly, but even though I've seen lots of other rainbows, this one really looked like it was where it belonged, like maybe all of the rainbows I saw at home were actually Irish exports. I couldn't help wondering out loud about the pots of gold at the end. Felicity said drily that there'd be a lot of competition for it if there was one.

Felicity's bedroom was next—smaller than mine but also with its own bathroom. The bed was canopied with what I thought at first was mosquito netting until I saw the fine web of silvery threads worked throughout, sparkling dewlike with beads or sequins or—maybe it was dew. I couldn't imagine a spiderweb that large inside a new house, much less wanting to sleep under one, but that's what it looked like. Felicity didn't seem to think it was the least bit remarkable, however, and just said, "It'll be more personal once I've unpacked."

Then she opened a door at the end of the hall.

It smelled like fall, spicy and rich and earthy, *winelike* I think poets call it. It reminded me of cinnamon and popcorn and cider, that smell. But what it was, actually, was a long wide stone walkway with yew trees arching to completely canopy it. Felicity flicked a switch and a hundred tiny white lights sparkled in the arch.

"Fairy lights!" she said, clapping her hands like a little kid. "Delightful!"

I was less interested in the leftover Christmas tree lights than I was in the trees themselves. "How old are those trees, anyway?" I asked Felicity, who was still admiring the little twinkly lights shining on the shaded pathway.

"Hmm? Oh, hundreds of years old, I suppose," she said.

"But—didn't the building bother them? I mean, look at the mess it made of everything else in the yard."

"Ah, yes. That is a wonder in itself, isn't it? However, I understand Dame Prudence herself remained on the site, brandishing the organizational cheque book, to make sure the builders didn't commit any unacceptable expediencies. You do know that yews are quite magical trees—"

"Well, I heard the bark has something in it that cures cancer," I told her. "The lumber companies in Washington have been burning yews as waste for a long time, and now they've got people poaching them from old-growth forest."

"Remarkable! This yew walk leads us into the heart of the house."

I was pretty puzzled by that, since it wasn't even inside the house, and said so.

"Never mind. You'll see," she said and I tagged behind her as Felicity wafted ahead, flitting along as ghostly as a close relative of the Addams family between the arched trees, and at the far end opened a disappointingly normal door to . . .

A swimming pool!

From the buildup I'd been expecting something different, though I wasn't sure what. It couldn't have been as welcome a sight as that rectangle of turquoise was to me, though. A pool! Some actual normal civilization and fun—and exercise. Maybe Ireland wouldn't be too bad after all. Not all self-sacrifice and doing good for others while being lorded over by sassy cats and horrible hoptoads. The pool was surrounded by normal, unmagical white walls, and was overhung by a glowing wooden ceiling lit with mundane modern track lighting. There was a changing room next to the door, with a shower. It was great. I was glad it was there. But it didn't look like the heart of anything except maybe a health program.

"This is great," I said. "A swim would feel good right now."

"In a bit, then," Felicity said. "First, there are some things we need to discuss. Come, let's sit down." We sat by the edge of the pool. The turquoise wasn't actually water, but a pool cover. To keep the heat in, usually. A little steam did rise from the edge into the relative chill of the room.

Felicity folded her feet under her and turned her holographic eyes on me. I was reaching down beneath the pool cover to feel the warmth of the water with my fingers. It was like a bath. She gave a little cough that I recognized as a tip-off that the teacher was about to begin the lesson. I drew my hand back into my lap and faced her.

She smiled. "You could remove your slippers and wet your toes if you wish while we're talking about this, Sno dear."

"Do I have to take notes or anything?"

She shook her head in a gentle way. "You could hardly carry notes with you wherever you are apt to encounter the need to consult them."

"Good. I'm glad. Some teachers want you to go through the motions, but actually I've got a really good memory."

"Excellent. Then just listen for now. I hate to start off speaking of what we can*not* do but it saves disappointment, in the long run, to know these things, so that we can apply our talents where they will be of use.

"We cannot stop wars, though we can perhaps save one soldier from the consequences of battle, or prevent a family of innocents from being utterly destroyed, if we learn of it in time. We cannot bring the dead to life nor can we cure plagues of diseases, drug or alcohol addiction, though we might be able to save someone from falling prey to those diseases or addictions."

That seemed to cover most of what counted. "But you could—I mean, we could—stop crimes and stuff?"

She laughed. "Some of them, certainly. But we're not the police force, nor did anyone die and make us Superman. You saw for yourself what the sorority's like. Some of us are quite ordinary with a rather small sphere of influence and some of us are—not entirely of this world. There are far more people suffering for one reason or another than there are godmothers, or than there is magic.''

I felt let down, Rosie. No Santa Claus. Again.

"But every person we help can help many other people. And the really magical part is, they usually do.''

"Like me?''

"Just like you. And Rose. And Fred. And Dico, who will give joy with his music, and Ding, who has so very much to offer.''

"So how do we know who we're helping will pass it on? I mean, do we make them sign something or take applications or what?''

Outside the long glass doors enclosing the pool on one side, the wind was whipping up the bits of paper and wood chips left behind by the construction. The rainbow and blue sky had disappeared into the roiling gray that threatened rain again. Out in the meadow, the horses were kicking their heels and chasing each other, and the sheep were baaing their brains out while the grass did the hula at their feet.

Felicity sighed and pushed her silvery hair back with her long fingers. Her ears are a little on the Mr. Spock side, did you notice that? Her hair usually hides them.

"No, you have to use your own intuition, your own judgment.''

"But you'll be here to help me, right?''

She was hedging, I could tell by the way she licked her lips before saying, "Often I will be, yes.''

I was beginning to feel a little panicky. I was beginning to feel that I'd bit off more than I could chew, as Granny Hilda used to say. "Because, you know, I've done drugs, I've been on the streets. Some people would say my judgment isn't always . . .''

Felicity laid her hand on mine. "Sno, all that began because you were lost and grieving and felt you had nowhere to turn when your mother and grandmother were killed and your father married that dreadful woman who tried to kill you. That doesn't mean you couldn't have handled it better, but you know that now. It's because of the mistakes you made that I'm certain you will with time and practice become a splendid godmother. Truly.''

I wasn't so sure and it must have showed.

''I'll be about, though not by any means with you every moment. If I guided your every move, it would not be *your* move, would it? Besides, I have certain tasks of my own to perform to get my magic back up to snuff.''

''How long does that take?'' I asked. ''If I make a wrong wish, we won't have much magic to work with.''

She touched my hand again, stirring up a sweet scent that clung to her, vanillaish but rich as chocolate, like a cookie. ''You can't make a wrong wish, Sno. Even on an impulse, like last night. I have to earn my magic back and accept certain limitations in the meantime. But there's plenty to do, nonetheless. Your wishes are to help you make your decisions. Communication with animals is a very good one.''

I pictured the animals unanimously suggesting that if I wanted to help them I could convince everybody in the country to become a vegetarian.

''Especially since,'' Felicity continued, ''we would not dream of leaving you totally unattended.''

Here came the catch.

''On the other hand, we do have to be discreet about our presence and our mission, especially here where Her Majesty's people have not always enjoyed a good reputation. If it was known you were under her tutelage you might possibly be subjected to suspicion and superstitious nonsense and we can't have that.''

A fairy godmother who turned people into frogs worried about superstitious nonsense? Just what would be something *she* would consider superstitious, anyway? I wondered. A misinterpretation of real magic?

''So it seems to me that your wish will be most convenient when it comes to providing you with a travelling companion.''

With that, the toad hopped out of Felicity's robe pocket and sat on the swimming pool tarp as if it was a lily pad. ''Ree-

deep," he said. Sarcastically. I definitely detected a note of
sarcasm in that croak.

"Come on, Felicity, *he's* supposed to help *me* with my
judgment? I may have smoked a couple of joints but I'm not
looking at an attempted murder rap the minute I grow hair and
get six feet tall again like some people. He's going *nowhere*
with me. How could you even think that, Felicity, when you
know what he tried to do to me?"

"You needn't worry. Puss will usually be along to monitor
his behavior—"

"Oh, great! I'm going to look like Barnum and Bailey's
coming to town for sure!"

"Puss is very good at attracting help. She is experienced at
being an assistant in our various endeavors and can help if
you should you run into difficulties."

"So much for my good judgment! You're just like Raydir—
you don't want to have to bother with showing me anything.
So you give me this big song and dance about how you have
so much faith in me that I'll do this wonderful job! I guess
that's why I need a condescending cat and a psycho toad for
baby-sitters. I mean, the toad is American too. He won't know
anything about Ireland. Why does he have to be along? To
protect me from leprechauns?"

"Don't be silly! Given Bobby's recent history, I rather think
it would be you who'd need to protect the leprechaun from
getting mugged. However, leprechauns are as careful as cer-
tified public accountants so I doubt you'll encounter one."

I was glad she hadn't bit on me telling her she wasn't paying any more attention to me than Raydir. Because, obviously,
she was just then. "Well, okay," I said. "But I'd still like
you to be along at first. Are we going to go look for folks to
help pretty soon?"

"Oh, yes. I just have a few things to see to here. I was
thinking tomorrow might be a good time."

"But—won't the people we need to help be getting in
deeper trouble every minute?" I was thinking what would
have happened to me if it hadn't been for Doc and the guys
being there right when I needed them, both when the hit man

was after me and later, when I was poisoned.

"Some trouble will deepen, of course. But though I'm sorry to say it, there's always a limitless supply of trouble, even here."

"Even here? Is Ireland really so peaceful, in spite of everything you hear about the war? Is that why I'm here instead of home, where I know the ropes? To kind of break me in gently? The girls at school thought it was pretty dangerous over here."

"That's because only bad news gets the notoriety, dear. Naturally, just as many bad things happen, per capita, in Ireland as in other places. But there aren't as many capitas to worry about and many people to assist in the worrying. Do you know that during the recent unpleasantness in Africa, Ireland, which has only three and a half million people, contributed four and a half million dollars toward relief whereas Germany, the richest country in the European Community, contributed a mere fifty thousand?"

"That's pretty good participating. What did they have, a telethon or something?"

"No, they have long memories here. The potato famine has cast a long shadow and people whose grandparents and great-grandparents were affected by it still remember and care for other countries in trouble. And here there's dole as well, the government social welfare program for pretty much anyone who isn't otherwise provided for. Since there are a great many people and comparatively few jobs, not to mention real careers, it's necessary. Of course, it's equally necessary in other places where people aren't provided for at all. And it doesn't cover everyone of every age and some of the restrictions are drawbacks and there are some who take advantage, but it's better than nothing. There's also national health care, so the sick can get medical care even if they've no money. And of course, the churches sponsor a great many projects to help out in other areas. Not to mention that country folk particularly are apt to look out for each other. Kindness, charity, hospitality and courtesy are all much valued here."

"So why do they need fairy godmothers?"

"Most people would say that they didn't. You must under-

stand that Her Majesty's race is thought of differently here
from the characters in the Disney films. In fact, the Irish tend
to regard fairies and Americans in much the same way—as
foreign relations with strange ways of doing things that would
be laughable if they weren't rather frightening. Both are to be
treated with flattery and courtesy for the boons they have to
offer and with fear and distrust for the harm they might do.
It's also well known that if you disappear into the realm of
either race you're likely not to return or to be very changed
and much older when you do.''

''Sounds like a pretty tough attitude to break through to
form any kind of, you know, trust, respect or intimacy or any
of that stuff Rosie's always saying's so important.''

''It is important. So is thinking well enough of yourself that
you needn't find fault with others to feel better by comparison.
That's a major difficulty with the world in general but with
wicked stepmothers, evil sorcerers and our other antagonists
in particular. Often it's what has to be overcome to find the
good that needs to be brought out in those we're helping.''

''Like the California Commission on Self-Esteem?'' I
asked, grinning at what always seemed to be a joke around
both Gran's house in Missouri and Raydir's hip crowd in Seattle.

Felicity didn't seem to be amused, though she smiled at me
in a tolerant kind of way. ''The only funny thing about that,
Sno dear, is that self-esteem is unfortunately something that
can't be commissioned. And remember that here in Ireland,
our people have been not only oppressed but *com*pressed, from
kings and queens and heroes and heroines, down to the lowest
working class, the servant class, the not-quite-human, by the
government and armies of another country. One can't be told
for years that one is worthless without beginning to believe it
on some level. So here the joke isn't self-esteem, it's the other,
more common trait, begrudgery. Not wanting others to succeed or get ''above themselves'' because they might show you
up. That's the flip side, if you will, of the courtesy and kindness.'' She paused, and took a breath.

''The concept of fairy godmothers is more European than

Irish in fact. Fairy anything here used to be feared and punished.''

"I know. I read about them burning babies they thought were changelings in the old days . . .''

"I doubt anyone would have done that who was not the sort of person to commit child abuse these days, but you can see that we must remain undercover here, as Her Majesty's people have stayed underground for centuries. Here the 'fairy tales' are about fortunate or unfortunate encounters with Her Majesty's people, about heroes and battles, with a beautiful woman thrown in occasionally to fight over. Tricksters and chancers and supermen and alien races don't provide much need to look into your own life and solve it—very comforting, I'm sure, when you're helpless to change things because your land is held captive. Not very useful at all when it isn't.

"That's one reason this is a place to rest and recover and teach recruits—very seldom does anyone actually wish for us. People pray to saints and other religious figures, and we are sometimes able to help, if the prayer is for something that falls within our scope of influence. In those cases we assume the guise of guardian angels.''

"Felicity?''

"Yes, dear?''

"Are guardian angels real too? Somehow I thought it was one way or the other—you know, fairies being considered pagan and angels . . .''

"Sno, dear, the two are only mutually exclusive to those who have to catalog the universe and sort it into comfy little niches. Of course there are angels, just as there's us. There were guardian angels long before Christianity came to Ireland and fairy godmothers long before Her Majesty's commission. They were just called different things.''

"Oh.''

"But there's no use in me trying to cram into a nutshell what you've come to learn for yourself. So to answer your initial question: For all the times when courtesy prevents people from inquiring too closely just when a bit of nosiness would be beneficial, and when seeming kindness and charity mask less savory motivations, we have a purpose here. We also try to protect people who extend themselves to do the right thing for others from those who would take advantage of them.''

''And make sure the bad guys don't get away with it, huh?''

I was surprised when Felicity shook her head. ''It takes far too much effort to weed those out, so mostly we try to reward the deserving and leave the police to sort out the bad ones.''

''So we—godmothers, I mean—only help out when bad things happen to good people, not when good things happen to bad people, is that it?'' I asked.

''More or less.''

''How about him, then?'' I nodded to ol' Bobby the bad toad hopping nervously from one spot to the other at the door, on the lookout, no doubt, for his enemy, the cat.

''He was a special case. Bobby is not truly wicked, you see, he's simply made several lifetimes' worth of unfortunate career choices.''

''He's near enough to wicked to suit me,'' I said and gave her my best *Night of the Living Dead* shudder by way of emphasizing my point. ''When I remember how he tried to cut me, I have a real hard time thinking of him as simply vocationally disadvantaged. Come on, Felicity. This guy worked as a Norwegian mobster! Give me a break!''

''I'm doing just that,'' she said. ''And though I'm giving him one as well, he doesn't always look at it that way. He has seven years within my service, not counting any possible time-traveling we might be doing in the line of duty, to redeem himself by good works and prove to us that he is completely rehabilitated before he'll be allowed to resume human form.''

''And what if he's not? Do you punish him then?''

''No, but there's a limited amount of damage a toad can do.''

''Ah!'' Felicity said as a sudden waterfall of harp music chimed throughout the poolroom, though I didn't see any stereo speakers. She stood up. ''That'll be the doorbell. Perhaps it's the plumber or the builder, come to sort us out.''

I didn't say anything or move. I had a lot to think about.

She left, closing the door to the poolroom behind her.

The toad leered up at me from his plastic lily pad and I lifted my feet from the water to kick the cover back up over him. He croaked and leaped for the pool edge. But where I'd kicked the cover back, the water shimmered blue and blinding white under the lights—and as the shimmers broke and the steam tendrils parted, I glimpsed what I thought must have been a mosaic in the pool tiles. It was of a castle, a river, women in long gowns and men on horseback. It seemed to move with the moving water and then, as the water stilled, it disappeared.

I must have said something aloud or looked funny.

"What's the matter, kid, having a flashback?" the toad asked in his usual nasty tones.

"None of your beeswax," I said in my most mature fashion. "I'm going for a walk and you're *not* invited," I told it— him.

* * *

Cunla hid in the hedge and giggled to himself as the girl walked past. Ah, he wished it might be night so that he could leap from the bushes and scare the straight black hair of her head curly. He didn't at all like folk going in and out of his house. He'd have to put a stop to that. The ringing thing— telephone they called it—really must go. It seemed to summon the invaders. He'd have to sneak inside when one of them left the door unlatched and banjax the poxy thing.

CHAPTER 8

The funeral procession for the King of the Cats was of necessity a ponderous body. Not only did the cats bearing the coffin need to trade their precious cargo off to relief pallbearers every few minutes to avoid injury from the unaccustomed burden, but the entire procession had to pause many times during the day and night to find a suitable place, large enough to shelter them all while they took their necessary naps.

Puss rejoined them after she had checked in with Felicity. The procession then was skirting the southern end of Dublin, on its way down the coast. Its mission was to carry the King's coffin the length and breadth of Ireland, so that all would know the King was dead and there'd be none of that twaddle there'd been about Elvis, for instance.

Puss's journey was perilous. To travel such great distances, she hitched rides under the hoods of cars travelling in the proper direction, having to trust luck that she would not be carried all the way to Belfast or the Giant's Causeway before her transportation stopped and she could safely jump out. Less canny cats trying the same trick had died for less pressing reasons.

The noise and the smells were dreadful, and the rattling along the road shook her to her bones. She was careful to always run down to the N11 to hitch her rides along the smooth dual carriageway. Rock and dirt lanes, she had found by experience, could be as hazardous as the fan during such journeys. One could drown in puddles, or be stoned to death on rough road, or knocked from one's perch by a bump, or at the very least arrive with one's coat a muddy and unpalatable mess.

Puss therefore had been careful to make friends with the neighbors and find out which people worked where and what times they came and went. It was a simple piece of research that she always conducted in a new place. She had selected a neighbor who went to work at Priority Travel in Stillorglin bright and early every morning. The procession would be passing through a little stretch of woods near there just at dawn, whereupon they would hide the coffin among the roots of a particular tree. Then all would climb trees and rest among the boughs until time to move on again.

She knew this because the funeral route of past Kings was a part of Irish feline history handed down from queen to kitten as a birthright.

The little stretch of forest was easy enough to find. It wasn't far from the mall, being situated on the remains of a large estate. Puss had no doubt that the procession had preceded her. A cacophony of purring and snoring shuddered through the leaves. By now a great many cats indeed had joined the procession, which had been going on for a very long time, particularly by cat-reckoning. It had circled three quarters of the way around Ireland already, from Cahirciveen to Killarney, from Killarney to Killorglin, from Killorglin to Castlemaine, from Castlemaine to Inch, from Inch to Dingle, from Dingle to Tralee, from Tralee to Listowel, from Listowel to Limerick. From Limerick it had gathered cats all over the county, and on they'd travelled to County Clare with stops in Ennis, Kilrush, Kilkee, Liscannor, Kinvarra, Gort and Galway. From Galway they circled, through Claddagh and Athenry, joined by all the cats of Connemara, and from Connemara up to the County Mayo to gather cats along Lough Mask, through Westport, Newport, Castlebar, and Ballina, then over to the flatlands of Roscommon where farm cats from everywhere came with gifts of fat mice, birds and rabbits for a mighty feasting for their fellow footsore felines. Cats came down from Sligo to join them there, and over they went east to Longford and north again to Leitrim, along the shores of Lough Erne in County Fermanagh, and up to Donnegal, Letterkenny and Derry. They skirted County Tyrone but those cats joined them as they passed nearby, up to Coleraine and Port Stewart, where they spent the night on the beach, staring at the waves of the wide sea and the great pale moon weeping wisps of rain.

Another night they spent upon the columns and stepping stones of the Giant's Causeway, where Finn McCool himself had once faced down a Scottish giant. Then down the coast they went, through the Glens of Antrim, gathering strength until Larne, where they were met by the rugged cats of Belfast with their battle scars and their continual peerings over their shoulders, as if afraid of their own tails. From Larne the procession passed north of Lough Neath, along the shores through Londonderry and the extreme eastern border of Tyrone, down into Armagh, where another night was spent leaving Himself in consultation with the ghosts of the Kings of Ulster at Ewain Macha, the great hill once guarded by Cuchulain, the Hound of Ulster himself. The Hound hadn't the decency to put in an apparition in honor of the King of the Cats, but that was to be expected. They travelled east a short way into County Down, but crossed over again into Armagh at Newry, where some musicians out late on the sentried roads spied them.

The funeral procession paralleled the musicians' route home through the Mountains of Mourne, and they were very pleased to find, as the lights went out in the house, that many offerings of canned tuna, salmon, chicken and milk had been left along the walkway for them. Not enough, of course, to feed everyone, but indicative of proper respect for the mission. The treats were ceded to the Nobility and those who had come furthest.

Then they swung down through Armagh on to Dundalk in County Louth and across County Monaghan via Carrickmacross, into Meath and West Meath, stopping at NewGrange and spending the night atop the mound of the oldest structure in the world, and on the Hill of Tara to pay respects to the ghosts of the High Kings.

Down through Mullingar and to Tullamore in County Offaly and over to County Kildare, swinging far north of Kildare and into Naas, where they passed south of Dublin, gathering followers, always.

And Puss had been with them much of the way, being previously unoccupied until Felicity arrived. It was a long, grand journey, one she had performed in previous lifetimes, but seldom.

And sure her pads were tender from the walking and her fur not so glossy as it was at home with nothing to do but eat and sleep and groom, but she was in fine shape, she was. Better than the carcase of the King, which must be near rotted away from the stench of him in the coffin. Her teeth felt loose from tugging the coffin cloth several turns over, honor though it was to bear Himself on his last royal inspection.

Cats came running and cats dropped away to return home along the route of the procession but always there were multitudes. Puss doubted, now Felicity was in occupation of the house, that she could finish the journey all the way back to Cahirciveen, where Himself would be laid to rest among the bogs at last. But she'd stay with it until she was needed elsewhere. For it was she, and had always been she, throughout her various lives down through the years, who, when some human stumbled onto the procession and asked, "What is this?" replied, "The King of the Cats is dead."

She was just in sight of a stand of trees when she heard a galumphing behind her and turned to see a battered black tom racing toward her. She took not a bit of the alarm she normally might, since this was a sacred mission, under royal protection and respected by all the cats of the country.

But this big fellow charged onward, almost falling on top of her until he suddenly noticed and skidded to a weed-pulling, ground-clawing stop. "Good day to you, Missus."

"Good day to you as well, Tom," she answered civilly.

"And would you be joining up with the funeral procession of the King of the Cats? I've only now heard he's dead."

"I would be, yes. And dead he is, indeed, Tom."

"Then it's King Tom to you I am, Missus. For I was his eldest son and I am heir to the throne."

Before she could debate this she heard the whiny feeble voice of an elderly human woman calling, "Thomas? Thomas! Oh, Thomas, where are you?"

"And that would be?" Puss inquired.

The self-declared King licked his paw. "Aw, sure, she's an oul' one I go to visit. I was there when I heard about me royal Da. She's followed me, I'm afraid."

"We can't have that," Puss said. "You must lead her back home. Her people will be sick for her."

Tom bounded into the woods, calling back, "If you're that concerned, you lead her home, then. I've no time. I must take my place at the head of my kind."

"Well," said Puss to herself as she trotted toward the poor old tinker lady tottering across the field. "For all his royal assumptions and his airs and graces, he's no better than he ought to be. A fine King he'll make indeed."

*   *   *

Aren't I the great one, though? Jack thought to himself as he walked back to the halt to tell his mother how he had chased away—well, it wouldn't make much of a story to say it was snotty-nosed schoolboys—an army of brawny men, then. No that was too much even for poor oul' addled Mammy, bless her—so, seven or eight of the blackhearted feckers anyway, and saved the Swan Princess Fionula and her brothers, the great-grandchildren of Lir. He never would have believed he had it in him before this, frankly, even to chase off the boys. The little ones could be as vicious as the big, and he had reason to know. But with right on his side he'd bested them all and the security guard as well, and so was gifted in return by their swanships with their special song, the tune of which even now he was humming over and over to himself. He was all the while thinking how to play it on his squeeze box and wondering if perhaps a whistle wouldn't be the better instrument for such a grand tune.

These thoughts warmed him from the wind and weather: they were the usual way of things, such grand deeds and tunes were not. And so he made his way through the city, up the road, past the dump and the various caravans illegally parked beside the legal halt with its shabby little new-built houses. No streetlights lit the way, but lamp and candlelight poured out of the caravan windows and from one or two of the houses a television blared. Children played ball on the bare dirt, while the acrid smoke of a trash fire blew into their faces with the force of the wet wind.

As he passed the Collins's caravan, he tried to ignore the great ruckus shaking the metal sides on their axles. He walked quickly, but not before he heard Davey Collins's voice give a mighty roar. Then there was the sound of a solid smack, along with the eruption of crying from children. At the same time, the flimsy metal door to the caravan bowed out with a mighty thump, then opened and dumped Maeve Collins on the ground, one side of her face red with the print of her father's hand. ''And not another bite will yez have at yer mammy's table till you earn yer kaype, ye great fat ugly article. No nayde for yez to snayke in again when ye think me back is turned.''

When the door slammed, Jack bent over the girl and helped her to her feet. Maeve gave him a grateful, cowlike look. He wasn't taken in by it in the least. She was a tough one, was Maeve. Had to be. They hadn't exactly grown up together, since both of their families had travelled when they were younger, but now that they were settled into the halt, Jack had got to know her a bit. When his Mam had her health, she hadn't liked him talking with any of Maeve's people. The Collinses were a huge travelling clan and were good folk on the whole, but Davey was a bad 'un. You could always tell, travelling, when you'd followed Davey Collins. The halt would resemble a garbage dump, with all sorts of ruined scrap spread over the countryside instead of thriftily piled for the next family to pick over. The local settled folk would be extra stirred up against you, not just silent and wary, but stone-throwin' mad, and not a mouthful could you beg, no matter how generous the area had been before, and not a mouthful of grass could your horses take, neither. The gard would be there to shift you before you got your caravan parked. It was like that, more or less, a great deal of the time, but markedly more so if you followed Davey Collins to a spot.

Maeve was Davey's oldest. She was big for her age, and had looked like a grown woman since she was ten. She was homely and rough and in the last year had organized her brothers and some of the other younger children into a gang. Usually they did very well, for what they didn't earn by begging, they got by purse-snatching and pocket-picking.

"Yer da turfed you out?" he asked her.

"What d'ye think?" she asked belligerently, then sniffed with self-pity and mopped her face on the sleeve of her blanket coat, now muddy from the ground. "Sod 'im anyway. If ever he'd worked the strayts in his life, he'd know it's no good in winter. No tourists, like."

"He's kept you other winters."

"Oh, yeah, but that's before I turnt sixtayne and he lost me dole money." She cast him a sly glance, which might have looked flirtatious on a prettier girl. "Say, Jack, ye wouldn't want to be gettin' married, would yez? If we had a babby, I'd get me dole back and we could have a flat of our own. The council would see to it."

Jack backed hastily away, "I got to see to Mam, Maeve. You know yer family would never think me a match, what with havin' Mam to think of." He was sweating, trying not to show how he really felt. The thing of it was, Travellers married young. Neither of them were too young to wed, and they both knew that while Jack would not be a match for a pretty daughter who was from a good family, he might be the best Davey would think Maeve could do. Jack didn't want to marry young and fall under the influence, for want of a father of his own, of the likes of Davey Collins. He had plans to be like Finbar Furey someday. Someday soon, now that he had the swan's songs to impress folk with.

Maeve said nothing, didn't even meet his eye, but grunted angrily and turned away, stalking up the road away from the halt. She wasn't stupid, by any means. She could read some and even write a bit. Father Ambrose, the one they called the Tinker's Priest, had taught her. She worshipped him more than God, the other lads said, making fun of her behind her back. Jack never had joined in, as much out of self-preservation as kindness since she and her gang operated very close to where he played his squeeze box. On the other hand, he didn't want to be on the bad side of Maeve.

He ran after her, and grabbed her arm again. She shook him off angrily. "Wait, Maeve. If ye've no place t' go, I s'pose you could stop wit' me 'n' Mam."

She was silent for a moment, licking her lips, and he feared she'd take him up on it and regretted he'd spoken. But then she said, "Tha's daycent of yez, Jack, but ye know yer mammy can't stand the sight of me."

He said, "If that's the way you want it, Maeve," as if placating her, and backed off, as she squared her shoulders and continued down the road. After four or five steps, her street swagger returned and he reckoned she was herself again.

He walked slowly back to his mam's house and ducked inside. No lamp was lit, and the remains of her supper sat beside the turf fire. There was nothing strange about that. Sometimes she was awake all the night, other times she was in bed when he came in, while still others she was lucid and waited until he arrived, sat with him awhile, and then went to bed or didn't, depending on her mood. He'd been hoping this would be one of those good nights, but the hope was such a vain one he wasn't even disappointed really, just let down at having to wait until morning to tell her about the swans. He thought of waking her—a year ago he would have done, for she kept no schedule, even of a loose kind, since she'd settled. But she'd become so bad lately that there was no point in it. He might wake her and she wouldn't even know him, much less make sense of what he said.

The little house had a second room, for a luxury, and Mam preferred it, for it was long and narrow as a grave—or a caravan—and had a great window with a view of the dump. Jack didn't bother to fix himself a bite, but finished what she had not in the bowl brought in by friends. Then he threw another peat tile on the fire, rolled himself in his blanket on the thin bare mattress beside it, and after a time, fell asleep.

It wasn't until morning that he realized Mam had gone, her bed as untidy and bare as ever it had been. No one had seen her leave. "Maybe they come for her and dragged her to hospital," someone suggested.

But no, they'd never have come so late without being called, and no one had called, and no one had seen them come, and no one had seen her taken.

Everyone helped Jack look, all the women and the children and all of the men in the camp and the halt, but no trace of Moira Daly was to be seen in dump or field or road or ditch.

He and every able-bodied, lucid person in the halt covered the neighborhood, and they searched all day and all night without discovering a trace. They did find an unusual number of paw prints in a muddy field, which made Ann McDonagh jump up and down and point and yelp as if she had a poker up her arse. Her mother swatted her, 'til she fell quiet. Jack never did find out what all that was about. He was too busy brooding on the unfairness of his lot and the lot of his mother and the lot of travelling people in general.

Had Mam been a settled woman, she'd never be left out in the rain and cold like this. There'd be gardai and soldiers and whole parishes out beating the brush for her, Jack thought. But no gard was likely to shift his lazy arse searching for a poor old tinker woman, was he? Not on the say-so of her tinker kin, leastways. They were hard folk, the gardai were.

But—a plan began to form in Jack's mind—the doctors and nurses at the hospital, now, they weren't so hard as that. They knew Mam some and they knew her condition, for hadn't he taken her to the emergency room himself when she was very bad? What if he was to call them on the telephone and demand to know if they'd taken her away? What if he was to insist they produce her, or—or what? Facing a tinker's curse didn't usually bother folk like that. But they cared about public opinion. Maybe he'd organize a picket line. Something. He'd think of something if they didn't get upset enough by the fact that the old woman was missing. So upset that *they* called the gardai and insisted that a search be conducted. Jack kept the idea to himself, because he knew his neighbors wouldn't approve of a plan that involved the gardai.

And in truth, it wasn't the best idea in the world but he could think of no other. So he hitched a ride into Dublin in Gerry McCann's van. Even if the telephone plan failed as he expected it to, some stranger might have met Mam on the road and likely as not would have given her a ride into the city. He'd ask everyone he knew to watch for her. Sure, they'd spot her if she was anywhere close by.

A flock of crows flushed from the field up the road ahead of the van, and he thought for the first time since he'd discovered Mam was missing of the swans. He'd go back to the pond and see were they there. Maybe he couldn't hire a helicopter, but if they *could* talk, and they were sensible creatures who knew they owed him a favor, as he remembered them, and they were not simply a real-seeming daydream, maybe he might just organize his own aerial surveillance.

CHAPTER 9

The Fortunes of the Youngest Son

The way the story went, there was once a man who owned a plot of land and had three sons and only one to inherit, and he sent the three of them off to seek their fortunes and the one to return home with the best food, the prettiest bride, the most money, the magical cure or the most of whatever was required would be his heir and the others might shift as they would. Usually they were conveniently killed on the quest, leaving the youngest, handsomest, bravest, most modest and devoted to inherit, the poor sod.

Joe Dunny's father had more than three children: six in all he had, and still Joe hadn't been able to avoid inheriting, even though he was the youngest. Young Donny, as opposed to Old Donny, Joe's father, was the eldest, and should have inherited, but he went into the Church instead and was now Father Gabriel somewhere in Kenya. Liam and Michael had gone into partnership with a lad from Lisannor they met in a pub and the three of them'd bought a fishing boat which sank in a storm the first trip out, rest their souls, poor fuckers. Maurice, who'd really wanted the farm but had no hope as fourth son, had at the age of eighteen gone to America to find work in-

95

stead and stayed. Bridget had fallen for a Scottish lad and lived outside Edinburgh with her husband and four children. And Joe, who'd been an afterthought baby, was left.

He'd been twelve when Maurice left for America, fourteen when Bridget married, fifteen when Liam and Michael were killed and eighteen when Father Gabriel was ordained, which Mam lived long enough to see, praise God, before the cancer took her. He hadn't the heart to take the scholarship to University in Dublin by then, and Da needed him at home to work.

And work he had done and still did, though the land was no better than it ever had been and Da was in his grave six months now, God rest his soul. And Joe was fifty-one years old and lived in the middle of nowhere and everyone in the county, it seemed, was either older than himself and God together or some posh couple from England or America or Germany come to sample the peaceful country life.

Peaceful! Ha! He grinned to himself as he slogged through the swampy field in the storm. Peaceful was in your bed with a hot water bottle at your feet, a pleasure he hadn't known since the death of his mother many years ago. He was always too tired to bother just for himself, though he used to do it for Da. Peaceful was not the reality of wading through the muck to keep your ewes from breaking their legs under the weight of their own wool, or getting so bogged down they drowned in puddles. He had lost four lambs this spring before he took to doing a regular patrol at twilight and sunrise as well as the daylight hours in between. Someday soon he must get another dog to replace Da's old Meg, the black-and-white Wicklow collie who had expired a week after her master's death. His hands and face were cold, chapped red. In this weather he had little feeling in the skin of his hands, so callused were they by the years of hard work.

One bog had claimed several ewes, sheep being what they were, and now more than ever he missed the dog to herd the sheep away while he extricated them. Otherwise the others were apt to replace the ones he freed. He began struggling with the sheep, his bare hands grubbing deep in the mud to find the feet while his nostrils were clogged with the pungent odor of wet wool mixed with a hearty dose of excrement.

"Here now, oul' lass, aisy does it," he said to the ewe, who kicked and wriggled her way deeper into the mud.

The wind and rain lashed him and thunder cracked in his ears. He smacked the ewe on the rump and sent her onto safer ground while he extricated another, and another. Three times he had to go back and pull out one of the sheep he'd just liberated from yet another mess.

By the time he was done, the wind had calmed a bit and the rain fell more lightly. The sheep had worn themselves out with their bawling.

A brilliant flash of sheet lightning receding over the hill showed that the field seemed to be moving, alive with forms that seemed familiar, and yet were too dark and indistinct to make out properly.

That was when he heard the peeping, mewling cries of newborn kittens. He found them sheltering by a rock about a hundred feet from where he'd been working. The mother cat was nothing but skin and bone, and both of the babies shivering. Joe took off his own jacket and gently laid the cat and kits inside it, taking the rain and cold upon himself through the holes in the Aran jumper Mam had been knitting for Liam before he and Michael were lost.

He made a place for the cat and her new ones by the fire. Her coat was torn and her pads bleeding, her claws worn away to almost nothing. He feared she wouldn't survive the night. He fell asleep in the big chair beside the fire, watching them, lest the mam slip away and the kits need him to warm them and dripper-feed them in the night. He needed a dog for a working partner, but a cat or two would make the house feel homey again and keep down the mice as well.

CHAPTER 10

Journal Entry—Saturday Afternoon, Continued

The godmother's house was in a good neighborhood, anyway. I could see that as I walked along the little lane outside. Six-foot hedges lined the road in places, low stone walls in others. Flowering trees interspersed with the leafy greenery and little wild daisies dusted the meadows. Along the road grew bell-shaped purple foxglove, which I'd learned about from all those Agatha Christie novels about little ladies in gardening hats picking an overdose of digitalis for crooked family solicitors.

Nor were the fields empty. Some held sheep, some cows and lots of horses. As I walked further, I saw that in one of the fields back away from the road, a brown-and-white pinto with a girl in jockey gear on his back was sailing over horseshow jumps. The horse took them in an almost lazy way, as if he was bored and wished the jumps were higher.

I climbed over the fence and sloshed through the field. The sky was as gray and forbidding as the hair of an elderly Conservative Republican Fundamentalist Christian lady, but a brisk wind kept the trees and bushes dancing.

I called out hello to the woman just climbing off the horse, but she called back, "This is private property, you know," in an Englishy accent. "And animals such as this one are extremely valuable and quite temperamental."

This was obviously not one of the kind, polite, flattering people Felicity had been telling me about.

"Well, pardon me, I'm *sure*," I said, feeling like the stupid, shallow child the stuck-up bitch obviously thought I was. She just turned her back on me and walked over to two men who stood watching.

Then, and I swear this is true though I had a little trouble believing it myself, the horse's head swung around and he slowly and quite distinctly gave me a wink of the same kind Raydir gives other pickers he recognizes in the audience when he's just pulled off some flashy trick.

Was this the beginning of the interspecies communication Felicity mentioned? Nah, the horse probably had something in his eye.

I beat a retreat across the field and climbed back over the fence. There was a little road to the right, a lane even smaller than the one I'd been on. I turned off between two hedge-trimmed fields that gave way to stone fences, houses and a long steep hill dead-ending in a field. About half a city block into the field stood a square stone tower. I wanted to go investigate it, but on the left-hand side of the road there were several houses between me and the field, and on the right there was a forest.

Well, I couldn't pass that up. I love forests. The forest hid me from that miserable little toad, back when he was a hit man, until Doc and the other vets found me. It was one of the most real times in my life, out there in the woods with the campfires and catching fish from the Nooksack River while sitting on a tarp to keep the snow off my butt. It was great. All except when the guys went off to talk about the war and I felt left out. But *mostly* it was great. Anyway, like I said, I love forests and here was one waiting to be explored.

I took a path that sloped into a muddy bog surrounded by trees. Old-growth trees, ancient forest I think environmentalists call them. I looked up into those sweet-smelling leafy branches, letting the leftover rain fall on my face.

A flock of crows swept in from the road and swarmed on the tree branches like so many Christmas ornaments. One of them, I swear, looked down at me with this cocked beady eye and asked in this kind of flat, nasal-sounding, Irish accent, "So, how long are you here on holiday, then?"

Before I even thought about how weird that was, I started to answer. "It's not really a hol—" I said, then caught myself.

"Oh, brother. You *do* talk."

"Talk?" it said. "Talk? Of course, I talk. Sure, I pecked the Blarney Stone with me own beak, would you believe it?"

"Not that. It's just I knew I could understand the toad and the cat and they know about me but how did you know I could understand you and that—well, that I'm not from here?"

"Oh, that. Dead easy," the crow said, preening its feathers.

"We'd have heard there was a young American lady who'd've been granted the gift of speech," another crow answered. "And American girls wouldn't be all that thick on the ground out here, now would they? It would've had to be you, wouldn't it?"

"Well, yeah. But how did you know I was American? I didn't say anything."

"Somethin' in the walk it was. You can always tell Americans by their walk," the first crow said.

"Not to mention that he overheard you givin' out to herself over there in the field," a lady crow added.

"Why do I get the feeling I'm in the middle of an Irish Heckle and Jeckle cartoon?" I muttered to myself. They heard me though.

"Who might that be? Relatives of yours?" another crow asked. "You've family here in Ireland, have you?"

"No, no. Look, this is a little complicated. I appreciate you guys coming over to say hi, but this is the kinda thing that's s'posed to happen to you on drugs and—I'm not. So I think I'll just go back to Felicity's and get used to the idea, okay?"

"Certainly, dear, you'd be tired after your long journey, wouldn't you? We'll just follow you back a ways, shall we, and we'll be sittin' outside your window in the mornin', watchin' over you like?"

Wonderful! Just what I needed! Guardian crows. Wasn't there some old Joan Baez song about crows talking over a battlefield, discussing a dead knight whose eyes and other tender parts they were going to pluck out? I was not crazy about these birds. Don't they call a bunch of crows a "murder" of crows? If you talked to them the way I did, you'd know why. They sounded like the kind of critters who'd cackle through the part in the Hitchcock flick where Tippi Hedren gets half pecked to death.

Felicity was just showing the lady she'd been interviewing out when I came in. A strong odor of booze trailed behind the woman as she marched for her cab.

"I'm afraid we can't use her," Felicity told me. "She had, as they say here, drink taken. Habitually, I should think."

"I noticed."

I also noticed the leak in the hallway had stopped. All that remained of the waterfall was a large soggy spot.

"So, how was your outing?" Felicity asked ne.

"I got yelled at by a snotty woman in a riding habit, winked at by a horse, and made boring small talk with some crows."

"Crows?" Felicity's eyebrow rose meaningfully.

"Yeah. They talked a lot but didn't say much except they think all Americans walk alike. They knew I could talk to animals but for some reason thought I was on a holiday. I dunno. I thought talking to animals would be more interesting, somehow."

"I think, dear, that perhaps you should delve more deeply into the books on Irish Celtic myth and fairy tales."

"I did read some already, remember I said? About the Hound of Ulster."

"Well, read further. And pay particular attention to the significance of crows."

Journal Entry—Tuesday

So I've spent the last couple of days holed up reading while Felicity deals with workmen and builders.

There's actually two different types of "fairy tale" in Ireland. The most modern ones are about the encounters of regular, usually poor farm people, with fairies, talking animals and so forth. The people are almost always good Catholics and often get out of trouble by invoking their religion. Sometimes, though, they resort to performing certain superstitious rituals, like turning their clothes inside out to find their way if the fairies have made them get lost.

I read Yeats for this. The same Yeats I had to read in English Lit also collected Irish folklore and fairy tales. These are the stories about witches, leprechauns and their cousins the cluricaun and Far Darrig, Merrows (like mermen), ghosts, fairy doctors (people who knew enough about fairies to remove enchantments), the devil, giants, the enchanted lands of Tir-na-Nog and Hy Brasil, phantom islands and talking animals. There's a story about the death of the King of the Cats and his funeral procession. There are a few, but not many stories of princes and princesses. Some of these refer back to the old kings and queens from the legends, some to medieval ones, and some to visiting European royalty. But most of the fairy tales are about ordinary people, I guess because the time these stories were supposed to have taken place, the Irish royalty had all killed each other off. There are however a lot of stories of tricky little guys sort of like Jack and the Beanstalk or Jack the Giant Killer or even Puss in Boots, who win over giants, witches, fairies or other beings with more power than they have, by using their wits. And there are stories of fairy songs and fairy musicians and of people who get wishes granted by the fairies or lose years and years of their lives when they fall asleep on a fairy hill and wake up, Rip Van Winkle style, to find out that everybody they knew is old or dead. Some of the Irish stories reminded me a lot of Native American stories, because the animals could always talk and had personalities and like, agendas of their own. Just like they really do, I guess, even if they're just boring old crows.

But I didn't really find out anything about crows or why certain meanings are attached to certain animals till I started reading the second type of stories, the myths and legends of Ireland. These take place a really long time ago, some of them back before Christianity.

There's four story cycles, as they call them. The first one was called, in the book I read, the Mythological Cycle and it's about how Ireland came to be, how it was populated, who fought who to gain control of the land.

This is where the Tuatha de Danaan come in. The thing is, the Tuatha de Danaan were invaders who came to take the land away from the Fir Bolg, who were living in Ireland at the time. The Tuatha de Danaan won, but their king, Nuada, lost his arm. Meanwhile, the Fir Bolg went to live with some people called the Fomorians on the islands around Ireland. The Fomorians had the ancient equivalent of a nuclear weapon. Their king was a man named Balor, who was a pretty ordinary king until one day he passed the magicians' lab when the magicians were making a death spell. He accidentally caught the fumes and they blinded him. Now, I can't figure out from the account if he had one eye to begin with or two and only one was affected by the fumes, but the Fomorians were supposed to be very ugly and misshapen so maybe he only had one to begin with. Anyway, the magician told him that because he'd caught the fumes, his eye would bring death to anyone it fell on. So mostly he kept it shut. But in battle, he'd open it and it would completely demolish anyone in range. A handy guy to have on your side.

Meanwhile, back with the TdD, because poor King Nuada was wounded in battle and lost his arm, according to the rules of kings he couldn't be a king anymore because kings had to be perfect. No equal opportunity employment there, folks. My friend Doc would be really pissed on behalf of a fellow vet. Nuada didn't give up, though. He went to the best doctor he could think of, who made him a silver arm. A little sidebar was that the doctor's *son* was an even better doctor and he was actually able to reattach and reanimate Nuada's original human arm to his body, but the father wasn't into alternative medicine and besides didn't like the competition so he killed his own son. The kid was such a good doctor he was supposed to have cured himself three times before the old man finally done him in. Even then, he tried to leave behind a legacy of healing herbs and stuff, growing them up from his corpse after he was buried. His sister tried to harvest them in order of the body part they were growing out of and over (and, presumably, would cure) but the father caught her and scattered them. How Nuada felt about having his reattached arm chopped off again and replaced by the silver one, it doesn't say.

While Nuada was out of commission, the TdD hired a gorgeous airhead named Bres to be king instead. Bres wasn't much of a king. He just let Balor have anything he wanted and sent TdD kids to be slaves. He didn't think anything could stop Balor, and neither did the others of the TdD.

However, Balor got unreasonably greedy and stole a cow belonging to a guy named Cian. Cian got on the good side of a witch named Birog. Well, Birog must have been kind of a yenta, because she had just been itching for some dude to come along and free up Balor's daughter, Eithlinn. Eithlinn, unlike other Fomorians, was not deformed, but gorgeous. She was shut up in his tower, a little like Rapunzel, and never allowed to see men. Birog sneaked Cian in, though, and Eithlinn instantly fell in lust with him and they did the dirty, which resulted in Lugh, who was the next hero of Ireland, since only Balor's grandson was supposed to be able to kill him.

Balor tried to kill Lugh, of course, when he was a baby, and did a sort of Moses trip on him, sending him out to sea, but he should have known that never works in any of the stories. Sure enough, his own fairy godmother, Birog, rescued him and took him to Cian, who farmed him out to a princess who raised him to have all kinds of talents. He became known as Lugh of the Long Arm. I think arms were really important then, because of all the fighting they did, which was why they were always calling their heros things like Silver Arm and Long Arm.

Lugh went to court, where he could do everything better than everyone, and eventually defeated Balor and put out his evil eye and helped Nuada be king again.

Lugh won at the Second Battle of Moytura, which is the first time crows come in. The crow was really the war witch, which was in some ways a good thing back then. Her name was Morrigu. She was Lugh's girlfriend. In some versions, the Morrigu (or Morrigan, meaning Phantom Goddess) is only one of three battle goddesses called the Badhbh (which means crow, actually) and has sisters named Macha (she comes up later) and Neman.

It goes on and on through the generations, but there are a couple of good side stories. There's one that might be the model for the story of the swan princesses, about the children of a king named Lir who are transformed into swans by their evil stepmother and are made to live on lonely wind-tossed lakes, seas and other wet places for thousands of years until finally a saint helped them turn back into people again. Oh, and while they were swans they could talk human speech and sing beautifully but it didn't do them much good because the curse took them away from people. When they finally were turned back into people, they were like the scene in that great old movie *Lost Horizon* when the woman leaves Shangri-La and turns really old and falls apart like a vampire in the sunlight. But by local standards it was a happy ending because they converted to Christianity first, which was considered a plus.

Also, and here's where the animals really come in, there's a story about this other gorgeous woman named Etain who was loved by several men and, surprise surprise, wasn't liked at all by jealous women, with the result that she spent a lot of time being turned into other things like pools of water, worms, flies, birds and so forth. Eventually, she managed to live happily ever after by solving a riddle. There's a lot of riddle-solving in these stories.

Then there's the story about the Milesians coming to Ireland. They're supposed to be the ancestors of the people who are now the Irish. They fought the TdD and split up the country eventually, with the Milesians taking the aboveground part and the TdD taking belowground. It sounds a little like the arrangement in *The Time Machine*, which I also had to read in English Lit, except that living belowground seems to have given the TdD some magical advantages and they're supposed to have become the people we think of as fairies, or the sidhe. It doesn't say how, of course.

Okay, so that's the Mythological Cycle. Next we get into the Ulster Cycle. That's the one I read parts of earlier, that takes place in the time of King Conor Mac Nessa at Ewain Macha. King Conor is the sexist old goat who drove poor Deirdre to suicide. He is also the idiot who made Macha (remember Macha) in the guise of the pregnant wife of one of his followers, race with one of his chariot horses, just for the sake of a bet. The result was, she won the race, he lost the bet, and she put a curse on him that he and the men of Ulster would be as weak as she was when they most needed to be strong. Oh, and she had twins on the spot. Ewain means "twins." Which is why Conor Mac Nessa's hill got to be known as Ewain Macha.

Fortunately for King Conor, the boy originally named Setanta was not born in Ulster. I say fortunately because the boy grew up to be Cuchulain, or the Hound of Ireland as he was called because when he accidentally slew the watchdog and the king said, "Hey, that's my best watchdog," he told the king *he* would be his watchdog from now on and he was.

He was very important in protecting Ulster when Queen Maeve decided to do some cattle rustling too. All the king's men, being under Macha's curse, immediately came down with really bad cramps, but Cuchulain was able to hold down the fort. Then he made the mistake of dissing the Morrigan when she came to him in disguise to tell him she wanted to sleep with him. She got back at him, of course, and a little while later, Cuchulain met one of the Badhbh (who apparently double as banshees) washing his bloody clothes, which meant he was going to get his in the next battle, which he did.

A lot of the Ulster Cycle would make a really good Schwarzenegger movie. It's full of battles and heroic brawls and the attitudes toward women really suck. But then, that's what eventually did those guys in, isn't it, when you stop to think about it?

The next cycle is named either after Finn Mac Cumhaill, another hero and king, or Oisin, the hunko-champion Niambh of the Golden Hair took a shine to and carried off to Tir-na-Nog, the Land of Youth. He could live happily ever after as long as he didn't want to leave. Guess what? He got lonesome for his drinking buddies and wanted to go home. She said, okay, as long as you stay on your horse, you'll be fine. But he had an accident and fell off the horse and did another one of those Shangri-La or Dracula special effects where he turned instantly from a hunk to a handful of ashes.

Much of this cycle is a lot of bragging about boy stuff which I suppose they had to do since they didn't have professional football or soccer or anything back then (although I read someplace that soccer came from when they used to kick their enemies' heads around after battles). There is one more interesting story about a girl named Grania who was supposed to marry Finn Mac Cumhaill (who, of course, already had at least one wife and several mistresses). She had other ideas and fell for a guy named Diarmid. It would have been the same story as Deirdre all over again but Grania was a much craftier little number than Deirdre and she and Diarmid eluded Finn long enough to work out a peace settlement so she lived happily ever after with Diarmid until he got tricked by Finn, who killed him, and then she lived happily ever after with Finn. Talk about your survivors.

The next cycle is about the medieval kings. I haven't gotten to it yet.

I came out of my book in time to overhear a conversation between Felicity and the contractor, who not only didn't know what the Keep Out sign on the door upstairs means, but claims he didn't even put that door there. This sounds all too *Alice in Wonderland* to me. I'll have to ask Felicity what she thinks of it.

CHAPTER 11

Dear Rosie,

What a drag! The godmothermobile has been in the shop since before we arrived—it was supposed to have been driven to the airport for us and left there, but it wouldn't start, so the person the FGMs hired to drive it to the airport took it to the garage instead. So we haven't been able to go anywhere. Meanwhile, the toilets still won't flush and the refrigerator is on the blink. And it rains *all* the time! Felicity must have had every dysfunctional woman in Ireland apply for the job as housekeeper. Some of them look like their last job was as room service at the Bates Motel. The only good thing is, I don't feel like I'm missing much when I'm reading. And I've been doing a lot of reading. Except now that I've read about these places and stuff, I want to *see* them. I'm uploading my journal entries so far for you on E-mail—you'll see what I'm talking about.

It was really a kick to hear from you. Fred sounds like a quality kind of guy. I haven't heard a single thing from Raydir so far, though Cindy wrote and said she was taking off for an endurance trail ride someplace in the southwest. God, I am so homesick! Only the weather is like Seattle. Man, I want a latte so bad! Tea is *not* the same.

In spite of the lack of my usual caffeine overload, I'm not sleeping very well. I keep hearing noises in the night. I also hear music and voices when I swim. There's something very strange about the swimming pool. For one thing, there's no chlorine—not that I can smell anyway. Felicity says it's fed by a natural well and the water is very clear and clean. Isn't that against the law or something at home, for a home pool I mean? It's cool but it's a little—I dunno. Not unnatural. Maybe *too* natural. Also, every time I close my eyes I can almost see the bottom change into—something. The minute I open my eyes again it's gone. Meanwhile, the builder took off on his vacation to Switzerland and won't be back for another week. And the godmother fax line is on the blink, and the phones ring at odd hours of the night, except there's nobody there. The milk is delivered every day, big deal. I don't like milk and anyway, it's always sour. We're almost out of groceries.

I woke up last night and heard someone stomping around upstairs—too loud to be the cat. I went to find Felicity and she wasn't in her room or in her office. And no, it wasn't her upstairs either. I couldn't quite bring myself to look at first but I did after Bobby did. I accused him of making all the racket and he hopped upstairs to prove I was wrong. He was right. There wasn't a soul there and the only thing that was any different was that door you're not supposed to open was a little ajar. I wondered if Felicity had gone in there and was about to peek in to find out when Bobby flung his warty little self against it. I told him he'd picked a hell of a time of life to start following rules.

I never thought I'd say it, but he's been more use than that cat. She doesn't seem to live here after all. I haven't seen her since that one night. I sort of thought maybe once we got to know each other we'd be friends, but she hasn't shown a whisker.

Anyway, about the time I was going to peek in the door, I heard a noise downstairs—seemed to be coming from the guest room, and when Bobby and I looked down there, there was Felicity again. I asked her where she'd been and she was pretty vague. Anyhow, I'll cut this short for now since the upload is going to take a while and I'll continue with the journal and send you more later. Okay?

Sno

*   *   *

Journal Entry—Thursday

I slept most of the day yesterday. Today, it was a total waste getting out of bed. I went into an empty kitchen and there wasn't even any of the plain old ordinary coffee left. We haven't had a chance to do any shopping. I didn't feel like tea, dammit. All this PBS atmosphere here is fine, but I'm from Seattle. I have a constitutional right to coffee. So I stomped back to my room and got my raincoat and went outside to find the horse that winked at me—I just needed somebody different to talk to instead of that damned toad. But it was raining so hard I couldn't even *see* the field across the road and the wind blew my raincoat up so I was soaked in a couple of minutes. When I sloshed back into the house, I decided to go swimming, but the heat had gone out on the pool and it was fuckin' freezing.

Anyway, finally I'd just had it and I walked into Felicity's office where she was consulting her crystal ball and said, "Look, I understand everything's going wrong and how you don't have much time or anything. But even if you can't actively teach me anything, I can learn by watching, can't I? Just clue me in and I'll check it out for myself. Who knows? I might even be able to help."

When she turned around to look at me, she wore that same out-to-lunch, half-depressed expression Raydir does when he needs to make a new album and has been doing too much promo and not enough music. Or when his agent had been calling too many shots and getting him to play gigs he hated, record songs he thought were crap. It busted his chops. Hey, just because he never paid much attention to me doesn't mean it was mutual. Felicity looked like that. In the week we've been here she's come way down from being the upbeat savior of everybody to looking like she could use a couch herself.

"Poor Sno!" she said, fluttering her hands like a couple of moths. "I've been neglecting you dreadfully trying to organize things."

I didn't agree but I didn't disagree either. I just said, "Where do you go when I hear noises at night and you're not in the house? Got a boyfriend next door or what?"

She stopped fluttering, gave me a guilty, half-quizzical glance, then decided I was joking, by which time I wasn't sure I was. She laughed. "I wouldn't say that, no. Confronting old memories, you might say."

"I really want to know about how you became a fairy god-mother," I told her.

"Another time I'll show you that, dear," she said, then straightened up as if she'd had a sudden backbone transplant. "But for now, I think perhaps we should see about our trans-portation, even if we have to involve headquarters in Bath. If we can organize that, we shall run into Greystones and Bray and if you like, you can take the DART in to Dublin."

"What's that?"

"The commuter train."

Sounded super to me. I like trains. There's all those train songs in Grandma's—my—collection and I sing them to my-self when I ride—"City of New Orleans," "Freight Train," "Way Out There." I mean, you *seldom* run into good plane songs.

Well, once Felicity decided to organize something, as she put it, boy did she ever organize! Our phone was out but the fax was running so she faxed Bath that if "our time here in Ireland is to be spent at all productively and Dame Prudence cannot see fit to countenance magical expenditures, then it is vital that she release sufficient fiduciary funds for us to rent a vehicle to maintain ourselves. The site of the new headquar-ters, while conveniently located to many useful facilities, has only a tenuous link to public transportation."

Then we braved the rain and went to meet the next-door neighbors. It shows our luck was changing that they were home. Anyhow, the man was. His name's Tim O'Connor. He's on TV but he does the evening sports program so he works odd hours, he said. Felicity introduced us and went to ''sort out'' the garage that had been messing with the god-mommobile for far too long.

A pretty little black-and-white dog with sides bulging and tits dragging the ground was right on Tim's heels.

''Nice dog,'' I said, when she jumped up on me and started sniffing and yipping.

''*No*, Hannah. Where're your manners? What kind of a mum are you going to be if you teach your children such filthy habits?''

''Get along with you,'' the dog said. Anyhow, *I* heard her say it. ''I'm only greeting our guest!'' She jumped down and looked up at me with big brown eyes. ''Such a *fussy* man, but what am I to do? He's master, is he not?''

I petted her and didn't say anything, not certain how to handle the conversation with her master there.

''You will have some tea and biccies, won't you?'' Tim asked. ''The wife will never forgive me if I don't ask you where your mouths are.''

''Thanks,'' I said, not sure what else to say.

Hannah was wagging her tail. ''The wife'll never forgive him if he doesn't find out all about you, where you come from and what you're doing here, he means. And a good thing it is too. What *have* you brought to the neighborhood?''

''What do you mean?''

''Why, the strange comings and goings at all hours. The peculiar little creature scuttling around the side of your house, stealing things and looking in windows and breaking things and tearing bits off the roof and all other manner of hooligan-ism. Why, if I weren't locked in at night to protect my own folk and the lives of my wee ones, I'd chase the living day-lights out of the baysht and have an accounting of such she-nanigans.''

''Stop that whining, you bold bitch, you!'' Tim O'Connor called from the kitchen. I took it he was talking to Hannah.

"What peculiar little creature?" I asked her. "You mean the toad? Or the cat?"

"Shush, no! Do you think I wouldn't know the likes of a cat or a toad when I see one? I mean the bitty little thing like a burly child—never have seen such a thing. Hairy all over except where the clothes are."

"It wears clothes?"

"Did I not just say so? And all hours it roams—inside your house too. Would you not be knowin' about it, then? And the strange lights and the funny music that comes from there. I confess I liked it better when your house was just another field and the hill not cut into and the old pool not housed over and refilled."

"Here we are then," the man said, carrying in a tray with three teacups, a teapot, and a plate of flat round cookies. "I expect you'll like the little chocolate covered biscuits," he said, pointing to the ones covered in brown.

I took one. It didn't look like any biscuit I've seen. The gravy wouldn't soak in at all. I wondered why on the British programs they were always having biscuits at weird hours of the day, and sometimes when they were also having scones, which are a lot *like* biscuits, only triangular. This explained it. They really meant cookies.

I wanted another word or two with the dog but Felicity came in just then, smiling, so I said to O'Connor, "I really like your dog, sir. Are all the puppies promised or do you think maybe I could get one to take home with me? I'd sure like to come and see them when they're born anyway."

"I don't see why not," he said.

"That's that," Felicity announced with a look of grim satisfaction. "The car will be brought around in about twenty minutes and then, Sno, if you'd like, we shall go see the flesh-pots of Greystones and Bray and buy groceries as well!"

We left without having much tea but apparently that wasn't real unusual. Felicity said the thing was, it was expected that you offer it or people would think you were mean—not as in vicious, as in stingy.

I tried to tell her what the dog said. "Felicity, Hannah told me there's been something odd skulking around outside the house."

She just looked vaguely guilty and said, "I wouldn't doubt it at all, dear. Now then, we need coffee and popcorn and what else?"

"Aren't you worried?"

"Not especially. Without my usual magic, and having drained my supply of good luck, I've no doubt attracted some sort of gremlin. I expect it will go away as we progress in developing your magic and reviving mine."

That was easy for her to say. She seemed to be MIA most of the time. But I guess if it was serious, she wouldn't be so casual about it and if it was really dangerous, she wouldn't leave me alone. So I shut up and let her keep making her list out loud and trying to find a ballpoint pen that hadn't dried up or a pencil that wasn't broken to make the list with. In the end, she had to go back and type it on the computer in the office. About then the car came and I finally got a chance to see some of Ireland.

The villages looked familiar, again like the sets of the British mystery programs with the stone houses and fences. Lots more quaint and picturesque than Felicity's house. "How old are these houses?" I asked her.

Felicity shrugged. "Varies, I suppose. Most of the grandest architecture is Georgian but there's a cottage that's still thatched around here someplace. And some of the buildings are quite old indeed. Have you ever heard the song 'The Vicar of Bray'?"

"I've got it on an old Theodore Bikel album I inherited from my Grandma Hilda," I told her. "This isn't *the* Bray . . . ?"

"The very one." Felicity agreed and began in a deliberately shaky soprano, "In good king Charles' golden time when loyalty no harm meant . . ."

"A zealous high churchman was I and so I gained preferment," I joined in. "To teach my flock I never missed, Kings are by God appointed and damned are those who dare resist or touch the Lord's anointed." And we chorused, "And this be law that I'll maintain until my dying day, sir, that whatsoever king shall reign, still I'll be the Vicar of Bray, sir.''

Felicity looked at me, I swear to God, with new respect but I just looked around and said casually like, "So this was his town, huh?'' It was a pretty town, the stately entrance of each Georgian unit individualized with different colored trim and a bright door. It never occurred to me that doors could be painted so many pretty colors! Turquoise ones, purple ones, lime green, kelly green, marigold yellow, rose, brilliant scarlet, mauve, every color of paint imaginable, really. And each teensy yard has its own little fence. Sometimes the section of house and its fence are a slightly different color from the adjoining section, but mostly, I'll bet it's the pretty colored doors that let each person find the right unit to go home to.

Felicity said, "I'm very impressed that you know the song. I shouldn't think it would have a lot of relevance for a modern young lady.''

"Well, I wrote a paper on it," I told her. "As an illustration of realpolitik for my Western Civ class. You know, like Richelieu and Machiavelli and those guys. 'The enemy of my enemy is my friend,' and all that. Seems to me to be about the way it is now too, except of course most of the time the presidents dump everyone who was already in power to put their new buddies in and nobody has a chance to be as flexible as the Vicar. But that doesn't mean they wouldn't change their spots if they could. Pretty cynical, I guess, but that's how the world works, isn't it?''

"Sometimes," Felicity said. "Though we do our bit to make it otherwise. I shouldn't think they'd teach about such things at your level.''

"I've got some good classes. The school wouldn't be too bad if we didn't have to wear those dorky uniforms.''

"Like those girls?" Felicity asked, nodding at a stream of girls in teal-colored skirts and sweaters.

"Ours are red," I said, and that was all I managed to say before Felicity pulled into the center of town and I was busy holding my breath and grabbing what she called the "Ojaysus'' strap while Felicity ran a slalom course right there on the main drag, dodging buses, parked cars, pedestrians and cars in her own and opposite lanes. It was weird enough that she was driving on the wrong side of the road but she was passing on the wrong side too when the car in front of her didn't move fast enough to suit her. It was like being in a rally, except that people were much nicer about letting each other in and out of tight places than they usually are in Seattle.

Finally, Felicity swerved past a van and ducked behind a block of shops and then swooped up into a parking lot, which fortunately wasn't very full. "There now," she said, not even breathing hard. I thought I understood now why the godmothermobile might have developed a few technical problems. "Let's see. I have to go to Dunne's Store for more towels and duvets and covers, and then to Anvil for reading lamps for our rooms, and to the news agent for the paper until ours can be delivered."

We walked through a little alley which had a butcher, a baker, no candlestick maker, but both a jewelry store and a fabric store. On main street we passed more jewelry stores, what looked like countrified minimarts, fruit shops, bakeries, banks and something called a turf accountant.

"What's that?" I asked, reading a sign that said that whatever it was, Michael Keating was one.

"A bookmaker," Felicity said.

Dumb me. I thought that meant a publisher or maybe a printer and I looked in the window. The inside was grimy with lots of chain-smoking men studying lists printed on pieces of paper tacked to the walls. "Doesn't look all that literary to me," I said.

"It isn't a maker of books, Sno dear, but a . . . er . . . betting agent."

"Oh! A bookie. Right." Why didn't they just say so?

"The sorority sometimes finds them quite useful when we wish to distribute the luck, you know. The lotto and scratch cards are other prime resources."

"You guys must love Vegas."

"In moderation."

I kind of hate to admit it but I didn't exactly find the town thrilling, or even interesting, and other than the stone fronts, which I was getting used to, and some cute curtains here and there and some fancy printing on a few of the shops, it didn't even look especially Irishy. Just kind of like a small town before the mall gets built. Most of the stores sold normal practical stuff, except for the green leprechaun house shoes and plastic thatched cottages the news agent kept for tourists. I restrained myself.

We stopped at a bank and I cashed some of my traveler's checks for Irish money. At another news agent, I bought some magazines, *It* and *D'Side*, aimed at the Irish babe trade, and a magazine called *In Dublin*. I bought that because it had Raydir's picture on the cover and an interview about his TV special—the one he made at Snoqualmie Falls. It's airing in Ireland next week.

"You look as if you're expecting more, dear," Felicity said. She must have been reading my mind. "I understand the Bray Bookshop is quite nice and there's a Golden Discs here if you'd like to purchase some music, but I'm afraid most of the trade here is rather on the utilitarian side. Local people find most things they need here or in Greystones or in Kiliney or Stillorglin, closer to Dublin."

"What if they need something from farther away and they don't have a car? Are there buses?"

"Oh, goodness yes, and there's also the DART."

"Oh, the train you were telling me about! Where can you catch that?"

"The station is here in Bray. If you like, I can take you over there now and you can go into Dublin to explore while I'm organizing things. I'm afraid I'll need to use the car until we're a bit more settled."

"You don't need me for anything? I haven't seen the cat all week and—well, I mean, the toad's not here. Can I go without him?" I was surprised to find I sort of wished the little creep were along. I liked the idea of being free to go where I wanted, but I guess my post-traumatic stress thing was kicking in and I was a little worried about going out in a foreign country full of total strangers.

But Felicity didn't seem worried at all. "Sure, you'll be perfectly safe!" she said with more Irish lilt to her voice than usual. "Students ride it back and forth to school all the time. Besides, Puss is never as far away as you think."

We returned to the car, both of us loaded with billowing plastic bags, which Felicity stuffed in the trunk or the "boot" as they call it here. Then she drove me to the station. "Off with yez, now!" she said still in her Irish accent as she pointed out the entrance. "Have a good time and ring me when your train returns and I'll come collect you."

I grinned back at her through the car's lowered window. "Right, and if I don't do it by midnight, the train turns into a pumpkin, huh?"

"No, but I don't believe it runs after half eleven so I'd advise you to return before then."

Before I could say goodbye, she drove away.

*   *   *

After dropping Sno off at the DART station, Felicity returned to Bray to finish the errands she wished to achieve unaccompanied. This involved both shoe stores in Bray and a shoe repair shop as well. With these errands accomplished, she returned to the house, where she found that the telephone had indeed been repaired as promised.

She checked messages in the control room and, finding none, cleared the rubbish from her bedroom and put it in the trash bin at the front gate for collection. She took her new purchases and carefully spread fast-drying glue all over them, and liberally sprinkled them with dime-store glitter. Then, slipping out of her errand running clothes and into a silver spangled gown and the newly glittered Doc Martens she'd bought in Bray, she entered the guest room, opened the French doors, and disappeared into the hillside that opened at the same time as the doors.

She didn't hear the fax buzz or see the sheet of paper emerge with the words: "Advised by Magic Comptroller of S. Quantrill's difficulty. Coming to sort it out at once. P."

*   *   *

To Cunla's eyes, the wires going into the machinery room sparkled with magic as the ringer rang and the paper-spitter spat its words in a long sheet onto the desk. Cunla watched from the doorway but he did not dare to go in, no indeed.

He had seen where Herself went, through them double doors in that red red wall, and he knew what that meant.

Trouble for poor Cunla. Trouble indeed.

Herself had left the front door ajar slightly and Cunla did not have to touch the cruel cruel iron to go back outside.

The absence of Herself and the girl had given him time to have a wee gawk around the place, to see the grand frame that had been built for the oul' scrying pool, to see the strange forbidden door in the attic that led to a place not even Cunla would venture, and to see the glassy doors in the red red wall leading into the hillside.

Trouble, great trouble. Poor, poor Cunla when Herself returned.

Just to make certain, he checked the rubbish bin, which was of plastic. Inside he saw the fatal items, all be-glamored and well worn away. He touched a bit of the glamourie. It fell from his fingers to glitter in a mud puddle beside the bin.

CHAPTER 12

Dear Rosie,

I finally got to Dublin. It was quite a trip and I'm uploading the following journal entries to let you know what happened. *Please* read through it and don't freak, okay? I'm fine, really. Okay, get ready for the upload. Here goes.

Hugs, Sno

P.S. I'm writing what people said the way it sounded.

*   *   *

Journal Entry—Dublin

At the Bray DART station, the crowd standing around the train platform didn't exactly look like the same kind of crowd you'd find in the bus tunnel in Seattle, but they didn't make me think immediately, "Wow, I'm in a foreign country." There were more girls in several different school uniforms, some kids with knapsacks, ladies dressed like World War II movies, and other girls and guys dressed like anybody you'd see in Seattle; jeans, T-shirts, loose sweaters.

Felicity had told me to tell the ticket agent that I needed a "day return to Dublin," and I did. I took the ticket, and started to walk through the turnstile but it didn't seem to be working, so I did what everybody else was doing and handed it to the most stress-free-looking uniformed individual I have ever seen, who was standing in his little box, punching holes in tickets as if the automatic turnstiles had never been invented. By the time he got mine punched, the train had pulled up to the platform.

The people-watching was excellent, and the listening just as good if not better. Almost everybody carried umbrellas, I noticed, even the kids, and once on board the train an awful lot of people pulled out a book to read, which, except for maybe in the U district is something you only see occasionally in Seattle, where people on ferries or buses tend to be working out of a briefcase, typing on a laptop, or scribbling in a notebook.

After a couple of minutes, I started checking out the people on the train. The first thing that struck me was how many of the Irish girls had big hair without even trying. At home girls who don't want straight hair will braid it at night to make it kink or perm it but here about ten of the girls had this really great hair—so thick and curly you could get a whole department store full of hair accessories lost in it, and full of energy, like it not only had a mind of its own, it had a whole separate agenda from the head it was on. Most of the girls had made a halfhearted attempt to control it with barrettes or velvet scrunchies but usually only a small portion seemed to be under arrest at any one time. What I had expected was that Ireland would be full of redheads. I saw only two, and one of those a guy. Most of the girls had dark brown hair or black, like mine. Hardly anyone was wearing makeup, which I don't either, but a lot of them *did* wear jewelry—fistsfull of chunky silver rings and, I saw lots of girls wearing velvet scrunchies as bracelets. We do that at home too but with the local hair gene, I suspect their reason here is more practical than trendy. Never know when you'll need that extra scrunchie to corral the locks.

Except for the hair and jewelry thing, I fit in okay. I was wearing my fadedest jeans, and a really cool net sweater that looks like it's woven out of binder's twine over a black turtleneck. I had a navy bandanna around my neck and *my* hair French braided into a scrunchied ponytail. I was carrying a knapsack, with my camera, a wallet, and stuff in it. And my wish-box, of course. I didn't have on a windbreaker, which most of the kids wore, and I hoped that wouldn't make me look too American, like the crows said my walk did.

Because I figured if you're going to learn about people, you need to blend in a little, right? Except for my straight hair, I didn't look a lot different from the Irish girls.

I seemed to blend okay, except for some of the guys checking *me* out but that was cool. I mean, I'd have been a little worried if they hadn't. Nobody actually tried to pick me up or anything, but some of them were pretty cute.

The older men tend to dress up way more than the ones not rushing off to do the corporate thing do at home. Even the ones not in business suits wore jackets. The younger guys mostly wore sweaters or bomber style jackets though, like they would at home. Even the people who didn't have their noses stuck in a book looked like they had a lot on their minds, even if it was just meeting buds to hang out with. The train wasn't very crowded, so I got to have a seat all to myself.

After a couple of minutes, I abandoned people-watching for staring out the window. The tracks run along some truly choice scenery. No snow mountains, mind you, but nice, very nice. There were more Georgian houses along the track, but there were also a couple of the Martello Towers, which are these squat round towers. I wondered which one had belonged to U2. The guidebook had given me the names of them and also said that the one in Dublin used to belong to James Joyce. I can't stand his stuff, what I've tried to read, but it was interesting that he and U2 both lived in the same kind of towers, I thought. On one side of the tracks it seemed like there was one big sprawling hotel with one golf course after another, castellated houses and church spires, and on the other side, downhill from the tracks, miles of beach with people and dogs sauntering along. Beyond was the sea, the water a deep teal green shading to silver, with another shore hazy in the dis-

tance. Funny to realize the shore could belong to another country instead of another part of the same state, the way it does
when you see land in the distance across the Sound. Even
when the train was in its ditch and you couldn't see the houses
or the sea, the tracks were banked with flockings of soft green,
bright green, and clusters of pink, rose, purple, yellow and
white flowers. All the trees had these little skirts of ivy. In the
stone walls that shored up the banks, the builder had deliberately left holes for bouquets of flowers, their colors blazing
up against the old stone like torches set in some fairy-tale
castle wall. I'm not much into gardens, but these flowers made
me feel like maybe some day I might want to be.

The train stopped at several cute turquoise-and-blue-painted
stations with names like Kiliney, Shankill, Dalkey, and
something that looked like you'd have to gargle it but turned
out to be pronounced Dun Leery. Later we passed this big
rusty crown of ironwork on the outskirts of the city, and pulled
into Pearse Street Station, a huge open brick barn of a building
with a roof sheltering the tracks.

I asked one of the other girls if this was where I ought to
get off to see Dublin.

"It is, yes," she said. "It's near to Trinity College, where
you can see the Book of Kells and Grafton Street and all."

I thanked her and followed her until she disappeared in the
crowd ahead of me. I was wishing again I had someone, even
the toad, to talk to. Maybe I was having a premonition of how
the rest of the day was going to go.

The street curved past two or three entrances to Trinity College, and onto Nassau Street, a bus-filled road with a long wall
on the college side and shops lining the other side. The light
at the crosswalk was just turning red, but everybody who'd
just arrived hurried out into the street anyway and crossed.
The vehicles didn't seem to mind and the people coming behind us were patiently waiting through the green light to cross,
it looked like to me.

There were signs to the National Museum. That sounded
pretty interesting but I didn't think it would give me what I
was looking for, which was a feeling for the social structure

of the country. I wanted to find people who had problems and figure out what a rookie FGM could do to help. The museums could wait. I wanted to deal with here and now and real life.

Nassau Street seemed to deal more with past lives, however. You could buy brass replicas of things people didn't use anymore, like door knockers and horse brasses, and there were two places offering to tell you the story of your Irish roots. I intend to do that for Raydir before I go home.

Outside this big gift supermarket called the Kilkenny Design Shop, a woman sat on the sidewalk, a baby cradled in her arms and a plaid blanket spread over her lap. The poor thing was begging for change. She didn't look drunk or spacey or anything. My idea of what Ireland was like got a rude shock right then. In the States, you know there's lots of homeless people but Ireland's supposed to be little and friendly. You'd think people would look after ladies with little kids like that. I dug out as many pound coins as I had in change from the DART fare and dropped them in the woman's lap.

"There you are, ma'am," I said in my most beneficent voice, and added, just so I wouldn't sound like I was lording it over her or anything, "Good luck."

She raised her eyebrows, as if the money was more than she expected, and like, she wasn't sure it was entirely in good taste for me to give it to her. But all she said was, "Thank you, dear," like I'd just run an errand for her.

While I was puzzling over that one, I came to the next corner, where I saw another woman, with another baby, and another plaid blanket. "I get it," I told her. "Quaint local native custom, huh?"

"Could yiz spare five pence, dear?" the woman whined.

But by that time I figured it was a racket and kept walking. I passed a bookstore that took up three shopfronts, one section devoted to best-selling paperbacks, the next to school texts, and the third to hardback fiction, history and books of "Irish Interest." It seemed like a good idea to bone up on that but there were so many books I couldn't figure out what to buy and decided to ask Felicity later.

Then I forgot all about my mission and got consumed with

my basic shopper/gatherer instincts as I passed store windows full of Celtic knotwork jewelry, heathery tweeds, capes and shawls in red, kelly green, and purple and the kind of Aran sweaters worn by the Clancy Brothers on their old albums. I almost succumbed to a sweater, but I didn't because what with all the walking around I was doing I was plenty warm and I was afraid it might look touristy.

Wandering down three more blocks, a woman, baby and plaid shawl at each and every corner, I arrived at Grafton Street, which is closed to all but foot traffic. At the entrance to the street an artist did chalk paintings on the pavement. A little farther on, a woman wearing dreadlocks and lace sleeves pumped her breath into a diggeridoo. Raydir used one of those on his last album and Dougie Maclean uses them a lot. It's very cutting edge to use weird ethnic instruments in pop music, y'know.

Further up the street, an old man sat playing good blues on a guitar with levers positioned over the strings so that he fingered it like a piano. Beyond that, four little kids played Irish tunes on whistles, drums and a fiddle. Street stalls sold cheapo Celtic jewelry along with stuff from Peru and woven friendship bracelets like the seven I wear on my left wrist above my watch, gifts from my vet buddies, Doc and the guys. Flowersellers presided over plastic buckets crammed with daisies, lilies and carnations.

I wandered down a side street and immediately got jumped by a kid who couldn't have been more than seven, begging for change.

I wondered why a kid that age wasn't in school and where was his social worker at first, and then I realized, hello, that I'm in a different country and maybe kids don't have to go to school and are actually allowed to live on the streets without interference from a truant officer. So I gave the kid a pound. I never learn, do I? Two steps later another kid held me up for more change and I gave him twenty pence.

"Haven't yez got any more?" the little monster demanded.

Before I became an FGM I'd have told him to take a hike but I tried to be patient and explain, now that I was supposed to set an example. "Look, I just gave that other kid something. Give me a break, will you?"

"You give him more," the kid argued. He was no older than the first one but he acted like *so* entitled, as if I were cheating him of what was rightfully his.

Then four *other* kids about the same age closed in and right then I knew I'd made a big mistake. I ducked into a nearby shop to lose the little piranhas.

I felt like a worm, frankly. Here I was a fairy godmother, almost, and I didn't want to give these kids more money because they weren't asking pretty. Well, that was part of it. The other part was I thought it was a scam. So I asked the girl behind the counter about it—who were these kids? Weren't there any national social programs to help them? Weren't they supposed to be in school? Where did they live? Who were their parents? I mean, we talk about how bad it is in the States but when I was on the streets, one reason I didn't stay there too long was that there were a whole lot of interfering people like the cops and you, Rosie, who kept asking a lot of questions I thought were dumb then. Of course, I didn't ask the one poor girl everything but I did, as Felicity would say, try to "suss out" the sitch.

The shopkeeper, who was a little older than me, looked beyond me into the street and shook her head. "I wouldn't want to sound harsh, Miss, but those are tinker brats and you're not to give them anything. It only encourages them. They have money enough from the government, and their parents won't be far away, you can be sure, waitin' to collect the money for the drink. They're an awful thievin' lot. If they see you've money, they won't leave you be."

That made me really feel like Miss Rich Bitch. Here I was begging on the streets myself only a couple of years ago and now, not only did the kids have me pegged as a mark but this girl was calling me "Miss" like she thought I might buy something. I thanked her and left.

The kids had disappeared but a bigger girl—maybe my age, maybe a little older, maybe a little younger—grabbed my arm before I'd gone two steps and sort of bent over like her stomach hurt her and whined, "Please, Miss, I'm turrible hongry. I wouldn't be wantin' your money, I wouldn't touch it, only I need something to eat so bad."

She didn't look like she was starving. She looked like she could have done with a diet, if you want to know the truth. Her dishwater blonde hair was scruffy and matted, her face was chapped red, she wore baggy-kneed pants and an enormous bulky jacket that looked as if it was made out of a saddle blanket.

I didn't feel very sympathetic. She was old enough to get a job. So I said, "Sorry, I'm fresh out."

She might have been short of cash but she had plenty of nerve. "That's a fine wristwatch you're wearin' there," she said, like I had no right to have it when she was telling me she was hungry.

"It was a gift from my dad. Look, really, I can't give you anything. I haven't got any more change."

"The shops would change money for you," she told me like a teacher blowing my excuses for not doing my homework.

It sounded like an out to me. I was a little worried about this broad. She was bigger than me and tough-looking and while it's true I've had martial arts training, I didn't really come here to fight. So I wussed out and shined her on. "Okay," I said, and headed for an antique shop.

"I'll wait," the girl said, crossing her arms and planting her feet as if she intended to stay in the middle of the street until she turned into a statue like the bronze sculpture of Molly Malone at the head of the street. Somebody told me the nickname for that one in Dublin was "the tart with the cart." What would they call this brawny babe in her Indian blanket jacket? The thug in the rug?

The guy in the fancy antique shop wasn't quite as impressed with my foreignness as the girl in the other shop had been and he didn't even want to give me the time of day, much less change when I hadn't bought anything (as if I would in that overpriced dump). I thought he was great toad material and said so, but quietly. His glare bored holes in my back all the way out to the street.

The big girl stuck out her hand.

I told her sorry, he wouldn't give me any change.

"I'm sorry too. I'm hongry and you promised."

"Look," I said. "You seem to have mistaken me for someone who adopted you or something. I gave up the street already. Why don't you get your little brothers and sisters to share?"

"Maybe I will then," the girl said with a nasty smile, and whistled. A squad of the street brats, including the little ingrates I'd already donated to, ran toward us. I started to beat a fast retreat but the big girl grabbed my arm. "Not so fast, Miss High and Mighty."

The little ones swarmed around us. It was like the scene in this scary old movie called *The Naked Jungle*, when all the ants attacked the plantation. The kids were too small individually to do any harm on their own, but together they were lethal. They jerked at my clothes, arms and legs and one grabbed my camera, another got my knapsack, while others were in my pockets and one ambitious little letch of about eight copped a feel. Meanwhile the big broad grabbed my hair with one hand and my watch with the other. I may know a few moves but I'm no Karate Kid.

I tried to knee her but the bitch butted me right on the bridge of the nose with her very hard head and I went down, gushing blood and shrieking.

The kids all jumped me again and then, all of a sudden, this guy starts yelling, "Layve her be, ya little haythins!"

The kids all backed off and some of them ran away but the big blonde stood over me like a dog with a bone and she said, "Who'reya orderin' around?"

"What's the matter witcha, Maeve?" the guy asks. "That's assault you got there, that is. The gardai'll lock every one of us up for good they see this."

"Who's gonna tell? You?"

"If you don't layve off, yes, I will. Me mam's gone missin'

and I can't afford to be spendin' me nights in jail because of your bullyin'. Now layve off.''

"I'm kaypin' the camera for me trouble."

"Do and I'll tell Father Ambrose."

"Jack, you wouldn't!"

"Try me."

Then she stepped away and I could breathe again. I heard her size 13s pounding off down the street. The guy knelt down and put his arm under my shoulders and pressed a grubby rag against my nose. I was glad my sense of smell was out of commission.

"Are you hurt bad, Miss?" he asked.

Before I could answer someone else hollered. "Here you, leave her alone."

"Go for the cops, Harry," someone with a New Jersey accent advised.

"Now, Trix, they're probably married and had a little . . ." Harry's matching New Jersey accent answered.

"Filthy knacker!" someone, not from New Jersey, screamed. "I saw it all! Filthy knacker brats attacked that poor girl and now this young scoundrel is out for what he can get."

"I never!" My knight in nappy blanket coat yelled back, but all of a sudden, when I needed them least, I seemed to have acquired this audience. I was expecting CNN to show up any minute. The guy started to bolt but I grabbed his arm and faced all the people so willing to help me, now that I didn't have a camera or a knapsack or anything.

"Hey, wait. Stop it. He's okay. He didn't do anything. He scared the others off. They're the ones who mugged me. He helped me out. No, wait . . ." The guy had sprinted for the edge of the crowd and when I unstuck my hair from the blood pasting it across my eyes, I saw him grappling with a man. I climbed woozily to my feet and a Japanese girl reached down to help me up. I staggered over to where my hero was still tussling with the man.

In my politest Clarke Academy voice, somewhat nasal because of my nose injury, I said, "Let him go, please sir." The man retreated and I grabbed onto the sleeve of the guy's jacket. "Wait, will you? Jack? Didn't she call you Jack? You said something about your mom's missing, didn't you? You helped me when I was in trouble. Let me help you."

"You've helped enough as it is," he said, like I'd started it and asked his girlfriend to mug me! Over his shoulder of the man I saw a cop being led toward us by a lady wearing a Scottish kilt and tam and an Aran sweater.

"Here's the gard now," the woman who had been screaming about "knackers" called. "Here, officer, where were you when you were needed? Knackers assaultin' tourists in broad daylight in front of our shops on the main streets of Dublin! It's a scandal, is what."

"They were just street kids," I said. For God's sake, I was the one who looked like a walking traffic accident and I seemed to be the calmest one there. Even the Japanese girl looked as if she was about to explode. A noisy crowd had gathered. No one seemed devoid of an opinion on my situation.

I told the cop, "This guy helped. And he's got a real problem, officer, sir. His mother has disappeared."

This did not endear me to my rescuer, who threw me an even dirtier look than before.

"I've no doubt she is, Miss," said the policeman, or gard. "His sort tend to go missing all the time. The point is, how badly are you injured, and do you want to press charges? We'll just hold onto this lad as a witness since it's likely that he knew your assailants."

"They're all in it together, filthy knackers!" someone spat.

"They were not. He tried to help," I insisted. The boy's eyes were shooting me full of knives by now. He had very dark eyes and when he wasn't glaring at me his glance darted from one face to another. He looked like a lab rat at a cat show.

"Look," I told them. "I was a witness too and the kids who attacked me are long gone. I'm not preferring charges and I'm not going to sue anyone, so relax. This boy helped me and if you try to lock him up I guarantee you I will raise hell and have Ray"— I stopped long enough to assume my best Valley Girl Princess voice, glad that my friends and Seattle were a whole ocean away—"have my daddy hire the best lawyers in Ireland to see that he's freed, you lose your job, and he owns half the country by the time it's over."

The Irish cop decided we were a waste of time when he could be eating donuts, I guess, and walked off. So did the rest of my audience, including the boy, but he wasn't getting away that easy. It may have cost me a nose job, but it looked to me like I'd found my first FGM client.

"Wait a minute. You didn't let me thank you."

"I'dve done as much for anyone," he growled back at me. "You kept them from throwin' the knacker in jail, Miss. You have my gratitude, Miss."

"Oh, knock it off," I told him. "And stop calling me Miss, for godssakes. My name's Sno."

He turned around and it was very clear he was still pissed off at something, me, the world, I didn't know what. "You can call me Rain, then, Snow, since we're after bein' so honest and all with one another."

"Cut the sarcasm, will you? If my nickname offends you so much, you could call me by my whole name, Snohomish, but I'd rather you didn't."

"I never said I had any wish to call you anythin' at all."

"You're a real pain in the ass, you know that? Not very easy to make friends with."

"Your kind isn't to make friends with my kind. Didn't the shopkeepers tell you that when you were after askin' them about Maeve?"

"I wouldn't exactly say she was your kind since she tried to mug me and you stuck up for me."

"She's my kind all right. She lives in the same halt."

"Halt?"

"You don't know much, do you?" he asked and added mockingly, "How long are you planning to be here on your holidays, then?"

"You sound exactly like a crow I met recently. I'm—working—with a lady down in Wicklow. A nice lady. She helps people. I thought maybe we—me, that is, with her help, could help you find your mom.''

"You don't seem to be able to find your own arse, the way it looks to me," he said.

"So I'm stupid and you're real popular with everyone around here. Seems pretty even to me. But look, if you don't want any help, okay. It's only, I thought you really were worried about your mother. If mine were still alive and in trouble I'd be worried. Just pardon me for asking, okay? And thanks a lot for your gracious intervention. Now excuse me while I go find a bathroom and clean up my face.''

"No one's going to let you in anyplace, looking like that.''

"I'll use the one at the DART station.''

He didn't look so certain or so hostile now. In fact, he looked worried sick and as if he was about to cry.

I took a deep breath and tried again. "Look," I said. "I'm sorry you got into trouble with that cop but it wasn't my fault your girlfriend beat me up. I'd really like to help you find your mom. I really would. And my friend, the lady I work with, she'd help too. What does your mom look like? When did you see her last? What was she wearing?''

"It's been days now. She was at the halt, feeding her old cat. The McDonaghs were going to look in on her. She must've gone missing a little before I came home but none of us could find a hair of her. I called up to the hospital, thinkin' she might have been took bad and they came to fetch her but they know nothin' about it and they say they can't start a search themselves—it's me would have to go to the gard. Well, you can see for yourself how much use that would be! Word's gone out among our people in case she goes back to places she used to stop by in her travellin' days. She's old and remainin' in one place has made her crazy . . .''

"Alzheimer's?'' I asked.

But he shook his head. "I don't think so. I've seen it with other Travelling people when they can't take to the road any more. They just get sadder and sadder and end up crazy. Mam isn't well either, her heart is that bad, and her legs swell like an elephant's. She's not fit for the road but it grayves her somethin' awful.''

''Where do you live?''

''North a' here.''

''Show me.''

''You won't like it. And we already know she's not there.''

''She might have come back.''

He brightened a little. ''That she could've, fair enough.''

''Let's go look for her, then.''

He shook his head. ''Not you.''

''Why not?''

''Think I fancy spending the whole day through defending you from Maeve and her like?''

''I'm not worried about her,'' I lied.

''Then you're a bloody fool—literally.''

''Maybe so, but I'm not the one with the missing parent who's turning down real help.''

He thought for a moment and his expression changed. I could see he was trying to overcome his prejudice against what he thought was my prejudice so he could get help for his mom.

''Give me your number then and the address of where you're stopping and if I don't find Mam, I'll ring your friend and see can she help, okay?''

''I—uh—don't have anything to write with,'' I said, delicately not mentioning it was because his good friend Maeve and her elves had run off with my knapsack. And my magazine. ''Shit,'' I said.

''What?'' he asked, startled.

''Oh, I bought this magazine that had Ray—my dad's picture on the cover. I just thought of it because I could have scribbled in the margins. But they even took that.''

''That's awrigh'—I can't read. Tell it to me. I remember good.''

I told him, adding, ''Now be sure and do it, will you?''

''Right,'' he said and turned and walked off. It wasn't what I wanted out of my first client—I was hoping more for something in the nature of impossible odds, quick success, and undying gratitude, I guess—but at least he didn't stomp off, or run. He just walked.

I'd wanted to spend more time in the city scoping out potential clients, but I thought I'd better return to Felicity's to be there in case the guy called, desperately seeking my help. Also, I wanted to get home in time to ask Felicity just what godmothers did in such cases, and how. Calling the cops was out, for sure.

The thieves hadn't been interested in my DART ticket, or else it was too small and they overlooked it. Unfortunately, I reached the platform just as the train did and I was feeling too strung out to go clean up and wait for the next one, so I climbed gratefully on board the train, and used spit and my kerchief to clean up as well as I could, with my reflection in the window as a guide. I had no change, but I figured that I could probably con someone into letting me make a local call to Felicity once I got to Bray. I wished I could just have transportation when I needed it, instead of having to wait on other people all the time. And then I reminded myself that wishing carelessly wasn't a good idea.

And then I remembered the little box had been on me when I left for Dublin earlier and now it wasn't.

Damn! Maeve or one of her little buddies had my magic box. What was I going to do? Even if Felicity and I could do without my remaining wishes, I was pretty sure leaving the box in the hands of unauthorized non-FGMs would be severely frowned on by Her Maj. Dame Prudence would have a cow, for sure. And poor Felicity would probably catch more shit as a result.

I wanted to go back to Felicity's and put ice on my face and take aspirin and lie down, but no way was I going to let Maeve have *my* magic wishes. *So,* hoping that no conductor would be checking in case it was illegal, I stayed on the train when it reached Bray and rode all the way back into Dublin again.

CHAPTER 13

Balor sometimes wished somebody else could see how funny it was, when he was contacted, first by the one side, then by the other. Of course, when he was out with Reilly and the lads, they knew him as a Taig named Carnahan. When he was with the Loyalist crew he was McWilliams. And it was among his special gifts to look totally different to each group and be unrecognizable, even in broad daylight. So he'd be planning what needed doing with the boys, one group or the other, and word would ascend the ladder or descend it in the chain of command and if the job in question was a special one, a delicate one, pretty soon he'd be contacted under his code name. Balor. He was such a bloody secret among each group that they both used the same code name and no one ever caught on. His password for accessing the locked computer mailbox was different for each group—for the Loyalists the name of his first South African target, for the Taigs his first Guatemalan. He'd been in the business far and wide, had Balor, though Ireland was his natural habitat.

And now, having received his commission, he headed south, following first the bus, then the route of the first car to give the girl a ride as far as Dublin.

He stopped briefly short of Dublin at a Traveller's halt. He was known to some of the Travellers, though not as well as they thought, and had used their help in the past. But that day, oddly, the caravans and houses stood empty of all but the younger children and two or three older girls left to mind them. "Where is everyone?" he asked one of them, the daughter of one of his contacts. She didn't want to speak at first but he sweetened her up with a couple of pounds. She had been witholding the information on general principle, it seemed. She was actually eager to talk and grew excited as she told him about the disappearance of the old lady and how Jack Daly had gone to town again to try to find help there while everyone searched here.

"Daly?" he asked. "One of Johnny Daly's?"

"The very same. It's old Granny Moira gone missing."

"I'll keep an eye out for her," he said in a friendly way, and he continued on into the city.

*   *   *

Jack caught up with Maeve and her gang at their corner by the upward arch of the Ha'Penny Bridge. Since the Dublin landmark metal footbridge was for pedestrians only, and fairly narrow, it was an easier place to snatch a purse or pick a pocket than the larger and more heavily travelled O'Connell Bridge a few blocks down the Liffey, the river that was the liquid artery of the city's heart. Maeve's gang was huddled together, snapping and snarling at each other like a pack of wild dogs.

"Come on, yiz, let's see what you got," Maeve growled at them.

"Get on with ya, Maeve. I took it meself and it's mine," one of the boys said.

Jack knew Maeve wouldn't let the kid get away with that. She needed the money bad as any, and some he figured she'd use to try to buy herself back into her family.

"I'll take that!" one yelled.

"It was his. Give it back," Maeve ordered while a caterwauling in some ungodly tongue was set up and a general scuffling ensued.

Jack reckoned that was the best diversionary action he was going to have if he was to take them by surprise. He busted in and took hold of Maeve's right arm—at the end of which she had her best punch. "You got to give her stuff back to that girl, Maeve," he said.

"Oh, and who's to make me? And don't threaten me with Father Ambrose again. He knows a girl has to make a livin'."

"Not a soul will persuade you to do it but yourself if you've any brains at all," he said, and spread out the magazine he'd found on the street after the girl left.

"Here—I took that," Maeve said. "Musta dropped it, but it's mine."

"What would you be wantin' with a magazine?" one of the boys asked. "You can't rayde."

"Can so," she said, "a bit. Father Ambrose had Sister show me."

"Then rayde the inside. Tell us about yer man on the front there," Jack said.

"I *know* 'im!" One of the younger boys said. "That's Mr. Raydir shaggin' Quantrill himself, that is!"

"So? Who is the tosser when he's home anyway?" Maeve asked.

"What're ye? Thick? He's only the biggest rock sensation since U2," the younger boy said. "Me sister in Warwick went to see him when he was in London. There was riots!"

"Look inside, Maeve, and see if it mentions about his family. Like a daughter who's the spittin' image of that young one you just mugged."

"So what if it does and what if I did? If she's his daughter, she can afford to trait me to a mayle, snotty little tart."

"If she's his daughter," Jack said, "He'll have the gardai hunt you down. Beggin's one thing, pickin' a pocket or two's another, but that was out and out assault and theft, that was, and she saw your face. She told me her address here. Post it back to her and she'll forget about it. She's stayin' with some lady she said would help me find me mam."

"As if you weren't lucky to be rid of the crazy old cow," Maeve snorted.

"Here now!" Jack said as a matter of form, though he was only acting and wasn't, in truth, all that offended. Maeve wasn't likely to have a lot of respect for mothers, the way hers was drunk all the time, and beat up besides. But she caught his eye and looked sorry, and looked down, and he saw to his dismay that she really did fancy him, at least a bit. She handed over the passport and a few plastic cards. "Here. You can give this back to her. It's of no use to me anyway. They cancel them cards right away. You lot, what do you have? Stand and deliver here!"

"Only the money she give me," one boy said.

She turned her glare on another child, who looked up at her with frightened eyes. "You, John-o, what did you get?"

The boy muttered something unintelligible and began digging frantically through his clothes.

"What's with him?" Jack asked.

Maeve shrugged. "Dunno. Eoin found him under the bridge one morning. Can't talk proper but he catches on real quick. Dunno where he come from. Says his name's John-o though."

The boy held out a little golden box.

"Well, la-ti-da, ain't this a piece of work?" she asked, shaking it. "Doesn't rattle, so it's not pills."

"Maybe it's cocaine," one of the boys said. "All them rock stars use it."

"Or ecstasy," one of the others put in. "Open it."

"Don't be daft," Jack said. "Drugs on top of theft! You'll never get out of jail!" He grabbed for it but Maeve tossed it to one of the others, who tossed it over Jack's head to another, who tossed it over Maeve's head and . . . into the Liffey.

"Take what I give ye and go," Maeve said. "You've plenty to kiss arse with now."

"If you see me mam, you'll send for me?" Jack asked in parting.

But Maeve only snarled after him. Jack didn't care. He had a definite plan in mind now. He would contact the girl and her friend and they'd help him find his mam and then she'd tell her da about this musician she'd met and how he'd saved her and they'd use his squeeze box on an album and he'd go to America and be rich. He might have to marry the girl, but that would be all right. Musicians weren't at home much at all, and everyone in America got divorced pretty often.

He went straight to a phone box to tell her he'd risked life and limb to reclaim her credit cards and passport and how about that help she'd promised? But there was no answer. Well, perhaps she wasn't home yet.

Maeve and her gang had caught up with him and were lurking round the phone box, practicin' bein' menacing, he guessed, when he emerged. He was about to head back down Dame Street when a car pulled up alongside him. "Get in," the man inside said.

CHAPTER 14

Joe Dunny awoke as he usually did at five A.M. The cat and her kittens lay curled together in the box he'd made them. He pulled on his muckers and his slicker and headed outdoors.

The sheep, for a change, were huddled together in one pasture without boggy places. They were all on their feet for a further wonder. He was relieved and was about to go back to the house to finish his other chores when he noticed the tracks in the mud along the fence. Tiny little tracks, but hundreds, thousands of them, running all along the fence, then up over the fence, and continuing on the other side.

There was nothing for it but Joe had to follow them. Apparently whatever it was didn't hurt sheep, but you couldn't be too careful. He trailed them all along the fence line, up over three more, and down across the field until it turned to the neighboring farm, where a crop of rape had been sown. Normally, Joe would never trespass on his neighbor's property on a whim, but this mystery was something he had to see the end of or know the reason why.

The rape field ended in a tangle of brambles that totally encased an abandoned house. You could only see the chimney and part of the roof. On the other side, he knew, was the ruins of the old abbey and the little caretaker's cottage the American priest was to live in.

A short detour down the road and a peek into the abbey yard and the priest's yard assured him that the tracks did not follow in that direction. They must have gone through the brambles, then.

Well, they were small animals after all, whatever they were. Looked like cats. When he found the first tufts of fur on the thorns, he was even more sure of it. But so many of them? Were they still in there? Now, he really *was* curious.

With great reluctance, he turned his back on the brambles and returned to his own place long enough to fetch a scythe. He didn't know the American chap who owned the adjoining farm, but he'd never miss a few brambles, Joe was sure, and just as certain he was that the brambles would grow up thicker than ever where he'd cut them in no time at all.

But cut them he did, quietly, efficiently, cursing only inwardly. Bleeding, yes. He did a fair amount of that. But he did it quietly.

When he'd cut his path to the door, he tried to open it, but the weeds and brambles had laced it tightly shut. So he made a path to the broken window and, looking inside, allowed his eyes to become accustomed to the dimness of the room. And then he beheld a very strange sight indeed.

Cats, hundreds of cats, all colors, shapes, sizes and breeds, lay sleeping all over the house, on the staircase and in the windowsills. And in their midst, lying near the fireplace, lay a pile of carpet with a long tangle of blondie hair hanging out. Cats snuggled close on all sides.

Joe swung himself up over the windowsill and landed in the room. And as he did, a geyser of cats shot up into the air, and rushed past him to erupt out the window. And the bundle of rug sat up, tossed back the blondie hair, and a girl about as old as his brother's middle girl looked around her at the cats jumping madly about, saw him and started screaming.

CHAPTER 15

Jack had hesitated to enter the car as others lined up behind it, waiting patiently, as almost all the cars save taxicabs tended to do. Seeming to be in a hurry was akin to admitting weakness. Let the other fella get flustered.

"Jaysus, it's *him*," Maeve breathed behind Jack.

"Him who?" he asked, turning away from the driver.

"*Car*nahan, ya eejit."

"Does your friend want to come too?" Carnahan asked patiently, and with a smile.

"Dunno. Maeve?"

But she hung back, looking uncharacteristically coy. Afflicted with shyness? Hero worship? It was hard to tell. Jack shrugged. "Whatcha want?" he asked Carnahan. Anyone Maeve thought so highly of was likely not to be up to much good. And the name was ringin' a bell.

"You're Daly, aren't you? Your mammy's gone missin'?"

"That's right, I am. She has. What's it to ya?"

"One of the girls at the halt told me all about it. I thought maybe we could join forces, like. I'm searchin' for someone too."

"Go with him," Maeve muttered. "He's bags of money."

Jack flapped his hand behind him for her to keep quiet,

thought it over for a moment, and hopped in.

"I thought we could troll the streets, like, and look for both your mammy and my little sister at the same time," Carnahan explained as he pulled away from the curb and Jack settled into the seat.

"Your little sister?"

Carnahan held up a photograph of a pretty young girl with blondie hair. "Her. Seen her?"

Jack had, somewhere, recently, but only in passing. He considered for a moment, then shook his head. "No." He had a clearer view of Carnahan as the man turned to show him the photo and now he did recognize him. From the north he was, and a friend to the Travellers, some had it. Though he mostly expressed that friendship by showing up with strong drink. After he left, one or two families might shift rather suddenly and other families might have more money than was usual. Jack had seen him with the other men perhaps once or twice a year. Jack's mam, when she was in her right mind, had made excuses to keep him with her when Carnahan was around, though once one of the other men had mentioned something about Jack's da having once done some work for the man. Jack had always figured it was her mistrust of outsiders, Mam actin' that way. But somewhere he'd picked up the general feeling that the man was IRA and that's where the money came from. That would explain Maeve's attitude as well.

"Your mam's been missin' how long?"

"Three days or so. My folk have searched the countryside round, and I've been searchin' the town. I tried the hospital where she goes sometimes and they haven't seen her but they'll send no one to look—they say they can't and nothing I said made a difference. I've told everyone and looked every-where else as well. I don't think she's here. I think she must have snagged a ride and gone further on."

"Maybe so, but I don't know the same about my sister."

They drove up and down the streets for the better part of an hour and a half, Carnahan asking Jack's opinions on a great many topics and listening with flattering attention.

"Your father and I worked together once, you know," the

man said. "He was a brave man until the butchers cut him down."

"Until they what?"

"Did your mam never tell you?"

"Tell me what?"

"Ah, shoite," he said and thumped the steering wheel with the heel of his hand. "Now I've gone and done it. I'm sorry, lad. I never meant to spill the beans. If your own family never told you I reckon they thought it best that you not know. They wouldn't want to be hardening your heart at such an early age."

"What're you on about?" Jack asked, but respectfully. He wasn't sure what Carnahan was up to, but he *was* sure it was essential to his own health that the man remain pleasant.

"I might as well tell you now. Your da was going to deliver a few items to me at my place in Armagh. The soldiers took him in and that was the last was seen of him."

Jack had heard something about his father dying in jail, but he'd never heard about the delivery Carnahan mentioned.

"I just thought you should know," Carnahan added. Then he changed the subject and talked about sports and then music. Jack told him about playing the squeeze box.

"Just like your daddy! Oh, he was a fine musician, that man."

They were passing the Westland Row DART station then, the one they called the Pearse Street Station on the train—everyone else in Dublin knew that the Pearse Street Station was the garda station and preferred not to confuse the two.

Just as they passed the entrance, Jack saw her. What was she doing back in town? Oh, sure, without her money the girl couldn't get home, could she?

"Stop for a minute, would ya?" Jack asked Carnahan.

"Sure, why, what is it?"

"I see a friend of mine I got to go talk to . . ." Carnahan hesitated and he added, "about Mam. And I can show the picture too, if you like, and tell her to watch for your sister."

"No, that's okay," he said. "You go on. I'll tell you what.

I'll go find some food and I'll be back in an hour and we'll
head out of town, all right?''

Jack agreed quickly, though he wasn't sure if he wanted to
return to the car with the man or not. Still, having a ride
around the countryside to look for Mam was better than trying
to find her on foot.

The light was fading and the wind picking up, puffing light
drizzle into his face as he climbed out of the car. He pulled
his blanket jacket closer around him, and ran in a low crouch
toward the girl's back. It took him a minute to remember her
name. "Wait up, you! Sno!" he said.

When she turned, she looked so bad he almost didn't recognize her. Her eyes had puffed up, and the redness was
quickly turning dark. Her nose was even larger than it had
been before, and her attempt to clean herself had merely
smeared the blood around on her face.

Carnahan's car prowled slowly past.

"Hi," she said, in a stuffy, nasal voice, but sounding glad-
der to see him than he could ever remember anybody being.

Before she could say any more though, he dug in his pockets and pulled out her passport and cards. "I got some of your
kit back from Maeve," he said, handing them to her.

"How'd you do that?" she asked wonderingly.

Modestly, he told the truth. "She's mad for me, actually.
It's me bein' a musician, I s'pose." He hesitated a moment
and added, "She wouldn't give back the cash though."

"Then I may have to try her begging technique to get back
on the DART," Sno said. "I used up both halves of my ticket
and then some." Her face fell as she took back her things and
held them in her hands, her slitted eyes obviously searching
for something that wasn't there. "I don't suppose she had a
little gold box, did she?"

"She did, yes, but . . ."

"It was a gift from a friend. A really important one. I have
to have it back. Tell her I'll buy it back from her. Whatever
she wants. But I have to have it back."

Jack hung his head. "She hasn't got it anymore."

"Then we have to find out where she took it and get it

back. She didn't . . . open it, did she?''

"I don't think so . . ."

"Oh, you'd know if she did."

"The truth is, Sno, I'm sorry. I was tryin' to get it back for you and had a bit of a scuffle with the others and—it landed in the river."

"The river!" she wailed. Then she said. "Well, but, look, it's light and it probably would float. Do you think it might still be there?"

He shrugged. "Unless the tide's carried it away. But Maeve and the others, they might be there still, too."

"Screw them!" Sno said, and started running. She wasn't running very fast or very straight, though.

Then she seemed to suddenly realize that Jack was the only one who knew where the box had gone and she turned back and yelled, "Well, come on, hurry up!" Thinking of her paternity and his own career, he pelted after.

They were both winded by the time they reached the river, upstream somewhat from the Ha'Penny Bridge where Maeve and her lot were still hanging out. The tide was lifting the Liffey's flow to the scummy high water mark on the bank. They both scanned the water for a glint of gold, but couldn't see anything but the diving gulls, ducks and swans on and above the water's surface.

The girl was as frantic as any human being Jack had ever seen, and began stripping off her shoes, socks and sweater.

"What are ye, daft?" he asked as she headed for the water. "You can't find it like that."

"I have to," she said. "You don't understand."

"I don't at that. How could a trinket be so terrible important you'd risk your life for it? That's high tide, that. You could drown. I heard Americans were all crazy but I never saw a girl so vain she'd die for the loss of a bauble."

"It's not a bauble! It's magic. But I wouldn't expect you to understand anything about that!" she shot back, sounding half-comical in her nasal, strangled voice. But the fierce determination in her reddened eyes wasn't anything he cared to laugh at. He saw then that she was not only frantic, but worn

out from the quick journey to the river, and half-drunk from
the blow she'd taken.

And this pitiable creature was telling him *he* didn't understand about magic? He, practically captain of the guards to the
great-grandchildren of Lir. How often did a man get such an
opportunity? It was perfect. If only the swans were the right
ones! He could at once show the girl he knew more than she
thought *and* ask Princess Nuala and her brothers to help him
find Mam. "Oh, do I not, just?" he challenged and began
singing the song he'd learned from the swans. Casual like.

Instantly, four of the graceful white birds stopped and changed
directions in mid-glide to sail toward him.

At the same time, the gang at the Ha'Penny Bridge, Maeve
in the lead, spotted them and came, first walking, then running,
toward Sno and himself.

The lady swan's beautiful voice carried from river to shore.
"Ah, Finn, would you look here? It's Jack come to pay a
visit."

"Princess Nuala," Jack answered her, making such a
courtly bow he almost fell in. He didn't even look at Sno's
face and nobody else paid him much mind, except for that
little group running down the sidewalk from the Ha'Penny. "I
was wonderin' if yer highness might grant a small boon to her
humble servant," he said in the courtly language he'd learned
from the telly.

"Name it, Jack," the lady swan said.

"My companion here, the Princess Sno, she's lost a little
gold box she says is magic. It got thrown in the Liffey by
some—highwayparesons, I suppose you might say."

The lady swan fluttered her wings in assent, and then she
and her brothers set up a ruckus and all dove into the water.
It took a few tries, but it was Princess Nuala herself who came
up with the little box in her beak. Which she proffered to Jack.
Which he turned and proffered to Sno, who was too irritatingly
nonchalant about the entire matter altogether.

She was quick enough to snatch the box away from him,
though, and polite enough to say to the swans, "Thanks a lot,
guys. Thanks, Jack." As if he'd introduced her to a group of

the lads and they'd given her a pint.

Maeve and the boys arrived just then. "What if I wants it back?" Maeve demanded nastily, grinning at Sno's bruises.

And that was when the taxi pulled up and the little granny in the gray business suit climbed out, carrying a clipboard.

CHAPTER 16

Journal Entry—Dublin, Continued

Jack's buddies, the swans, had just given me back my magic box when the last fairy godmother in the world I wanted to see arrived.

"D-Dame Prudence!" I said. I couldn't have been more blown away if she had drifted down from a cloud rather than alighted from a cab with a sniff and a bare ten percent tip.

"Good gracious, young lady, what a state you're in. You're a disgrace to your calling," Prune-face said to me. I was not in the mood for that. I felt like shit warmed over but I did have the box again. What did she want from me anyway? I was about to find out.

"Spare a quid or two, Missus?" Two of the boys in Maeve's gang whined.

"Bugger off, you old cow," Maeve said.

"You. Be still," Prune-face commanded and Maeve was *really* still, like *spell* still.

Prune-face turned to me. "I'm glad to see that even in your current sorry state you're not a total disgrace. However irresponsible you were to allow yourself to be parted from your gifts, you had the good sense to befriend a suitable stalwart companion who could assist you with his own gifts and well-earned magical favors.'' She nodded to Jack and raised a hand and waved a white hanky at the swans, who were still looking on with interest. "How do you do, your highnesses. Fair winds and calm waters to you all!''

"And to you, my lady,'' the swans chorused back in this really awesome four-part harmony. Jack first looked confused by her compliment, then grinned.

"Your educational fund still has two wishes in it, Snohomish,'' Prune-face informed me. "However, since you were attempting to act in your capacity as a bona fide godmother trainee when your magical enabling device was wrongfully separated from your control, you are entitled to an additional enchantment.''

"How come?'' I asked, suspicious.

"Why, to punish your assailant, of course. We can't allow this sort of thing to pass, you know. Godmothers would become targets everywhere. If I may make a suggestion, it's traditional, when someone insults or harms one of us to a somewhat more minor degree than is involved in incurring transformation to amphibian state, to have objects fall from the perpetrator's mouth as a sign of wrongdoing. Snakes and toads, for instance.''

I was confused, Rosie. Hadn't Felicity told me already we don't punish people even for crimes, that there's not enough magic? And here was the mystery miser herself telling me to lay a double whammy on Maeve in the name of self-defense. "Does it *have* to involve toads?'' I asked. I looked at Maeve. She was standing like a statue, but her eyes were wide and showing the whites all around.

"Don't be too hard on her, Missus,'' Jack said to Prune-face. "She's been kicked out by her family and she's got no place to go. She can't help bein' big and rough. She did give some of Sno's kit back already. She didn't know about the box. She's never had nothin' pretty, has she?''

My head felt like someone was using it for a bongo drum and I could hardly breathe. I wasn't sure how long I could even stand up, at this point. Honestly, part of me wanted to nuke the bitch but then, I could hear me telling this to you,

Rosie, and to Felicity and the two of you asking me if people like Maeve don't pay for being how they are every miserable day of their crummy lives. And why give a person toads to fall out of her mouth if she already looks like a toad? Or have snakes fall from her mouth when she already has a personality worse than a cornered rattler?

"Isn't there some sort of diamonds and pearls spell you can do too?" I asked Prune-face. With my face in the shape it was in, I didn't even have to try to look all innocent and eager for knowledge. Nobody would have noticed.

"That's a reward."

"Only for whoever's catching the jewels. It's my punishment to mete out, right? Since I'm the injured party?"

"Within reason."

Maeve managed to cringe without moving so much as a corpuscle.

I was tempted. I really was. Everything hurt and it was gonna keep hurting and be real ugly for a long time, I knew this. Maeve didn't seem to me like a defenseless waif at all but a big strong gangster with this major hostility problem. However, I have a hostility problem of my own and I definitely needed more practice doing good than I did being pissed off. Besides, Prune-face obviously was totally freaked by Maeve swiping my magic and wanted me to do something horrible to her. So I tried to think of something I could give Maeve to change her in a good way and still make it sound like a curse. Grandma Hilda's folk music collection came to the rescue again.

"Well," I said, and by now I was having trouble getting out the words but I was determined to do this right. "There's this song called 'True Thomas,' about a minstrel the Queen of Faerie curses to always tell the truth. Which, trust me, is a bad fate for a musician. So how about if I—let's see, ahem, Maeve, you gangsta girl, henceforth every word you speak shall be a truth as clear as a diamond spoken in a voice as smooth and perfectly shaped as a pearl, just to make you easier to listen to."

"Very well, young lady, but while you're being so bountiful, I suggest you make one of your own wishes so that if this young lout relieves you of your wishing vessel again it won't have been a total loss.''

"Then I wish I could get around this country wherever I need to whenever I need to without money or a driver's license.''

I looked to Prune-face but she was nodding impatiently. She twiddled her fingers and Maeve opened her mouth and begged, "Jack, make her take it off! I don't want no witch curse on me. Here, girl, take back your money. This is all I kept, honest!'' She shoved a wad of bills in my pocket. But the funny thing was, she begged so beautifully—her whine was like a cry for all the lost souls of the world and her voice was like a cross between Kathleen Turner's and Mary Black's. I was glad I'd given her the diamondlike truth (I thought that was a very cool and poetic touch) as well as the pearl-shaped tones. Otherwise the big oaf would just use her new voice to beg better or advance herself up in the world and take a job doing phone sex.

Jack was impressed. He looked at her as if he'd never seen her before and put his arm around her shoulders, even though he had to reach up to do it since she was taller than he was.

I turned to Prune-face again. "I particularly wish to be someplace else before you let Maeve all the way out of the chute and she beats the living shit out of me again.''

Prune-face sighed a put-upon sigh. "So be it.'' And she vanished.

And the driver of her taxi leaned over and said to me, "Where to, Miss?'' I was so messed up that I only asked to go to the train station.

*   *   *

Jack felt outdone and unappreciated. Here he had showed that girl his talking swans—royal talking swans, no less—and she had actually produced some magical city council lady who put a curse on Maeve, then disappeared like a shaggin' Tinkerbell. And to add to it, the girl then took off in a taxicab without so much as considerin' she had promised to help him find Mam. The swans had flown away also. Well, he still knew her address and number and he would hold her to it. If he hurried, he could still meet Carnahan and have him take him there. Maybe Sno's friend would even help Carnahan find his sister. If that's who it was he was huntin' for. Maybe it would be better if she didn't. But right now, Carnahan was his best chance for getting Mam back. "Gotta go, Maeve," Jack said.

"No, Jack, don't layve me. Please. I'm scared. I don't know what to do," pleaded Maeve. It was disorienting, was what it was. The same big ugly awkward Maeve he'd always known talking in that sexy silky voice that begged him to help. Jack had always been more sensitive to sound than to sight. She still had her Traveller's accent, but it was the most beautiful accent in all of Ireland now.

"You'll be okay, Maeve. You've still got your fists and your gang." He looked around, but the boys were nowhere to be seen. They must have run off when the witchy council lady froze Maeve into a statue. "I've got to go find Carnahan. He's helpin' me search for Mam."

"What'll I do?" Maeve cried, and the beauty of the cry wrung Jack's heart.

"I don't know, Maeve, but Carnahan'll skin me if I'm late," he said. He raced back to Westland Row, arriving just as Carnahan pulled over and handed him a bag of fish and chips and an orange squash.

"So, how was she?" Carnahan joked.

Jack's head was still back at the river and he was a bit slow on the uptake. Then he realized from Carnahan's grin and wink that he figured Jack had been shagging Sno.

Since Carnahan seemed one to keep on the good side of, Jack returned the grin. "Good," he said, wondering at it himself when he thought of Maeve's sexy new voice. "She was very good."

CHAPTER 17

Arriving in Dublin, Deirdre was welcomed by a young second cousin, Fiona, who ran a guest house. Though Fiona was far too busy to entertain, she made Deirdre very comfortable indeed, and insisted that she stay at least a week and see the city.

Deirdre did her best. She saw the golden Treasures of Ireland and St. Patrick's bell and the Tara Brooch and the Book of Kells and Brian Boru's harp and the whole city bustling with energetic young people.

When she was worn out with walking and ready to go, Fiona mentioned that it was a shame she couldn't stay in Bray long enough to take a bus out to see Glendalough, the home of St. Kevin, and the famous Powerscourt Gardens. She could go out by the DART, spend a night or two free at a guest house owned by Fiona's friend, Noreen. The two had an arrangement, you see. Fee usually put Noreen up when she came to the city and since Fee rarely got out to Bray, cousin Deirdre was welcome to her favor instead. That was too good to pass up. Both places were said to be spectacular, with a splendid waterfall at each. Several films had been shot there.

In order to get an early start the next morning, Deirdre decided to take the DART down to The B&B at Bray, which was what Noreen had pragmatically dubbed her establishment, and spend the night there.

As she walked into the station, a taxi pulled up across the street and a young girl emerged, paid the driver, and entered the station. Shortly after, a young man, a tinker from the looks of him, ran up to the station. At about the same time a dark gray car swooped up to the curb to collect him. It was nothing to her, Deirdre thought, but young people here in the city today lived much differently than she had when she was younger.

The train platform was crowded, and when the train came, she found her way through the crowd and captured a seat. The girl she had seen entered the car, but all of the seats were gone. That was when Deirdre noticed that the child had been injured—her eyes bore huge bruises and were swelling shut and her nose was swollen and bruised as well, with a fine smear of blood around the nostrils. Her hair was matted too. And this was the child who had been riding across Dublin in a taxi?

Just then, the girl let go her hold on the metal pole, her knees buckling, and toppled forward. At first Deirdre thought she might be drunk and about to vomit, but then she thought perhaps the injuries were enough to make anyone woozy. Especially stuffed back in the car amid the crowd, where it was comparatively airless. Deirdre slid out of her seat and knelt to help the girl up. Everyone else stood around with their arms up their sleeves.

"Come on, one of you stout fellows, give me a hand with her. The girl's hurt, can't you see?" Someone did help, and then several more, but all she wanted was to ease the girl into the seat. Her seatmate stepped over the girl's body to exit at the next stop, and Deirdre and the others slid her into a half-reclining position.

"Come along now, pet. Mustn't drop off and miss your stop now," she said patting her cheeks very gently and wishing she had water instead of a half jar of jam. The chocolates were long gone, not that they'd be of particular use.

"Shall I pull the cord for the driver to stop?" a lady asked.

"I shouldn't think so. We wouldn't want her put off in the middle of nowhere."

"Someone's clobbered her a good one, looks like," a boy volunteered.

"Try this on her," a woman said and handed her a little capsule. "Break it under her nose. It'll bring her round."

It did.

"Where are you headed, pet?" Deirdre asked her.

"Bray. Where am I? What's going on?"

"She's American. Poor dear, what a way to start a holiday. What happened, child? Were you mugged?"

"Yeah. Ouch. Oh, this thing is lots worse. I need to get home and put ice on it."

"Did you make a police report?" someone asked. The girl nodded, whether in assent or to field the question, Deirdre wasn't sure. She still had money enough to pay the taxi, so the mugger mustn't have taken much. Perhaps she'd put up a fight and that was how she was injured. Anyway, she clearly didn't feel like being cross-examined just now.

Deirdre didn't feel she could just leave her, however, once they reached Bray. She might need medical attention after all. She was able to get off the train with only a little help, but she still looked lost. "Is there someone I could ring for you, pet?" Deirdre asked. "A doctor, perhaps, or a friend or relative at your lodgings?"

"Felicity," she said. "I gotta call Felicity to come pick me up."

But when Deirdre dialed the number the girl gave her, there was no answer.

*   *   *

As Carnahan drove past the Greystones exit Jack said, "We need to stop near here for a bit."

"And why's that?" Carnahan asked.

"Sno's stopping there and . . ."

"Sno being the pretty little piece with the black eyes, I'd wager? Can't get enough, can you, lad?"

"That's not it," Jack said. "She has a friend she said could help find Mam."

"You've already got a friend."

"Her friend helps people, she said," Jack added. "Maybe she's seen your—sister."

Carnahan said, "Then I'll stop and you can ask. But don't involve me. I don't want the settled people knowing I'm down here. You don't suppose that other girl—the ugly one—will blab about me, do you?"

Jack shrugged. "Dunno. She's a few other things on her mind at the moment though, has Maeve."

Carnahan drove them up one lane and down another, past pastures full of sheep and horses and large, posh-looking houses. Twice they drove into the hedge to avoid being run down by a horse trailer.

Finally, they found the house of Sno's friend. The entrance was very grand. Stone dragons squatted on big square pillars on either side of fancy goldy-tipped wrought iron gates. An orangey gold car, something like a Volkswagen, sat in the driveway. The grounds had a barren war-zone look about them except for quite an old-looking yew walk connecting the house and another large, blocky building. A third, smaller building, was set off to the side, down the hill a bit. A dog barked up a horrible ruckus someplace nearby.

Jack went to the door and knocked. No answer. He signaled Carnahan that he would go round to the back and he did, looking in the kitchen door, and on around, where the house was jammed right against the side of a hill. Jack scrambled atop the hill and over to the other side, where the back of the house showed more of the war-zone landscaping. Beyond a stone wall, in fields spreading in every direction, fine horses wearing raincoats nicer than anything he or Mam had ever had were grazing on long green grass. Jack looked around through all the windows, patio doors and into all the rooms, rapping and knocking but he could see no one. He took a detour and looked around the smaller flat too but it was empty. He returned to the main house and tried another door. Once, he thought he heard an answering knocking but no one came to greet him.

He walked along the outside of the yew hedge and circled round the low building. Inside was a big field of blue plastic. Some sort of tarp it looked like to him. That was all. He was so interested in trying to figure out what it was doing there that he didn't hear Carnahan till the man was all but on top of him.

"*I* know this place," Carnahan said with an unpleasant grin. "Used to be an old pool here. Looks like they made a proper swimming pool of it, the fools. I don't remember the hedge before, though."

Which was a funny thing to say, since the swimming pool— of course, that was what it was—looked new and the hedge old. And why were they fools to make a swimming pool? Sounded lovely to him.

Carnahan cupped his fingers on either side of his face to cut the glare and looked through the glass. Jack followed suit in the next window, though there was nothing to see. He thought he heard a splash, though, and the plastic cover quivered and rocked a bit.

"We might as well go on," Jack said. "No one's here."

"Too bad," Carnahan said. "I liked the looks of that girl. Nothing sexier than a porcelain-skinned, delicate-featured girl with a bit of a black eye, to my mind."

Jack sat close to the door until the next stop. He was sorry he'd insisted on stopping here, not liking the idea of Carnahan knowing where Sno lived.

*   *   *

Bobby the toad was hopping mad. When Sno went for her swim that morning, he'd followed and she'd locked him in. They'd left him out here without leaving so much as a transom open for him to catch flies. Nobody even thought to look for him. In fact, he was pretty sure he heard them leave the house. Now the damn phone was ringing off the hook and it was driving him nuts.

He'd been squatting on top of the plastic liner for hours. He was not, in human form, a worrier. Mostly when he was human, other people worried. About him. Coming for them. But if anything happened to the godmother, he was a wart factory for life. A shortish life, at that. It was a no-win situation, the way he saw it. He formerly never thought much about human spirituality, animism, anything like that, although the process of death interested him in a professional way. But he got a little worried when he considered that if what died when a human being died was a spirit or personality—that same himness that had been transferred into the toad's body—then did it die according to the schedule of its own species, or was it the body it was in that decided when? Being turned into a toad was also turning him into a goddamn new-ager, wondering this kind of thing, but hey, it was personal. 'Cause if a toad spirit, or whatever, croaked after a few years, and it was a toad spirit hanging out in his former body . . . well, what if he got disenchanted only to find he had no home to go to? And if it was the body that decided, he had no idea how old this hopper he was in had been at the time of transfer. How long did this toad have, in toad-years? They should be required to provide a guidebook or an instructional video when they did these things to people. He intended to tell Felicity so the next time he saw the drifty old broad.

He'd been bouncing off the walls, checking out the doors and windows and even the drains, having a good think on the big blue pad covering the pool, and now he decided it was time to go for a swim. The lack of chlorine in the pool was the only good thing about this whole heap, in his opinion.

He dove in the pool in the crack between the pad and the water along the edge, the cool wetness gladdening his amphibian heart. Once he thought he heard the door open, and he surfaced in time to see what looked like a hairball run past the glass doors. He hopped out and looked around, but couldn't see anything, so he dove back down again.

Then he heard noise outside the poolroom. Footsteps. Voices. Not Felicity. Male voices. Workmen maybe. Bobby surfaced and peered out over the edge of the plastic. They were people he'd never seen, though there was something disturbingly familiar about one of them. After a time they went away.

Ringing phones! Strange guys running around the place playing Peeping Tom! He had a fair idea what guys like that were up to, and if he had his human form, he'd make them sorry they'd ever set foot here. Of course, if he had his human form, he'd be outta here and who gave a damn who came here. Still, he had been a careful man, and the sloppiness of Felicity's operation pissed him off. He'd like to see her right now. He'd give her a thing or two to think over. He dove again, fast and hard.

And then, through the ripples in his wake, he did see her—all silvery and shimmering, on the bottom of the pool.

She was dancing.

With some long-haired guy in green velvet tights.

What kinda deal was this? What was she doing dancing? Where was she? He didn't remember any ballroom big enough to hold all the people in fancy dress dancing with her—not to mention the pillars spiraled with ivy and roses and a floor that looked like it was made out of gold, silver and jade tiles. Maybe this was some new rich-people toy—a TV screen in the bottom of your pool. But what was she doing on TV? He was under the impression godmothers kept low profiles. Maybe it was like a surveillance camera hidden in a special room there. He hadn't thought the secret attic room was as palatial as this one seemed to be, but then he hadn't looked inside, and what showed through the crack was dark.

He dove for the bottom of the pool, and the image shimmered and disappeared, then reformed. He dove into Felicity's likeness, projecting for all he was worth, "Hey, godmama, stop screwin' around and get back here. The phone's ringin' and I'm locked in the fuckin' pool."

Then he surfaced.

A few minutes later the phone began ringing again and stopped in mid-ring. Shortly afterwards, the door of the poolroom unlocked and Felicity, standing there in her dancing dress, said, "Thank you for the reminder, Bobby. Time is very treacherous down there. Come along now. We have to go fetch Sno.''

*   *   *

Cunla had been making faces at the dog next door when he heard a car come puttering down the lane. He ran for the hedge. A man who stank of old magic and a boy who plain stank climbed from the car and started snooping all about the house. Cunla followed them along the hedge, as best he could. He couldn't allow them to do the house or its inhabitants harm. That was his own job.

But they did nothing at all but look. Most puzzling, curious and disappointing. And all too quick. Cunla had no opportunity even to give them as much as a wee flat tire before they were back in their car and away again.

And only moments later, Herself appeared from the house as if she'd been there all along, climbed into her squashy little car and drove away.

CHAPTER 18

Dear Rosie,

I just finished my journal entry about what happened to me in Dublin and will upload it to you along with this letter. It actually was a couple days ago. See, on the way back on the train, I passed out. This nice lady from a little village in County Kerry got me into a seat and helped me off the train and when we couldn't get ahold of Felicity on the phone right away, took me over to Noreen's B&B in Bray. Noreen's really a sweetheart too.

The two of them cleaned me up and put ice on my nose and gave me aspirin, and of course a "nice cup of tea" which is apparently the chicken soup of Ireland. Noreen offered to call a doctor but I said Felicity could do that in case I got, like, critical or something.

"Who did this to you, pet?" Deirdre asked.

"I got mugged," I mumbled. Well, you'd mumble too if you had a nose as big as a summer sausage and an ice bag on top of it.

"Now, dear," Noreen said, "I want you to think about this carefully. I know we've no divorce here but if it's your husband's been beatin' on you, there's steps can be taken. The shelter is full at the moment but the Sisters are always willing to help a woman in need..."

162

"She's only a child!" Deirdre said.

"I've known many a married child, and some children with children who wished they were married. I just want her to know help is available."

"Thanks," I said.

Noreen went on, "I was only a child myself when I married, you know, and I put up with beatings for years before I threw the devil out. He drank himself to death at last, I'm ashamed to thank God for the favor, and I'm widowed now but—it wasn't your father, was it, dear, did this to you?"

"She's American," Deirdre said. "Isn't that right, pet?"

I muttered "yes" because it hurt to nod, then added as clearly as possible, "I told you. I got mugged. By a female perfect stranger. Could we try Felicity's number again, please?"

Two cups of tea later, Deirdre, smiling triumphantly, returned from the hall phone. "She's on her way."

Felicity was as low-key as I've ever seen her when she came to the door. She wore a gray overcoat and galoshes and had one of those tacky plastic rain scarves on her head.

When she saw me she nearly had a cow. "Oh, Sno! My goodness, what happened to you? You poor dear. Your first trip to Dublin too."

"You know, dear," Noreen put in helpfully again, "if your things were stolen, there's a special tourist assistance branch of the government now to help you continue your holiday and get home. They started that so tourists would know that we don't take crimes against our visitors lightly here in Ireland."

"How lovely you are to take her in and offer so much wonderful information," Felicity said to her. "We really must have a talk sometime."

"It was Miss O'Sullivan here found the child on the DART," Noreen told her. "She's up from Kerry, lodging with me while she's seeing a bit of the country."

"Seeing the country?" Felicity looked a little confused. "But—aren't you yourself Irish?"

"Indeed I am," Deirdre told her, "but that doesn't mean I know the country as well as I'd like. Ah, I know, a most un-

Irish thing it is to play the tourist to be sure, but since my
mother died, I find myself between responsibilities and decided to take advantage of it by seeing what I could see. I
could afford to see nothing farther afield than my own country
but it's been a very good trip, thank you.''

"Are you going home directly after this?" Felicity asked.

"Well, now, that depends. I'm getting a bit weary of travel,
to tell you the truth, but I've yet to find what I was looking
for, which is a new place to live and a bit of a job to keep
body and soul together. I thought perhaps I might work in a
shop, though a hospital would be more appropriate, I suppose,
since all I've done for years is look after my ailing old ones.''

"Well, nice to . . .'' Felicity began but I was tugging on her
raincoat and pointing at Deirdre and outside. If ever there was
a prime candidate for housekeeper, a nice, calm person who
knew what to do in emergencies and was used to looking after
things, I thought this lady was it. And she was kind and brave
too. How many ladies travelling alone these days would stop
to help a strange teen who looked like she'd been in a barroom
brawl? She seemed perfect to me for an FGM household.

Felicity caught on at once. "What a grand idea! Miss
O'Sullivan, we've just relocated here and are looking for a
housekeeper. I don't suppose you'd consider coming back to
the house with us to take a look and see if you might be
interested . . . ?''

"Just like that?" Noreen asked. "How am I to stay in business if you hire my customers right out from under my roof?''
But she was laughing.

"I'll be happy to bring her back if she doesn't like it, but
perhaps you'd like to bring your suitcase just the same?" Felicity suggested.

"It'd be a live-in position, then?" Deirdre asked.

"Yes, but there's a little flat you can have to yourself," she
said. I didn't remember such a thing, but I hadn't really toured
the grounds yet.

So that's how we found a housekeeper. I told Felicity a little
about what happened to me on the way home, but frankly, I
wasn't up to a big narrative then. Before the two of them took

off together to tour the house and the flat, they put me to bed with an ice pack. Then as I was trying to fall asleep, Bobby hopped onto my pillow . . .

*   *   *

New Window
QueryQuantrill@aol.com
Dear Raydir,

Please arrange my ticket home *now*. This is not working out and I'm really bummed. Felicity said she'd teach me what I needed to know to become like her and she's just *ignored* me all the time I've been here.

Yesterday I went to Dublin and I got mugged while I was there and when I finally made it back home, after fainting on the DART, Felicity wasn't even home! If a nice lady named Deirdre hadn't helped me, God only knows what would have happened to me. I might have died even. When Felicity finally did come, she said she couldn't hear the phone. Well, she hired Deirdre to be housekeeper (and now, I realize, baby-sitter for me as well), they tucked me in here with my ice bag and the damned toad, and I haven't seen Felicity since! (God, if Gerardine could see me now, she wouldn't be the least bit jealous, let me tell you. I look like a cross between a panda and an anteater.) Deirdre came in a time or two last evening to offer aspirin and tea, but neither of us even knows where Felicity is today. What kind of fairy godmother is she anyway?

Well, I hate to say it, but the toad knows what kind. He told me this weird story. He says if it wasn't for him she would probably have never answered the phone. Apparently while I was struggling for breath through my probably broken nose Felicity was out partying at some masquerade party shown— here's a new techno toy for you, Dad—on a closed circuit TV in the bottom of the pool. Then he claimed there was a trail of glitter from her room out the door to the trash cans.

I told him he had warts for brains and to go away and leave me alone and he said if I didn't believe him, it was my nose that was swollen, not my feet, and I should go look.

So this morning I did. Know what I found? Boots. Covered in glitter—well, lots of it had fallen off and left bare patches. Not as bare as the soles, though. They were almost danced through. There were at least a dozen pairs in the trash. Even if I wasn't already pissed at Felicity about everything else I'd be really p.o.'ed at her for not recycling or resoling or something. That's a lot of leather!

I grabbed a couple of pairs and took them back in the house with me. Deirdre was vacuuming, so I went straight to Felicity's office, but she wasn't there.

I tried to talk to her about what she wanted me to do, Raydir, but she's just so secretive.

So send a ticket like, yesterday. I want out of here.

Luv, Sno

Send/Cancel/File
New Window
QueryQuantrill@aol.com

Dear Raydir,

Hi, Hope your tour is going well. Have you heard from Cindy and the horses lately? Hope the trail ride goes well for her. Everything is great here. I went into Dublin the other day and made friends with one of the local kids. Also met a nice lady on the train who is now keeping house for us. My lessons are proceeding slowly but I'm sure I'll learn a lot.

They had your picture on the cover of a magazine in Dublin. In fact, I think it was called *In Dublin*. Just thought you'd want to know you were getting good coverage.

Luv, Sno

File/Copy/Outbasket/Send
New Window

Dear Rosie,

Well, I just finished writing my second letter to Raydir and E-mailing it. I had to interrupt the first one I wrote to you because Bobby told me something last night—it's in the first letter to Raydir, the one I didn't send. I wrote it in a dead heat, first thing this morning because I was confused and pissed off at Felicity, but then I realized he wouldn't have a clue what I was talking about and besides, I hadn't really had much chance to talk to her about anything first either. And you keep telling me that you can't have a relationship with anybody without communication. So I figured I'd give it one more shot. After I did, I wrote the second letter and sent it. In the interests of having a good relationship with you, I'm uploading copies of everything so you can see where I've been coming from.

I had just canceled my "send" message on the first letter when Felicity came roaring in. You'd think I'd been shouting for her, the way she looked.

She sat down on the bed and took both of my hands and said, "Oh, Sno, dear, I'm so terribly sorry. I've been so preoccupied I wasn't even picking up on your feelings until you began sending so strongly. What's the matter, dear, and how can I make it better?"

I pointed to the pair of glittery worn-out Docs I'd salvaged from the trash and said, "The toad says he saw you dancing in the bottom of the pool while I was trying to call from the train. He said you had on boots like these. Felicity, we found *twelve pairs* in the trash, all worn to pieces. What the hell have you been doing to wear out twelve pairs of Docs in a little under a week?"

"Fund-raising," she said with a deep sigh.

"*Fund*-raising?" I repeated. "How? Where? Why?"

"Let's start in reverse order, shall we? Least difficult first. Why should be perfectly obvious. I'm out of magic, out of luck and it's my responsibility to replenish it. I don't just sit here passively and wait for it to come back, as perhaps we led you to believe. If so, I'm sorry. I must go forth and—er— schmooze, acquiring power from those who have it to give so that I can carry on our work. As to where, well, Faerie, of course."

"Faerie? Like fairyland? Where Her Maj used to dwell and rule and like that?"

She nodded. "Very much like that. She still does. But she's an absentee ruler much of the time. And her aristocracy doesn't give power simply to fuel her projects because she wishes it. The power must be earned, coaxed, won. They must be persuaded to part with it. So part of what one does here is network, I suppose you might say."

"By dancing in glitter-covered Docs?"

"That's about it, yes. And I couldn't take you with me yet because I had not yet wangled you an invitation to court. Lord Robin was just promising to arrange it when Bobby got my attention. You're to come with me tonight, by the way. If you're not up to it I'll make excuses, but it really would be best if you could manage."

"The show must go on," I said like a good plucky heroine. "But why the dancing? And how did you wear out the Docs?"

"Well, they're fond of dancing in there, you know. And partying in general. Normally a mortal who goes inside for an hour ages seven years and comes out old, both because of what your *Star Trek* people would call a space/time continuum and also because the parties are really quite strenuous for mere mortals. Those of us who are in the employ of and under the protection of her Majesty are permitted a different time relationship with Faerie, however. When we go into Faerie, we may spend infinite amounts of time without much passing out here. You may miss me for an hour, and the equivalent of seven years has passed within there. Of course, no one ages so no one notices. But shoes of human manufacture really aren't up to so much dancing. That's why I choose the heavy boots to begin with. Regular dance slippers would be a dead loss."

"Yeah, but what about the swimming pool? I knew there was something weird about it, but closed-circuit TV?"

She laughed. "This country is not quite that high-tech yet, dear. Did you not realize it was a scrying pool? Surely you saw images in it when you swam?"

"Well, sure, but I wasn't expecting a scrying—what's a scrying pool?"

"It's the model for the crystal ball—a pool that shows you the image of someone or something you seek in the past, present or future. Ireland has a lot of them. This property was no doubt chosen because the old pool was located here and the fairy knowe as well. That's what I meant when I said the pool was the heart of the house.''

"Well, you could have explained it. And what's a fairy no? Like N-O?''

"Like K-N-O-W-E, dear. It's the hill outside—that's why it has doors up against it instead of a regular wall or a window. It's an entrance. So you see, I haven't been far when I've been away. Not in physical terms at least. I never meant to neglect you. It was just until I could arrange for you to be included. You'll have to cadge your own magic from them as well, you know.''

I took a deep breath. I realized then that I hadn't been communicating too well myself. I could keep blaming it on the fact that she wasn't around long enough for me to tell her everything, and that I hurt and couldn't concentrate on telling my story straight, but the fact was, I hadn't wanted to mention Prune-face. In the back of my mind, I guess I thought she and Felicity had already traded stories about me maybe—that maybe Felicity called her in (though why I'd think that, I can't tell you) or Prune-face called Felicity after I saw her. But talking to Felicity now, I could tell she didn't know or she would have said something so it was my turn to come clean.

So I said very casually, "Speaking of my own magic, you'll never believe what happened in Dublin. After I got mugged? Look, did you know that Puss and Bobby-boy aren't the only talking animals around here? My friend Jack has four swan buddies who got my wish box out of the river. As if that wasn't weird enough, I was just thanking the swan princess for fishing my magic wishes out of the river when your pal Prudence pops out of nowhere and tells me I get to lay a double whammy on Maeve, the bitch-uh-girl who bopped me with her head? Felicity, she *gave me an extra wish.*''

"Maeve did?''

"No, silly. Prudence. Can you believe it?''

I thought she was going to go into shock. She got very quiet for a minute and then said, "Honestly not. But it does rather fit, now that I think of it. When I returned from my fund-raising jaunt, just before I came to fetch you, I found a fax from her saying she was coming to sort something out. I never dreamed that she'd already made her appearance. And you say she *gave* you an additional wish? That's extremely irregular. She must like you.''

''You couldn't tell it. She bawled me out for being bloody.''

''Speaking of which, how are we to get you presentable for court?''

''Beats me,'' I said, then I got an idea. Have you seen the videos of the English *Robin Hood* series? You know how on the covers the characters have like this blue bandit's mask painted on? That's the concept. I took a quick shower, washed and rebraided my hair. Then I got out Gerardine's industrial strength model's makeup kit—she would not be needing it where she was, so I borrowed it, partly because it supported Raydir's idea that I was going to cosmetology school but mostly, I admit, because I thought it would make her profoundly unhappy if she knew I had it. Anyway, it took me a couple of tries to get the war paint on evenly, but the results were truly awesome.

Felicity clapped her hands and jumped up and down a few times. ''Oh, Sno, that is lovely!'' she cried, looking first at me head on, then each profile to get the full effect of my mask. ''Positively Druidic! The Fey will be so pleased you remembered. And it hides your bruises marvelously.''

''So, when can we go?'' I asked.

''Did you bring a dancing dress and some very sturdy shoes that will last through seven years of dancing?''

''Wait a minute,'' I said, thinking this over again. ''I won't be voting age when I come out, will I?''

''Not here. And Faerie is a monarchy. But you will be an hour older, and we don't want Deirdre to worry, so I'll tell her we're just popping next door for a moment.''

So we're leaving now. I'll update you later.

Love, Sno

CHAPTER 19

Cats exploded from everywhere as the blondie girl screamed at the sight of Joe in the window of the ruined building.

"Shush now, lass, I'm not going to hurt you," Joe said, climbing through the window. "It's just me, Joe Dunny. What are you doing here? And how did you come by so many cats?"

The girl stopped screaming as soon as the cat that had tangled itself in her hair got untangled and bolted off after the rest of its kind.

"They're not mine," she said.

"How long have you been in this old place?" Joe asked her. "It's a wonder you haven't frozen or starved."

"A few days," she said.

"With all them cats?"

"No, they must have come during the night. I was dreaming of being—you'll think it's silly—well, kissed by Bono except he had this really long mustache and when I woke up there was this cat's nose in my mouth and whiskers tickling my face and they were everywhere. Very warm they were. I slept something brilliant. Is this your house? Do you mind if I stay here a bit?"

"Mine? No, not at all. But as for minding, well, this is a

desperate poor place for you to be.''

"Not as desperate as where I came from," she said.

"And that would be where?"

"If I told you that you'd make me go back and I won't. She'll kill me. I know she will."

Although Joe realized he wasn't overly used to teenage theatrics, the girl's protest sounded like more than that to him. She sounded as frightened as Mam had sounded telling them about the storm at sea before they found out his brothers had drowned.

He didn't know what to say to that, so he said simply, "Well, you can't stay here. There's cat shit and bits of dead things everywhere. It's no place for a human person."

"I maybe could smarten it up?" she said in a small voice, half-wistful, half-doubtful.

"Best you come home with me before you catch your death," Joe said firmly. "Are you injured at all? Can you walk?"

"I'm fine," she said.

He ducked back out the window again and, when she was through as well, picked up his scythe.

"You're quite sure you're not the grim reaper?" she asked, making a small, shy joke.

"Yeah, sure. Didn't know his cloak was a slicker, did you?"

"I was supposed to meet my doom on me sixteenth birthday," the girl said. She was getting chattier as she got used to him. He figured she was glad to be out of that rotten place in spite of her reluctance to leave. "I was thinkin' it might be you, and you were a bit late."

"Not I," he said. "It's nothing to me if you stay or go, but you may come back to my house and use my sister Bridget's room if you like, until you can think what to do with yourself now that you're apparently not doomed."

She grabbed his arm suddenly, coming up behind him. "I wish that were true, but it's not. There's someone after me. I'm sure of it."

"Is it the law?" he asked. "I'll not be hiding a criminal."

Of course, he didn't expect her to admit it if that were true and, though he knew from the telly and the papers that crime was rampant, the young were lawless and godless, and you couldn't trust anyone at all anymore, he didn't care to live that way.

"I'm no criminal," she said. "But I am hiding."

"I'd never have guessed it. I thought you just had a very poor house agent." They came to the fence separating his property from the neighbor's. The overcast sky had melted into drizzle and then rain. A flock of crows circled overhead, cawing to each other. The girl scrambled more agilely over the fence than he could these days, with his joints stiff with the wet and cold.

They had to stop to release first one ewe, then two others, that had wandered into bogs. The girl was helpful, but he could see that she was weary and underfed. She was also walking with a slight limp, as if her feet hurt.

Once the ewes were free Joe and the girl proceeded to the house. She flopped down on the floor to admire the kittens and pet the cat, her fellow strays. He made up Bridget's old bed and pulled out more of his siblings' cast-off clothing. His brothers' would fit her better than his sisters', he thought. Fortunately, these days it didn't matter.

Later he would go into the market and fetch enough food for them both. Perhaps she would relieve him of his own cooking for a short time, at least.

* * *

"What's the matter with you, bringing that old one along?" Puss had snarled at Prince Tom the first time she laid eyes on the poor old woman he'd trailed behind him out of Dublin. "Anyone with the sense God gave a goose can see she's not up to it."

"And how was I to stop her?" Tom had demanded. "She's human you know, and bigger than me. Not that she's fed me once so far."

"How long have you been gone?" she'd asked him.

174 Elizabeth Ann Scarborough

"A half day if it's an hour," was his reply.

"Well, you'll have to take her back, there's no help for it," Puss had told him, plain as day, but he wouldn't listen even then, when it would have been easy to take the poor old thing back.

"Can't," he'd said, insolently intent on washing under his tail. "I'm the new King. I have to follow the funeral to the end. That's the rule, that is."

Puss had scratched behind her ear to show him what she thought of his self-importance. "Funny how I've been to King Cat's funerals many times before and that's the first I've heard the rules explained *that* way.

"Well, then, but you're not a prince, are you? If you want her returned, you'd best do it yourself. In fact, that will be my first command."

"Get on with you," she'd told him, and spat at the high-and-mighty chancer. But one rule she and all the others did know was that there was to be no fighting during the procession. Otherwise the procession would be impossible to keep secret, and for that matter, with so many cats involved, Ireland would be a great long claw mark from one end to the other.

So then Puss had gone up to the old woman and said, "Come along, woman. You must go home."

But the old one was daft, and had looked at her blankly.

Tom by then had run off to lord it over his new subjects.

Puss had made an attempt to question the befuddled human. "Where do you live, woman?" she'd asked.

About then the procession had begun moving again, and the woman moved with them. She was old and slow, but so many cats take a long time to move from one place to the next. Puss kept trying to persuade her to go home.

Once she'd used her claws to try to turn the old girl, but that counted as fighting, and she was immediately chastised by the five cats nearest her. That set her ears back good.

So for a day or two the woman drifted along with the procession as it wound down into the country. But then, having had some sleep but little to eat and drink, she began to fall farther and farther behind. And Tom would not stay to guide her, so it fell to Puss, who was the only one who seemed to notice or care.

Finally, when the others were far out of sight, the old woman sat down alone in a field with her legs outstretched and her hands in her lap and her head bowed with weariness. Puss decided that the only way to handle the situation was to involve Felicity. Even without magic powers, she was human and she could do something. But meanwhile, Puss would have to leave the old woman to go fetch Felicity. She couldn't properly guide her psychically without a magic link, and also, she'd no idea whose field she was in or where it was exactly. They'd been cutting cross-country since they left town.

"Stay where you are, woman, or it will be the worse for you," Puss told her, and ran off, hoping that the old woman would obey her.

*   *   *

When the bossy little cat what spoke proper human speech had hightailed it away across the field, Moira Daly rose at once to her feet.

Imagine a cat fancying she could give orders to a human person! This was a peculiar and cunning lot of cats, and that was a fact. But they couldn't fool old Moira, the mangy beasts. They might be faster than she, but she knew well enough how to find them. She had been the best tracker in her family, had she, and she'd taught her chiler the same. The momentary lucid thought of Jack popped into her mind. Where was the boy? Didn't she always tell him to keep up? If he was wanting his supper, 'twas only himself he had to blame, never about when she needed him. Old Tom and his little friends were up to something, and she would know what and why. The more he eluded her, the more she determined that she would find him. He hadn't finished his supper at all, the bold cat.

Tracking them was dead easy, if she kept at it slow and steady. There was so many of them, and the ground was very soft and they went overland always, avoiding the roads. She wasn't aware of much except those little paw prints. When she sat or lay down to rest she did it right there on their track and when she moved she followed those little prints, no matter what.

She might be tired and she might not find enough to eat sometimes, but she was free, finally free, the way she had been as a girl. No concrete buildings nor barriers. Just the mud and the grass and the trees. A flock of crows flushed from the trees ahead of her. That was smart of them. Cats didn't mind eating crow. Ah, that sly old Tom knew how to live.

It took her two days tracking to find the ruined house in the brambles, which was as good a place as any to lay her down and rest. Someone had obligingly cut a path through the stickery thorns right over the little tracks, though larger, human tracks were sunk in the mud on top of them.

That was where the cats would be, all right, but none of them were there right then. Nothing at all was there but a little box in the shape of a coffin with a little purple scarf on top of it and a little golden trinket in the shape of a crown. She opened the box and sure enough, there was a dead cat—a very dead cat at that. She replaced the lid and fastened it and tucked the box into her apron. ''Now we'll see who must find who,'' she said to herself, grinning happily to have such a trick to play on Old Tom, and the bossy cat, too.

CHAPTER 20

Journal Entry—Faerie

"What's Fairyland like, Sno?" the girls at Clarke would undoubtedly ask me when I told them (as if!) about what I just saw, right before they called the asylum to arrange for a straightjacket and a padded cell.

If I were going to answer I'd have to say, "It's just like the postcards would be, if there were any." What I mean by that is that it has all the features the poems and fairy tales and songs describe, but you really can't exactly capture the feeling of being there by making a list of its chief exports and imports and natural resources. But I'll try.

It smells like autumn, sounds like Christmas and looks like twilight on a clear evening in late spring, when everything is in blossom.

I wore my black spandex mini and velvet leggings with my Docs. Felicity had another glittery pair and brought a spare pair under her arm. When we were dressed, we walked into the guest room, opened the patio doors and walked into the hill.

As soon as we opened the doors, there was a hallway that hadn't been there before, like a tunnel in the dirt. Very plain. I thought for a minute there I was going to be wildly overdressed to go spelunking. But it was that way to fool anybody who opened the door accidentally, Felicity said. She closed the glass door carefully behind us and we walked a few steps into the tunnel, where it took a sharp bend. Bells tinkled like Santa's sleigh somewhere far off. There were wind chimes too, but at first all we heard was the bells.

Fireflies the size of hummingbirds flitted around us, lighting up a fork in the path. There was a rough, rocky-looking one on the right, a broad smooth one on the left. The middle path had a trickle of a stream zigzagging back and forth down its center, hard to see sometimes because the whole thing was overgrown with wildflowers.

"And which do we follow?" Felicity asked.

I grinned at her and sang—I can't remember my French verbs for dirt but I remember every word of some of the longest ballads on Grandma's records:

O see ye not yon narrow road
So thick beset with thorns and briers?
That is the path of righteousness . . .

"But," I added, "it looks to me like it's for experienced hikers only, and me without my gorp."

"You wouldn't care for the company there, I should think. Many early Irish saints were a bit on the misogynistic side, though St. Brigit was good fun."

I pointed to the superhighway, trying to sound like Maddy Prior as I sang, " 'And see ye not that braid braid road/That lies across that lily leven?/That is the path of wickedness/Tho some call it the road to heaven.'

"Nah," I said. "Been there, done that. It'd be—whadday-acallit?—redundant to do it again."

"Yes, and the climate's a bit warm at the final destination," Felicity said.

"So . . . how about this one?" I pointed down the middle path and went into my Maddy Prior imitation again.

"Oh, see ye not that bonny road/That winds about the fernie brae?

"Is that the road to fair Elfland?" I paraphrased. "Where thou and I this night maun gae?"

"The very one," Felicity said. "After you."

I have to tell you something here, Rosie. All the kidding and quoting aside, if Felicity hadn't been behind me, I don't know if I'd have set foot on that path or not. It's one thing to hear about it in a song, or read about it in a story, but I mean, there it was. The actual road to Elfland. It was a heavy moment and I felt a little dizzy there for a bit.

"How about the eating thing? I thought mortals couldn't eat or drink anything in Fairyland or they'd have to stay."

"You won't be able to eat any of their food, but Her Majesty has a special menu, for those of us in the sorority, of food items imported from the surface."

After the first step I was okay, concentrating on not stepping in the stream and soaking the boots I'd be dancing in for the next seven years.

I never knew there were underground forests, but there are, and boy would the lumber companies love to get their hands on them! We came into this oak grove with these massive trees—big as redwoods almost. On the other side of the grove, the stream fed into a little river and there was a boat waiting by the bank. And a dreamboat in it to pilot it, if you'll forgive the trés retro expression. The guy looked like one of the long-haired studly dudes on the covers of romance novels, only better. His hair was long and bright bronzy-colored and curly and he was wearing swim trunks, which they never tell you about in fairy tales. But it was warm down there, balmy even, so why not, when he was working in the water?

He gave Felicity a look that was so incredibly hot. I don't know about icebergs or stones, but I was melting. "G'die, Flitters," he said. "How's it goin'?"

"Not so bad, Bluey," she answered. "How are things going with you?"

He shrugged gorgeous shoulders. "No worries."

I raised my eyebrow meaningfully, forgetting that the whole area around my eyes was blue and not likely to show off my expression to best advantage. "An Aussie elf?"

"Lord Bluelagoon of the Southern Star, may I present Sno-homish Quantrill of Seattle, Washington. Sno, Bluey is great-grandnephew to Manannan Mac Lir, the sea god."

"So *this* is her, then?" Bluey asked, giving me a medium-well look. "Raydir's daughter? Looks like 'im except for the blue bits."

He stopped talking to row then while Felicity and I sat in the back of the boat. "Is he for real?" I asked her. "And what about Raydir?"

"Many Irish and Scottish people were forced to emigrate to Australia. The Sidhe have always been a subversive group here, so it's little wonder that a good many of the ones who strayed aboveground during that time period were deported along with the more prosaic races. And the Sidhe are very fond of music so of course they know of your father. Also, you have a bit of Sidhe in your bloodlines, I've been told. Your paternal ancestor to whom Raydir seems to be a throw-back was a changeling."

"That would explain a lot," I admitted.

The little river broadened until it was almost as wide as a bay.

Bluey rowed us out to an island where a couple billion more of the hummingbird-sized fireflies lit up the scene. I looked at one of them close. It didn't look like a firefly much after all. The wings were more like a butterfly's, and they were the part that lit up. If you looked carefully, there were a lot of subtle pretty colors inside the light.

What I remember most was that the whole island looked like a pillared ballroom but the pillars were actually birch trees and their leaves made a ceiling overhead. Massive rhododen-dron blossoms hung down at intervals and the butterfireflies seemed to like these and clustered on them, so they glowed like candlelight. Most of the floor was grassy carpet but there was a tiled dance floor of what looked like gold and silver and a green substance I didn't recognize. "Jade?" I asked Felicity, touching it with my toe.

"Connemara marble," she said. "A kind of serpentine. It's more precious down here than gold and silver."

The music was beautiful and the air smelled of hazelnuts and cinnamon, apples and autumn leaves. The walls were a yew hedge, the branches twined with white moon flowers and morning glories. The yews arched into graceful passages opening out to a sunset that lasted the whole time we were there, always reflected on the water.

I was prepared to just start dancing but no, my first visit wasn't that easy. If we were there seven years, as Felicity says, I bet six and a half of them were spent in the reception line. I "came out" I suppose, FGM style. People with slanting eyes of—well—Connemara marble green and the bored expressions of stars having to make nice to the plebes asked me how I was liking my stay in Ireland (again!), what brought me here, what I wished to do when I finished school, how my wishes were working out, where I got the idea for my unusual toilette (this from a lady with what looked like a purple Afro but turned out to be lavender rhody blossoms massed all over her head). "Woad?" she asked.

"Maybelline," I told her.

Others in the line asked if I would care to eat, dance or make love as soon as the reception was over. "You can dance," Felicity said. "Period."

"If seven years pass I'm going to get hungry, aren't I?"

But I didn't. I got bored, though, after I looked at the clothes. What appeared to be green velvet the men wore was actually a fine coating of plushy moss or lichen they must have grown for the occasion. The lady's lacy dresses were real flowers strung together with spiderwebs. They had to change fairly often. Especially after the polkas and the set dance numbers.

I danced some of them but I found that I preferred dancing the way we do at home, with our hands free. I couldn't seem to dance with my hands in somebody else's, the way some people can't talk without gestures.

Finally I went and sat down beside one of the flowering bushes. A beautiful lady was already sitting there and when I joined her, she said in a rough, heavily accented hostile voice I remembered only too well, "Aren't you the clever one, thinking of giving that nasty strayt girl a lovely voice that told the truth besides? Why couldn't you listen to your betters and give her toads and snakes? Well—worums anyway, since we've no snakes handy. Plenty of toads, though.''

''You've got Maeve's voice!'' I said, gaping at her.

''That I have and she's bloody well got mine, thanks to you. Where do you think magic gifts come from? When I pledged to support Her Majestay's work I'd no idayea it would cost me so dayre. It'll take me centuries to train my voice back to where I'm fit to be heard and as for singing! I could wreck ships by driving them onto the rocks to get away from me!''

That was when I noticed that the tight strapless blue-green sequined evening gown she was wearing wasn't made of fabric and she didn't have any need for dancing slippers since she already had dancing flippers.

''Sorry,'' I said. Just then Felicity gave me the high sign and we waved goodbye to everybody, and climbed back into Bluey's boat. I wasn't sorry to go, to tell you the truth. I guess seven years must have passed, like Felicity said, and it was all kind of a long drawn-out blur—for instance, I only remember making the boat trip once, don't remember sleeping or eating or doing anything but dancing and meeting people. The way I figure it, it was like one of those lecture classes where according to your watch, you're only there an hour real time, but it definitely feels like a lifetime. We thanked Bluey for the ride, tiptoed through the tulips and other flora down the middle path again, back through the tunnel and to the glass door.

I opened it and ducked as a frying pan came sailing past my skull.

CHAPTER 21

Journal Entry—Friday Afternoon

The pan fell with a clatter and Deirdre stepped back in a mock faint, her hand over her heart, "Praise be to Jaysus, it's only you, Sno! And Felicity! Where have you been? I heard noises in there. I thought it was wild animals or ghosts."

"We're fine, Deirdre," Felicity said, laughing. "There's an old bunker in there. Sno wanted to explore it but it's quite dangerous and I—"

Deirdre simply looked us in our finery up and down. "So was it a victory celebration you were attendin', then?" she asked, and turned on her heel and went to the kitchen. I'll tell her about it later. I don't want her to leave.

My feet were very sore and my shoes as worn out as Felicity's discards. Another part of me, however, wasn't sure Fairyland hadn't been one big hypno-high. I ran to my room and looked into the mirror in Gerardine's makeup kit. Under the blue shadow, my nose was normal size and no longer tender to the touch. I washed my face and all the blue came off. No lingering bruises. Super.

Felicity and I both changed into more normal clothes and she came down to my room to tell me she thought I'd done well and she had been promised that she would be growing stronger in her own magic soon. I started to tell her about meeting the, I guess mermaid would be the only correct term, and how she had Maeve's voice.

Deirdre came bustling back and said, "Felicity, there's a cat scratching at the door. It's desperate skinny and raggedy-tailed. Does it belong here? Shall I let it in?"

Puss came streaking in a short time after crying at the top of her lungs, "Flitters, Flitters, I need your help at once!"

"What on earth is the matter, old dear?" Felicity asked, and scooped her up. She was pretty much a mess with her fur full of burrs and her nose scratched up and looking as if she hadn't had a good meal in ages, even though she was here at the house just about a week ago.

"One of yours is in trouble from following one of ours who thinks he's a prince but is no better than he ought to be," Puss told her.

"Then I suppose the one who is ours will discover his or her error soon," Felicity said.

"I don't think she can," Puss said. "She's old and not at all reasonable. Pixillated, I would say. Daft. I gave her ever such a scratch on the legs to send her home and she kicked at me and almost fell down but kept following. I've left her alone in a field but, Felicity, it took me two days to get here and I don't know how long she'll last."

"Who was she following?"

"Prince Tom, he calls himself, and it seems to me his heart is as black as his fur. This poor old thing was his food provider and he's let her follow after without a bit of thought to whether or not she can survive. I gave him a piece of my mind, for all the good it did any of us, which was not much."

"Where were you when she joined you?" Felicity asked.

"In the park near Stillorglin. I did *try* to turn her then, but she kept up pretty well to begin with. Tinker women are used to walking."

Well, duh. It took me that long to get it but I finally did. "Jack's mom!" I said. "Puss, you found Jack's mom!"

"She found *me*," the cat said, washing the blood from her paw pads. "I say, I'm famished. Is no one going to feed me?"

"Deirdre," Felicity called into the kitchen. "Have we any meat or fish of any kind we could fix for Puss? She's starving."

I don't know what Deirdre thought we were doing, standing there in the hallway having a two-way conversation while we both looked at a ratty-looking cat. Bobby was nowhere in sight. He didn't like Puss when she was her normal self. I guess he *really* didn't want to face her when she was hungry.

"Felicity, the boy I met, the one who helped me, that's *his* mother who followed the cats. He's worried sick about her—been looking all over Dublin. We ought to let him know we know where she is."

"Yes, I suppose so. Where exactly did you leave her, Puss?"

The cat looked at us like we were nuts. "I told you. In a field two days from here. She won't have gone far."

"Where was the field?" Felicity asked.

"Next to another field which was three fields from a little wood and fields on the other side."

I began to see the problem.

"What county is it in, Puss? What town is it near?"

"Waterford, I think. Or maybe Clonmel. There was a wee village not far but I'm not sure which one. It's changed since the previous dynasty."

"Will tuna do?" Deirdre called from the kitchen and Puss streaked away at warp speed.

"Now what?" I asked.

"There's nothing for it but to use the scrying pool," she answered. "With that we can at least look at where the woman is and see if there are any identifying sights or sounds that would lead us to her."

"Scrying pool?" a little toady voice said. I looked and there was the hit toad, up on the staircase. "What's that supposed to mean?"

"It's like a crystal ball," Felicity told him. "You see things in it."

"Like you, for instance."

She nodded. "And now we must try to see the old woman who followed the cats."

"I wish I knew how to get ahold of Jack," I said. "If it's his mom, he'd want to be in on it."

"There'll be time enough for that when we've fetched the woman back again. If she's old and disoriented, she'll need food and rest. Then we can worry about locating family members. Now then, to the pool."

We heard this shriek from the kitchen and Deirdre came stumbling out, Puss tangled under her feet. "It—the cat—she spoke to me."

"Yes," Felicity said. "She does that. Puss, were you rude?"

Puss sat washing her right front paw as if nothing at all had happened. "I merely suggested she bring my food dish along so that I could view the scrying pool too."

"What sort of place is this?" Deirdre asked. Felicity told her.

I held my breath. She listened to Felicity with this shocked look on her face, shook her head, crossed herself, then turned on her heel and walked away.

About two minutes later she emerged from the kitchen carrying a tea tray with three cups, a carton of milk, the sugar bowl, a plate of cookies (biscuits) and Puss's dish. "I knew all them cats was up to something and of course, I'd always heard of fairy godmothers and stories of the Good Folk and that, but I never imagined when I thought perhaps I needed a bit of an adventure I would end up mixing in such matters," she said. "I thought we could do with a cup of tea while we're having a look at that pool of yours, Felicity."

I grinned and picked up Puss and carried her so she wouldn't get tangled in Deirdre's feet while she was carrying the tray. Puss immediately dropped her dignity and purred like the furry slut she is.

When we got to the pool, I kissed her on the nose and set her down while I helped Felicity and Deirdre remove the pool cover. When we sat back down, Puss crawled back into my lap, and I heard the pushy note in her voice even though she forgot herself and actually spoke in her native tongue instead of English.

Felicity touched the water and said, "We wish to see the place where Puss left the woman who followed the King of the Cats' funeral procession." When the ripples she created with her hands stilled, green fields rolled under a predictably cloudy sky. Sheep schlepped around in the meadows and crows did an air show overhead while swans posed in a small pond. But there was no woman. "Show us where she is now, then," Felicity said. And there was a picture of an old lady with a plaid shawl, carrying something bulky in what looked like a worn and patched apron. In the background was a house with a roof half-fallen in and behind it, slightly downhill, earthmoving machinery rumbled and workingmen shouted orders.

Puss washed the tip of her tail. "I've no idea what she's doing there, wherever that is."

"Wherever it is, indeed," Felicity said.

"This thing doesn't have like caller ID or anything on it then, huh?" I asked. "Maybe we could get it to pan backwards until we can see a signpost or some kind of marking you'd recognize."

"I'm afraid this sort of thing is less cinematic than what you're used to, dear," Felicity said.

"Well, now," Deirdre said, "of course, I don't know anything about it, but it seems to me that if you asked to see where the men were working, perhaps one of the vehicles or machines might have a name on it."

Felicity beamed at her and rippled the water with a dramatic sweep of her hand. "Show us the workmen near the ruined house from which the woman walked," she said to the pool. Over her shoulder she told us, "Scrying pools are a bit like computers in that you must give them very specific instructions."

The pool re-formed to show the work site, a stone cottage, some roofless buildings and a number of machines, one of which said, "Clonmel Builders."

"Clonmel it is," Felicity said.

Leaving Deirdre to guard the house, Felicity, Puss, the toad and I all piled in the godmothermobile and set out down the road—for about a quarter of a mile. That was when something clunked and clattered and the godmothermobile shuddered to a halt.

"Aw, shit!" I said.

"Exactly," Felicity agreed.

"What is it with you humans and your machinery?" Puss asked. "We must find that poor old soul and you must remove her from our fur so we can get on with our procession in peace. At once," she yowled for emphasis, paddling her front paws against the window.

"We're doing the best we can, Puss, but our machinery keeps failing. Sno has been informed we have a gremlin."

Bobby hopped up and down with excitement, and I realized I hadn't actually told him about my conversation with the dog. Listen to me. I was rude, teacher. I didn't explain to the toad what the dog next door told me about the supernatural nuisance at the house where I'm staying. Sheesh.

"I knew it was somethin' like that," Bobby said smugly. "I *know* breaking and entering when I hear it."

"Very perceptive, Bobby," Felicity said. "A shame you said nothing about it to me. Customarily there is a guardian on duty to protect a house where the godmother is temporarily drained. However . . ."

Puss flipped her tail with annoyance. "I have urgent business somewhere else for a few days, and everything falls apart."

"Look," I said. "All this isn't finding Jack's mom. One of my wishes is that I have transportation whenever I want it and I want it *now*," I said loudly to like, put it out there to the universe as the new-agers say.

That was when I saw that brown-and-white spotted horse, standing there in the field, looking interested in all these people sitting in the middle of the road.

"Just a sec," I said, and hopped out of the car to go talk to the horse.

"I was wondering when you'd get round to me," the horse said.

"You the same horse that winked at me before?" I asked.

"The very same," he said.

"I need to find an old lady who's become lost following some cats," I said.

"Would that be the funeral procession of the King of the Cats you'd be after?" he asked.

"How did you know?"

"How could it be anything else when there's a swath runnin' round the whole of Ireland and hardly a fayld mouse, rat or rabbit left alive nor a songbird what dares to touch ground for fear of its life?" The horse talked just like Jack and Maeve.

I'd left the car door open and now Puss and Felicity got out and Puss bounded over to us. "He can't help you, Sno. They're many miles from here and I am too knackered to run always ahead and lead the way. He'd be much too slow."

The horse winked again. "Not a bit of it. You don't know who you're daylin' wit', Puss cat. There's toime enough and to spare, if only you knew. Climb up on my back now, Miss, and you, cat, layde us to the trail of your cronies and I can follow it well enough."

"This is really nice of you," I said.

"You haven't a friend for me, I suppose?" Felicity asked the horse with a sigh that was becoming long-suffering. The horse snorted and shook his head which we both took to mean no.

"Well, then," said Felicity, "I'll just have to see about organizing another car and I'll be right along. We'll need something to transport the poor lady in at any rate."

"But how will you find us?" I asked.

"Why, there's no magic in that. I'll simply look up Clonmel Builders and ask where that work site is and meet you there. She can't have gone far from there on foot, even if it takes us hours to reach the place."

"I hope it won't be too much for you," I said to the horse.

"Shush, shush, not at all, not at all. I love a bit of a jaunt," the horse said. I climbed up on a rock and mounted.

But Puss didn't budge. "Too much for him indeed! Nothing to do but stand here all day and munch grass while I'm wearing my paws to the bone. Well, if you think I'm going to scamper over that trail again on these sore pads of mine with barely a morsel to keep body and soul together, you've another think coming. Sorry as I am for that old fool of a woman, she made her own choice and I'm not killing myself in any cross-country chase. I'll ride with Felicity, thank you very much."

"But how will we . . . ?" I started to say "find her" but the horse had already wheeled, bolted across the pasture and jumped a fence into another field, a jump so smooth I hardly felt it. Cindy Ellis would have been proud of me but it was really the horse. I just sat there yelling, "Wait, whoa." But I had nothing to hang onto or enforce my commands. This horse obviously had his own agenda.

"Never you mind them, dear. We'll make out fine, we will. I wasn't too keen on having that sharp-clawed little bugger hangin' onto me backside anyway. Now then, all we have to do is find the trail and it'll be clear as glass how they went. You can't hide thousands of cats that easily. I believe I heard about them passing by the round tower just a bit aesht of here."

And find the trail we did. The track wasn't real definite, because the rain had washed the mud flat, but in places you could see the definite imprints of hundreds, maybe thousands, of little kitty paws.

"Wait, wait," a voice said from my sweatshirt hood. "I don't think this is the mission for me after all. I should maybe hop down and go back to the house and see if the god-dame needs any help."

"Ugh, yuck!" I said. "Like, who *asked* you to come?"

"I got to do good in order to lose the green warts, remember? And I can't do much when certain thoughtless individuals lock me in the swimming pool."

"It's a scrying pool."

"Whatever."

"So you're here. So stay put and you won't get bounced off. But don't get in our way."

"Not unless I need to save you from getting your neck broken which, trust me, is an intellectual challenge for someone with my physical attributes. But hey, y'know, this ain't bad. This is a very smooth gait you got here, horse. No bounce, no pounce, I like it."

"Thank you, I'm sure," the horse said. He *was* giving us a very smooth ride considering that he was running so fast. "It's not something I do in mixed company all that often but since you're the young lady as talks to bayshts and you're a talkin' toad, I figure you're the right sort of paypul to understand and you did say the matter at hand was urgent."

I didn't really catch on, even then, until I noticed that he didn't lift to sail over the next fence. There was, in fact, no change in the level of his back at all. Then I looked down. "Am I nuts or are you flying?"

"That I would be, yes," he said. "But not to worry, I'm mindin' the trail well enough."

"Oh, hey, then that's okay," Bobby said. "That was all I was worried about was if he was payin' attention to the trail. You god-babes are fuckin' amazing! How in this whole country did you manage to end up aboard the one horse who could fly?"

"It's not that uncommon," the horse said.

"It's not?" both the toad and I asked.

"Not in Ireland, no."

"Why?" I asked. "Did some magic horse like Pegasus come over here and sire a herd of Irish flying horses maybe?"

"Oh, no. Sartinly not. Otherwise we'd have wings. No, it's much simpler than that. Some of us are air pookhas is all."

"What the hell is that?" both the toad and I asked.

"Well, you've no doubt heard of yer water pookhas, them as looks like beautiful horses what invites paypul to clamber upon their backs and then takes them for a bit of daype say divin'?"

"Yeah," I said.

"Go on," Bobby said. "Deep-sea diving doesn't worry me much."

"Well, that's not the kind I am. The kind I am likes takin'

to the air instead of the water. Just a matter of preference really.''

"Where do you come from? Are you part of Faerie, because I was just there and I can tell you, they're cooperating fully with us on this mission.''

"Are they really? How fascinatin'. But no, it's nothin' t'do with them. It's just some of us, soon's we get our legs under us, start laypin' over things and a more select group, of whom I must say I myself am the foremost, like laypin' over things and not comin' down again until we're good and ready. Of course, when I'm with most folk, I just jump me jumps and they're all impressed somethin' turrible, but the truth of it is, I'm foolin' wit' 'em. They think I'm a great jumpin' horse when actually I'm an authentic air pookha flyin' horse who's tryin' not to show the others up.''

"Lucky I happened to meet you then,'' I said.

"Luck had little to do with it, young lady. You go to live in a house built by fairy godmothers, abuttin' a fairy knowe, adjoined by a yew walk specially sprouted aboveground from its old home below just for the sake of landscapin' the place, and use an ancient scryin' pool for a swimmin' pool, then you go around convairsin' with all the bayshts in the neighborhood just as if they was human bein's such as yourself, and still you're surprised there's a flyin' horse in the field across the lane?''

I had to admit he had a point. "I just thought all the magic stuff would be more like, you know, secret,'' I said.

"Oh no, not atall!'' the horse said. "Now, some folk are superstitious because their clairgy have taught them that there's somethin' bad to magic, somethin' un-Christian and wicked. But the truth of it is, there's angels, see, and there's miracles and all that so if you look at it a sartin way, not only is magic holy but it may even be said that the churches lay claim to inventin' it. The other half of the paypul, well, if they never see anythin' magical in their whole lives, they'll make things up just to be entertainin'. So no, the magic isn't very hidden here. And when you think of it, life itself is magic, is it not?''

"A horse who flies *and* is a philosopher," Bobby said. "This is some country they got here."

It was easy to see how you'd become a philosopher if you could fly the way the horse could—he told us people had called him a lot of things but he liked being called Ace the best—low altitude, sailing over those ivy-grown fences, past ancient towers set out in the middle of fields, over the tops of castle ruins, through beautiful gardens and over sheep and lambs. It gave you a sense of the timelessness of the country and life. Of course, Ace had to avoid villages and he said he usually didn't fly a lot in daytime. If the odd shepherd saw him, it didn't matter. People usually just figured the shepherd had been hitting the jug a little too hard.

We kept on the trail of the cats pretty well. They avoided water, of course, and only crossed at bridges and stepping stones or at low tide if they strayed near the sea. Looking back and forward, I could see that the trail stretched on and on forever, winding, twisting, braiding back on itself, and I imagined a Celtic knotwork border, like the ones knitted into sweaters, only made of the twined tails and whiskers of cats tying Ireland together as they passed through.

The fields all looked pretty much alike to me, though, and I was absorbed in watching the sun start to sink into a pinky coral blaze on the horizon when we saw a familiar-looking chimney in the distance and heard the sound of machinery that I realized meant we were near the site where we had first seen the old woman. It must have been about four-thirty, five o'clock then. Maeve hadn't given in to Jack so far as to return my watch, so I didn't really know exactly. It was the Kama Sutra Swatch that Duck Soul, Raydir's lead guitarist, gave me for my birthday too. The watch, I mean.

Ace set hooves to trail then, but not before he was seen. "Ssst, you there!" a voice said from behind a clump of the brambles that separated the house from the area where the men were working.

"Me?" I asked.

"That's right. You with the opposable thumbs and the gift

of feline understanding. You're that American girl, aren't you?''

"How can you tell? By the way I ride?'' I asked sarcastically. A big black cat crawled out of the brambles.

"No, on accounta you're ridin' a flyin' horse and have a toad in your hood. Besides, Puss told me about you. I presume she's over her hissy fit and has come back with you.''

"She'll be along later,'' I said.

"Divil take her anyway,'' the cat said, which was just about how I felt about it right then too. "It's you I'm wantin' to talk to, Miss. You see, this mornin' as we was sleepin', a man broke into the house where we'd stopped. There was some noise ensued, don't ask, it's a long story, and anyway, we all ran away. In our haste, we forgot a certain object. A—rather awkward object. And by the time we'd regrouped and discovered it was left behind, those tossers down there decided to do a day's work for a change and we couldn't very well move it in plain sight o' them. So what I was thinkin' was, it would be no unusual thing for a girl such as yourself to go pokin' into the old house, now would it? Matter of fact, there was another girl in there when we arrived, though she was asleep. And I thought, that is, We thought, to use me official position as Crown Prince of the Cats and I'm sure you'll take my meanin' since you've been consortin' with Puss, that you could do us a favor and go fetch the item.''

"What item? Is it heavy?'' I asked.

"Not for you. It's my royal father's casket and without it the funeral procession cannot proceed, I cannot succeed him on the throne, and meanwhile I got all these subjects to feed.''

From the concealment of the brambles, thousands of shiny cat eyes peered out at me like little gold Christmas lights strung along the ground.

Right about then engines started up, men laid down their tools and climbed into trucks, and began driving away.

"There's a path over there,'' the Prince cat said. "But it leads to a window. It was a bit of a struggle getting the casket in there but I says, let's be safe. After all, anyone could pick it up out here. And I'm glad I did it, since that man came by.

He had the look of a thief to me."

So did the black tomcat. Just then a tuxedo tom sashayed out from the brambles as if they were a carpeted kitty bed. "Your highness, it's time we were movin' again."

"Do you think I don't know that, Bronski?" Prince Tom asked. "But it's no good us movin' without me royal da's carcase. So how 'bout it, Miss?" He looked at me out of big wide gold eyes. If he'd had lashes, he'd have batted them. This had to be the kitty Puss had complained about, so I wasn't as sympathetic as I normally would have been. Just the same—it was important to all the cats, I guessed. So I had Ace land long enough to let me traipse across the brambles and stare into the window. There was enough daylight coming in through the windows so that I could see the place by the fireplace clearly.

"Zippo," I told the cats.

"What do you mean?"

"Just what I said. Zip, nada, nothing there, and you can look for yourself if you don't believe me."

"Go inside. Look under things," he said in a voice of command.

But Bobby bravely said from the protection of my hood, "Look, bird-breath, the lady already told you there was nothin' there. She did you a favor despite our heavy schedule. Now excuse us, we got things to do, places to go and people to see."

"Yeah," I said. "It's a matter of life and death." I wanted to add that it was also mostly his fault, but guilt-tripping cats is impossible, so I left it at that. Ace knelt again and I climbed onto his back. We left Prince Tom complaining about how it was so hard to get good help these days.

Chapter 22

Maeve's mouth might as well have been dripping toads and snakes the way she stood there gawping as first the rich girl, then the witch in gray, then Jack, left her standing on the riverbank. The boys clustered round her. Some of the younger ones were so confused they forgot themselves and started bawling. Normally she would have fetched them a clout, but now she just sank to her haunches and stood staring out at the river. The four swans hovered offshore. She remembered them speaking to her but she had no idea how to reopen the conversation.

There was a tug at her sleeve. "I'm hongry, Maeve. We give that girl back her kit, and now we can't buy nuffin' t' ate." That was Wee Donny.

"Worse'n'that," said eight-year-old Eamon, "Oi've naught for me da t' get pissed on. He'll skin me."

Normally Maeve would have sorted something out, found another mark or two, but now she was too preoccupied by the curse the dirty witches had put on her. "Don't whinge at me, yez," she commanded in the voice of one of the ancient women poets criticizing a king. "You're best off larnin' now that if yez want to ate, yez can't go givin' it to your old man to piss away. What ya want to follow the loikes o' me for? I look a bayg success to yez, do I? Yer young yet. Go to Father

Ambrose. Get him to put yez in school so you won't be blee-din' eejits.''

"But ah'm hongry," Wee Donny insisted again.

A passerby dropped five one-pound coins beside Maeve. "Here's some money to help feed your brood, young woman. I can tell you're a cut above most, encouraging your children to get an education."

Maeve tried to whinge and wheedle more out of the man who gave her the coins, but what came out of her mouth was, "You think foive pounds will feed us all? Would it feed your family? And they're not my family. Shoite, man, I'm only sixteen years old and look at me! Out on the strayte because I can't bring drink money to me own fam'ly and there's no dole money for me now. And an education don't solve every-thing. I larnt to read and wroite me own nayum but ah'm still beggin', you'll notice.''

To her surprise the first passerby didn't look disgusted and run off but stood for a moment with tears running down his cheeks while he pulled out a twenty-pound note and added it to the five. A second passerby meantime said, "What a fine brave girl you are to look after these children though you've no home of your own. And it's sad that you've had to beg, but you know, my dear, you've an absolutely beautiful voice and with a little training, why, I see no reason why you couldn't use it to good advantage in broadcasting or even the stage. Here's my card. Call me sometime and we'll talk. Oh, and please accept this twenty as a contribution to your future.''

"Me Dad will prob'ly bayte it out of me, sir, but I thank you for the card even if you do mayne to lord it over me or maybe take advantage of a poor girl."

But by that time, both men had hurried off. Meanwhile sev-eral other people had crossed the street to see what was hap-pening and the boys set up a clamor that their poor mama, who had just starred in a production at the Abbey Theatre, had learned she'd been widowed and they were all left on the street. Eleven-year-old Tim wisely pulled Maeve's head against him and wouldn't let her speak until the people had donated whatever they could to the plight of the widow and orphans. Normally, they'd not have considered giving to a pack of knackers, but the previous two gentlemen had obviously learned something that moved them to give generously, and it was a sin to deny charity to the needy.

That night Maeve and the gang members who had family still there returned to the halt with almost seventy pounds among them. They didn't notice the small flock of swans flying above them from the Liffey to the stagnant little pond near the dump.

Maeve had divvied up another twenty pounds among Wee Donny and John-o and told them to make it last, that she doubted she'd be back the next day. She didn't even know why she said it. Second bleedin' sight maybe.

She'd told herself she wouldn't go to the caravan if her dad was home but even though she heard his voice from ten feet away, she jerked open the door, her money held before her like a shield.

Her dad and mam were passing a bottle between them while baby Nancy squalled on the floor. There was no pot on the stove nor food on the table, nor did the caravan smell as if anything like food had been near it lately. It smelled of booze and baby shit. Her mam fished on the couch behind her and came up with a baby bottle. She took a swig from the whiskey bottle and poured it into the baby bottle until it was half full. Then she stuck it back in Nancy's mouth.

"Tol' yez t' stay away," her da growled.

"But I brought the money, see," she said, waving it. "Like you said, to pay for me kaype. Twenty-five pounds, Da. I'll just go back to town and fetch us some groceries, wha'?"

Her father was squinting at her as if he couldn't see her clearly. "Who the sod are you?"

" 'S Maeve, Davey," Mam said. "Our Maeve come home with a fortune."

"Why the devil don't she sound like Maeve then?" he demanded, pushing the table over and almost spilling the bottle before Mam caught it. Maeve was relieved. If he'd spilled that bottle, everyone would get a wallopin'.

Her brother Jimmie pushed in behind her then. "Wha's for tay?" he asked.

"Here now," Da said. "You're a man of the fam'ly. Wha's yer sister up ta, soundin' loike the soddin' Qwayne?"

Jimmie grinned. "Oh, she got witched, moonin' after Jack Daly and some rich American girl he was after."

"Witched!" Mam crossed herself and pointed to the door. "Witched, is it? I'll have no witchin' under my roof. Out wit' yez!"

"And don't come back till you sound yerself agin!" her father cried; then, as she stumbled back through the doorway, he caught up with her long enough to snatch the money from her hand and give her a smack across the face. "Ye great ogly hoor you."

Maeve cursed herself silently for losing the money. She ought to have known better. Did know better, but she couldn't help hoping. Still, her da was like that. He'd never change.

She decided to ask around and try to find Jack again. The American girl owed her. If he and Carnahan had found her so her rich friend could help Jack find his mam, then she could bleedin' well help Maeve as well. They should be back by now, if they'd gone out to Wicklow. They could bleedin' well turn around and take her down there with them this time. It wasn't them the witches had cursed to sound like a bleedin' duchess, after all.

Maeve pounded on the McDonaghs' door. Mary answered, a baby on her hip and two more kids clinging to her skirts. "Yah?"

"Mary, I'm after lookin' for Jack Daly. He took off wit' yer man, you know, that Carnahan bleeder. You got any idea where that one lives?"

"Maeve?"

Mary peered at her as if she'd suddenly turned green.

"Never mind me voice, Mary. Got a bit of a cold. About Carnahan?"

"He's from the north, Maeve, didn't you know? He's a bad lot, that one. Murtherin' bastard. If Jack Daly's wit' him then yer best off stayin' clear and prayin' for Jack."

She asked at several other houses and caravans, but by then the boys from her gang had spread the story about her being witched and people wouldn't open their doors, though some of the window coverings lifted at her knock. She was tempted to just knock down the bleedin' doors, but what good would that do if they wouldn't talk to her?

Hungry, tired, and not sure where to go next, she turned away from the halt and down the road. She walked and walked until she was well away. When she couldn't walk any more, she lay down in the grass beside the road and slept as best she could.

Lifting her head the next morning, she saw that she'd stopped beside a park. Only a few feet from her was a pond with swans swimming on it.

"Good morning to you, Maeve," said a lady's voice coming from one of the swans, as it had the day before.

"Layve me alone," she said miserably. "Haven't yez done enough?"

"Why, evidently not. You still seem very upset. But any friend of Jack's is a friend of ours, and we're prepared to help you however we can."

"Then help me find Jack," Maeve said. "He's gone off with Carnahan."

"Carnahan?"

"A hard man from the north. Has a red car, loads of money. Friendly with Travellers, though some say he's a bad lot altogether."

"If that's so, then we'll find him for you, dear."

"It won't help," Maeve said miserably. "They'll be long gone by now."

"Have you any idea at all where they might be?"

"Might've gone to the place where that girl is—the American. Out in Wicklah." She fished in her pocket and dug out the scrap with the address and read it aloud. "His mam's gone missin' and Carnahan and the girl both promised to help him find her."

"Very good, then, dear. We'll go find his mother for him and him for you then, shall we?"

The kindness in the swan's voice hurt Maeve in a way she didn't understand. "Get on wit'cha then. I don't care what you do."

The swan princess wasn't offended. Instead, she arched her long neck and bit at her tail and pulled out one of her own feathers, which she extended to Maeve. "Here then. Take this and we'll be able to find you by it when we return. Right, lads?"

The swan princes inclined their heads and one of them says, "It's just like our Nuala says. We'll find yer man, and his mam, though it may take us a bit, and if you hang onto Nuala's feather, we'll find you as well when we return."

"Yah, sure, right," Maeve said. But somehow she believed the swans would do exactly as they said.

*   *   *

The swans flew south from Dublin to County Wicklow and circled the house Maeve had told them about, but although they sensed magic seeping from its pores, they saw no sign of Jack and so they flew on, circling first one section and then the other, separately and together, high and low, over fields and towns, farmhouses and mansions, expanding their circles further east until they touched the ocean and further west and further south, until at last, near County Wexford, Princess Nuala was nearly knocked from the sky by a flock of speeding crows. Though she was only the descendant of a mythical creature, and not from the time of myth and legends herself, still they were all in her blood and that of her brothers. Such a great flock of crows homing in on one area like some of those smart missiles the soldiers polluted the airspace with these days! Forboding filled her. Two or three things such flocks of crows had meant throughout time, and in none of those matters did she like to think of her friend Jack being involved.

*   *   *

In Wexford town, Balor left the boy to his own devices while he found a call box and reported to his true mortal masters, the men so high and so wealthy that they were far beyond the petty affiliations of Irish politics—or any politics, for that matter. Their motives were their own. This did not mean they failed to take an interest when their interests were threatened. They were taking an interest now in the gropings toward resolution of the Troubles. They were not pleased. They liked the Troubles to stay troubled.

"Can you not speed things up?" they asked him. "It's getting dangerously peaceful up here. The IRA has stopped retaliating and even those in sympathy with the Loyalist movement can hardly continue to support it when the sloppy bastards keep accidentally executing Catholic grannies watching the telly and young Protestant girls with the same names as legitimate targets. People are merely bored with that level of violence, and disgusted. We need a highly controversial atrocity to keep them properly terrified of each other."

"I'm working on it," Balor told them. "What's going to happen to this girl should liven things up a bit again. But first I have to find her and bring her back."

"It's going to be increasingly difficult to make it look like that soldier you killed last week did it. Perhaps you should return and choose a new target."

But that hurt Balor's professional pride. He saw his assignments through. Always. Also, like his masters, he had his own motives for choosing his targets and executing his missions as he did. "I've a new angle," he told them. "We'll give out that the soldier had accomplices—spies among the tinkers. The killer-to-be has been asking for the girl from here to Dublin."

His masters rang off with more impatient words. Did they not trust him, when he had always done their will, and his own, without fail? Still, the search was a time-consuming process. While he enjoyed the stalking, he could no longer afford to depend on the ordinary methods. There was another way, but it involved indebting himself to a force, an unstable, unpredictable, demanding female force, a natural ally but one that could turn on him at a whim. She had first offered her help through a whore he met in Belfast. He'd been skeptical, but the proof had left even him howling and shaken. He'd been given a token, invited to use it. Perhaps it was time. He walked out into a vacant lot, then pulled a feather from his shirt pocket and stuck a match to it, smelling the acrid stench of burning protein. Ah, napalm in the morning, he thought with a grin at his own joke. As the feather burned, crows suddenly rained down over his head from nowhere, to flutter to the earth like ash.

The servants of the Mistress Morrigu saw everything, knew everyone, and they gossiped incessantly from one flock to the other. He told them what was required and they first dispersed to the four directions, to return a short time later, ready to guide him.

What he didn't see, of course, was the white wings high above the black. But if he didn't see the swans, they saw him well enough, and by his commanding of the crows they knew him for what he was.

*   *   *

On the second day of their search, Carnahan and Jack reached Wexford, and Carnahan went about his own affairs, to Jack's great relief. The man's mind was a great smelly sewer, and when he left Jack alone, the air cleared of the stench of him and Jack felt he could finally breathe easy for a time.

All along the way, Carnahan had stopped the car beside one halt or the other and sent Jack to the caravans to talk to the people inside about his mother and the young girl in the photograph. He wondered that Carnahan didn't get out of the car himself most times, but sent himself in alone. After all, wasn't yer man supposed to be a great one among the Travelling people? But in a way, Jack was glad of the time alone with his own, and something kept him from ever telling them who the man was in the car.

The great man was gone for a long time at the stop in Wexford. Normally, Jack might have taken out his squeeze box and busked for a time to earn a few coins, but Carnahan had locked the squeeze box in the car. Jack threw stones at things for a while. He was very good at throwing stones and could hit what he was aiming at with great strength and accuracy. When he was small and the family still travelled, he brought down birds or hares for the pot with his throwing. He was throwing rocks into the bay, trying to throw them farther and farther out to improve his arm, when he saw the swans land.

"Jack, lad, you must come away," Princess Nuala said.

"Come away where?" he asked.

"Away from that awful man. He's not at all what he appears."

Jack walked to the edge of the water and hunkered down, leaning out over the bank to whisper to the swan, "I'm not a fool, you know. He's a terrorist, I know that. But he's helping me look for me mam."

"He's no such of a thing, lad," said one of the brother swans, he didn't know which; he couldn't tell them apart as yet. "He's a murderer. The worst murderer in the history of this land. Worse than all your British soldiers. Worse than your landlords. Worse than the famine. He's not a man, that one. He's a bloody nightmare. You must get away from him."

Jack looked over his shoulder. Carnahan was walking toward the car. He was throwing crisps to some crows. "He doesn't seem so bad when you get to know him, but he makes me nervous, I'll admit."

"Jack, back in the car," Carnahan said. "Time to hit the road again. Some friends of mine think they saw your mum."

Jack looked toward the swans, but they were already airborne.

What the swans had told him wasn't exactly concrete. Not that he disregarded it. But if Carnahan knew where his mother was, Jack didn't dare cross him, did he? So he climbed back in the car. Carnahan drove slowly. Up ahead of them, a flock of crows flew down the highway, then turned left. Carnahan braked suddenly and turned left too. When the crows swooped in another direction, Carnahan followed as well.

While not exactly a wild-goose chase, the situation had its comic side. Jack decided he'd laugh once they'd got Mam back.

CHAPTER 23

Felicity scooped up Puss, and the two of them watched Sno ride away on the brown-and-white spotted horse. "I suppose she does have to do these things herself," Felicity says. "But it's frustrating not to be in the thick of it."

Puss was about to make a catty response when a taxi drove up the lane, stopped and honked. "You order a taxi, Missus? Get in, me meter's runnin'."

Felicity started to say there was some mistake, and then she looked at the driver more closely. She knew that husky voice, the cocky angle of that head, the pugnacious set of that jaw and the tilt at which that eyepatch was worn. This man had been around as long as the godmothers. "Cormac?"

" 'Lo, Dame Felicity. I'm your answer to young Sno's wish."

"But she's already got an answer—the horse is carrying her where she wishes to go."

"Ah, but that wasn't the transportation wish did that. That was the talking to animals wish. So since she's gone, and doubtless wishes you were with her, as who wouldn't, I ask you, no sense letting a come-true go to waste, is there?"

"That's very good of you, Cormac. Will the fare be much to go to Clonmel or thereabouts?" she asked facetiously. Cormac was still so much the warrior, after all these years, that he needed teasing at times to leaven his mood. He had a very good sense of humor actually, but he forgot about it sometimes in his single-minded concentration on his mission of the moment.

"You can bet it would be if the meter was running. But it's my cab and I fancy a drive in the country today instead of braving Dublin traffic for a quid here and there. So Clonmel it is."

*   *   *

Hearing the squat orange car wheeze to a halt, Cunla peered around the stone pillar and down the road and saw the women climbing out of it. That was a funny car indeed, with no iron in it at all, and very easy for Cunla to fix. Give him enough time and he'd make a proper jack-o-lantern of the pumpkin-colored vehicle, he thought with a gleeful chuckle. They'd have to stay home now, the hussies. Home to be victim to his bedevilment.

But no, the young one was talking to that nosy spotty horse Cunla had seen in the pasture. No sooner was she gone than a taxicab drove up and the silver-haired one was away again too. At least they'd been good enough to leave a fresh-up-from-the-country new housekeeper to entertain a poor lonely house spirit. Now Cunla would just have to see how good the woman's nerves were.

*   *   *

The kittens Joe Dunny had rescued were lovely, though very young, Grania thought, as she played with them in front of Joe's fire while he biked down to the little market near the old abbey to pick up a few things for them to eat.

The mother cat basked in Grania's admiration. She took time out from nursing the kittens only to wobble upright and totter to her bowl to eat voraciously, before flopping back down to let her babies suckle once more. There were four of them. A wee red one, a calico like its ma, and two black-and-white, one a tuxedo cat and one with a saddle on its back.

Grania felt as if she could finally draw a breath. Joe Dunny was a good man, she could tell. He reminded her of her da a bit and her favorite uncle, the one who teased her only a little. When the world had been particularly harsh on her, Uncle Dermot would find a lamb for her to feed or an old dog to coax into eating. Her father's cure had been planting things. He'd listened better than her uncle had, although he couldn't bear her crying. He was apt to cry along with her.

Joe's matter-of-fact going about his business had almost convinced her that her danger was all in her imagination. If her aunt truly thought Grania was kidnapped, why would she send anyone after her, hating her as she did? But though Grania's head asked what could possibly happen in a peaceful place like this, her sixth sense kept her looking toward the windows, listening, waiting, watching for something . . . something.

A sharp rap at the kitchen door nearly made her jump out of her skin. Very carefully she rose and tiptoed to the window of the tiny kitchen and peered out—only to be peered back at by an extremely ragged, skinny and dirty old woman.

The old woman rapped louder. She looked like death warmed over, but she didn't look like doom. Grania opened the door a crack. The mother cat began meowing in a demanding way. Grania could hardly believe the cat was so jealous that her attention was diverted away from her kittens.

"Please, Missus, have ya got a bit of bread to spare? I'm so very hongry, y'see. I've not had a bite to ate in days."

"It's not my house," Grania said fearfully. Her aunt would have beaten her for as much as opening the door to a tinker. "The man who owns it will be back soon and he'd have to be the one invitin' you in."

"Oh, I'd not soil your foireside if it comes to that, it's only food I'm after."

Grania hardly felt able to turn away someone as hungry as she had been until a few hours ago. She reached over to the counter and grabbed the half loaf of bread and the apple Joe had left for her. As she turned back to the woman, the wind whipped the door wide, driving rain into the house. The mother cat streaked out past her. Poor thing probably needed to piss.

*   *   *

"Is it that hard you've been workin', Joe, that you need all that food?" Mrs. O'Toole at the market asked.

"I've a guest—my sister Bridget's girl's over from Scotland to see the old place. You know how teenagers love to eat. I'll be havin' to sell off land soon if she keeps eating so."

"Is that so? Well, there was a young girl come by not long ago lookin' for a place to stop. Funny that is. Seems that for a time all the young folk move away and then suddenly there's new ones comin' by."

She was fishing for information with her usual delicacy and subtlety—which was, not much. It didn't help that she had already seen the girl, though, and knew her to be no relative of his own. He had hoped to pass her off as Bridget's girl and keep her safe under that pretense until he could gain her confidence and find out who she was and what was to be done to help her.

He thanked Mrs. O'Toole and placed the groceries in the milk crate he had fastened to the back of his bike. He waited at the corner of the lane leading from the old abbey as a covey of workmen left for the day. Then he pedaled across the lane and down the main road.

He hadn't gone far when he heard a dreadful caterwauling ensuing from somewhere back near the abbey. Perhaps the girl's cat friends were distressed to have returned and found her missing? He'd have to see about taking some milk out to the site. Maybe he could tame a few of them away from the place and keep them as mousers at his house. Otherwise they'd probably be killed. Feral cats in such numbers were not welcome to most farmers.

Rounding the corner into his own lane, he saw a rider outlined in the distance against his field. Another girl—female, anyway—to judge from the braid flopping at her back. Ah, what a time in his life for so many young women to be attracted to him, and him old enough to be a grandfather, he thought with a smile.

The wind blew up in a sudden hammering gust and carried knifing rain on it as he turned off the lane into the kitchen yard. An old woman stood at the kitchen door, talking to his "niece."

He pulled the sacks of groceries from the crate and ran against the wind to the door. The old woman turned and looked at him, her eyes oddly vacant. She was raggedy and soaked with more than the recent rain, skinny and dirty beyond the usual for a beggar woman. She carried some burden in her apron.

He nodded to her and inclined his head to the kitchen. "I see I'm back just in time," he said to the girl, who backed away from the door to permit the two of them to enter. The old woman crossed immediately to the fireside, set down her burden, and began to warm her hands before the fire. "Lass," he said to the girl, "there's another lady ridin' up to the house just now. Would you be puttin' the kettle on and invitin' her in while I go fetch some clean clothes of Mam's for the both of our guests before they catch their deaths?"

The girl looked frightened, and he could hardly blame her. After all, she was apparently trying to hide. And here he had been feeling lonesome from having no company from one year to the next, and all of a sudden had more than he'd seen since his father's wake.

Chapter 24

Journal Entry—Friday, Continued

They're not just kidding when they say Ireland is a hospitable country. I was only going to ask at the farmhouse if they had seen Jack's mom and by the time I got to the door and jumped off Ace's back, a girl about my age had opened the door to invite me in.

Not only that, but the old lady I recognized from the scrying pool as Jack's mam sat warming her hands at the fire and sipping tea. The girl handed me a cup and pointed me toward the fire too. Bobby wasn't too crazy about that, since there was a nest of kittens snuggled near. The girl gave a little shriek and then a giggle as the toad hopped out of my hood and out the door before she shut it behind me.

"Hi," I said to the old lady, hunkering down beside her. "I'm a friend of your son Jack's. He's really worried about you and asked me to help find you."

"Jack?" she asked. "Ah, Jack's a good boy. I'm sure he meant nothin' by it, Missus. He wouldn't do any wrong, my Jack."

"No, ma'am, he's a nice guy. Saved my life just about." I thought it was kind of sad that the first thing she'd think of when I mentioned Jack was to say he was innocent of all charges, but then, that must have been what she'd been used to. And also, I already knew from Jack that she was one leaf short of a shamrock.

The girl came back in the room.

"It was sure nice of you folks to take Jack's mom in," I told her. "He's been really worried about her."

She shrugged and looked confused, then took a seat on the footrest near the kittens who were mewing and teetering around on noodly new legs.

The mewing of new kittens, however, sounds a little different to me since I started understanding animals.

"MaMA! Come back!"

"Where is she?"

"I dunno. I'm blind, I think. At least, my eyes won't open."

"Ow! Get your paw out of my nose!"

I reached over and picked up the one who had its paw in his sister's or brother's face, and scritched its belly. "Help!" it cried. "A giant's got me! Put me down, let me alone. Oh. That feels nice. Like mama licking. That spot over there's kinda itchy."

The man came downstairs carrying a bundle of clothes, which he dropped on the floor. Then he walked outdoors to give us privacy while the girl and I struggled to get the old woman out of her wet things and into the dry clothing. I decided I'd rather die of pneumonia in my own clothes, thanks. It wasn't just that the man's mother wasn't exactly a fashion plate, but I'd need to stay in my jeans and hooded sweatshirt in case I ended up doing any more riding.

"Your dad is really nice to let us both in," I said to the girl while Jack's mom changed.

"He's lovely, isn't he? I wish he *was* my dad."

Right away I could tell, from the way she said it and the way she looked, that this chick was another potential fairy godchild. "So, is your dad, uh, *not* lovely?" I asked. My tone was tactful even if the words weren't quite right. But she was so caught up in her own thing, the tone seemed to be all she picked up on.

"He's dead. My mum too. They died in a car accident and

I lived with my horrible aunt. I think she's coming to kill me.''

"Wow, you too? My stepmother tried to do me in last year.'' I thought of telling her all about it and then decided that maybe she'd think I was making it up, like, to compete with her story the way people do sometimes to try to top each other? I figured she especially would think that if I told her the guy Gerardine hired to do me was out in the yard catching flies even as we spoke. "So, how come she has it in for you? Jealousy?''

"Oh, no. She wouldn't want to be like me. She thinks I'm horrible bold and thick besides. She's turned everyone in the village against me. She was convinced I was going to be an awful tart if I got a chance. Though I guess that doesn't worry her anymore because she's also convinced I met my doom on my sixteenth birthday. I didn't, not then at least, but a poor young soldier I smiled at turned up dead. And she saw me, you see, Mrs. Reilly next door to Aunt Gobnait, she saw me smiling at the soldier. It was just a little smile, you know, but somethin' about the way she was watchin' me, well, I knew she'd be makin' somethin' hidjis of it, somethin' that would make my aunt's doom come true. So I ran.

"Later on, I felt a total nutter for running off like that, and I probably would have returned home but then I saw my picture in the paper the next morning and saw where the soldier was dead. It was awful! He was so young and he was just lonely and all we did was smile at each other.''

"She's jealous all right," I said.

Jack's mother patted the girl on the cheek as she helped the old lady into a cardigan sweater. "Such a lovely little lass," she said. And she was, or would have been with a shampoo and soap and water in the right spots. Good bones, nice skin, if you didn't count the scratches on her arms and face, but no acne or anything, genuine blonde hair that a hairdresser never touched, I swear to God, in a thick braid down her back, big blue eyes and the kind of mouth lots of women try to get with collagen injections. If she didn't grow up to be a tart, it wouldn't be for lack of opportunity. And Gerardine's agent would be crazy about her.

"We need to compare life stories," I told her. "My name's Sno Quantrill, what's yours?"

"Grania," she said. "Grania O'Malley."

"Like the pirate?"

"She was an ancestress."

"How did you happen to come here? Is the man a relative?"

"No, he's just a kind farmer who took me in. His name's Joe Dunny and this is his farm. Seems to make a habit of taking in strays—the cat and her kittens, me, the old lady. You. Why are you here?"

"I came looking for her," I said, nodding to Jack's mother, who had wandered off into the kitchen and seemed to be trying to cook something. The wet apron was still bundled around the bulky object and, in the warmth of the room, it began to stink really bad. I unwound the apron and pulled free a little box shaped like a coffin. A sodden scrap of purple velvet with a crown embroidered in gold came away with the apron.

"Would you look at that," Grania said.

Joe Dunny poked his head in and when he saw that everyone was decent, came over to check out the coffin. From outside came the sound of tires on the dirt lane and then a knock at the kitchen door.

Grania shrank back, her nails going to her mouth.

*   *   *

Jack thought he'd heave, the way Carnahan took the roads in pursuit of the crows. From Wexford to Waterford they fairly flew down the road themselves, then fought with several lorries for right of way on the way to Clonmel. In Clonmel, Carnahan jerked the car onto the road to Cashel that passed the old Templar's castle and the village of Fethard. Through the village and over it the crows flew like a black arrow aimed at the heart of whoever Carnahan was trying to find. Jack knew it could not be his mother. The girl, then. It had to be the girl. He twisted in his seat once or twice to see were the swans following as well but he couldn't tell. Perhaps the birds of the air had drawn up sides the way the people seemed to have done. They did things like that in the old legends. The crows now, they were the birds of the Morrigan, goddess of battle, were they not? He was sure his mother had once told him so. But that was daft, to think that Carnahan had any such mythical motive to following them. Perhaps they were homing crows. Like homing pigeons, only crows. He'd never heard of such a thing, but that didn't mean there wasn't. It was a better explanation than that an ancient war goddess had sent perfectly ordinary birds to guide this nutter to find some poor young one.

Which was almost as daft an idea as that he had been warned against the man by the talking, singing, great-great-plus-grandchildren of Lir. So far as he could remember, the children of Lir and of the Morrigan never had anything to do with each other, but there was a first time for everything, wasn't there?

At last, around twilight, Carnahan jerked to a stop outside a little market. The crows had sailed a bit further on, but seemed to be circling an old chimney and caved-in rooftop Jack could barely see sticking up above the trees in back of the shop. The market looked as if the people were getting ready to close up but Carnahan pointed first to it, then to the chimney and the crows.

"Go ask inside what's in that place over there, Jack," he said. "Show them the picture of the girl."

Jack didn't want to, but he did want to get out of the car. He wanted as far from it as he could go. "What if they don't serve Travellers in there?" he asked.

"Oh, they will. One way or another," Carnahan said with a smile that showed his long side teeth. He looked like a vicious dog when he did that.

Jack left the car and went inside the market. The lady behind the counter gave him a suspicious look, but she didn't say anything. "Excuse me, Missus, but what would that ould place be over there with the chimney stickin' up and the roof all hoved in?" he asked.

"An old house, and what else would it be?" she asked.

"But if you're thinkin' to halt there, I'd forget it. Someone else has already gone that way and there's workers in there every day, restoring the property next to it to be a farriery school."

"That person who was inquirin'," he said, his stomach churning again as he dug out the picture of the girl. "It wouldn't be this girl here, would it, now?"

"What's she to you?" the woman said, now really suspicious.

"She's nothin' to me, nothin' at all."

"What's goin' on here now, young man? First there was the girl, and then there was Joe Dunny from down the road buyin' extra groceries as he claimed for his niece, though none of his family ever comes to visit anymore, and then there's a Dublin taxicab draw up with a fine-lookin' lady askin' after the same house as yourself. I've given all the information I intend to give until I get some meself."

Jack licked his lips. In his experience, whatever he said he'd be blamed, but he leaned forward and said in a low voice. "The truth is, Missus, I don't know about none of these people. Me mam disappeared and this bloke offered to drive me around to help find her but he says he's lookin' for the girl in the picture. Says she's his sister. But between you and me, I don't think so. I think he's after her, like, chasin' 'er, though don't ask me how come. Please, ma'am, where does this Joe Dunny live? Maybe I can steer Carnahan away from him or warn the girl somehow."

"The next lane up, you keep on till you get to the house, but don't you go lookin' for handouts. Joe's poor as dirt, he is." She took out her reading glasses, held the picture away from her, and squinted at it through her glasses. "Looks a bit familiar, somehow. Who is she?"

Jack shrugged. "He's not even told me her name. I've just been told to look for her at every place I stop to ask after me mam. If you see Mam, Missus, please help her. She's not right in the head—oh, not that she'd harm a soul," he said, seeing the alarm deepen on the woman's face, "but she's confused like."

The woman backed further away from him and said a bit too firmly, "That's as may be, but I haven't seen her. Get away with you now. It's time for me to be closin'. And I'd stay off that property if I was you. That American lady what owns it won't be likin' trespassers."

Jack shrugged. "It's not up to me, Missus. I expect yer man out there will insist on havin' a look."

The horn sounded and Jack headed for the door, the woman close on his heels to slam it behind him. The light was fading ever more rapidly and he could just make out a cluster of crows perched on the chimney of the distant house.

Carnahan'd stay on the trail of those crows no matter what, Jack thought. They drove down the bumpy lane, into the abbey yard where building machines were parked among the debris of construction in progress. "I'm going to go look in there. Stay back and don't come until I call you," Carnahan said, and he tried to be careful about it but Jack saw that he was pulling a gun from under the seat.

"Oh, never mind me," Jack told him, or rather, told his back, for the man was already striding up the hill. "I'll just stay down here and look for scrap." Which was no doubt what Carnahan would expect of his tinker accomplice.

But as soon as the man was out of sight, Jack hightailed it into the woods and paralleled the road until he found the farm lane that he hoped was the one leading to Dunny's house.

CHAPTER 25

Joe Dunny was having an unusually sociable day for himself. First the cat and kittens, then the girl, then the old woman and the other beautiful young girl, as dark as the first one was light, riding on a tinker pony and carrying a toad. Now, before he could answer the new knock at his door, the old tinker woman opened it wide. The wind and rain blew in yet another woman, this one with silvery hair curling where the rain had wet the tendrils not protected by a jaunty cap. Like a landed ladyship, she wore heathery tweeds, only slightly damp with the rain—like all good handwoven woolens, they retained enough lanolin to repel brief exposure to the elements. She took off the hat of her head and shook it outside, and with the other hand pushed at the unruly curls. "Hello, Mrs. Daly darlin'," she greeted the old lady in a cheerful voice. "Are you quite all right after your long journey?"

"I'm desperate tired and hongry, Missus, if you could spare a few pence," the old woman whined, slipping automatically into her beggar's Cant.

Joe found himself apologizing for the slander to his hospitality. "She was wet and cold and I thought we'd best get her dry before we fixed supper. I'm just back from doing the marketing."

The blondie girl—Grania, she said her name was—said, "I'll just put on the kettle, shall I, Mr. Dunny? Cuppa, Missus?" she asked the elegant newcomer.

"Felicity!" the dark girl, who had called herself Sno, cried from the fireside. "You made it!"

"Your second wish—er, your alternative arrangements conveniently reached fulfillment just in time to get us here. There's a taxi outside, but I'm sure we can wait until Mrs. Daly has had a bit of sustenance. And I wouldn't mind something myself."

"Me neither. It's been a long ride, though it would have been a lot longer on any horse other than Ace. Did you know about Ace, Felicity?"

"Know? I don't believe so, but you can tell me all about it later. You might introduce me to our host and hostess." She gave Joe a bright smile that made him think of his mam, his favorite teacher, and every other female who had ever had the slightest regard for him. Her eyes were a bit odd—gray-blue, but they picked up the colors around them and reflected them back. Perhaps the poor thing had some sort of cataracts.

"This is Joe Dunny, Felicity."

"Felicity Fortune, Mr. Dunny," she said and extended her fingers. He didn't know whether to shake them or kiss them and felt embarrassingly like tugging his forelock. He touched her hand and made a wee bow over it, in compromise. He was not an obsequious man by any means, but this was a real lady, not like your poor befuddled, self-involved, scandal-fodder of an English gentility, but the genuine article, and Irish to boot he could tell by the face of her.

Sno was continuing. "Mr. Dunny owns this place. He found Grania here and took in the kittens and just brought Jack's mom in out of the rain too. And this is Grania. She has an aunt who sounds a lot like Gerardine. We gotta do something for her."

Grania looked wary of this last assertion, but passed the cups around. Everyone was preparing to troop back across the lino to the fire again when yet another person, this one wet, sweaty, and breathing hard, burst in through the door.

"Is it O'Connell Street in Dublin they're cuttin' through me own kitchen?" Joe wondered aloud, but nobody seemed to hear him.

"Jack!" Sno, cried, running forward to drag the boy further in. "How'd you find out your mom was here?"

"I never did till now, but it's sorry I am to see her here. And you too. All of yez." The young man gave her a brief wild glance and grabbed the old lady. "You have to get out of here, Mam. You know Carnahan? You always thought he'd somethin' to do with Da's death? Well, he brought me and he's up to murder to be sure."

His eyes were dark and hunted, and he flipped the water from his longish dark hair with one hand and said to Grania, "It's you he's after, Miss. I come to warn you, never knowin' me own mam would be here too, in the line of fire as it were."

"Wait," Felicity Fortune said as the boy tried to hustle his mother out the door. Nobody seemed to mind that the rain was pourin' in and all the warmth from the fire was goin' out. The kittens was meowin' their little hearts out, nearly frozen from the wind and rain let in, Joe thought, and he wondered where their mother might be. It was time for him to go do his evening rounds of the fields as well. Everyone turned to face Mrs. Fortune, however, though the boy looked as though he was about to pick the old one up in his arms and bolt with her. "Who is this Carnahan? What does he want?"

"He's one of them terrorists. Mam's never liked him, always s'pected he had somethin' to do with me da's death. And now he wants to kill this girl here. He's a queer one too, daylin' with somethin' dark. Crows led us here. I left him back at an old house but he'll not be far behind. I have it from reliable sources"—and to Sno, the dark girl, he said, "the swans, you know. They flew all the way from Dublin to tell me that he's a murderer of the worst kind. I tell you we must all go now."

"Princess Nuala said so, huh?" Sno said. "Felicity, that's good enough for me. Look, if Grania's his prime target we have to get her away fast. Ace and me can take her back to

headquarters and hide her there. He's real strong. He'll be able
to carry us both.''

"Good plan," Felicity said. "The rest of us shall take the
taxi and lead him a merry chase."

Drugs, Joe Dunny thought. Must be all of them on drugs.
The old woman was daft, he had known that from the first,
but it must be young Grania had been on drugs and now these
other children were as well. Felicity Fortune, for all her la-
dylike looks, must be their pimp—no, that wasn't the word—
dealer. That was it. She was the head of a drug ring, which
was a shame, because he couldn't help feeling nevertheless
that she was a very great lady. Maybe it was the cost of keeping up her ancestral castle drove her to it.

"I'm afraid you must come too, Mr. Dunny," the woman
in question was saying to him.

"Oh, no, Missus. I couldn't do that. Who'd tend the sheep
and them kittens? Their ma's not back yet."

"Nobody's going to tend 'em ever if you're dead, mate,"
the boy said. "But I shouldn't like to think what he'd do to
you to get you to tell where we went."

"Mr. Dunny, once we've reached safety, you can call a
neighbor to come look in on your sheep. And I'll have the
taxi return you as soon as we're sure it's all right to do so."

Joe smiled and shook his head, amazed at how wound up
they could get over their own delusions. "And how would
you know a thing like that, Missus?"

From the dooryard a new voice, melodious and fine, sang
out, "We'll watch for you, farmer. But hurry. Even now, the
Morrigan's thrall is driving toward us, the crows flying van-
guard. Fly! Fly!"

"That's very kind of you, but . . ." Joe said, looking around
the people clogging his door to see four swans among his
chickens. "Beg pardon?"

"Make haste! Make haste!" the swans all cried. It *was* the
swans who cried it. Definitely the swans. Perhaps one of the
girls had slipped something in his tea, but Joe knew for sure
that it was the swans who were speaking.

About the time he adjusted to that a new voice said, "Don't

forget the kittens. I'll stay too and warn my people but I'll not be burdened with the offspring of some irresponsible queen.''

At this speech, Felicity Fortune bent and picked up a gray cat, crooning to it, ''Oh, Puss, you are ever so brave. Come home as soon as you can and stay safe.''

And the cat, pausing to preen as it was petted for just a moment, seemed to say, ''You know how it is, Flitters. A cat's gotta do what a cat's gotta do, and right now I gotta get *down.*''

Another motor roared in the distance, and Felicity Fortune's back straightened and her strange eyes took on the steel of command. ''Quickly but calmly, now. To the taxi. Mr. Dunny, the kittens, sir. One at a time, that's right now.''

Joe scooped up the kittens, holding his hands over them in his coat pockets, and was ushered ahead of the others, without so much as time to close the door properly. They splashed across the half-cobbled dooryard and into the waiting taxi, which now had its motor running. Joe saw that a very rough-looking individual indeed was behind the wheel of the taxi, and as soon as the last door slammed he revved the motor and took off down the lane. About a hundred yards before reaching the highway, a black car came barreling up the lane toward them and the driver swerved just in time to avoid a head-on collision. He did wipe out a couple of birds from the thunderhead of crows scudding just ahead of the bonnet of the black car.

*   *   *

Balor knew as soon as he saw the taxi bumping down the lane toward him that the boy had betrayed him. As the taxi passed and he saw Jack's face against the window in a car crowded with people, he shook his head, smiling indulgently. The boy had done what he himself would have done were their positions reversed and someone else required of him something he was unprepared to deliver. A very normal, human mistake for the lad to make. A very unfortunate choice for him, one that he would have but little time to regret, though Balor was an expert in making that short time seem like an eternity.

He stopped the car in the middle of the lane and leaned out the window. "Follow that cab!" he yelled to the crows. They wouldn't get the joke, of course, though it amused him mightily to be able to use the line from so many gangster films, his favorites. Still, the crows took his meaning and half of them swooped away from the main flock and disappeared down the road.

Balor continued driving up to the farmhouse. He stopped the car and gazed thoughtfully at the house for a moment. It all looked very peaceful. Chickens in the yard, sheep in the meadow, a toad sitting on a stone. Although it did seem disquietingly as if the toad was actually watching him. But that was just his creative imagination, getting the best of him, like. He slowly opened the door, unfastened his seat belt, climbed out and stretched his legs, then walked into the house through the kitchen door. It pleased him to see that they had been so panicked they'd failed to close it properly. The rain was blowing in and the kitchen floor was awash. The kettle was still warm, as was the tea in several cups.

He walked into the parlor. The turf fire was blazing away, and the warmth prompted a fearful stench. The smell seemed to come from a little box. A damp and crumpled piece of purple cloth lay over it. He straightened the cloth. It bore the design of a crown embroidered in gold thread. Curious what some people would keep in their houses, wasn't it? Judging from the dampness, it hadn't been indoors very long. He lifted the lid, and the stench hit him full force. There had been a time when he would have paid no mind to such a thing, have disposed of it without a thought, but since the time when he had met his mistress, he paid better attention. No one would keep such a thing as this stinking up their house for no reason. And the reason couldn't be sentiment. This was an item of power, power that might be of use to him.

He left the box for the moment, and poked around a bit more. In one of the bedrooms he found the skirt and jumper

Grania O'Malley had been wearing when she left her aunt's. The girl was a blonde, and he found long blonde hairs, still damp, in a brush. Very good of whoever lived here to take her in. Something should be done to repay such kindness.

He took the shovel and carefully poured glowing coals from the fire onto the hearth rug. Taking a handful of the paperback books from the shelf by the couch, he fed the pages to the fire until it had a good hold and began to eat into the floor. Meanwhile he lit the curtains with his cigarette lighter.

He picked up the box and its little cover, closed the parlor door, and stopped in the kitchen long enough to turn on the gas, though he didn't light the hob.

Then he opened the door and was smacked in the face by something hard and feathery. "Back in there with you, varlet! Knave! Quisling!" several voices said at once. "What have you stolen now?" Swans. Four of them, though it felt like hundreds. What were they, rabid? They whacked and bit him, his hands, his face, pulled at his hair. One concentrated on the hand holding the box, which made him more determined than ever to hang onto it.

He charged through them, beaten by bones and smothered by wings full of featherbeds. He swung his free hand, clutching the power object with the other. The house was about to blow. He had to break free.

He did, finally, and stumbled to the car with wings and necks and beaks still beating at him. It was with great satisfaction that he slammed the car door on the tip of a wing. The engine turned over and he backed out, just as the bird's companions tore it free of the door and used their wings and bodies to block his view from the windshield and the rear window.

Flames licked out the windows of the house.

He backed toward the field, and for a moment the swan blocking his rear vision flew up to avoid being run over. The scene he saw through the window was incredible. Thousands of shining eyes surging toward him like a candlelit parade. He jerked the gearshift into drive, gunned the engine and took off down the lane. A piece of window frame struck the boot of the car as the house expanded and bloomed into a ball of flame behind him.

CHAPTER 26

"My kittens!" the skinny little calico queen screamed as Joe Dunny's house exploded. She ran straight toward the fire while the rest of the cat horde tore back across the fields. Puss saw her and took a flying leap, pounced on her, rolled her over and slapped her back.

"My kittens are in there!" she screamed. "Let me go!"

Puss asked in her calmest and most matter-of-fact tone, "What kind of eedjit do you think I am, queenie, that I'd not see that the kittens were cared for? The man himself bore them away with him before ever I went looking for you."

"Oh. Look out!" the little queen cried as a piece of burning debris hurtled toward them. Both cats scrambled back into the field with the others.

The chaos was no less in the field.

"What to do? What to do?" Prince Tom was wailing even less attractively than he did when he was courting. "Me royal da's royal carcase has been cremated, far away from the royal boneyard where it needs to be before I can claim me royal crown."

"Yer a royal pain in me noble arse, if you ask me," spat Lord Bronski, all pretense of courtliness blown away with the explosion.

The mother of the kittens hissed at Prince Tom too. "He doesn't seem fit to be King," she complained to Puss.

"He's not, of course," Puss said, pretending to clean the ashes from her fur but actually engaged in the deep contemplation of stratagems. "They never are. Any cat fit to be a ruler would have no business ruling cats, if you take my meaning. We're a bit like the French that way."

About that time six of the youngest, fastest cats could be heard quarreling at the entrance to the lane.

"It's mine, I saw it first!" one screeched.

"No, it's mine!"

"Let's all drag it into the bushes or some of the others will want a share," said the youngest.

"Let . . . me . . . go, you feline savages!" cried an achingly beautiful, human-sounding baritone.

"I told you you should have finished it off," complained the first cat voice again.

"If I hadn't pulled it out of there, we'd have had *roasted* swan, and tartare is much nicer!" said the second.

"Swan?" Puss cried. "Oh, no! Stop!" She ran full tilt to where the four young cats were trying to drag the injured swan down the lane, away from the fire.

Just then three other swans swooped down and began beating the youngsters with their wings. "Let him go!" cried a lovely human soprano.

The other two were singing at the top of their range.

"What's that music?" asked Lord Bronski.

"A swan song. They're singing it for their brother. Lay off, you little hooligans!" Puss said.

The four young cats abandoned their prey and furiously began washing, but their ears were laid back flat on their heads and they were obviously offended to the tips of their tails and whiskers.

"Why did you stop them?" Prince Tom demanded. "Our people need to eat too before they begin their long journeys home. We outnumber the swans. See how tired they look? We can dine royally . . ."

"If you wish to dine, Pretender to the Hibernian Feline

Throne," said the female swan, "and if you wish ever to retrieve your former ruler's remains and finish the procession and thus become King yourself, may I suggest that instead of devouring your allies you instead eat crow?"

"We beat the flock guiding the black car until they fell to the side of the road from sheer exhaustion, but the man they guide still holds a little box with a purple cloth. It seems to me very like the one we saw you carrying outside of Dublin."

"Attack!" the Prince screamed to the other cats. When that failed he screamed instead, "Food! Follow me!" and the other cats surged past the little island of swans, the injured one protected by his brothers, his sister, Puss and the little queen.

"What a fool," the little queen said. "If he hadn't argued so when I told him about the old woman taking the King's coffin into the house, if he hadn't tried to assign blame for leaving it behind instead of following me when I told him, he'd be off on his foolish procession now and I would be with my kittens."

Puss gave a spit, turned to the swans and said, "Can your injured brother fly at all?"

"I don't know," said the lady swan, Princess Nuala she was called, as Puss remembered from past encounters. Ireland being a small country, the animals who were magic in and of themselves rather than as minions (like the crows) generally knew one another, though the horse was a newcomer to Puss. But then, he was a tinker pony and no doubt travelled a lot, and of course, the godmothers had only just moved their headquarters to its current location across from the field the horse was stopping in now.

"I can," said the injured swan, "without all those wild cats weighing me down."

"We'll go slowly, dear," the princess promised.

"Not I," said Puss. "I'm going home to be there when Flitters and Sno return."

"And I'll be with you to comfort poor Joe Dunny and be with my little ones," the queen said.

"In that case," Princess Nuala said, "let us fly."

*   *   *

Balor had felt quite sure of himself when he set out to follow the taxi, even though it zigged and zagged down the back lanes and byways. But then it turned off just as the swans attacked again, this time invading his phalanx of crows, beating black wings from the air with white ones. The crows dispersed without a quarrel or an attempt to reform while the swans dived the windshield, so that all Balor saw was snowy feathers and long necks. "I have the cure for you," he growled, and reached under the seat for his piece.

It kept eluding his hand. He touched something cold and pulled, but it didn't feel quite right. It wriggled. When he yanked it out, he saw why.

"Reedeep," the thing in his hand said. It was a toad. The toad from the rock outside the house. And there was definitely something funny about it.

He stared at it. It stared back. Threatening. The car lurched as the lane turned and it didn't. It plowed into a ditch that the heavy rain had turned into a streambed. The hood struck the stone fence beyond the ditch and popped open with a hiss and steaming of the radiator.

The car wouldn't budge. The doors were stuck in the mud. Balor pushed the button for the windows to open, but they didn't respond. Whatever happened in the crash, the electrical system seemed to be involved.

He flung the toad aside, but it was ready for him and hopped as it was thrown so that it landed uninjured and hopped back into hiding. Damnedest toad he'd ever seen.

Fortunately, this car had access to the trunk through the back seat. He crawled over the front seat, lowered the back one, climbed into the trunk and unlocked it to crawl free.

The swans were nowhere in sight, and the crows were scattered over the last three meadows. He swore and kicked the car, then climbed back in to retrieve his piece and the little wooden coffin.

It was the dead of night by then, and sheets of rain soaked

him in waves. He pulled a slicker out of the trunk and put it on, though it was a bit late for that.

The funny thing was, although the night was full of rain and the sky full of clouds, down the road he saw a patch of night clear enough for him to make out hundreds of shining stars—shooting stars, perhaps, because they seemed to be, no they were definitely, coming his way. But they weren't growing a great deal larger. Not stars, of course. Cat's eyes! Well, he was a good marksman. He'd see how many he could take out before they ran home to their firesides.

He felt the gun under his slicker.

Larger, brighter lights came at him from another direction, then halted a few feet away. "Problem, mate?" an older man asked in a jovial voice.

"Yes," he replied. But not for me, he said to himself.

"Hop in," the man told him, and he did.

By the time he had killed the helpful motorist and left him by the roadside with a Loyalist terrorist trademark carved into his forehead, the cats were nowhere to be seen. He settled himself into the driver's seat and turned the key in the ignition.

The clouds broke over a hunter's moon, large and bright and bloodred, hanging just over the trees. A form flew across it—the outline of a horse in mid-jump, two riders clinging to its back.

Now there was a jumper he could sell for enough money to buy his own dictatorship in some banana republic. That could wait, though. Since tracking Jack and dear little Grania had become impossible, he would simply have to outthink them, which shouldn't be hard.

There'd been a taxi. The O'Malley girl had no money. The boy certainly had no money. And there had been others in the cab with them. Where would he get money? From the girl with the black eyes and her friend with the fancy house, that's who. If he returned there, he'd shake some answers out of someone.

Abandoning the lanes and byways taken by his quarry, he made his way as directly as possible to N76 and connecting motorways.

*   *   *

If ever a house needed a keeper, Felicity Fortune's house was certainly the one. Deirdre had spent the day washing and putting away dishes, taking down and rehanging the curtains properly, coercing the builder into replacing the carpet ruined because he hadn't put the roof on properly, and generally putting assorted bits and pieces to rights. She had a list of questions to ask and details to discuss with Felicity when she returned. The windows rattled like mad, even when there was no wind, and the doors seemed loose on their frames and tapped and knocked so that several times, she went to the door to find nobody there. She refused to consider any further oddity that wasn't architectural. And the dog next door never stopped barking for more than twenty minutes at a time.

She had already decided for the sake of her own peace of mind to pretend to herself that there was no cave leading to Fairyland through the guest room door, that the swimming pool did not show moving pictures on its bottom, and that the room in the attic had unsafe floorboards, which was the only reason the Keep Out sign was up there.

For now she'd relax with a nice cup of tea and a telly that showed two hundred channels, many of them in foreign languages and many featuring the fascinating, if disgusting, antics of people speaking foreign languages and wearing either tight, uncomfortable-looking bits of leather or nothing at all.

The machine in Felicity's office beeped again. The foolish thing kept spitting bits of paper whether anyone was there to read them or not. Actually, the office with its machines and lights and ringings and automatic thisses and thats intimidated her much more than the otherworldly destinations through the guest room.

She was drowsing in the only comfortable chair in the house, the wicker one already liberally endowed about the cushions with microwave popcorn, courtesy of young Sno, when the neighbor's dog, who seemed on the verge of a nervous collapse, started in again.

She jerked awake and looked out in time to see a horse land in the drive, and young Sno and another girl, a blondie lass, dismount. In the time it took her to go from chair to door to let the girls in, four swans also landed. One of them was all in, its feathers broken, disarranged and spotted with blood. The other three carried a tarp between them. Two cats were curled tightly together in the middle of the tarp, their fur standing up with fright.

"Hi, Deirdre, this is Grania," Sno said, as if she'd just got off the bus instead of a flying horse. "Oh, look, it's Puss! Hi, old cat, long time no see. Who're your friends?"

Americans were very strange people. They got used to odd things entirely too quickly. No doubt the result of being constantly bombarded by mass media from the time they were babies.

The other little cat set up a row and the blondie girl, Grania, was down on her knees scooping the cat up. "It's the mother cat from Joe's, Sno. She's missing her kittens."

Then Puss looked up at Deirdre and said, saucy as you please, "My companion and I are fatigued, dear. I trust you have some more of that lovely tuna and a nice saucer for us? Afterwards, if you'll just leave the door to the guest room open, we'll make ourselves at home on the duvet until the others arrive."

"We got any carrots?" Sno asked, heading into the house for the fridge. "Ace here has gone above and beyond the call of duty, flying us back and forth."

Stare as she might, Deirdre could see no wings on the quite ordinary-looking broken color brown-and-white tinker pony licking water from a puddle on the gravel.

"How about them?" she asked, nodding to the swans. "I suppose we could put them up on the pool for the night. The heat's still out, but they're no doubt used to that."

"That would be ever so kind," one of the swans said to her. She shouldn't have been surprised to hear it speak by now. "My brother's had rather a rough time of it."

"I can see that. Shall I call a vet?"

"Perhaps later," Puss said. "There may be a bit of a mass

casualty situation at some point, but I don't think we need to get anyone out of bed over it now." The other cat was still crying, and wobbled to her feet to come to Deirdre and paw at her legs and rub against them. Deirdre reached down to pat her. Puss said impatiently, "I told you the others will be along with your kittens soon. You must rest now and gather your strength for the time being, dear. I have a feeling this isn't over yet."

Sure enough, Deirdre had no more than settled the swans in the swimming pool with a couple of heads of lettuce to eat, fed the cats, the girls, and located carrots and apples for the horse, who nuzzled her hand and repaired to the field across the lane, when a taxi drove up. It disgorged Felicity Fortune, a raggedy-looking tinker woman and her blanket-coated son, and a nice-looking country man who was holding a couple of kittens and weeping.

"What's the matter, Joe?" young Grania asked, putting her hand on his shoulder.

"Did you not hear the explosion and see the fire?" Felicity asked. "We fear that was poor Mr. Dunny's home."

"That would be just like the bastard," the tinker boy muttered angrily.

Felicity Fortune saw well enough that Deirdre didn't approve of such language, at least not before she found out how the lady of the house felt about it. Felicity said, "Deirdre, I'd like you to meet Jack Daly and his mother, Moira Daly, who will be staying with us temporarily, and Joe Dunny, who was kind enough to assist Moira and Grania O'Malley, Sno's young friend, when they became lost near his property."

Jack Daly nodded sullenly, and the old woman looked off into space and talked to herself. Joe Dunny juggled the kittens who were crawling out of his pockets. They were hungry, curious and blind, attempting to make their way to their mother via his jacket. Deirdre plucked them from him. "They're lovely and their mother's been cryin' after them," she said.

"She's here? Already?" Joe asked, looking somewhat dazed.

"She and Puss flew in with the swans a few moments before you arrived. I expect they're sleeping in the guest room that leads to Fairyland by now so I'll just go put the kittens with them and then we'll all have a nice cup of tea before bed, shall we?"

Deirdre examined the kittens in her hands. "This one is marked very much like my poor Popsy," she told Joe as they walked back to the guest room.

"Is she?"

"Yes. One night right after my mother died, I went looking for Popsy and found her with a great many other cats. The next morning every cat in the village was gone. I think they were all doing something together, because I went travelling meself shortly afterwards and on several occasions saw numbers of cats trooping the land. Most uncatlike, I'd have said."

"They ended up in an old house near my property," Joe told her. "The mammy of these couldn't wait for shelter to deliver her kits, and the others left her behind. I found her and brought her home. The talking cat made me bring the kittens with me. She has a good head on her, for a cat."

"I've always found cats to be very sensible on the whole," Deirdre said. Puss opened one eye as they entered the room, but the other cat sat up meowing like mad.

Deirdre, thinking the little animal was wild to see her kittens, set them down by her at once but the cat ignored the kittens and snagged her hand with a paw.

"Would you be after gettin' the light, Mr. Dunny?"

Joe obligingly switched it on and Deirdre took her first really good look at the new cat. It was scrawny rather than fat, raggedy rather than sleek, bony and tattered and fallen on hard times altogether. But the coloring was the same. "Popsy?" she asked it, and it purrrowled mightily and licked her hand, then settled back to feed its babies. She caressed the frail fur-covered skull and kissed her long lost cat on the nose.

"Mr. Dunny, I want to thank you. It's my very own Popsy and her kittens, that you've saved."

He sighed. "It's a good thing I saved somethin' at least."

They left one cat nursing and the other sleeping and returned to the kitchen.

Deirdre poured the tea and most of the people in the kitchen had a few sips. But then Sno said, "I'm all in, folks. Come on, Grania, you can bunk with me."

"Show Mrs. Daly and Jack the beds upstairs, please, Sno, on your way," Felicity suggested.

There was a knock on the door. Deirdre saw that the taxi was still parked outside. The driver stood on the threshold, his cap in hand and said, "I'm needing to use the facility, please, Missus."

Felicity called, "Oh, Cormac! I forgot. Just a moment, Deirdre, I'll show him where it is."

Deirdre thought that very odd that Felicity would show the man to the toilet instead of just tell him, but she didn't take him to the toilet at all. She led him into the main guest room, past the cats, and Deirdre heard the glass door sliding. Felicity called back, "Tell Sno I'm going with Cormac just long enough to pop in and make my report. I won't be that long. Ta!"

Joe Dunny looked mildly quizzical. Deirdre shook her head and said, "A very good woman, as near as I can tell, but she's away with the fairies about half the time. Not in the sense of the old one upstairs either. So tell me, Joe Dunny, did I hear someone say something about your home blowin' up?"

He nodded. "Yeah. Though we didn't go back to check, I've got this awful feelin'. Do you think Mrs. Fortune would mind if I called the gardai station at home to see if they've any news? I'll also be needin' someone to look to the sheep."

"Not at all. I'm sure she wouldn't mind in the slightest. She seems to get lots of correspondence from all manner of unlikely places."

He placed his call and returned with tears running down his face, though his expression was stony. "That's it, then. The house is gone. Not a stick nor stone of it saved. My nearest neighbor, an American lady, has promised to have her tenant care for the sheep until I can return. But how shall I do it? There's nothin' there. All these years . . ."

Deirdre patted his hand and rose to search the cupboard for a bottle of something to take the edge off the pain, but she found only a little Norfolk Punch, which she heated in the microwave oven she'd spent half the morning figuring out how to use.

They toasted. He told her about the farm and his father and his brothers dead at sea and the other in America, his sister in Scotland. He told her how, when he was little, people had said that he was a changeling because he cried constantly. People had urged his parents to do this or that to him to rid themselves of the fairy child and get their own baby back. But his mother had said, "Human or fairy, he's mine to keep, and keep him I shall and I'll murder anyone who dares raise a hand against him." And how for years he thought people had been right, because he never fit in with the community, he dreamed and read and secretly wrote a bit of poetry. How funny that in the end he was the only one to remain and care for his parents. He finished his story without the rambling you might expect of a pub tale, and grew quiet.

And then, for a miracle, he asked about herself and listened while she told him of the long slow death of her mother, her feeling when Popsy left that there was nothing to stay in that house for, and the trip she had made discovering her own country.

"Aren't you a wonder, though?" he said when she'd finished. And he said it admiring, not sarcastic. And why should he not be admiring? The streaks of silver in her hair were highly becoming, she'd been told, and she was not at all unpleasant to look at, even if she had put·on a few pounds. "Think of the sand of ya, taking off on such a journey and you newly bereaved. Me, I stay in the same old place nursin' the sheep as I nursed me da. To think we're so alike and yet so different in the way we'd handle a thing such as bein' orphaned at our great age—excuse me. I don't mean you, of course. But I've felt a thousand years old if a day. Today, with the kittens and the girls and all, has been the first day I haven't thought I might lay down and die at the end of the day."

Deirdre gave him a speculative look. The muscular build

from hard work, the hair white but still thick, the green eyes with their rings of gold around the pupil. A fine-lookin' man altogether and not a one to reach for a bottle at the first crisis, from what she'd seen. "Get on with ya, Joe Dunny. You look to me as if you've a great deal of life left in you yet. Perhaps all of it, if only you've a little help in bringing it out."

He wasn't stupid either. He grinned broadly and winked at her, turning his hand over to clasp the one she'd kept near his own, for comfort. "And would you be knowin' who I could apply to for such help as you describe?" he asked.

CHAPTER 27

Journal Entry—Through the Looking-Glass

I started this entry once before with, "It's finally over and we're home safe." I thought we were then. Felicity was off in Fairyland and Deirdre and Joe Dunny were talking in the kitchen. Puss, Popsy and Popsy's kittens were sleeping in the guest room and the swans were recooping in the swimming pool while Jack tried to sleep through his mother's babbling upstairs.

Grania and I talked for another hour or so until she fell asleep but me, I couldn't quite close my eyes. Something, someone was missing. It's like having a splinter and all of a sudden you knock it loose and you miss it, you know?

By midnight it was blowing a gale, shucking the slate tiles off the roof like corn kernels and crashing them onto the gravel. The wind was actually shrieking, with the little dog next door howling a feeble harmony. I hadn't noticed if the O'Connors were home or not.

I started worrying about Ace and hoped he wouldn't try any more feats of aerodynamic impossibility in this storm. I was afraid he'd blow clear to Oz like the Wizard in his balloon. Part of me said, Ace is an Irish horse, he's been in storms like this before. But another part of me was afraid maybe we'd worn him out with all that flying. Not that he'd looked worn out. He'd actually seemed friskier and more coltish when we finished than he had when we began.

Then I realized that it was another critter that was really bothering me. Bobby. Old Toad-face hadn't made it home with everybody else. Well, it was quite a hop. Maybe he was in Felicity's pocket all along and was just sleeping or something so I hadn't seen him, but just in case, I propped my window open a crack so he could come in if he wanted to, the little slimeball. The cats could use it to go in and out and do cat things too, I thought. It made me kind of nervous, having an open window with all that wind pounding at the house, but the window opened in such a way that it wouldn't catch on a gust and fly open and break.

I went back to bed, wishing Felicity would return from Fairyland, then thought maybe I should check. What if she had come back and and I hadn't heard the sliding door because I was in the bathroom or talking?

So I walked in my stocking feet down to the office. I was wearing leggings to bed with heavy socks and a sweatshirt. It wasn't really cold under the duvet but I got chilly when I had to get up and use the john. I'd loaned Grania a similar outfit to sleep in but either her bladder was bigger than mine or she needed to sleep worse than I did.

The office was dark when I got there, except for the little lights twinkling like mini-Christmas lights, red and green and clear. There was a long streamer of fax paper dragging across the floor and I turned on the overhead to read it. Then all of a sudden the lights were gone as if someone had put them out with a bucket of water.

I left the office and padded toward the kitchen where Joe and Deirdre were hunting for candles and fuse boxes like this was any normal night.

As I passed by the guest room, my leg was snared by a claw. "Please be kind enough to open the door into the hill," Puss said in a voice that brooked no argument. "I don't care for this wind and I heard the power go out and it didn't seem natural to me. I'm going to fetch Felicity."

I did as she asked and then whispered to Popsy, "Maybe you and the kids would be better off *under* the bed for now, huh?" and moved them.

Popsy purred at me but didn't say anything.

It was getting colder by the minute, since the heat was electric except for the kitchen fire and the big fireplace in the living room.

I jogged back to my room to grab the flashlight from my bedside stand. Grania was sitting up rubbing her eyes. "What's the matter?"

"Power outage," I said.

She groaned and sighed. "Not an unusual sort of thing in this weather, surely?"

"No, but indulge me. I'm feeling paranoid."

She sat up. "Yeah. Me too." She flipped the covers off herself and shivered.

Just then something moved at the window and the voice of the wart-prince himself croaked, "What the hell's wrong with you, leaving a window open when that guy's out there hunting for your heads?"

Grania shrieked and I jumped back three feet. When my heart stopped thumping in my tonsils I shined the light on the toad.

"Close it," he said. "That guy's prowling around outside looking for a way in right now."

I hesitated just a moment, afraid a hand would come out of the dark and grab me like they always do in the horror movies. The windows were black distorted mirrors running with bright worms of water. I couldn't see a damned thing. It could have been another dimension out there, a sharp dropoff to nothing, and we'd never have known the difference. I saw no lights across the fields stretching in back of the house. There weren't many ordinarily, only one or two, but now there was nothing but blackness.

I grabbed the window latch like it was a snake, pulled it and latched it tight. Like a little glass was going to bother that nut if he decided to come in and get me. Just for good measure I drew the curtains, then worried about what they'd hide from *me*. I realized I'd feel much better if we were totally away from the windows.

"I'm gonna go check on the swans," I told Grania. "Why don't you go see how Jack and his mom are doing?"

"Right," she said and we were both in such a hurry that we ran into each other trying to go through the door at the same time.

As Grania bounded up the steps, I heard the door slide in the guest room and saw the glow of a candlelight and heard Joe and Deirdre murmuring to each other. I ran in just as Deirdre was about to step through the sliding doors and into the hill.

"No! Wait! You can't go in there," I told her.

"And why not, pray? You and Felicity did and are none the worse," she said. "I need to tell her she's wanted before her house ends up like poor Joe's."

"Puss has gone for her already. And you can't go through there because, well, because you can't. When Felicity and I go through, we've got protection but if you go without it you'll age seven years even if you're only there an hour. Felicity explained it to me."

Deirdre jumped back and held onto Joe for dear life. I stepped into the dark hallway, lit only by flashes of lightning through the windows, and down to the end where the door to the yew walk led to the pool. I really didn't want to leave the safety of the main part of the house and the other people, but with no means of escape, the swans would be sitting ducks.

The door was a little ajar and when I opened it, I caught my breath as I saw at the end of the black yew tunnel a man's figure outlined against the open doorway to the pool.

The man twisted to look at me and said in Jack's voice, "They're gone. He's got them, the bastard."

"The guy you warned us about? Maybe. But what I don't get is how he found us."

"I brought him here," Jack said miserably. "When I was lookin' for you to help me find Mam again, before I knew what he was. He had a high old time lookin' in here."

I joined him, staring into the empty poolroom and out

through the open glass doors where the wind rippled the un-covered water, its vacant surface holding nothing but the neon reflection of the lightning.

For a moment the wind was quiet enough that I thought I heard what could have either been a sob or a low chuckle, and then a shout from back inside the house.

Turning toward the shout, I saw a little lick of flames dart up at the far end of the yew hedge. I grabbed Jack and bolted for the door to the house. Once we were through I slammed it after us and threw the lock. Locking the barn door after the horses got out, Grandma would have said.

As wet as the weather was, the fire wouldn't do much dam-age to that sopping yew hedge and the house and poolroom are both made of cinder block with slate shingle roofs. I watch TV. I watch movies. I know a diversionary tactic when I see one.

Jack was down the hall ahead of me, Grania leaning over the stair railing. "Your mam, Jack, she's gone. I saw the tail of her disappear through that door that says Keep Out but when I looked in there, I couldn't see a thing. Deirdre and Joe are up there with the light now."

I followed as fast as I could but the lightning stopped flash-ing as I groped my way up the steps and I felt my sock squish against something. It took no genius to figure out it was my former would-be assassin.

"Hey, watch it," he croaked.

"You're lucky I had only my socks on," I said, picking him up and carrying him so I wouldn't step on him again and probably trip and fall down the whole flight of steps. Just then I heard the crash of breaking glass from below and a scuffling and a cry from the room where Jack and his mother had been.

As I swung around the top of the steps, Grania's foot dis-appeared through the forbidden door. "Hey, I don't think we should do this," I said, but realized that Jack and Joe and Deirdre must already be ahead of Grania since I didn't see any sign of them or their light. As I went through the door myself I heard the sound of footsteps in the hall.

The inside of the room beyond was dark save for a sliver

of light way far down at the end, farther down than I thought a room at the top of the house could stretch. It was another door. Grania must be following the others, I figured, so I headed for the light. The door was slowly closing, but I grabbed it just before it swung shut.

It was very quiet up here. I heard a foot creak on the first tread of the stair. Then, toad in hand, I stepped through the door.

The light was a little better on the other side. I hadn't realized in the storm that dawn was so near, but I could see the coraly crimson of the sun trying to rise through the ceiling of leaves high above us.

"Hey," Bobby said. "Where is everybody?"

"Shhh," I told him, not wanting whoever was on the other side of the door to hear us and follow. They had to be close by. I looked back anxiously toward the door. It wasn't there anymore. Stretching back as far as I could see was a little path through the giant trees, a path paved with moss, small white flowers like the ones in Faerie, and fallen leaves.

Ahead were more trees. I walked and walked, putting as many trees between me and where I'd come in as I could, in case our uninvited visitor found the door I'd come through. The path was clear but with all the little soft things underneath, my footsteps were almost silent. The rustling trees, the slight wind teasing my sweatshirt, the toad making little nervous "reedeep" noises.

An owl hooted and I dropped the toad.

"Gee, Toto—" Bobby began.

"Don't," I said.

"You don't think this could be the top of the hill the sliding door leads into, do you?"

"Nope. That's just another field. I'm sort of afraid we may have taken the backdoor-emergency-exit into Fairyland. The trees and the flowers are the same."

"And the climate and time of day took a sudden change," he said. "Lift me up again. You don't have a pocket in that outfit, do you? I think we'd better stick together here."

"Why? You afraid some puckering princess will make you marry her?"

"Very funny. Wait. Listen. Hear that?"

"What?"

"That. Crying. Somebody's crying."

I checked but it wasn't me. It didn't sound like Jack, who might be crying if something had happened to his mother. It sounded like a woman. Grania, maybe, crying in sympathy? But no, this sounded like someone had the blues bad, sobbing, choking, and making a horrible reverberating sound like feedback when the monitors are turned up too loud.

"That's keening is what that is," Bobby said.

"What? How can you tell?"

"I go to a lot of horror flicks, okay? And you know what always keens, especially in Ireland? Banshees."

"Right."

"No, I'm serious. I read up on them. If you find one crying over your dirty laundry, it means you're gonna die. I've kinda wondered if some of my targets of the Irish persuasion might not have, you know, seen one before ..."

"Well, I didn't see any ghostly dry cleaners before you tried to snuff me and I'm part Irish. But I'm also part Indian and for us it's owls calling our names and that one back there definitely said, 'Whoo Whoo,' not 'Sno Sno.' So let's see whoo it is who's crying."

He huddled close to my ear, like a pet parakeet, as we walked further and further from where we'd entered.

The longer we walked, the louder the noise got. The more human and less bansheelike it sounded too, and after a while we came to a clearing.

We were both, I'm sure, relieved to see that there was no seaside, lake, stream, river, pool or twenty-four-hour laundromat of the sort where a banshee might like to hang out. Instead, the clearing was filled with a hill that looked as if it might have been man-made.

A low grave-shaped mound, definitely man-made, crowned the hill. It was covered with little plants that made it smell like The Body Shop, all herbaly smells, sweet, savory, spicy, minty and something a little like Italian food. That reminded me that we hadn't had much to eat back in the house and that if this were an annex of Fairyland, it wouldn't be safe eating anything here, a detail I hadn't had time to warn the others about.

The source of the sobbing was this woman who was stretched across the grave.

"I admit she doesn't *look* like a banshee," Bobby said.

"No, she looks more like one of the ladies in the ballads who are lying on their sweetheart's grave for a twelvemonth and a day, alas."

She heard us then and looked up, and I about fainted with relief. Her eyes reflected the sunrise, and the long pale hair looked platinum blonde instead of silver, and the light made her look younger, but I ran up the hill to throw my arms around her, I was so glad to see her.

"Felicity! What are you doing here?"

CHAPTER 28

"I am mourning my brother, so lately slain by my father," she said, though not in those words exactly. She was talking some other language that sounded something like the little bit of Gaelic I'd heard in this country so far and also something like the Old English they use in the Chaucer audios at school. The same kind of Scandinavian lilt to it, like you hear from all the Norwegian sailors in Ballard. But I understood her any-way. So did the toad, apparently. "And as you are one of the Folk of the Air, I beg you to help me gather my poor Miach's legacy, that its healing powers not be lost to mankind."

I had climbed the hill to give the woman I thought was my mentor a hug and now I looked down at the grave. The little herbs grew in the perfect picture of a man, muscle definition, facial features and all. "Wow," I said. "I'm sorry. I didn't know you had a brother, Felicity. Did you do this grave dec-oration yourself? It's really cool, I mean, as that kinda thing goes. What are these little plants?"

"They are the herbs my brother alone knew how to use to heal the ills of mankind, before our father slew him in his jealousy."

"I'm really sorry. I'm from a dysfunctional family myself." I sat down beside her. I could see now that though this woman looked like Felicity and her voice was even a little like Felicity's, she wasn't. She wore a long dress of gray natural-sheep colored wool held together at the shoulders with some bronze pins the size of softballs and she had a matching crescent-moon necklace. All her jewelry looked like it came from a museum shop to me. It was tempting to treat her as if she wasn't real, but someone in a play or maybe in a Society for Creative Anachronism event, except that she was clearly in a lot of pain. Her face was as shocky and numb as Trip-Wire's when he's having a flashback, and she'd say three or four coherent things and then her voice would break with a little sob. "Do you want to talk about it?"

"I thought the whole Island knew of it! How my father the King's physician tried to cure Nuada when his hand was struck off by replacing the hand with a silver one. My brother Miach has long outstripped our father in the healing arts but because his methods differ from my father's, his knowledge of herbs and the spells that can speed the healing much greater, our father called it evil sorcery and tried to forbid it."

"Too bad your brother couldn't live where I do," I told her. "Seattle's pretty accepting of alternative medicine."

She went on as if she hadn't heard me, reliving her brother's last days. The longer she spoke, the more I realized I knew her story already, from reading the myth cycle. "Miach grafted Nuada's original arm back onto its stump, with all movement restored. He labored for many hours him but at last Nuada was cured, and could resume kingship. But father was so jealous, so very jealous, that he was determined to kill Miach. He tried three times and each time but the last, Miach, being such a great physician, was able to heal his own wounds. At last when my father spilled his brains out on the floor, even Miach's art could not save him. And so we buried him and then came the insane plan to send my other brother Cian to court the daughter of Balor of the Evil Eye!" Her hand softly touched the image of her brother rendered in herbs. "And what you see here is that even from the grave Miach would heal us. If only I collect these herbs in their proper order, whatever harm befalls Cian in the giant's house, I can cure him."

Even though I'd read the story in the book, it was different hearing it from her—the difference between reading about other people getting kidnapped and getting kidnapped myself. "Aren't you afraid of your father?" I asked. Keep her talking, I thought. Who else in this time is ever going to let her work her grief out by talking it through?

"I am only Airmed, his daughter, to be bartered off for what lands or power he would possess, but still I would have the fruits of Miach's skill to protect me and mine," she said. "Help me gather."

I did and tried to remember the name and function of each one as she recited them while we laid them out on her cloak. I have a pretty good memory, but I wished I had a pen and paper because there were over three hundred.

We just about had them all sorted and the shape of Miach laid out on Airmed's cloak when there was an angry shout, by which I gathered the Doctor Was In as a big white-bearded man in a swirling cloak came running toward us, straight up the hill. This had to be Dian Cecht, Airmed and Miach's father, the physician who killed his own son out of professional jealousy. He didn't say a word but grabbed Airmed's cloak and shook it so that the herbs went flying everywhere. Then, without a word to me, he grabbed his daughter by the hair and dragged her back down the hill.

"Hey, you, cut that out!" I yelled and ran down the hill after them, taking a flying leap at the learned doctor, fully prepared to beat on him until he let go of his daughter's hair. I don't care how many silver arms you make or babies you deliver, nobody's got a right to kill their kids or treat them like that. And he wasn't getting away with it while I was there.

But as I ran a mist sprang up at my feet and I overshot Airmed and her father, or so I thought, because when I turned, they weren't there anymore. There was only a wall of the mist as high as the lowest leaves of the trees.

"If I still had hands I'd applaud you in your infinite political correctitude," Bobby croaked from the ground. "But as it is,

I'd just like to remind you there are two of us here, your vision is bound to be impaired, and I am underfoot.''

I picked him up a little roughly, because I was still steaming. Apparently they gave women a certain amount of status back then, let them own land and have professions and so forth, but they still pushed them around when they thought they could get away with it. It might be history but it teed me off.

We kept walking through the mist, it didn't seem very long, but the sun never came up. It was like the time Mom and I flew with Raydir to Australia and chased the sunrise the whole way—it didn't get any closer to day for the whole trip. Always sunrise. Also, there was a beat to the air in here, like a big heartbeat, and a little breeze that seemed like breath. The rustling in the grass and trees sounded as if someone was moving in the mist beside us, but I couldn't see anything for the grayness. I thought it might have been Jack, Deirdre, Joe, Grania or even Mrs. Daly fumbling along beside us but surely they were in deeper than we were by now? Only one person had any catching up to do. Bobby and I both shut up, without talking about it. And whatever was with us in the mist seemed to pass us and leave.

Pretty soon the mist began to smell like smoke, nasty smoke. Then a huge heart of orange flame showed me that part of what I'd mistaken for sunrise was an enormous fire. By its light I saw it was set next to a giant statue—no, idol. It was an idol. An idol of a dragon. Men were feeding the fire and when I finally made out what they were feeding it I was glad I hadn't eaten very much or I'd have barfed. Arms, legs, halves of torsos, just big chunks of flesh. And piled around the dragon idol were all these heads, hair and rivulets of dark blood indistinguishable in the fitful firelight. Ugh. I'm not going to go into any more detail. It was sickening.

A tower had been erected in front of the dragon idol. Not a pretty tower or a quaint tower or a round tower or a square tower or one of those Martello towers you see in Dublin. This was a wooden tower, made of logs, still with bark on them, even leaves in some case. Ropes and wooden pulleys and levers and gears were prominent architectural features of the structure. There was a stump at the top, like a seat, and what looked like a flagpole.

"Be careful or I'm going to spew all over you," the toad said in my ear. "These people did real sloppy work, didn't they? In my professional opinion that is."

"They went into battle to defend themselves and their land and families, toad, not because some sleazeball drug dealer or jealousy-crazed, over-the-hill supermodel paid them to kill unarmed people."

"Okay, okay, take it easy. Just a little gallows humor there. Watch out. You were about to step in a disembowelment."

I was. What with the smoke and fumes from the horrible bonfire, my eyes were tearing. Well, also I was crying. I thought again about Doc and the vets, if it was anything like this for them. It could have been one of them I was about to step in. My own skin was crawling. I kept telling myself this was some sort of diorama, some holographic TV historical drama, and I didn't know anybody there.

Then I saw Jack being led out by a band of warriors, clapping him on the back and pushing him forward, shouting things. Encouraging things, I think, like at a football game. Ace the flying horse was waiting for him, except that he had a mane halfway to the ground and a tail to match. A bit overpowering on such a little horse, I thought. Then Jack saw me. "*Jay*ney Mack, but you took your time! I'm sorry about Nuada and your sisters, but can you not do some sort of spell for me?"

"Spell?" I asked.

"Look down," croaked the toad. I did. I was wearing a bloodstained red cape and armor over my sweatshirt and leggings, and my hair had grown ass-length in a matter of minutes.

"Well, what's a war witch for if not a victory spell? Not that it did a great deal of good for poor Nuada. I wish they hadn't hoisted his silver arm to the top of the tower givin' us the bird like that . . ."

"I thought it was a flagpole," I said, but looking back, I saw that the star on top of that gruesome Christmas tree of a tower was actually a silver arm, the middle finger of its hand raised in a gesture that was very familiar and a lot older than I'd thought.

Jack was easier to look at. He was kinda cute without the blanket coat. Bronze and multiple tattoos became him.

"So, I suppose an incantation before I go into battle with Balor and the Eye of Death is out of the question, eh?"

"As if it would do any good," I said. "But—uh—break a leg. Oops, sorry. That wasn't appropriate. I mean, give 'em hell, keep your powder dry, whatever."

"Some war witch," said the toad. "Look, kids, I'm a professional. You shouldn't try what I'm going to tell you at home without expert guidance but since our boy here doesn't have any choice, he'd better take me along as advisor."

Jack was sweating despite his lack of clothing and the chill of the morning. "I'll take whatever help I can get," he said. I handed Bobby over to him.

"Now then, what have we got for equipment?" Bobby asked.

"This sword," Jack said. "It's called the Answerer. No man can survive a wound from it. But I don't think I'll get close enough to try it."

"Maybe we can't get you close enough but we might be able to get the sword close enough," Bobby said. "What's our time frame here? And how good are you with a slingshot?"

Everybody else probably thought Jack was hearing voices, wandering out there, looking at the tower, discussing the merits of different materials at hand to build a slingshot with.

So, if Felicity was Airmed, this must be one of the Battles of Moytura, the second one, it had to be, since Nuada lost his real arm at the first one. Jack was Lugh, the champion of the Tuatha de Danaan. Like Felicity, he could see and speak to me but he only recognized me as a Celtic war witch. He was totally locked into what was happening—he was Lugh. Whereas, I knew I was only playing the war witch. Which witch? The Morrigan was the most prominent one. But there were also Macha and Neman.

I was still wondering about it when I came to the wreck of a chariot, on the far edge of the battlefield where the frightened horses had dragged it. A little girl's decapitated body lay near a childish blonde head—the face was Grania's. A woman's body lay half over her. The woman had silver blonde hair. I didn't turn her over. I was afraid to.

A warrior with a face half like Joe Dunny's and half like a cat's, complete with a slitted eye, said to me. "Your sisters are a great loss to us all, Morrigan. May the Il Dana wreak his vengeance on the one who slew them."

The last part of his sentence was drowned as shouts went up. The tower began glowing and people were running from it.

It looked like some kind of red laser beam sweeping from that tower, though how that could be I don't know. Then I realized that what I must be seeing was Balor's evil eye. I saw Jack/Lugh raise his sword and then heard him cry, over the screams and shouting, in a sudden moment of breaking through the time barriers, "Jaysus, Mary and Joseph, it's Carnahan!" and the sword went flying. There was a shattering and the red beam broke. So much for Balor, I thought. As if it was that easy.

So he was dead but so was Felicity, so was Grania. I tried to reach Jack again, to remind him who I really was, to see if he knew now who he really was, but he was being held aloft on shields while the other warriors did a victory dance. I couldn't get near him.

Let Jack have a victory celebration or whatever ancient Irish heroes did, I thought. I'd catch him later. I'd had enough.

I ran for the wall of mist behind the lines of the Tuatha de Danaan, leaving Jack with his magic horse and his magic sword and a toad with practical experience to protect him.

But I was out of there. It was not my scene. I ran into the mist and kept running. And realized very soon that I wasn't the only one. I had a feeling that if you could look down on top of that mist from a helicopter and blow away the gray, it would be boiling with people. I couldn't hear much above my own steps and my own heavy breathing, it felt creepier than a whole library full of Stephen King stories. I didn't know if my sense that I had company was true or not, but I didn't want to take the chance. All I could do was try to outrun it.

I ran so far that time I was pretty sure I should be coming to an exit, or maybe to the river that ran through Fairyland, something familiar, something to help me get my bearings. I seemed to be the only one here of all of us who really knew that we were still in Felicity's attic with a nut after us. Even the nut himself, Carnahan/Balor, must have been caught up in the roles we were playing to have pretended to be the old demon king instead of just shooting us. Did Jack, as Lugh, killing Carnahan mean we didn't have to worry about him anymore? Was all we had to worry about getting out of this combination psychodrama/history seminar and back to modern Ireland?

But how about Felicity? She was Airmed and then she was one of the war witches and she was dead this time too. So was Grania. I hoped Jack/Lugh's conquest of Balor had taken care of Carnahan but if so and he was out of the picture, then were Felicity and Grania dead in modern times too? Process of elimination to try to figure out who might be hiding three misty wisps away from me was not working. Insufficient data, as they say. And I didn't want to bite a bullet to collect more info.

Then all at once I had the feeling I'd had before, that I was alone in the mist and anything or anyone else who had been there was gone. A couple of steps later, I was out of the grayness and standing at the bottom of a hill where a bunch of people were gathered around several Ben Hur-type rigs hitched up to sweaty horses. Some people were cheering, some were swearing, everybody was exchanging money. I knew this scene too. I'd wandered into a horse race.

These people, like Felicity as Airmed and Jack as Lugh and the others I'd met before inside the mist, were all dressed in what my History of Art teacher calls loom-shaped garments and pieces of sheepskin and fur. Also, the horses were ever so slightly funny-looking, like they might have been the original models for what had later been perfected into the modern horse. Except for good old Ace, who stood next to a handsome thirty-something guy wearing more bronze than everybody else. He was smiling. It wasn't the sort of smile that made your heart sing or in any way brightened your day.

Jack was there. He seemed to be arguing with the smiling man—no—pleading with him. But the smiling man wore the expression of someone who had all the cards.

Suddenly it seemed to me that I had walked too far and my legs were like lead and I needed to pee and my back hurt and I felt really bloated and very very heavy.

And one of the men next to me said, "So, Missus, your man says you're fast. The King of Ulster, Conor Mac Nessa, wants to see just how fast you are."

"Fast?" I asked. "Look at me! I'm—oh. I'm pregnant." And I was, and this was news to me because whether anybody else believes it or not, I'm still a virgin. Not for want of opportunity, I might add. "I'd say that for once I haven't been fast enough," I told the man.

"I'd say so too but your man says you can outrun the king's fleetest chariot horse and the king wants to see it. Now."

Suddenly Felicity was at my side, and she was done up in lots of bronze too and this time her dress was dyed red. Conor Mac Nessa signaled, Jack groaned, and Felicity said, "Conor, brother, have you gone completely over the edge? This woman is due any moment. She can't run a race just because you've placed a few bets! She might lose her baby."

"Can she not? Then her man has lied to his king, a very grave offense. She runs, now, or he's put to death."

Jack whispered to me, "Don't worry, alannah, the king's bet against you. You needn't run very fast and he'll win and this will all be over with. Just toddle along a ways, there's a good girl, and he'll drop it all soon enough."

Me, Sno, I wanted to say, hell no I won't go and stage a sit-in but one of the guards had a blade at Jack's throat and I found that whoever I was supposed to be who was pregnant by him was really crazy about the guy.

The pregnant lady took over. Well, women sometimes run marathons up until their fifth month or so now, don't they?

But not when they're ready to pop, for chrissakes. That was nuts.

The king crooked his finger at me. That made me mad right there. He reminded me of Raydir's asshole friend Greece E.T., who crooks his little finger for the lucky groupie of the night to come running. We stayed in the same hotel with him once and I had to get up and go for a Coke. As I was going back to my room I saw a bundle of clothes come flying out his door and this naked chick lean over to get them and then, bang, she fell headfirst into the hall with a foot at her butt. She was starting to pound on the door when the hotel cops came running—the bastard had called them on her. I would have hidden her in my room but she was high on something and freaked and ran down the hall with the cops right after her. Greece even gave me the eye a couple of times, me, and I was a fairly young kid then! But I couldn't stand him. I didn't like this king at all either.

I tried to reason with him, though. "Your Majesty," I said really nicely, considering how I felt. "Obviously there's been a miscommunication here. Ja—my husband didn't mean to lie to you at all. Ordinarily, I'm like greased lightning, it's true" (No I'm not. Why'd I say that?) "but I'm just about to have a baby, as you can see, and it just wouldn't be really good for me or the kid to run right now."

He smirked at me, the fucker, like he thought it was funny! I used to think it was funny too, the way pregnant women waddled, but I didn't think so anymore. It hurt to walk, even, and I felt like I was juggling an elephant under my navel. "I can see that. Do you also see that it's not good for my subjects to brag to me that their wives are faster than my prized horses? Do you see, my dear, that it will not be good for your husband to be deprived of his skin if you don't run this race, or for you and your child, should you survive, to do without him when I cast you off the lands I gave him? You will run, if you have to be dragged."

The sonovabitch! I was so mad I literally saw red. I wondered if my hair was standing out, like the Hound of Ireland's did when he went into battle frenzy. And with that thought I knew who I was supposed to be in this little scenario. It wasn't like I was me anymore. I was someone else. Someone who was determined that if Conor was going to make me run in my condition, heedless of the harm it might do me or my babies, I was going to make fuckin' sure he didn't win his lousy bet. In fact, I was going to make sure he paid and paid big time.

Ace caught my eye. He, I should have known, was the chariot horse in question. He gave me a wink, like he had the first time I saw him. "Don't worry, little mare," he said. "They don't know how fast either of us can run—or jump—and I'll not be the one to show them. Don't kill yourself."

But he didn't even need to throw the race. Flying horse or not, I won fair and square. It was that berserker thing. Except for the horse's voice in my mind all I heard was a roaring in my ears and the pounding of my heart, so fast I thought it would burst out my eyeballs. My belly ached and waves of cramps swept through it strong enough to turn me into a pretzel under ordinary circumstances, but even though I felt it, it didn't affect me at all. I just ran harder. Until I crossed the finish line, just ahead of Ace, and fell screaming to the ground as something gushed down my legs and I began to rip apart.

I don't remember that part, I'm happy to say. But the next thing I knew I was waking up and Jack was holding two little boy babies. The king stood right behind him, looking mean, a little scared, pissed off and as if he could have done what I'd just done with one hand tied behind him.

"Congratulations," he said.

I couldn't stand it. "You're a worm, your Highness," I told him. "You and all of your voyeuristic, sadistic, misogynistic, psycho *crappy* soldiers didn't give a damn whether we made it or not. Well, let me tell you something, buddy. You know what I wish for you? I wish for you and every guy from around here that when you're in as desperate a spot as I am you'll be as weak as I am and, *unlike* me, you'll totally wimp out. That's what I wish, oh high and mighty warrior king."

"That's it?" he asked.

"Yeah. Except that you'll be out of it for five whole days

and four nights instead of just one and it'll happen for the next nine generations to you and yours. Have a nice day.''

So, having delivered the babies, I'd just also delivered the curse of Macha I'd read about early. The goddess Macna, who was killed at the last battle of Moytura where *I* was the Morrigan and Jack was Lugh and slew Balor, had been reincarnated in me. At Moytura, she had looked like Grania, and had been dead on (my) arrival. This time she was me. I didn't understand it but I was glad that both Jack and Felicity were okay and whatever was operating here seemed to be recycling people as well as goddesses.

And all of a sudden, Macha wasn't with me anymore. I was Sno, I had never been pregnant, and the kids the man who looked like Jack was holding had nothing to do with me.

Under my own steam, I got to my feet and ran away. Back in the mist, I had on my own clothes, wasn't sore, wasn't bloody, nothing. And as soon as I started running again, I now heard, definitely heard, other feet running too, other bodies coming through the mist with me. This time I stopped running and stood still, watching the mist flow around me as the ghosty steps ran past.

I was about to start walking again when I heard a single shot, just ahead of me. Somebody shouted and then everything was still again. I guessed that whoever else had been in the mist with me had gone into the next, I didn't know what to call it, scene, time zone?

Not quite everyone else, though. All of a sudden I heard a familiar toady voice croaking through the mist, "I guess you showed Carnahan that time."

"Who?"

"Carnahan, aka Balor, aka Conor Mac Nessa. Jack busted his chops at Moytura and Carnahan thought that as King Conor he'd get back at him here but you turned the tables on him. I wish I had pockets. I'd have bet on you."

"You would have?"

"Sure, I'm startin' to figure this out. Toads don't have a lot to do in Irish mythology the way they do on the Continent or even in England, so that gives me a little time to think.''

"How do you know that?"

"I may have a toad's body, but I can still read. Who was there on your pillow while you were doing all that research?"

"Well, I'd appreciate hearing about any theories you've got," I said. "All I know is that we keep acting out these Irish myths."

"Like this one?" the toad asked as we pushed through the mist again only to find ourselves back at the same damned hill. There were no more chariots and the King's beard was white instead of red now, so I knew we weren't running around in circles after all. We hadn't changed places but we had changed time, which is easy to understand for someone who used to be a Doctor Who freak.

Bobby was saying, "There's Carnahan, still being Conor Mac Nessa. Look at him! The poor sucker's so frustrated he's about to pop! See, he knows some of what's going on like you and me, and he's still chasing us but he can't just blow us away in here. That's why he took a shot in the dark a minute ago. I bet he spotted someone leaving the mist to come here, and before he got caught up in the story himself, he fired. But once you get into a special time this far back, bullets haven't been invented yet, so the shot never comes off. Get it? And even Carnahan has to play out the story according to how it happened."

"Yeah, I wouldn't have even been able to do what Macha did but it's like I didn't have any choice really."

"Except maybe you can choose who you get to be. This guy has connections in old-time Ireland, even in the modern world. The war witch and her crows have taken him under their wings. So it's possible he at least gets to choose who he becomes, whereas you and Jack don't. So he chooses to be kings and demons because he's got a good chance of winning and wiping you out."

"Yeah, but nobody dies really. Not us anyhow. So what's the point?"

"The point is only you and I seem to know that. Carnahan may be able to pull a few strings, but he's still learning how it works too. The others, if Jack is any example, are all hyp-

notized or something. Jack snapped out of it for a sec when
he recognized Carnahan but then he got caught up in Lugh's
character again. It's like serial possessions.''

"The transmigration of souls," I said.

"What's that?"

"Kind of like what happened to you becoming a toad—
your soul goes into another body or you become some new
person. It's supposed to be an old part of Irish myth. You even
turn into animals and things . . .''

"I knew that," he said.

I stopped watching then to watch Carnahan/Conor Mac
Nessa. He had Deirdre, a younger, slimmer, more beautiful
version of Deirdre, but Deirdre. Her hands were tied behind
her back, and Joe's head was on a stick.

This myth, at least, was sickeningly easy to figure out. Joe
would have been Deirdre's lover, Naoise. Felicity was her old
foster mother Levercham the poet, who was about to be exe-
cuted for letting Deirdre run off with Naoise. Conor Mac
Nessa/Carnahan was licking his lips over poor Deirdre. A fatal
attraction if there ever was one. I thought Bobby was right
about him getting to choose. He was a stalker in real life and
had chosen the most disgusting kind of stalker—not to mention a sexual harasser—as his old-time self.

King Conor had hassled poor Deirdre literally from before
she was born, using the excuse that according to a prophecy,
she was supposed to cause wars and men to die. But really,
the prophecy only came true because *he* betrayed his friends
and killed everybody who kept him from getting to Deirdre.

I didn't seem to be in this one. In fact, I could see out of
the mist, but I stayed inside it. I was just a ghost again. I
didn't want to stick around for the last little twist in his sick
treatment of her when he told her he was turning her over to
Naoise's killer for a year and they'd swap her back and forth.
That was what made her kill herself in the end of the story
and I couldn't stand seeing it actually happen.

"Come on," I said to Bobby.

"What's the matter?" the toad baited me. "Don't want to
get involved?"

"Why should I? I can't change anything. I thought the past would be colorful and interesting but it's just horrible. Sadists and rapists and psychopaths run everything."

"Yeah," the toad said. "Those were the days, huh? Or should I say, these are. Come on. Maybe he'll get stuck there for a while. I don't like the idea of amateurs like him shooting blind in the smog."

This time when we came through the mist I didn't even stop to see what the scene was.

"You're missing Jack as the Hound of Ulster," the toad said. "He's getting good at this hero stuff."

"You stay and coach him if you want to," I said. "I want out of here."

"I don't think so," the toad said. "Look down."

I was wearing the red cape again and now I could see that my hair was not only long but the same color as that horrible fire in Balor's camp.

"The Morrigan again, huh?" I said, recognizing her signature cape. If Jack was the Hound, we must be in the time when the Morrigan tried to seduce Cuchulain.

She was supposed to have disguised herself (either that, or he hadn't seen the Morrigan before and didn't recognize the cape) and come on to him, saying, "I'm the king's daughter and I claim the best for myself. Because of your great prowess and legendary deeds, as well as your great beauty, I'm yours tonight and happily ever after." Or something like that.

I frankly couldn't see the Morrigan saying anything like that and figured the old lady poet Levercham had to make a good male fantasy out of the story to please Conor Mac Nessa, who had apparently spared her life even though she screwed up with Deirdre. Because it was Levercham who stood there talking with Laeg, Cuchulain's charioteer, who resembled Joe, only this time Levercham didn't look like Felicity. Now she looked like Grania, older and wiser, but Grania.

Instead of delivering the message the way Levercham related it, I went over to Jack/Cuchulain and stood as close as I could, which probably made it *look* like I was coming on to him, and said, "Listen to me, man. You are not Cuchulain, the Hound of Ireland, and your name was never Setanta. You are Jack Daly and you live in Dublin and we're being chased by a terrorist who looks exactly like your boss, Conor Mac Nessa.''

"Is it mad you are?" the warrior wearing Jack's face asked me. "Any fool can see that I'm Cuchulain and I'm here to protect my king, whom you defame, against Maeve the cattle thief while the curse of Macha is upon the men of Ulster. Get on with ya, Morrigan. You're the war witch of Ireland. Can't you do something constructive, like take the spell off?''

"Forget it," I told him. "Conor Mac Nessa deserved that spell and worse, if you ask me. In fact, I think we can safely conclude that it's right about this point in Irish history when the Morrigan goes totally rogue. She's not about to work for the king who tried to kill her pregnant sister. When Lugh was alive and ruling, she was his lover. Once Conor became king, though, she saw that being the king of Ireland doesn't automatically make anybody a good person, so she started doing as she damn well pleased. Jack, I know this doesn't make a lot of sense but you have to get out of here. Come with me.''

"Go away with you," he said.

"Oh, go to hell, then," I said. And he did.

His wife Emer, who put up with more screwing around than my Mom ever did from Raydir, tried to organize his girlfriends to save him from Queen Maeve's soldiers, but in the end, I found myself getting dishpan hands from washing his shroud in the river. Maeve, the ancient queen and most famous cattle rustler in Irish history, looked like Mrs. Daly, oddly enough. I left before Jack got killed again. I'd read the story. I knew the ending. I didn't want to watch.

I ran into the mist and through it. Carnahan hadn't been in that particular place, which worried me, because he could be anywhere now in this crazy labyrinth. I had started to hate the way history was always tripping up the people I cared about and turning them into something and somebody else. I ran right through the next four stories, and didn't see Carnahan or Jack. I intended to keep running, not get caught up in any of the stories and find my way out the other side.

But pretty soon I had to rest and this was when I came out of the mist to the place where Grania was conniving Diarmid into fooling Finn Mac Cumhaill. This was a weird one. For a change Carnahan wasn't the king. Joe was, looking old and lonesome and sad. Grania Sr., whom I would have expected to look like our friend Grania, had our Grania's hair and face and figure but Carnahan's calculating eyes. This was King Arthur, Guenevere and Lancelot all over again in a less fairy-tale setting. And when Diarmid died, Grania married the king just in time to be the dowager, so she got the love of a young man and the wealth of an old one who adored her all in one lifetime.

Now I was totally disgusted. I fully understood why the Keep Out sign had been on the door. Being chased by a psycho was bad enough but this was hell. It was confusing. It was depressing and it made you feel like there was no sense ever trying to do anything. And we hadn't even got to the Battle of the Boyne yet.

"What's the matter, kid? Had enough?" the toad asked. I couldn't seem to lose the little sucker, no matter how many time zones we crossed.

"You bet I have," I said. By now I was crying and I didn't care if Carnahan heard me or not. I was frustrated and mad enough to chew his bullets up and spit them back out at him. "If I'm going to have to be around murderers and terrorists, I'd rather it would be in my own time when I don't already know they're going to win."

"Too bad you don't have any pockets," the toad said, narrowing his pop eyes slyly, which can't be that easy for a toad to do. "If you did, then you'd have your little golden wish box and you could just wish yourself out of here."

"I'd wish us all out of here, wart-face," I told him.

"You don't have to stress yourself out on my account, kid. I can leave any time I want to. In fact, I could go get your little gold box and bring it here to you if I wanted to."

"How come you can and nobody else can?"

"Because I'm a toad. I'm operating on a different level here than you are, see. Besides, I don't have to worry about bad guys, A, 'cause he's in here with us already, and B, 'cause he's got so many other fish to fry he's probably not gonna bother with frog legs, or rather, toad legs.''

"But I don't guess you'd go get it for me, would you?'' I asked. I thought he was just making it up to torment me.

"I might. For a price.''

"Like what?''

"Like a little respect.''

"Sorry. No can do. You tried to kill me.''

"There's a saying I learned from a buddy of mine who's in the San Francisco Tong. 'Happiness is good digestion and a short memory.' What we're experiencing here, babe, is a really long memory which, face it, has done this country no good at all. Everybody remembers that everybody else at some time or other tried to kill them. You got to concentrate on the here and now. So what do you want? A new ally or an old enemy?''

"What would be involved in this so-called alliance?'' I asked. Normally it would have turned my stomach to think about having to be nice to the toad, because I really enjoyed knowing that he was a toad after what he tried to do to me. But in the past—well, the past however long it was that we'd been in here—I'd frankly seen a lot that turned my stomach even more. On a badness scale of 1 to 10 he'd dropped from 11 down to about three and a half.

"To begin with, no more speciesist jokes. I don't want to hear about wart-face or toad-butt or any of those other little endearments you've been laying on me. Also, I want you to take my side against that damned cat. And otherwise, you do *not* have to kiss me, but you do have to stop treating me like doo doo on your shoe.''

"But this wouldn't mean we were like, engaged, once you get back to human form or anything, huh?''

"I'd rather marry the cat.''

"You got yourself a deal, war—Bobby.''

We came through the mist again just then and this time the technology was considerably advanced. It looked like a medieval city, with a castle and all. I was sitting on a windowsill.

"Oops, I don't care for your current persona," Bobby said. "I'll meet you in a few centuries."

"I want out of here neeoww!" I snarled at him. But he was gone. Embarrassed at having shown I cared so much, I washed my—paw.

CHAPTER 29

The Cat's Palace

My window was separated only by a wooden screen from a room where three ladies were having a domestic crisis.

The mother, who looked very much like Mrs. Daly, was saying to two young women who looked like Grania and her only slightly older sister, Felicity, "Sorry as I am to say so, girls, your father left only money enough for one dowry and that must go to Felicity. She is the eldest. Once she marries, maybe there will be a chance for her to save a bit of the household money and provide a dowry for you, Grania, in a few years."

"But I'll be *old* by then," Grania said. "Nobody will want me! Meanwhile, what are we to live off while she's living in comfort with a fine husband?"

"There's the will of your peculiar Auntie Maeve, she that was cousin to the last high king of Ireland, before the men sold us out to the English. She invested heavily in your father's shipping interests and she did leave the warehouse . . ."

Grania shuddered delicately, her golden curls bobbing with distress and tears welling up fresh in her wide blue eyes. "Oh, Mama, it's all full of cats, that place. They're dirty and stinky

263

and they'll scratch my skin and tear the few good clothes I have.''

''Yes, dear, but so will diggin' turf or pullin' potatoes damage your complexion and your clothing. And enough money is involved in serving the cats that we can live, you and I, until Felicity can organize something for us.''

Felicity gave her mother an unhappy look. Her dress was better than her sister's and her hair paler blonde, but she had that prominent nose and strong chin and pale eyes which make her more striking than pretty. Also, Grania was fragile and slender and Felicity, while not huge, was sturdily built.

''Now come along, girls. Felicity's future husband awaits us in the next room.''

This I had to see. I didn't know Felicity had been married though she did tell me she'd been alive a long long time.

I jumped down from my current windowsill and looked until I found one from the room the three women had just entered.

And there stood Carnahan, fawned over by two flunkies and looking extremely pleased with himself. He looked right at me through the window and raised his eyebrow, as if he knew he'd won.

The mother introduced Felicity to him as his bride-to-be and he drooled over her hand, her cleavage, and her dowry, no doubt, but his eyes never left Grania and she never stopped playing up to him. It was sickening.

In disgust, I hopped down from the windowsill and strolled home to the warehouse for a nap. The next day, who should show up but the three ladies. The mother said to Grania, ''Now dear, just fix the pussies a bit to eat and look to their wounds and messes and there's good money in it for their maintenance. You'll need to be sleeping here of course as well.'' And she left Grania there.

Need I mention that she was useless? She wasn't a bad girl or a mean girl but she was so bummed out that all she did was cry. Several of the kittens tried to get her to play with them and she batted them away. The top cat put his paw firmly on her knee to let her know it was time to get up and cook for us, but she picked him up and tried to cuddle him. When she fell asleep, several of my pushier roomies jumped on her, and one gave her a little scratch on the nose, which made her wake up, cry and cower worse than before. To tell you the truth, I was afraid what was going to happen to this stupid girl if she kept doing such a lousy job. I scooted back to her house.

Only to find the young Felicity, crying over her drawings and harp strings. I jumped into the room and did a slalom around her ankles. To my relief, I could speak to her. "Felicity, what's the matter?" I asked.

She picked me up and held me against her cheek. "Oh, Puss. I don't know. It seems I've been waiting forever to finally be the one who gets the prince, who lives happily ever after, and now . . . Heavens, but you're a skinny thing." She stood up and bustled off with me to the kitchen. "We can continue this conversation in here just as easily while you have a bite of this fish my intended sent over for our supper. Now, where was I?"

"The prince," I said, first sniffing the fish to make sure Carnahan hadn't poisoned it, then tearing into it.

"Yes, the prince," Felicity said. "Well, he's not a prince, actually, only a provisional governor, but he's powerful and has money. And he's nice-looking. But there's no—I don't know. He does not look on me warmly as he did on Grania and frankly, though he's a nice-looking man, I find him a bit autocratic. He actually laughed at the idea that I write songs about the hardships of our people during these times of transition. He said women should confine themselves to songs for children. He then said he hoped I wasn't over old for having children. He prefers my sister, I know it! Oh, if only she weren't around . . ."

I realized she was heading into dangerous territory with that one. Murders have been committed and folk songs written about them over that kind of situation.

"If she weren't around, *we* wouldn't have to put up with her," I told Felicity sharply enough, I hoped, to snap her out of it. I had a very grating meow when I wanted to. "She hasn't fed us once this week and two of us have died. All she does is bawl. We, that is I, would appreciate it very much if you'd come over and sort it out.''

"Mother won't like it," she said. "She wanted Grania to come and tend to you to get her out of the way. She knew Kerwin would prefer her to me. She actually even suggested something more permanent."

"Felicity?"

"Yes?"

"Would you really do that? Are you that different?"

"Different than what?"

"Never mind. Just come with me."

She did. And then, for a while there, we had *both* of them crying and carrying on, Grania because she was full of fresh scratches and Felicity, funnily enough, because her gorgeous sister had become such a mess and also, I am happy to add, because she was so sorry that said gorgeous sister had been such a slacker that us poor cats were in a mess too.

Good old Felicity went straight to the market and bought us fish and meat with her own money and cooked the food for us too.

She took a rag soaked in milk and fed the kittens whose mother had died because of Grania's neglect. And when we were all content and napping, except for me, and I seemed to be the most curious of all the cats, she took her sister back to her mother's house. I followed.

"What's *she* doing here?" the mother asked. "She belongs with the cats. Look at her! And you! You're a mess, and on your wedding day too!"

"We'd like to switch," Felicity told her.

"You'd like to what?"

"Switch," Felicity said. "She should marry Kerwin. Their tongues hang out when they look at each other. I'll see to it that the cats are *properly* cared for and collect the income from Auntie's estate to feed us. In fact, Mother, I suggest that you ingratiate yourself with Kerwin and get him to install you in his house too. Then I'll just move my bits and bobs over to the warehouse and that will be that."

"But you're the eldest. The dowry is yours."

"I'm the eldest, and having children at the advanced age of twenty-two could easily be the death of me."

"What will Lord Kerwin think of us, switching daughters as if they were horses or goats?"

"I very much hope that I'm wrong, for Grania's sake, but I daresay Lord Kerwin won't notice the difference. If you're that embarrassed by it, tell him that it's an old Limerick custom to wrap the bride in heavy veiling until after she's married. Then he'll think it's me, and be pleasantly surprised that it's Grania. Trust me."

And with that she snatched up her harp and her drawing pencils and papers and her favorite quill pen, an apron, a less costly dress, a warm cloak and some sensible shoes, and came to live at the warehouse.

Lord Kerwin and Grania were married that day and he was so delighted with the switch, it was said, that he invited the mother-in-law to come and live with them. People wondered where Felicity was.

At the time of the wedding, she was sweeping away cobwebs, cleaning up the mess from hairballs, drip-feeding kittens and cooking cod. And when the church bells finished ringing, the table was set with our dishes.

And all at once every cat in the place changed into a lord or lady, including me, though I wasn't in finery like the others but back in my leggings and sweatshirt.

"My dear Felicity," said a beautiful redheaded woman who had been a beautiful orange marmalade female. "Your kindness and good sense has prompted us to offer you a reward. Which would you rather have, a wealthy handsome husband we will provide for you or a very long life of adventure and usefulness?"

"Kitty, I mean, Madame, I hardly know what to say. I have always imagined I would like to have a husband to care for and who cares for me, but I have met no one and now I am overripe for family life."

"You're an infant compared to the great age you could live to," said another of the ladies at the table, one who had been a thin gray cat with shrewd pale blue Siamesey eyes. Now, except for her clothing and her age, she was the spitting image of Dame Prudence.

"Who would I be useful to, please?"

"Those worthy mortals who will make the world a better place if only they have a chance to survive their own difficulties. You will be the agent of that chance."

"But how will I do that? Will I be a queen or empress? Is it a kingdom you're offering me?"

"Nothing so limited. Your realm shall be the entire world, and your fortune endless, though, of course, strictly rationed."

"We like to call it a trust fund," said Dame Prudence. "Because we are entrusting you with funds, as well as your missions."

"It sounds lovely," Felicity said, but her voice was skeptical and stern. "But I insist on knowing what you have done to all of the cats who have also been entrusted to my care."

The red-haired woman laughed. I knew the answer of course, but Felicity was mortal. So far. "Why, dear Felicity, have you never heard that cats are often the Fey in disguise? *We* are your cats and I myself am your own Auntie Maeve."

"Then I accept your commission with a whole heart!"

"Good. Now the first thing you will need to do is help your sister, Grania. You see, dear, Lord Kerwin is not actually a very nice man ...."

I didn't see Carnahan again in that time, however. So far, Felicity seemed to be the only one of us who was acting out herself, which was a relief. It was funny that Jack had recognized Carnahan as Balor enough to pull him out of his own role as Lugh, but that didn't prove Carnahan actually *was* Balor. Anyhow, it seemed like Bobby was right and the bullets were no good in times when they had not yet been invented. Since no more shots had been fired, Carnahan must now be aware of that time quirk too.

I followed Felicity into the fog and up through the years. I appeared in her life in lots of different roles and watched how she helped people, sure that sooner or later she would get us out of this situation. She didn't know me as myself yet, of course, because I wouldn't be born for a few hundred years, but it occurred to me that maybe I was being some of my Irish ancestors. Sometimes I was an animal, sometimes a fairy. Once I was even a mermaid. But mostly I was a person, a girl about my own age. And the funny thing was that the more time I spent as other people, the more I started thinking like them instead of the way I usually did. It was like learning computer jargon or going out with the French club. I just got into it. Felicity herself changed too and became a lot calmer, happier, more confident. Her self-esteem rose with every mission she performed for the godmothers. I watched her help all kinds of people, veterans who'd lost limbs in various battles, widows who needed work, orphans who needed homes, people who were about to be evicted. But she usually did it as a fairly humble person and acted indirectly, through people she knew whenever possible. She used magic only when absolutely necessary. It was a serious thing back then to get labeled a witch, even a good witch, because the first time things started going wrong, people would turn on anyone who was supposed to have magical powers. The fairies were smart to stay underground and incognito and, as much as she could, Felicity did the same thing. The mist between these incidents lasted only a step or two and I didn't see Carnahan again, or Jack, or any of the others. I think it was because now we were reliving events that weren't significant to Irish history nor to the history of anybody but Felicity.

And then, all of a sudden, we were all brought together again, when the potato famine hit Ireland.

Felicity was working as a cook at the home of a wealthy landowner named Taylor, who lived in Wicklow. I was a kitchen girl.

"I'm sure we don't know what to do, Mrs. Fortune," the missus said while giving Felicity her instructions for the evening's meal. Unlike most fine ladies, Mrs. Taylor did not dispense her orders from the balcony high up the kitchen wall, but came into the room and sat at the table to talk. It made some talk, then, thinking that she wasn't born to the quality. I liked her better for it.

"Do you not, Mrs. Taylor?" Felicity asked mildly.

"No. Sir Dennis and Lady Helen are calling this evening to discuss the problem with Mr. Taylor, but frankly, we are not impressed by what we've heard of his solution."

There was a knock at the door then and there I was almost shocked to see Jack standing there with his cap in hand and Mrs. Daly crying, "Please, Missus, could you spare a bit of bread? My boy will work for it. It's only we've been turfed out and have nowhere to go. Oh! Pardon *us*, your ladyship," she said, quite shocked to see the lady of the house in the cook's domain.

"Moira Daly, you and yours have been on your holding for two hundred years. Are you standing there telling me you've lost your home?" Felicity asked.

"Oh we have, yes, Missus Fortune. And our house leveled. Still, we wouldn't like to complain," she said with a nervous glance at Mrs. Taylor. "We're better than the neighbors that was sent off to America on that ship His Lordship organized. Everyone died. Cholera. Me and my Jack, we're for the road. There's about ten of us families going."

"Ask them in, Mrs. Fortune," said Herself. "And add another loaf and a joint to the preparations."

Felicity nodded but caught up with her ladyship at the door, her own rough dark gray woolen skirts brushing her ladyship's violet taffeta with the French lace overlay. "It'll be as you say, naturally, Mrs. Taylor, but we cannot—that is, himself and you yourself, madame, cannot continue to feed folk so lavishly. There's many to consider. If I may speak to you later. I've a recipe of my ma's for a hearty soup that goes far with a loaf to fill the hole in a hungry body's middle."

"You're a treasure, Mrs. Fortune," Mrs. Taylor said.

I helped serve and was less than surprised to see that the infamous Sir Dennis, one of the architects of the deportation ships, resembled Carnahan. He talked to Mr. Taylor of the landlord's responsibility to his tenants and how, since the land could no longer support labor-intensive agriculture, sending the laborers off where they might make a living for themselves was the only reasonable and humane thing to do. He kept appealing to Mr. Taylor's humaneness, as Mr. Taylor was known to be a very humane man. Sir Dennis I don't think understood the meaning of the word.

"Frankly, William, I can't see how you'll continue to support yourselves here at your present rate. Why, the construction on your new wing has just begun and the masonry alone will cost the support of all of these people for two years. And of course, if you stop work, why, then you leave them unemployed."

"Thank you, Sir Dennis, for your concern. We'll carefully consider all that you've said."

But afterwards, Mr. Taylor and the missus stayed up late talking far into the night and the next day she came and asked Felicity what would be needed to provide the soup and bread for everyone per week.

Mr. Taylor allowed his own tenants to hunt his woods then, and stopped the stonework construction on the new wing of the house and instead used the stone he'd bought already to put his field-poor farmers to building walls and walks and fountains. Anything to give them work. And every day, Felicity would ring a big bell outside the kitchen and the people who worked for the Taylors would come fill their bowls with a hearty soup, augmented by whatever game had been caught on the property, and fresh loaves of coarse and filling bread.

Not a soul who worked for the Taylors died of anything but the usual causes and when the famine ended, they built a little castle turret folly for the garden to show the Taylors they knew real quality when they saw it.

Then one day when the guerrilla war for independence was raging through the countryside, destroying the landlords and their great houses and castles, the tinkers were seen out on the road. A short time later, Jack came to the door, hat in hand, looking nervously around him. "It's bein' said in sartin places, Mrs. Fortune, that the Fenians mean to burn the Taylors out tonight. But you never heard it from me."

"I never did, Jack Daly, but there'll always be meat and bread for you at this door," she said.

And she rang the big bell.

When, somewhat later, she informed the master of Jack

Daly's news, he was ready to meet the guerrillas with his gun, but Felicity said, "Never you mind, sir. You and the missus take that gun and sit in the parlor and wait. You've friends enough here. We'll sort it out."

They always did the burnings after dark. But well before twilight, every tenant, every casual laborer from the village who had ever had a bowl of the soup made by Felicity Fortune and paid for by the Taylors, was standing outside the big house, ringing it with a wall of people. In the front were Felicity, Joe, Deirdre, Grania and me. A moment later, Jack Daly and his mother came round from the kitchen door to stand with us.

When the Fenians came, I recognized many of them. Some had been turfed out by Sir Dennis, who'd been murdered during the famine. Many were known to our people. The leader I knew well enough. He didn't look like Sir Dennis any more, but he still wore the Carnahan look about those pale cold eyes.

"You get along with yerselves now," Felicity said, as spokesperson for the Taylor's tenants and employees. "These are not people with whom we Irish have a quarrel. They were good landlords who fed us and cared for us when every hand was turned against us and even our own land betrayed us. You'll not harm a hair of their heads or damage a blade of grass of this property or you'll have your neighbors to answer to."

While a murmur of assent spread around the house, I felt a sudden weight in my apron pocket and then on my shoulder. Bobby the toad blinked at me. "Reedeep," he said.

I reached into my pocket and pulled out my wish box, but I wanted to see what happened. Like their other employees, I cared very much about the Taylors.

Most of the rebels muttered and nodded among themselves and started to back off, but the Carnahan leader laughed at Felicity and raised his pistol.

And Jack Daly drew back his hand, which held a hefty stone.

And I said, "I wish every one of us from a future time safely back in Felicity's house."

CHAPTER 30

Journal Entry—Saturday

"Safely," I'd said, and the fulfillment of that part of the wish was debatable. I also knew before the words were out of my mouth that I should have excluded Carnahan.

But it was too late for second thoughts. Before I could blink, the house and all of the other tenants and rebels fell away and it was Carnahan with his automatic pistol facing Grania, Joe, Deirdre, and Jack, whose hand was still raised.

The only problem was the stone had been part of the past and his hand was now empty. He realized it, swore and looked for a projectile. Without thinking, I tossed the only thing of throwing size I had to hand, the wish box. Carnahan was caught off balance by the move and anyway, I don't think he intended to kill anyone immediately. He wanted to watch us squirm first.

We were all standing in the room outside the room with the Keep Out sign. Carnahan's back was to the door while Grania, Joe, Deirdre, Jack and I were up against the beds, facing him.

Jack caught the little box and, looking as much like Lugh or Cuchulain as he ever had in battle dress, let fly with a hard throw that caught Carnahan's hand with the wings of the little fairy and caused him to drop the gun.

273

Joe Dunny dove for it while Jack tackled Carnahan.

Unfortunately, Carnahan felled Jack with a swift karate kick.

However, just then the Keep Out door slammed open, into Carnahan's back, knocking him forward into Joe, who hit him with the pistol. Mrs. Daly sprang out from behind the door with a wild whoop and landed on Carnahan's back, riding him like a bucking bronco while pummeling his head with her hard callused old hands.

Everyone else tried to get in a punch as well and it was too much for Carnahan, who bolted for the steps, Mrs. Daly still on his back until they reached the landing, when he managed to throw her off onto her rear, which didn't stop her from shaking her fists and cussing him out in a mixture of English, Irish and a language I didn't recognize. (Jack told me later it was Cant, the Traveller's language.)

Carnahan stumbled down three stairs, the rest of us hot on his trail, when Felicity and Puss started up the bottom step.

Carnahan pushed Felicity aside as if she didn't exist and ran down the hall for the front door.

"I wouldn't if I were you," Puss purred.

"Shoot him! Would ya shoot him, Joe, for the luvva Jaysus, he's gettin' away! Plug the bastard!" Deirdre was yelling like the Morrigan herself.

Carnahan ripped open the front door and ran out. We were all right behind him and were a little surprised to see a baffled-looking Maeve standing in the driveway.

"Mr. Carnahan," she said in her newly melodious voice. "Help me, Mr. Carnahan. Make her"—she pointed to me—"take it back. She's ruined my life is what."

But Carnahan grabbed her, took a knife from his pocket and flicked it open near her jugular. "You, throw down the gun or this one's in pieces," he said to Joe.

Joe was willing enough to comply but about that time several thousand cats sprang from the hedges and fences nearby and surged toward the house. Carnahan tried to drag Maeve a few steps but quickly abandoned her as cats sprang onto his shoulders and back and tore at his pants legs.

"They'll be wantin' back the corpse of the King for proper haythen burial," Puss said, still looking unconcerned, and indeed, cats were now swarming over the car and the taxi as Carnahan ran for the side of the house. We chased after, unmolested by the cats except for maybe tripping over them.

Carnahan ran through the burned spot in the yew hedge. We ran after him as he disappeared through the open doors to the pool. The cats, though angry, weren't foolish and they still hated water. They stopped dead at the glass doors. Carnahan slid them shut with a "snick" and backed away from the mass of fangs and claws, laughing.

I was the first to reach the other door from the yew hedge into the pool room, and I never saw the hairy little thing run past me until it ran full tilt into Carnahan's legs, knocking him off balance. He flailed his arms and danced a few steps on the edge of the pool, but his shoes were slick and he fell in backwards, splashing like a sounding whale.

The little hairy thing jumped up and ran the other way, tangling my feet as I tried to get to the pool's edge. Then Felicity, Jack, Deirdre and the others all pushed in behind me and the creature got tangled in their feet too, delaying us further.

Carnahan surfaced once, and then it was as if he was sucked down into the water, which didn't actually seem to be more than four feet deep where he fell.

Jack ripped the doors open and the cats came flooding in, the swans almost breaking their wings flying in behind them.

"Oh, Jaysus, Missus," Maeve was yowling—but gorgeously, heart-achily. "I never meant to be layvin' the doors open like that, only when I come by earlier, them birds was callin' out to me that they was trapped and . . ."

"Whatsamatter, ya, are ya thick, ya?" demanded Mrs. Daly of Maeve. "Hosh!"

The eerie part was that as the swans swarmed in, they were singing a battle song, one I'd scarcely been aware of hearing on the field where Lugh met Balor. Their beating wings completely covered the place where Carnahan had gone under and they dived, all together, down and down, far past where the floor of the pool should have been.

When they finally shot from the water with a mighty splash that totally soaked several disgusted cats, they soared to the ceiling, and there was no sign of Carnahan.

Another man surfaced instead, and swam to the edge of the pool in two lazy strokes, shook himself like a dog, then grinned at Felicity. "You call a cab, Missus?"

Felicity acted as if all of this was perfectly normal and she knew the man well enough to give him a flirtatious grin. "Whatever has become of poor Mr. Carnahan, Cormac?"

"Ah, him," Cormac said with a dismissive wave that soaked several more cats. "Sure, he's away with the fairies, that one. You can have a look if you like."

We all edged forward to look into the pool, which definitely was now much more than Olympic depth.

Far far below, what looked like miles underwater, a red-headed woman with her mouth open in a wild laugh was whipping a team of chariot horses. Tied to the back of the chariot was the battered, barely familiar body of Carnahan.

"It doesn't do to disappoint some ladies at all," Cormac said as the two faded to a dot and disappeared in a ripple.

"Way to go," I said, taking what felt like the first deep breath I'd taken in centuries. "But, where did he go exactly, Felicity? I can see that the Morrigan got him, but how did she get in there and how'd the pool get so deep?"

"Well, dear, you may have noticed that one of the salient architectural features of this house, though the structure isn't particularly old, is that certain aspects of the landscape are inextricably interconnected. The old well over which our pool is laid, for instance, has been here longer than recorded history. It is fed, in fact, by the river that runs through Faerie. The other connections I leave for you to puzzle out for yourself. You no doubt will have realized by now that everything does *not* have what you might call a rational explanation."

"All I'm really interested in," I said, "is that Carnahan is—you should pardon the expression—history."

"Is he the one who destroyed poor Mr. Dunny's house?"

"Yeah, *and* he killed you and Grania when you were Macha

and Neman, *and* he made me run a race when I was Macha and pregnant and damned near killed me as well as killing poor Joe, I mean Naoise, and Deirdre just because they were in love and he—he—he—''

''You're raving, child,'' Felicity said. ''I think we could all use a nice cup of tea.''

So over tea at the kitchen table, once I gathered that Felicity had not been with us, I filled her in on what had happened in the little room. The others, not too much to my surprise, sort of remembered their own part in past events but more as if it was a dream. I was getting a little upset about it but Bobby winked at me and Puss rubbed against my ankles. The rest of the cats were out hunting the hares and shrews and birds on Felicity's place. Deirdre and Joe also quietly set out all of the remaining canned tuna, milk and the rest of Puss's food for them and made a note that we'd have to go to market soon lest Puss and Popsy and the kittens be slighted.

I thought nothing could get through Maeve's thick skull but she was nearly hysterical and kept gibbering about monsters murdering Carnahan and how the Travellers would probably get the blame.

Felicity intercepted the flat of Mrs. Daly's hand as she made to cuff Maeve one across the back of the head.

The old lady lowered her hand but gave us all an evil, absolutely sane smile. ''And if a hair or toenail of the murtherin' cutthroat bastard was left, who better than the knackers to take him? But there's not a fart of the hoor to be found, thanks to these ladies.''

Maeve let out another bawl. I don't think it was just the killing. It was everything, all the magic, all the cats, the swans, that funny hairy thing. We'd all had a chance to get used to it but it kinda got sprung on her.

Jack was good. He put his arm around her shoulders and explained to her, ''The swans said Carnahan was going to kill Grania here and blame it on me, Maeve, and don't be forgettin' the knife he held to the very t'roat of you when he grabbed you as a hostage. He put the torch to this man's house''—he nodded to Joe—''and didn't it just explode all over the countryside like a nuc'leer bomb it was as we drove down the lane. That he done just for wickedness.''

"And he had my man, Jack's da, foully murthered and that only because Pappy would not do his evil will," Mrs. Daly said.

Jack turned to his mother and said, "Ma, you seem to be feeling better today."

"Never have I felt better a day in me life, Jack. But I must tell you, I don't mean to stop here long. You'll be on your own, lad. The city life's not for the likes of me."

"Mam, the road is no place for you now, in your shape."

"Not in my shape, no. But I've ears in me head and I've been paying attention to what this fine lady and this young lass"—she nodded at Felicity and me—"have been sayin'. You two are like that with the fairies, are you not? And that was no dream I had of the road as it once was? It was, a true place long ago?"

Felicity just looked at her.

"Well, it's not me or mine will be jabberin' about it, only you must do a thing for me in exchange. I'll make you a bargain."

Felicity raised an eyebrow.

"You look after my Jack's future and see that he has a good one and I know you can do it, Missus. I've the sight and I can tell a thing or two about folk and you—you—well, just you take care of my Jack. As for me, I wish to go back into that little room and continue where I left off. Those was better times."

"What, the famine?" Jack asked.

"No, no, just after. Just after, when the famine was over and folk were open handed rememberin' that we all have troubles from time to time and it's bad luck to turn away your neighbor or deny a crust or a place to halt to a poor Traveller when you might be needin' the same yourself someday. There was space enough then."

"Mrs. Daly, that little room was not to be entered," Felicity said severely. "There will be consequences as it is. I'd have to speak—"

"Then do some fast spaykin', my lady, or it's Moira Daly will be after tellin' Travelling people the length and breadth of Ireland what you and your fine house are about and never will you have a moment's payce without caravan loads of my payful at your door aitin' you out of house and home and beggin' you for magical favors and wantin' to camp by that little river that runs through Fairyland you spoke of. Sure you'll never be rid of us."

"Ah," Felicity said, nodding knowingly, "the tinker's curse. I'll see what I can do, Mrs. Daly."

There was a scratching at the door. Deirdre rose and went to see what the cats wanted. Popsy and Puss went with her in case she needed an interpreter.

Someone shrieked and we all went running. Just outside the door, two of the feline funeral procession straddled a hairy figure a little bigger than them. They dabbed at it with their paws every time it tried to move. Next door at the O'Connors', Hannah the Wicklow collie was barking furiously and jumping at her gate.

"What in heaven's name is *that*?" Deirdre demanded.

"Ah," Felicity said, shifting aside the cats to lift up what looked like the hairiest, filthiest, smallest person in the world. It—he—was dressed all in brown with long dirty matted hair and beard and wicked little black eyes. "This would be bad luck himself. Formerly bad luck for me, and more recently bad luck that was the end of Mr. Carnahan. My guess is, little gremlin, that tripping up Carnahan was your way of telling me that now I've my magic fully restored I'll be seeing the back of you," she said pointedly, staring the little creature in his beetling brows.

"It's only me, ma'am, Cunla," he said and tried to pull his forelock. "My house, my grounds, I was here first, was Cunla. Don't tell the Gentry, Missus. Never have poor Cunla banished from his land. Cunla's land. Cunla's house."

"Hmm," she said. "Not a gremlin, then. A house spirit. Very well, Cunla. You have done us a service this day. Therefore, I won't ask the Gentry to remove you, Cunla, but I do lay a geas on you that from now on you cease your wicked tricks and do only good to the inhabitants of this house and protect it from harm. That was your original purpose, you know.''

"Yes, Madame, I understand, Madame. Only let me come in until them wicked nasty cats is gone. It was runnin' I was to hide from the savages when I tripped yer man. Butcherin' baysts has no business here on Cunla's ground. Yez scat yez!'' he yelled, squirming in Felicity's grasp as he waved his baby-sized arms at the cats.

"Speaking of us," Puss said. "It's time we were reclaimin' our King's body and finishing the procession. The only problem is, we've had to backtrack so far and it's such a great long journey that everyone is too done in to lift a paw. And yet, however tails may drag and whiskers droop, the King must be buried whence he came and the procession must continue.''

I had an idea. "Puss, can any cat at all be in the procession and carry the King?''

"There's no restrictions on that I'm aware of," Puss said.

"Well, in the past, I was once a cat. Does that make me an honorary lifetime cat in case I wished to claim the honor of bearing the King's corpse back at least as far as Joe Dunny's?''

"Let me confurrr," Puss said.

The other cats, with their customary practical feline self-interest, welcomed me into their ranks. Joe had to return to his house anyway to see what was left of it and figure out what to do with his sheep. Cormac waited for us in the taxi, though he grumbled about the stench arising from His Majesty's body.

It was Deirdre who emphasized Puss's point about how exhausted the cats were by pointing out that many had bleeding paw pads and were so skinny, despite the feeding, that they were unlikely to make it.

"Then we'll hire a lorry to carry them," Felicity said. "I'll just put in a call to Prudence to authorize the expenditure and speak to her on the matter Mrs. Daly and I discussed as well.''

I ran back in the house to get dressed. Grania had slipped

back to my room already when the cats first scratched at the door. She already had put her own clothing back on and was sitting on the edge of the bed staring into space and looking very sad.

"What's the matter?" I asked.

"Don't be takin' it wrong, Sno. I'm that glad to have that awful man dead and not after me anymore. But I can't return to Aunt Gobnait's lest she try again, and I don't know what's to become of me."

"Listen, Grania. I've got a secret for you. In case you hadn't guessed, I'm a fairy godmother. Almost."

"You? You're very young to be in that line of work, aren't you?" I could see that in spite of everything she didn't really believe me.

"Felicity and me are together. I mean, she's teaching me. So I'm sort of an apprentice godmother. But anyway, the point is, we won't let anything happen to you, so don't worry."

She obviously thought I was as nuts as Mrs. Daly used to be. She reached out as I pulled the sweatshirt over my head and said, "Here, what's this?"

"What's what?"

"This sprig caught in your shirt, and this one? They look like herbs but I've never seen the like."

"Oh, that. That's Miachwort. Airmed says it's good for the bodily defenses against ill humors. And this is Cianweed, which staunches wounds, and this—"

"Where'd you get them? I know herbs, and these are new to me."

"Maybe because they're really old," I told her.

"We should plant these right away," she said, and started brushing me off and asking for the names of things. I was more full of seeds and sprigs than I remembered and pretty soon we had to get a pad and pencil to write them down. I could still hear Felicity on the phone, arguing. When I went to the hall desk to get the pad and pencil I saw Mrs. Daly slipping up the stairs behind Felicity's back. The old woman saw me and put her finger to her lips. "Shush, dear," she whispered. " 'Tis aisier to beg forgiveness than to ask parmission.''

I ran upstairs after her but her legs seemed to be working much better than they had before she went through the forbidden door the first time. I made it to the landing just in time to see her bend down to scoop up something glittery—my wish box, dammit. I'd wanted to keep it for a souvenir. But then, the wishes were all gone for me and maybe it would come in handy for her back then and a fairy godmother, even one in training, shouldn't be selfish.

From below I heard Felicity call, "Oh, Mrs. Daly! I have your authoriza—" just as Jack's mother disappeared through the forbidden door.

I rushed back downstairs and told Felicity she'd gone already. "That'll be fine then," she said. "She'll be transferred automatically to the time she requested."

"How about Jack?" I asked.

"Oh, he's your little project, dear," she said. "Was there something you wanted?"

"Pad. Pencil. We found these herbs in my clothing from when you were Airmed, and Grania wants me to write down what they are so she can replant them."

"You'd best hurry along then. There's a convoy of suitably black lorries on the way."

It was a good thing Grania and I made the list because I found my memories of what I'd done behind the door were fading fast. She asked if she could stay behind and plant them in the yard and look after the house while the rest of us joined the funeral procession. First, however, at Felicity's request, Joe and Jack boarded up the forbidden door.

We heard the lorries driving in around noon. The day was still cloudy and rainy, and to tell the truth, I was a little afraid to ask what day it was, after we'd spent so long in the past and Mrs. Daly, at least, had been altered by the experience. But I checked the makeup case mirror anyway.

No gray hairs or lines, and it seemed to be business as usual. When I came to write this entry, I noticed that the date on my computer was the one following the night we went into the forbidden room, so there doesn't seem to be even as much time discrepancy as there is, say, in Faerie.

Anyhow, Cormac drove the cab with me holding the stinky corpse of the cat King in my lap and Felicity riding along in the front with Puss on her lap. Maeve and Jack rode with me in the back with Prince Tom using Jack's lap as if it was a velvet cushion. Joe rode in one of the lorries and Deirdre came along too, with Popsy and her kittens.

By that time many of the cats from Wicklow and Dublin and other nearby areas had decided to return to their homes. We loaded the rest in the lorries, several hundred cats per truck, which was a fairly amazing sight. Paws and tails and ears were everywhere at first, but after a while everyone settled into his or her nap spot, even if they were piled several cats deep.

It was quite a procession. No crows this time, but the swans flew overhead and we could hear them singing their beautiful lament over the wind. Jack sang along. I suppose everybody else thought it was the radio in the trucks and cab.

Bobby had remained at Felicity's. All those cats, all those *hungry* cats, made him nervous.

I enjoyed it, except for the stink, until we got to Joe's. Poor Joe! As he put it, not one stone of his house was left standing on another, and everything was covered with black slippery ash. The sheep were baaing their heads off and several were bogged down in the mud. I returned the Incipient King of the Cats to his subjects and we all went to help with the sheep.

When we came back from the fields, Puss was squaring off with the black tom while about thirty other cats looked on. All the rest of them were gone.

"I never heard that said before!" Prince Tom was saying to her.

"On my honor as the oldest cat here, it is as I say," Puss said. "The last quarter of the procession, the King is attended only by his successor and the court. You and all those who will be your officers have the sole honor of transporting your dear departed royal da from here back to Cahirciveen. Everyone else has to depart and leave you in peace to perform your sacred duty.''

"But, how can we be expected to go so far, draggin' that bleedin'—draggin' me royal da the whole way? We're all in as it is.''

"Isn't that just the wonder of it, though?'' Puss said, washing her whiskers. "Such a good thing it is that Princes are made of sterner stuff than we common felines. I wish you a very pleasant journey, sire that is to be, and rest assured that I will be sure to attend your Dublin coronation.''

"Dublin, is it? And how will I get all the way back to Dublin from Cahirciveen, I ask, on paws surely crippled by the doin' of this deed?''

"Oh, of course, you and your procession will stop to have other coronations on the way—same route as the funeral, as is customary, a coronation in each county, so that no subject will miss the fine feasts you'll catch for the occasion. I myself am partial to fresh haddock, my soon-to-be-King. Until then, I shall miss the honor of your exalted company. Ta,'' she said, and with a flip of her tail, jumped back into the cab beside Popsy and the kittens. The rest of the cats scampered off as well, all but a couple of bedraggled toms who, like the Prince, began pawing dirt over the coffin as our cab pulled away.

I hated to see a cat mistreated, but Popsy and Puss assured me he deserved it. Besides, maybe he'd be inclined to declare his reign a democracy and hitch a ride back to Dublin in one of the three lorries Felicity left at Joe's to help transport the sheep back to her house.

As the cab bounced away from his ruined house, Joe asked if we could stop in at Clonmel so he could pick up his mail. He was very excited to see that he had a letter from his brother Michael in America.

Once back at Felicity's, Joe popped out of the cab of the truck too excited to even see to the sheep before he waved the letter at us saying, "Michael wants to move his family back from America! Can you believe he was after askin' my permission to move back to our old place and said he hoped I'd not be insulted but he wanted a modern home for him and his second wife because what with his children and her children and their children they'll be needin' a great barn of a place!''

Deirdre, who had evidently been hearing all of this in the lorry on the way home, looked bummed out about it, though she put on a little social smile and squeezed his hand and tried to look pleased.

Felicity is not slow. ''Oh, dear. Then you and the sheep will be returning when your brother has built his place?''

''Are you mad, Missus?'' he blurted out, then said, ''Excuse me, Mrs. Fortune, I'm sure. I've been very bold not to speak to you of this before, but there's been no time, you see.''

''Oh, I do see,'' Felicity agreed fervently.

''Well, it's just, Deirdre and me were talkin' last night before all the excitement and she says as how there might be a caretaker's position here and frankly, Mrs. Fortune, I never thought I was cut out to be a farmer. What I'd like is to stay here and help Deirdre care for your place while you and young Sno is off on your travels.''

''Of course, Joe. I meant to ask you myself as soon as we had a free moment, but then, I suppose that's why I hired such an efficient housekeeper. What of your sheep?''

''I'd like to sell off most of them and keep just a few, though I'll still need a dog. One that would get on with the pussies, of course.''

''Hannah's pups are due any time now,'' I said. I was very excited. Finally after all that bloody past it looked like some folks were going to get a happy ending. ''Puss and Popsy and the kittens can bring up the pup to suit themselves.''

''Well, there's that taken care of then. Just one more thing, Missus. Could you tell me the name of the local parish priest?'' He turned to Deirdre. ''I know we just met but I feel I've known you forever and ever and—''

''I feel the same. Oh, Joe!'' and the rest of us had to turn away and give them a little privacy while they indulged in an unseemly public display of affection.

''Well, that's all very well for you lot, but what about *me*?'' Maeve wailed, the wail sounding like the soul-wrenching lament of the Morrigan herself for Nuada of the Silver Arm when he died under the evil eye of the demon Balor. "You gave me this posh voice and now me maytes is puttin' about that I'm witched and everyone is afraid of me and me own family won't speak to me, they're that convinced I've put meself above them!"

"I'd say losin' that family of yours is another thing you've to thank Sno for," Jack said. But Maeve looked genuinely grieved and he put his arm around her shoulders. "Don't worry, old girl. We'll sort something out."

Grania came into the kitchen, brushing the dirt from her hands, as we all sat down to tea again. Joe and Deirdre had gone off in Cormac's taxi to the market to get something for us to eat, which was a good thing since my back teeth were floating from all the tea I'd been drinking.

"Got them all planted just as you said, Sno, though the yard's an awful mess. It could be so pretty, though. A few daffs, some roses maybe."

"Oh, Grania!" Felicity said, clapping her hands. "*Would* you? I'll buy everything you need but I'm simply desperate with plants and I do travel so much. If you would stay here and do the garden for me, just to start it, mind you, until you go off to college or whatever it is you'd like to do, I'd be ever so grateful!"

"Yeah, sure," she said with a casual shrug but she was so pleased she was blushing.

Maeve and Jack were in consultation. I heard the words "squeeze box" and remembered that Jack had said he was a musician. That's when I remembered Rosie telling me that the street boy she and Felicity saved, Dico Miller, is also a musician and is down in Kinsale studying at a famous Irish school.

Guess it's time to stop writing to myself and drop a line to me dear ol' da.

CHAPTER 31

Dear Daddy,

I just thought I'd see how that sounded.. I finally got your E-mail message about what's going down with you and Cindy. I don't know what to tell you, Daddy. Cindy's been through a lot lately and if she says she needs space to go off and ride horses and get to know who she is before she makes any decisions about you guys, I think I'd just listen to her. Meanwhile, you still have a darling daughter who loves you. Why don't you take a vacation and come to Ireland?

Then we can see it together. I've been working too hard to do any sightseeing. I'll be graduating really soon from this school, I think.

It's been swell, though. I've made lots of new friends and had a really good time and learned lots. Ireland is just as wonderful as everybody says it is and I really really really think you should look into buying a place to live here. They don't bother celebrities at all, because everybody's too polite, Felicity says.

Anyway, I just wanted to ask you for a little bitty favor. No, not money. I'm doing fine there, thanks a lot, though I haven't got back into Dublin to buy souvenirs like I wanted to yet. If you had a place here, I wouldn't have to bring you stuff because you could pick out your own, couldn't you?

It would be really the *best* if you could come yourself but if you can't, weren't you telling me how your manager, Rob Tyrell, is getting really burned out and has always wanted to visit Ireland? Anyhow, if either one of you or both could come, I know how you can write it off.

See, I met these kids here and the guy is like from this very interesting ethnic group and plays dynamite squeeze box and has some wonderful songs and the girl has the best set of pipes I've ever heard and then there's Dico Miller from Seattle who plays flute down in Kinsale? Well, I thought if maybe Mr. Tyrell wanted to, he could get them together with a good lead guitarist and they'd have as good a band as U2 or any of those guys. Please, Daddy? Please?

I gotta know really soon. Both the boy and the girl are of the Travelling people and they don't stick around too long so please say yes right away. And come yourself! I miss you.

Love, Sno

*   *   *

Dear Rosie,

You what? Eloped? You and Fred eloped? Wow! Good for you. Any chance you might come to Ireland for your honeymoon? I'm trying to talk Raydir into buying a castle here. Maybe you could be like his first guests? Anyway, congrats and much happiness. I have a little news of a ceremonial nature myself.

To catch you up, I'm uploading all the journal entries since my last E-mail to you. Try not to freak out, as there is some truly weird shit in this batch. But it was worth it because (insert drum roll) . . . Ta Da!

You are now reading a letter written by a genuine graduate fourth-degree journeyman fairy godmother, ready to return to Seattle to do her residency.

Where else would you get career advancement like that at my age? Not even in the military, thank God!

The ceremony was held in Faerie, which made me a little

sad since none of my entirely mortal friends could come. But we had a little party at the house anyway. Dico Miller came up to meet Rob Tyrell, Daddy's manager, who was on the Concorde as soon as Daddy read my E-mail. Daddy's coming over as soon as he does this benefit gig in LA. Rob's been helping Dico, Maeve and Jack rehearse and Dico got a couple of other kids from the Kinsale school to come up and join the band. They are going to be so hot and Rob is already checking out recording studios for a demo. With Daddy backing them, though, they'll be cutting a CD even before they do any gigs.

So the party was great. Deirdre did Wicklow lamb and cul-cannon, a potato and onion dish, and for dessert there was chocolate cake. Deirdre also is knitting me a sweater from the wool of Joe's sheep and Grania showed me the sprouts in the Miach Memorial Herb Garden. Mr. O'Connor invited us all over to see Hannah's new pups and Joe picked out his and had orders from his brother in America to reserve another one for the brother's kids. They'll get one of the kittens too.

Which brings me to Puss's little surprise. Yeah, well, she did more than walk during the funeral procession. She particularly wants me to have a kitten in America, and Felicity said we'd sort that out later.

It was the best birthday I've ever had but now I have to go. It's time for the main event.

Love, Sno

EPILOGUE

(Courtesy of the Tir-na-Nog Grapevine)

Once upon a time there was a princess who became a fairy godmother.

At the stroke of midnight, arrayed in her most excellent finery, a sleek ebony garment, virtually skirtless, Snohomish Quantrill of the clan of Kinsale received her diploma as an official agent of Her Majesty's Godmothers Anonymous sorority. Mistress Snohomish was accompanied by her mentor, noted Godmother Felicity Fortune, who was clad in her signature glittering silvery array.

Lord Bluelagoon of the Southern Star and Lord Cormac Strongarm stood honor guard to Her Royal Majesty Tatiana the Everlasting at the ceremony, where sorority members from across the globe gathered around Her Royal Self in the grand ballroom to honor the new graduate.

A short business meeting took place before the honors were presented.

Dame Prudence, the sorority's treasurer, called the new member to task, reminding her that the sorority's purpose is to assist worthy mortals.

The quick-witted girl smartly responded to Dame Prudence, who is well known for her parsimony, "But don't you feel,

Dame Prudence, that some people need a little break in order to become worthy?''

Dame Felicity applauded the comment with a ''here here.''

Dame Merrilee was heard to giggle and observe that standing up to Dame Prudence was one of the chiefest trials of the fledgling godmother. ''I don't know how a Conservative Republican type like her ever made it into the Godmothers,'' Dame Merrilee has been quoted as saying with regard to Dame Prudence.

Her Majesty called for order and rapped her wand upon the table, commanding Dame Prudence to present Mistress Snohomish with the balance of wishes she is to bestow on her next three missions.

''You don't think a more judicious distribution is perhaps in order, Your Majesty?'' Dame Prudence inquired.

''I do not,'' Her Majesty responded.

''Oh, very well,'' Dame Prudence agreed, and with that, sprinkled Mistress Snohomish with a goodly amount of fairy-dust.

Tragedy nearly ensued as the honoree first inhaled the magical blend, then sneezed out a portion of it, but it was quickly recovered and reapplied to her person.

Her Majesty then gave the customary graduation speech in which she reminded Mistress Snohomish that her magical budget is to be supplemented by mortal means and contacts.

In her acceptance speech, young Mistress Snohomish observed puckishly that having a ''rich dad with lots of friends and admirers isn't going to hurt.'' She went on to graciously concede that ''This is not a field where anybody makes it on their own. This is a field where we all get by with help from our friends. ''

Though her tone was light, the honoree was seen to be weeping with emotion and was handed a lace handkerchief with the official Godmothers Anonymous crest on it. When Mistress Snohomish had dried that which was moist, Her Majesty asked Dame Genevieve of the Sparkling, Dangly Bits to make the final presentation.

Dame Genevieve handed Mistress Snohomish the first of two boxes.

A golden card case lay within the first, ornamented with the same tasteful fairy-on-a-flower design wrought in pearls, gold and crystals as was on the wish box presented to Mistress Snohomish at a prior ceremony.

In unison, the assembly chanted to the recipient, "Open it."

She did so. Inside were her personal sorority business cards, inscribed with the sorority motto as follows: "Mistress Snohomish Quantrill, Godmothers (Anonymous), Fair Fates Facilitated, Questers Accommodated and Virtue Vindicated. True Love and Serendipity Our Specialty."

"Gosh, thanks," the honoree said graciously.

"And now for your membership badge," Dame Genevieve said, and looked to Her Majesty.

"I think it would be most meaningful if Dame Felicity bestowed the badge," Her Majesty said, inclining her head.

Dame Felicity accepted a second box from Dame Genevieve and showed the honoree and the assembly that it contained, upon the customary crimson velvet cushion, a delicate lapel pin in the guise of a magic wand.

This Dame Felicity pinned to the shoulder of Mistress Snohomish's gown.

A reception followed and a good time was had by all.

*   *   *

Journal Entry—Endings

Everyone else was in bed by the time Felicity and I returned from the ceremony. Grania had taken the bed Jack's mother had slept in the first night, so I had my room to myself. I pulled off the spandex, and pulled on another pair of leggings and a sweatshirt. The little card case I stuck in my purse and the wand pin I set carefully on the bedside stand. I felt like it was mean, if Mrs. Daly really needed it, to regret the loss of my wish box, but the sisters had obviously meant for me to keep it since it matched the card case.

I cracked the window, in case Puss or Popsy might want in late, and pulled back the duvet with a sigh. I remember thinking as I pulled it back about something somebody smart had once said about it being a good thing we had time the way it usually is, or everything would happen all at once. Or something like that. I saw exactly what he meant, since everything had been happening all at once what with all the special dispensations for Fairyland and time warps to the past I'd been in lately. People changing faces and identities so fast it made my head swim. For instance, didn't Her Redheaded Majesty bear a striking family resemblance to the Morrigan? Were they sisters or was it maybe just that the war goddess had decided that keeping justice and good things going in the real world provided contrast for the bad stuff? That kind of cosmic thinking was what was wearing me out, so I dropped it. I figured I was about five or six generations worth of exhausted, minimum.

And then I saw it.

My little gold wish box, there on my pillow.

"Congrats, kid," said a voice from the windowsill. It had been preceded by the plop of a toad butt landing on the same sill. "The old lady sold your pillbox to buy herself a caravan, and so I sort of reclaimed it for you. Happy graduation."

I scared the hell out of him by scooping him up and giving him a big smooch right between the eyes.

"Hey, watch it! You'll get warts," he protested, acutely embarrassed.

"There just might be some prince material in that little green bod after all," I told him.

"Don't get sloppy on me, kid."

And so I went to sleep, grateful that when I finally fly home, I only have to cross eight time zones to get to Seattle. It'll seem like a snap, after Ireland. Maybe I'll write a book about this some day and call it "Once upon a Time Warp."

In the meantime, I guess I'll do my duty as a fairy godmother and make sure as many people as possible live happily ever after.